HELEN YENDALL has had dozens of short stories and a serial published in women's magazines over the past twenty years and now writes female-focused WW2 novels. She's a member of the Romantic Novelists' Association.

She studied English and German at Leeds University and has worked in a variety of roles: for a literary festival, a university, a camping club, a children's charity and in marketing and export sales. But her favourite job is the one she still has: teaching creative writing to adults.

Although a proud Brummie by birth, Helen now lives in the North Cotswolds with her husband and cocker spaniel, Bonnie. When she's not teaching or writing, she likes reading, swimming, tennis and walking in the beautiful countryside where she lives.

A Wartime Secret

HELEN YENDALL

ONE PLACE. MANY STORIES

This novel is entirely a work of fiction. The names, characters and incidents portrayed in it are the work of the author's imagination. Any resemblance to actual persons, living or dead, events or localities is entirely coincidental.

HQ
An imprint of HarperCollins*Publishers* Ltd
1 London Bridge Street
London SE1 9GF

www.harpercollins.co.uk

HarperCollins*Publishers*
1st Floor, Watermarque Building, Ringsend Road
Dublin 4, Ireland

This paperback edition 2022

1

First published in Great Britain by
HQ, an imprint of HarperCollins*Publishers* Ltd 2022

A catalogue record for this book is available from the British Library.

ISBN: 9780008523114

MIX
Paper from responsible sources
FSC™ C007454

This book is produced from independently certified FSC™ paper to ensure responsible forest management.

For more information visit: www.harpercollins.co.uk/green

Printed and Bound in the UK
using 100% Renewable Electricity at CPI Group (UK) Ltd

For Mum and Dad

Chapter 1

London, September 1940

Maggie Corbett lay face down on the open platform of the number 56 bus, the heel of another passenger's shoe an inch from her nose. It was a man's black brogue, probably about the same size as her dad's: a nine or ten. She watched it, ready to jerk her head back if it looked likely to move.

The siren, that awful banshee wail that she'd never get used to, had gone off ten minutes after she'd boarded at Poplar. She shouldn't have been surprised but, blimey, of all the mornings for it to happen!

It had been standing room only and they'd already been running behind, diverted due to rubble and craters from last night's raids. If they weren't all about to be blown to smithereens, she was going to be late on her first day and covered in dirt, into the bargain.

Her clothes must be filthy. She was stretched out, her head in her hands, her face two inches from the grimy, footprint-covered floor. What had been the point of carefully darning her best stockings last night, sponging down her mac and pressing her white blouse? She needn't have bothered.

Two minutes earlier, she'd flung herself to the floor as the clippie, frantically pressing the bell, had yelled, 'Oh Gawd! Everyone down! There's a nasty old man in the sky dropping stones!' Then the clippie had hitched up her slacks and got down on the floor herself.

The driver had veered to the side of the road and braked heavily, sending people flying.

A gas mask, in its cardboard box, fell onto Maggie's hand, making her grimace. An elderly woman to one side and a uniformed soldier on the other were struggling to find room to lie down. Maggie tried not to mind too much as she was shoved and prodded by elbows and knees.

'Sorry, Miss,' the soldier muttered. Honestly, at any other time, it would be a right rum deal to have a strange man lie down next to you, close enough to smell his ciggie-breath, but these days it seemed almost normal.

Maggie's nose itched. Dust. She turned her head and shifted her weight so she wasn't facing the soldier (it was too queer, like they were a married couple lying in bed). She quickly pulled her hand in, before it was stamped on from above by a spiked heel.

Finally, everyone was still. The bus stopped rocking. They were motionless, waiting for the worst to happen. Or, God willing, the all-clear. Someone sniffed; a man coughed. No one spoke. It was like some strange child's game. If she thought of it like that, it wasn't quite so frightening.

Dad believed that if your time was up, it was up. If that bomb had your name on it, there was 'nuffink you could do'. It was certainly fate that had brought Maggie here to this moment, lying in a bus, waiting, possibly, to be blown sky high.

If it hadn't been for that chance meeting with her old teacher from the secretarial college the other day, Maggie wouldn't be here now.

She'd popped up town to buy a few bits and pieces for Vi to

take with her, and as she was leaving Peter Robinson department store, she'd bumped into Mrs Leibervich.

'What are you doing now, Maggie?' she'd asked. 'Have you kept up your shorthand and typing?'

Maggie told her about the munitions factory. 'It's essential work,' she'd added proudly.

'And how do you like it?'

Maggie thought about the cavernous factory that was alternately sweltering and freezing, the infernal noise and the rotten smell of oil that clung to her clothes, skin and hair, no matter how often she washed. The flickering artificial light gave her headaches, and the stuffiness was so bad that sometimes, in her lunchbreak, she gulped the air outside like a fish out of water.

The wages weren't bad, though. She used to hand over her pay packet to Mutti each week and get some money back, for 'spends'.

'It's all right,' she said. 'Mustn't grumble.'

Mrs Leibervich narrowed her eyes. 'You know, there might be a position for a clever girl like you at a friend's bank.'

Maggie shook her head. 'No, really—'

But Mrs Leibervich had placed her warm hand over Maggie's and glanced around, as though checking no one was listening. 'This would definitely be essential work. I could put in a word, if you like.'

A week later, the factory was bombed out and Mrs Leibervich got her an interview for the job at the bank.

Today was meant to be her first day.

Maggie's nostrils were full of the smell of Cherry Blossom shoe polish and sweat. She tried to breathe through her mouth. Usually, down in the shelters, some bright spark wouldn't be able to resist a joke or a song but here no one spoke, apart from a woman lying a few feet away in the aisle, who tutted and murmured, 'I'll be late again. Bloody Germans, pardon my French.'

Maggie bit her lip. Everyone hated the Germans, of course,

especially now, since the bombing had started. There was an absolute rage against them.

'They ain't normal, you know,' the woman continued, to no one in particular. 'They're not like us. Oh no. My old mum says they eat babies.'

Maggie had to grit her teeth. She'd heard lots of comments like that recently, but it still made her burn inside. She wanted to stick up for the Germans, but what could she say?

Actually, I know some very nice Germans. They're not all Nazis. I'm sort of one myself. We're not all bad! No, she couldn't say that, she'd be set upon.

A soft breeze blew across the open platform of the bus, carrying an acrid smell of burning. Maggie lifted her head and glimpsed the deserted street, the coils of hosepipes, smoke and ruined buildings.

At any other time, the cool air would be welcome; the bodies next to her were generating an uncomfortable warmth. But Maggie could only think about how exposed they were. Could the enemy bombers see them … from the sky? London buses were such a bright red, they might as well have a target painted on them.

The old woman next to her must have been thinking the same; she suddenly started to shake and whimper. Maggie reached out to stroke her hand. She was as small and frail as a tiny bird.

'Shhh, love,' Maggie said, trying to sound perky, though her teeth were chattering. 'It'll all be all right.'

If she survived this, the prospect of what lay ahead at Rosman's was making Maggie's stomach twist. When she finally arrived, the typewriters would fall silent. The other girls would watch from their desks and listen to the inevitable dressing down she'd get from the supervisor, Miss Sharp. Maggie would turn scarlet, with all those hostile eyes on her. She'd have to put her hand up to her cheek, to cool her face down.

'You'll grow out of it, *Liebchen*,' Mutti used to tell her, with a reassuring smile. But she hadn't. Maggie was eighteen now – eighteen! – and she still blushed at the slightest thing.

Miss Sharp had interviewed Maggie only last week. She was poker-thin and angular, like her name, and she hadn't smiled once. Miss Sharp didn't seem the sympathetic type. Maggie had passed the shorthand and typing tests, but the older woman had seemed doubtful, pursing her lips and peering at Maggie over tortoiseshell spectacles as Maggie assured her that yes, the journey from Poplar was perfectly manageable. She'd have said anything to get that job, to be a business girl at last!

She'd left the interview feeling quite down, convinced she hadn't come up to scratch. So, it had been a surprise when the letter came, confirming her position at the bank. Even Dad, who was never impressed by anything, had nodded his head in something like a 'Well done' when she'd shown him the letter.

For once, it had seemed things were going her way. Mutti – when Maggie finally got the chance to tell her the good news – would be so proud.

But now, doubtful Miss Sharp was about to be proved right: the journey from home to the bank wasn't manageable, after all.

Maggie couldn't bear the thought of being late. She'd been told to arrive punctually. Could they sack her before she'd even started? Dad would go barmy. And, on top of everything, she'd be letting dear Mrs Leibervich down.

Oh, thank God! The warbling all-clear was sounding. There was a collective sigh on the bus and the tension lifted.

Other passengers around Maggie started to shuffle, moving their limbs and struggling to their feet. There were bangs and thuds on the ceiling, as people in the upper deck did the same.

The clippie waited, her finger poised on the bell, while everyone got up, dusted themselves down and retrieved their gas masks and bags. Maggie helped the old woman into a seat.

The bell sounded. 'Off we go, fella!' the clippie called to the driver, wiping dust from her trousers.

* * *

When Maggie eventually reached the panelled front door of Rosman's Merchant Bank on Bond Street, without further mishap or delay, she was over an hour late. And she couldn't find the knocker.

The interview had been at a hotel in town; she'd never been to the bank before. Maybe this wasn't the entrance? There was no one around to ask. Should she go down the alley at the side? Or perhaps there was a doorbell here, set into the stone wall? She couldn't see anything that resembled one.

She pushed on the huge door without much hope but it gave a little, so she shoved with all her weight and it finally creaked and then swung open, whereupon she tripped up the step and fell inside. Blast! She'd landed on the rough horsehair mat inside the door.

'Awww!' The cry was more out of frustration than pain. She seemed doomed to spend half this morning lying in a heap on the floor.

'Hullo there, do come in!' a man called out. He marched across the lobby towards her, smart black shoes clickety-clicking on the tiles and – before Maggie could push herself up – he lifted her, as though she were as light as a doll, and set her down on the floor.

'Oh, thank you!' she said, brushing herself down and checking her stockings for ladders, to hide her embarrassment.

Eventually, she had to look up at him. He was tall and thin, a little older than her and he was clearly amused by the spectacle she'd just made of herself. His slicked hair and black business suit marked him out as a bank clerk. They were so close she could see the dusting of freckles across his nose and smell coal tar soap on his skin.

He tutted and shook his head in mock despair. 'Not another young lady, fallin' at my feet.' He was a cockney like her and, clearly, he thought himself a comedian, too.

After the morning she'd just had, Maggie was hardly in the mood for jokes but she tried to smile. He was a colleague, after all, and almost certainly her superior; she needed to make a good impression.

She glanced around the lobby. There was a reception desk straight ahead, strangely devoid of a receptionist. A shining chandelier hung from the ceiling and beneath it, in the centre of a round table, stood a huge vase of flowers.

She looked back at the clerk. 'It's my first day. Maggie Corbett's the name.'

He nodded. 'Ray Maguire, at your service.'

Was he laughing at her? Maggie gazed at him. Those lips were definitely twitching, as though he were about to laugh. But perhaps he always looked like that.

Apart from Mr Maguire, the place seemed empty, the building silent. This wasn't like any bank she'd been in before. Where was everyone?

He rubbed his hands together. 'All in one piece, are we? Because—' he pulled a pocket watch out of his waistcoat and grimaced '—I'm ushering everyone through. Rounding up the stragglers.'

The jokiness of a minute ago had disappeared. He was suddenly awfully businesslike. 'Would you mind coming this way, Miss er … Miss? And if you don't mind, could you walk quite fast?'

'Sorry I'm late,' Maggie said, following Ray Maguire as he set off down a corridor at a fair lick. 'The bus had to go another way because of the mess on the roads and … Well, it was all Herr Hitler's fault.'

'Most things are,' he called back. 'I shouldn't worry. Let's face it, 'til we get here each morning, none of us knows if the place will still be standing or just a pile of bricks.' He held open a door for Maggie, followed her through and rapidly overtook her.

They hadn't shaken hands, had they? Should they have? Mr Maguire seemed in too much of a hurry for any niceties.

'His Nibs is here,' he said over his shoulder, as though that should mean something to her. 'Everyone's in the boardroom.' He tapped his nose. 'Important announcement.'

The carpet was thick and the corridor walls were covered in paintings set in ornate gold frames: landscapes and horses and bowls of fruit. Maggie inhaled. Even the air was different, it smelled of something exotic, like cigars. Or money.

They slipped in at the back of an oak-panelled room in which about twenty bank employees were standing with their backs to them. Ray Maguire seemed to forget her immediately: his attention was fixed on the middle-aged man standing at the front, addressing everyone.

Now, there was a proper toff, a real gentleman. He was speaking in a deep, rich voice, that carried clearly to the back of the room. Maggie's breath caught in her throat. It must be him: Lord Ashford, the owner of the bank.

She resisted the urge to take a look at her new colleagues and focused on what Lord Ashford was saying.

'… given the international situation … likely to continue for some time …'

'I knew it! What did I say? He's going to close us down,' a freckled redhead said crossly. She folded her arms across her chest and frowned. Someone nudged her and a couple of others glared at her to be quiet.

'My intention is to protect the bank and all its assets. There's no time to be lost. And so …' He paused and gazed at them all.

Maggie moved her head to one side to get a better look at him. He was ever so handsome. Like a film star. Like Clark Gable! She'd seen *Gone with the Wind* at the Troxy three times and yes, that was who he reminded her of: Rhett Butler, with his dark, Brylcreemed hair, side parting and pencil moustache. And those sparkling, intelligent eyes, scanning the room. They wouldn't miss a trick, those eyes.

He spoke clearly and loudly but he wasn't frightening, like an awful lot of bosses, he was more … what was the word? *Imposing*, yes, that was it.

'So,' he continued, 'I am proposing to move everything to

Snowden Hall, my place in the country, miles from here. Away from London—' he waved his arms '—and the bombs and this horrendous mess.' He nodded, took a gulp from a glass of water on a nearby table and waited for their reaction.

No one spoke. A few people exchanged frowns and worried looks. Then the redhead piped up again. 'And what about us, Sir?' she asked, tilting her chin. Her body was held rigid, her jaw clenched. She looked ready for a fight.

Lord Ashford hesitated for a moment, then his face broke into a smile. He was even more handsome when he smiled.

'You, Miss Davenport? What's to become of you?' He laughed. 'Why, didn't I say?' He held out his arms. 'You're all coming too!'

Chapter 2

'You ain't going and that's my final word!'

Maggie was lifting the pan of boiled potatoes from the stove to the sink as, behind her, Dad yelled and thumped the kitchen table. The plates and cutlery rattled. The cat, Tabby, shot out through the open back door.

Dad's face was beetroot, his fists tightly closed. He'd never used them – yet – but perhaps the day was getting closer.

She could kick herself. Why had she even told him the bank was moving? She should have made up a story about losing her job. She could've said the place had been bombed out, like the munitions factory. He'd have believed that. It wouldn't be out of the ordinary for two workplaces to have bought it. Not with the way things were going: every night now, enemy planes came and set a different part of the city ablaze.

And besides, it wasn't as though she even wanted to go. The other girls had been so excited after Lord Ashford's announcement that hardly a stroke of work had been done all day. Although the raids and dogfights overhead hadn't helped. Twice, they'd had to leave their desks and file down into the bank's basement to take cover for an hour or more.

As for the dreaded encounter with Miss Sharp the supervisor, she'd merely nodded in Maggie's direction and said mildly, 'Ah, there you are, Miss Corbett. Welcome to Rosman's.' She'd waved a finger towards a girl with blonde curls, a grown-up Shirley Temple type. 'There's your desk. Next to Miss Fry.'

The girls had exchanged smiles. Maggie needn't have worried about being late, after all.

No, the others could be as thrilled at the prospect as they liked but the thought of leaving London had left Maggie cold. How could she possibly go? She'd never been away from home before but, besides that, it would be like running away from the war itself. And who'd be here for Mutti and Violet, when they came back?

'Who'll cook me dinner, if you go gallivanting off?' Dad asked, interrupting her thoughts. 'First your mother disappears—'

As if she'd had any choice in the matter.

'—and then your sister.'

Maggie's chest tightened. That wasn't fair! She'd had to beg Dad to send little Vi away. He'd refused to let her go when war broke out, when her whole school was sent to Wales.

'No! Families stick together,' he'd said. Which was a joke because they never did anything together as a family, except eat their meals around the little kitchen table, in uneasy silence.

So, Vi had been kept at home, even though all her pals had been evacuated and there was no school to speak of. She'd been the only child down in the shelters and people had stared at them, no doubt thinking they were wrong for keeping a child in London when everyone knew sending them away was for the best.

It was only after those poor kiddies were killed in the shelter the other night, that he'd agreed, finally, that it was too dangerous for Violet to stay in London.

Maggie had taken Vi to the station but she wasn't allowed on the platform. No tears, no fuss, that was the order.

She'd watched through the railings with the other women – mothers with brave smiles and sad eyes. The other evacuees, five little boys all at least a foot shorter and five or six years younger than Vi, were driving the WVS woman in charge to distraction, bashing each other with their gas mask boxes and running amok on the platform.

'It goes against the grain,' one of the women said, crying into her hankie once they'd waved the train off. Maggie knew what she meant. She was a sister not a mother, but it still tore her apart to let Vi go.

Her sister had been gone for three days and ten and a half hours. Maggie was on tenterhooks; she wouldn't relax until the postcard arrived, telling them where Vi had been sent.

Mutti had gone, Violet had gone. There was no way Dad would let her leave too.

She suddenly felt a surge of indignation. Why shouldn't she go? She was eighteen years old, an adult. Other girls her age were serving in the WRENS and the WAAF, putting their lives in danger for King and Country, doing their bit.

Maybe this move, with the bank, to the countryside was her big chance? Once, after Dad had ranted and raved and slammed the door on his way out to the pub, Mutti had said, 'You and Violet will get away from this, one day.'

Maggie thought she'd meant when they got married and had homes of their own but perhaps neither of them had to wait that long. Perhaps some good could come out of this bloomin' war, after all.

But what about Mutti? she'd thought When would she get away? Maggie could never shake the feeling that Mutti would have left Dad a long time ago, if she'd had anywhere to go.

'You're staying here. Right here!' Dad said, banging the table again.

There would be no arguing with that. Maggie said nothing; answering back would only make things worse.

'What kind of man is he anyway, taking young women off to the countryside? What's he after? Some kind of harem?'

Maggie poured the water off the potatoes into the sink and

was immediately enveloped in a cloud of steam. *Harem?* It was almost comical. If Dad could only see the women from the bank, he'd soon take that back.

She pictured her new colleagues. There were a few women in their thirties, like the feisty redhead who'd turned out to be called Elsie Davenport, and some older, spinster types, such as middle-aged Miss Sharp the supervisor. The other girls, the typists, ledger clerks and secretaries, were mostly a little older than Maggie. Apart from Nancy Fry, who sat next to Maggie, she hadn't yet learned their names. They were all smartly dressed and well spoken and she felt a little in awe of them, but no one was particularly glamorous.

No, film star status, Maggie thought, was definitely reserved for Lord Ashford himself.

She smiled to herself at the memory, and then shook her head. 'It ain't like that, Dad. It's not only women, he's taking fellas too. He needs all the staff there to run the bank and help fund the war effort. Besides, he's a Lord, a proper Lord and a gentleman. And … and he's married.'

She'd guessed the last part. He was bound to be married, a wealthy, good-looking chap like that.

Dad's face twisted into a sneer. 'So what? In any case, what are the men doing, waltzing off to the country? Don't they know there's a war on?'

She sighed. 'Banking's reserved, Dad. Like dock work.'

He smacked his lips and frowned at her, as she stood at the sink. 'What about my dinner? Can't a working man get a decent meal around here?'

There wasn't much. A bit of cabbage, a few boiled potatoes and a piece of dubious-looking meat. Maggie had joined a queue outside the butcher's the other day and asked the woman in front of her, 'What're we queuing for?'

'Gawd knows. And by the time we get inside, it might be gone anyway.'

Another woman had tapped Maggie's shoulder, once they were closer to the shopfront. The window would have been full of refrigerated meat before the war, but was now empty. The woman pointed at the sign: *HORSE MEAT.*

Maggie sighed. It'd have to do. Dad always wanted meat, as though she could conjure it out of thin air. It might stop him moaning for five minutes if she got a cutlet, but she wouldn't tell him what it was.

After two hours of queuing, she managed it. She only had enough coupons for one piece. She'd go without and make do with veg. She didn't mind, she didn't have much of an appetite these days; her stomach was continually churned up with worry. Besides, if Violet knew she'd eaten horse meat, she'd never forgive her.

Now, she put Dad's dinner on the table in front of him.

'Did you slam that plate down?'

She had. She was cross with him.

'No, Dad. It slipped out me 'and.'

He didn't like her to talk properly ('putting on airs and graces'), so she dropped her aitches when she was with him and tried to remember to speak like the other women in the street.

He grunted, as though not quite believing her and then stabbed the cutlet with his fork. 'What's this, then?'

'Steak, Dad. Got it specially. Had to queue for bloomin' hours for that, I did. Eat up, before it gets cold.'

As they sat across the table from one another, Maggie remembered something she'd overheard at the bank today. She tried to make her tone conversational and casual.

'You know the fella who owns the bank, Dad? Lord Ashford?'

He looked up from his dinner, chewing vigorously. 'What bank? What you talkin' about?'

'Rosman's Bank. The place where I'm working now.'

He held his fork aloft and let a piece of potato fall onto the plate. 'Rosman's? What kind of a name is that?'

'I dunno. They're Jewish, I think.'

'Well, what about him?' He started eating again.

'He served, last time. He was a captain, in the Great War.'

That took the wind out of his sails. She knew it would. Dad had fought last time and he always thought well of anyone who'd done the same.

He frowned. 'What regiment?'

Fiddlesticks. She should have found out. 'I don't know.'

He scoured the tabletop, frowning. 'Any salt?'

It was usually Violet's job to lay the table. Maggie's stomach lurched; it did that every time she remembered that Violet wasn't here.

Maggie pushed her chair back from the table and fetched the salt from the press behind her. Tabby was slinking back in from the yard and Maggie bent and gave her a reassuring stroke. Mutti and Vi loved that cat. If she did nothing else, she'd make sure Tabby was safe and well, waiting for them both when they finally came home.

Dad let his knife fall onto the plate with a clatter that made Maggie jump. Tabby streaked off again, towards the front room. Maggie placed the salt cellar down in the middle of the table, careful not to slam it.

He grunted his thanks. 'You still ain't going, mind,' he said.

Chapter 3

Where the bloody hell was she?

Ray tapped his foot, crossed his arms and uncrossed them again. He fixed his gaze on the flight of steps leading down to the platform, willing her to appear. Behind him, all the train doors were shut and the guard was checking his pocket watch. Any second, he'd blow his whistle and the train would start to pull out.

Perhaps he should forget about her and climb on board? He mustn't leave it too late. A fine to-do that would be, if he got left behind with all the tickets in his jacket pocket. That'd take some explaining to his Nibs. It wouldn't be the best of starts.

He should've handed the tickets out when everyone arrived at Paddington and he'd crossed their names off his list. All present and correct, except one: Maggie Corbett.

He might have guessed she wouldn't turn up. She wasn't supposed to be coming at all but yesterday, everything changed. She'd come to find him in the banking hall, wanting to know the exact location of Lord Ashford's house.

Ray had frowned and tapped his foot. 'What's it to you? Last I heard, you said to count you out. But, seeing as you're asking, it's in the Cotswolds.'

Her face fell. 'We've had the postcard, see, with my sister's address. She's a vackie and she's been sent to Gloucestershire. But I've got it all wrong, then. I thought that's where Lord Ashford's house was.'

Ray sighed. He didn't have time for this. He had labourers to oversee and a hundred and one things to do. 'The Cotswolds and Gloucestershire overlap,' he explained. 'The house is in both.'

'I know it's a lady's prerogative and all that, Miss Corbett,' he said, 'but are you coming now, or not? We're leaving tomorrow, ten o'clock sharp, from Paddington. I'm in charge of travel chits and tickets. Should I get one for you?'

'Yes!' she'd said, eyes gleaming. 'Oh, yes please! I'll be there!'

But she wasn't here; she'd let him down. He'd quite liked her, up to now, Maggie Corbett. Oh, not in that way. A little cockney sparrow – practically 'the girl next door' – wouldn't do for him at all. He had his sights set higher than that. But she was down to earth, without the airs and graces of some he could mention, and he knew how it felt to want to escape the docklands and better yourself.

She must have thought she'd landed on her feet when she got the position at Rosman's Bank and then – the thought of it still made him smile – she'd fallen flat on her face coming through the front door. Pure slapstick. Ray had nearly burst, trying not to laugh.

He'd worked out from the other girls' tittle tattle that she lived with her dad, just the two of them. So, even though she'd assured Ray she'd be coming with the bank to the country, her old man had most likely put his foot down. And, of course, a girl like that wouldn't have the gumption to stand up to him.

The sound of someone rapping on a window pulled Ray out of his daydream. It was Pam and Nancy – the terrible twosome – laughing and pointing at him from inside a nearby carriage.

Pam stood up and slid back the top window. 'Hurry up,' she said. 'She's not coming and if you stand out there much longer, you'll miss the train. And all the fun!'

He rolled his eyes. He'd like to sit with Pam and Nancy. At least they'd have a giggle. That awkwardness with Pam seemed to be forgotten now, thank God, and this might be the last time their little gang could be together for a while.

Once they got to Snowden Hall, he'd be – Ray's stomach plunged at the thought – well, he'd be management and probably ought to keep his distance. It would be a sort of 'last hurrah' to spend the train journey with Pam and Nancy.

But oughtn't he really to sit with the other men? Without being too friendly? Ray bit his lip. He could see problems ahead if he was too pally. They mightn't take too kindly to him ordering them about, once they arrived at Snowden Hall.

It was all very well for Uncle Bob to have recommended him for this promotion before he retired, but no one seemed to have given it any consideration. No consideration at all.

According to Bob, this was Ray's big chance.

'This war's changed everything, lad,' he'd said. 'A smart fella like you can get on, if you play your cards right!' He'd jabbed his finger at Ray. 'So, act the part from now on, eh? No more larkin' about!'

It was good advice; Ray didn't want to waste the opportunity. But it might help if he was a little clearer on what he was actually supposed to be doing.

The chaps were sitting in the next carriage along. Big Bill was next to the window. Ray caught a glimpse of the swell of his stomach, his red hair and moustache. He – and Geoff and Norm – would most likely want to discuss how things would be arranged at Snowden Hall and Ray hadn't even thought that far ahead. It was all quite daunting, this sudden responsibility.

Funny how all the men were sticking together and the girls were doing the same. Would they be segregated like that at Snowden?

It reminded Ray of a Cub Scout camping trip to Essex, when he was eleven. There was a group of Girl Guides at the other end of the field and *Akela* had warned them that if any boys were found in the girls' tents, they'd be sent straight home. Boys and girls didn't mix. It was too dangerous.

Ray smiled. He'd enjoyed the Scouts. The last – the *only* time – he'd been in uniform. The following year, when his dad died, he'd had to leave the Scouts for good.

'You're the man of the house now, son,' Uncle Larry or Uncle Bob or someone had told him.

PFEEEEEEEEE! The guard blew his whistle. Blast! That was it, then.

But the next moment, the guard was yelling, 'Get a move on, Miss!'

Ray wheeled around and there she was: Maggie Corbett, staggering across the platform towards him. She had a small black suitcase in one hand, a bulky carpet bag in the other and the strap of her gas mask over one shoulder. Her felt hat was about to fall off, her face was flushed and she was grimacing, as though in pain.

'Here!' Ray leapt forward, grabbed the case and tried to take the carpet bag but she pulled it back.

'No, I can manage,' she gasped, straightening her hat.

There was a high-pitched squeal of brakes and a hiss of steam.

'Quick!' Ray yelled. 'It's moving off!'

They'd have to jump on and find their seats later. It was a disaster. This was exactly the scenario he'd planned so carefully to avoid.

Ray had a sudden image of himself falling down the gap between train and platform, squashed to a pulp or getting his leg stuck and being dragged along the platform, yelling in agony.

A woman – Pam, no doubt – was screaming encouragement through the window. There wasn't time to imagine more disasters; if he didn't act now, it would be too late.

They were running alongside the train, which was speeding up. Ray switched Maggie's case into his other hand, turned the heavy metal handle of the nearest door and yanked it open.

'Come on, I'll lift you!' He grabbed Maggie by the back of her coat and heaved and pushed her up onto the step. It was hardly gallant or gentlemanly but needs must. Then he threw the case in after her and jumped on board. The train gave a sudden jolt and Ray caught Maggie's arm just in time to stop her falling.

He was vaguely aware of shouting and cat calls. Men's voices. The open door was swinging wildly and Ray held onto his trilby with one hand and leaned out to try to reach it. The platform was flashing by. He grabbed the door, pulled it back using all his strength and slammed it shut.

Bloody hell, they'd done it.

A cheer rang out from a dozen or so soldiers further along the corridor. Some were sitting on the floor, playing cards, others were standing against the windows, smoking.

'Well done, mate!' one yelled.

Another gave an appreciative whistle. 'We were layin' bets you wouldn't make that!'

Ray tried to catch his breath. He gave Maggie a hard stare. This was all her fault. He straightened his tie and rearranged his mac so it was square on his shoulders. It wasn't the most dignified way to start the journey, entertaining the troops.

They needed to move on and get into a compartment. Ray felt uneasy around soldiers, with their quips and teasing and their strength in numbers. What must they think of him, in his civvies?

Damn, he'd really given his arm a good wrenching, pulling that door in. Almost pulled it out of its socket. Ray gave it a cursory rub. He'd like to take his coat and jacket off and inspect the arm more closely, but the soldiers' eyes were on them. It'd look feeble, after all his heroics, if he appeared to have hurt himself.

'Goodness! Thanks ever so much,' Maggie said, when they'd both recovered enough to speak.

Ray shrugged. 'Just doing my job. I'd almost given up on you.'

She winced. 'I'm so sorry. I—'

He put his hand up. 'Spare me the sob story. Come on.' He retrieved her case which had landed on its side. 'We've got seats in a compartment along here. The train's full to the gunnels, in case you hadn't noticed.'

He stopped. She wasn't following him. She was leaning against the side for balance and cradling the carpet bag.

'I ...' She glanced down the corridor. The soldiers looked back. One or two were smiling, encouragingly. She lowered her voice and spoke to Ray. 'I need to go to the lavatory.'

'Right. Shall I take your bag?'

'No! It's ... I can manage, thanks.'

There was certainly something very precious in there. It was threadbare and worn and her suitcase wasn't much to write home about either. It was battered and dented and the catches on the top were orange with rust.

Ray's heart softened. She was a pathetic little thing, with her shabby luggage and her obvious lack of money, so different from Pam and Nancy and the others. How on earth was she going to fit in?

She was standing in front of him, swaying with the motion of the train, as though waiting for permission to go.

'Very well,' Ray said. 'Come and find us. We'll be along here. I've got your ticket, so don't go wandering off!'

'No, "don't go wandering off", Miss!' one of the soldiers mimicked, making his pals laugh. Ray gritted his teeth. Was that how he sounded?

He watched as Maggie made her way unsteadily towards the soldiers. Those who were sitting on the floor, started to pull their legs in.

'Hello, sweetheart, is that your fella?'

'Come on, darlin', give us a smile!'

'Or a kiss!'

'What's your name, then?'

'Say, would you like to write to me? I'm ever so lonely!'

'Don't go wandering off now, will you, sweetheart?'

The jokes were accompanied by loud laughter, excited whoops

and yet more whistles. Anyone would think they'd never seen a girl before.

Ray hesitated. Should he wait, keep an eye on her? No, don't be daft; she was a grown woman. Maybe she was even enjoying the soldiers' attention. Ray's experience of the fairer sex was limited and somewhat disastrous. Who knew what women liked?

He made his way down the corridor. The train was rocking like a boat as it sped up and he almost lost his balance more than once. He nodded his thanks as he squeezed past yet more troops. The train was teeming with them. They were even using the luggage racks as hammocks.

London's grey skyline flickered past the dirty windows. He caught glimpses of silver barrage balloons with fins like giant fish and pulverised, half-demolished buildings. It was a shameful thought but he could barely believe his good fortune. There were constant twinges of guilt about Ma, of course, and it was too bad about losing the flat but, otherwise, Ray felt nothing but relief to be leaving it all behind.

He'd reached the girls' compartment. Pam and Nancy waved through the glass, gesturing to the seat they'd saved.

'Come on, twinkle toes!' Pam said, as he slid open the door and stepped between the other passengers' feet and bags. He sat down gratefully between her and Nancy and took off his hat. The compartment was now full. When Maggie reappeared, he'd give up his place for her and join the men.

Ten, fifteen, twenty minutes passed and there was still no sign of her. The train regularly ground to a halt and, having nothing better to do, everyone in the compartment – except a woman in the corner who didn't look up from her knitting – gazed out of the window.

'Where's this then?' Pam asked.

Ray shrugged. 'Haven't a clue. That's the idea of all the station names being removed, Pam, dear.'

She whacked him on the shoulder. 'All right, Sarky! I thought you might know, that's all. Seeing as you know most things. Bet you were a right know-it-all at school, don't you think, Nance?'

Nancy didn't answer. She was asleep on the other side of Ray, her mouth open, snoring gently.

It was a slow journey. As well as stops at unknown, mostly deserted stations, they had to pull into the sidings every so often, to let other trains through.

Maggie still hadn't appeared.

Ray couldn't relax. He stood up. 'I'd better go and see what's happened to her.'

Pam tutted. 'I hope she's not going to be trouble, that one.'

As he made his way down the corridor, Ray heard a commotion ahead: loud male voices and guffaws. It was bound to have something to do with Maggie Corbett.

'That's let the cat out of the bag!' a man called out, followed by raucous laughter.

She was standing in the corridor, red-faced, flustered and surrounded by half a dozen soldiers.

He'd reached her now. 'Miss Corbett? What on earth's going on?'

She turned and her eyes widened. 'Mr Maguire! Something … oh, it's such a nuisance. I'm afraid I've lost my cat.'

'You've lost your cat,' he repeated, deadpan. It sounded like code for something else. He knew, from growing up in a house with three sisters, that girls often had queer expressions for things. When they said they had the painters and decorators in, for example, that meant something entirely different, something mysterious and embarrassing. Perhaps this was the same, although he couldn't for the life of him think what it might be. The soldiers were certainly enjoying the joke.

'She's a sweet little thing,' Maggie was saying. 'She's called Tabby and I know I oughtn't to have brought her, but it was that or … and she's never been on a train before and she took fright. I only hope she hasn't jumped out of a window!'

Ray shook his head and looked out at the streets and buildings flashing by. At this precise moment, jumping out of a window seemed quite a tempting proposition.

Compartment doors around them were sliding open as passengers put their heads out, to see what all the kerfuffle was.

'Miss Corbett,' Ray asked, keeping his voice low and calm, 'are we talking about a real cat here?'

She grimaced and bit her lip.

'This is not a joke?'

'It's not a joke.'

In any other circumstances, Ray supposed he might have found the situation amusing. He liked a laugh as much as the next man. But not here, not now, when he was in charge. This was ridiculous and it was making him look ridiculous too. But at least it explained all the secrecy with the carpet bag. There was a cat in it! Or rather, there had been.

'So, to be clear,' he said, 'you've brought a cat with you, to Snowden Hall?'

He hadn't thought it necessary to add 'No pets' to the instruction sheet that he'd issued to all staff. Married couples were to be billeted around the estate or in houses in the village; the single men and women, or those, like Norman Keeling, who weren't bringing spouses, were to be put up in dorms in the house itself. No children, obviously. Clearly, he'd failed in his task. He should have also made clear: no pets.

He'd got it all wrong about Maggie Corbett. She was nothing but a silly little girl who'd brought her pet cat with her to work! With a bit of luck, the blasted cat wouldn't be found before they arrived at their destination and that would be the end of it.

Suddenly, a huge cheer went up. One of the soldiers, grinning broadly, held up the offending article – cradled surprisingly tenderly in his large hands – a striped brown and white cat. ''Ere he is! Found 'isself a nice warm corner in the guard's van!'

The guard's van! Ray slapped his hand on his forehead. It was getting worse. There'd probably be an excess fare to pay or a fine for bringing an animal on board.

Maggie took the cat back and then, blushing, she thanked all the soldiers. 'Thank you, Ted, thanks so much, Mickey … Well done, Sam …'

Blimey, she knew their names! They'd all clearly had a whale of a time. One of the soldiers who seemed especially solicitous, helped Maggie return the cat to the carpet bag.

'She doesn't seem any worse for wear,' Maggie said, turning to Ray.

'I'm so glad.'

She looked at him warily. 'I think I'd better stay out here in the corridor.'

'Yes, you better had.' He checked his pocket watch. 'Should only be another hour or so. Here …' He fished into his pocket and held up a ticket. 'If the guard comes, you'll need this. And hide the stupid cat, won't you?'

Chapter 4

Snowden Hall, September 1940

'Oh, excuse me! I do beg your pardon!' Joseph had almost flown into the parlour, expecting it to be empty, only to find he'd burst in on a knitting circle.

The women – seven or eight of them – looked equally surprised. Eyes widened in alarm, needles were dropped in panic. He stepped backwards and started to pull the door to, as Mrs Mason leapt to her feet.

'Your Lordship!'

Joseph put his head back around the door and smiled. They all looked so worried; he didn't want them to think he was cross.

He'd been searching for his Longines watch, a birthday present from Esther. He had to keep taking it off because the metal gave him a rash on his wrist. He was forever losing it.

Mrs Mason was peering at him over her spectacles, her face creased in concern. 'So sorry, Sir. I thought you'd be in London today, what with the move an' all. Otherwise, I'd never have presumed—'

'No, we'd never have presumed,' one of the other women said primly.

Mrs Mason shot her a look over her shoulder.

'We haven't touched a thing!' the other woman added. Her eyes were as wide as saucers.

Joseph coughed. 'At ease, ladies! As you were. No need to apologise, Mrs Mason. I was looking for something.'

'Your watch, Sir, I'll be bound.' She smiled. 'We haven't seen it, have we, ladies?'

'No!' they chorused. Some of them looked around the room and down at the carpet, trying to help.

'We're knitting for the troops, Sir,' Mrs Mason said. 'Balaclava helmets, socks, vests and the like.'

'If you can knit, you can do your bit!' someone chimed.

Mrs Mason coughed. 'And we thought this would be the last chance, before the bank staff arrive later today, so …'

Joseph raised a hand. 'Excellent, ladies. Doing your patriotic duty! You're more than welcome. I won't disturb you any longer.'

He started to close the door but one of the women – a snow-haired, hunchbacked creature – waved her knitting needles and croaked, 'I was only saying, your Lordship …'

'Yes?' Joseph asked. It was easy for the older generation to feel invisible, so he focused his attention on the old dear and smiled.

'I was only saying, Sir, how that Adolf Hitler should have his eyes pulled out with a couple of these!'

Joseph coughed, to hide his smile. 'Absolutely,' he said.

'I mean to say, we used to think he was rather a comical chap, didn't we? All that shouting and jumping up and down and the silly moustache? Like Charlie Chaplin! Well, we don't think that now.' She shook her head and to Joseph's relief, placed her knitting needles back on her lap. 'Not at all.'

Mrs Mason looked worried. She was like a shepherdess, whose flock had suddenly gone running in all directions.

He felt he should throw her a lifeline, despite his hectic schedule. The bank was moving today, the telephone hadn't stopped ringing and his driver was waiting for him to sign a pile of documents that were needed in Bond Street.

And he had to find his watch. The clock on his desk had stopped and it was driving him to distraction, not knowing the time. He kept forgetting and looking at the damn clock and seeing the same time – five past eight – and he couldn't keep putting his head out of the room to look at the grandfather clock in the hall.

'Do introduce me to the ladies, Mrs Mason,' he said.

The women shuffled in their seats. One or two touched the back of their hair and straightened their skirts. His mother used to host knitting circles and although Esther hadn't kept up the tradition, clearly Mrs Mason had.

Some of them looked familiar. Joseph had known many of the villagers, by sight, at least, most of his life.

'This is Mrs Enid Brown and her sister-in-law Joyce Matheson, your Lordship. They live in the old vicarage …' Mrs Mason introduced each of the ladies. Joseph smiled and made an appropriate comment each time, his mind half on the documents he needed to sign and the calls he needed to make.

Then, finally, 'And this is Mrs Nicholls. Gwen Nicholls. Her parents—'

'—ran the village shop,' he finished, feeling the blood drain from his face and then, in the next moment, his heart lift.

He could hardly breathe. *Gwen.* Gwen Tapper, as he'd known her. It was her, after all these years. He knew she didn't live in Snowden village any longer so what was she doing here? And then, his next thought was, *how can I make her stay?*

'Gwen, how lovely!' he said, not caring how that might sound or that Gwen's pale cheeks suddenly had roses. 'How … good to see you!'

He stretched out his hand and there was an awkward pause as she put down her knitting and shook hands with him. It was so formal, after all they'd been to each other. Her hand was warm and slightly coarse. She'd been working, all these years. No life of leisure for Gwen Tapper.

'What brings you back here?' he asked. He couldn't stop smiling.

'I … I came to care for my mother. She isn't – wasn't – too well,' Gwen said, eyes downcast.

'Oh, I'm so sorry to hear that. Do give her my best, won't you?'

Gwen nodded.

The room was silent. Joseph had almost forgotten where he was. He pulled himself together and stepped back, rubbing his hands.

'It's rather chilly in here, Mrs Mason. I'll send someone in to light the fire, shall I?'

'No, no, there's no need, Sir,' Mrs Mason said. She seemed anxious to be rid of him now. 'We'll be at Mrs Henderson's next time, so we won't be troubling you again. We take it in turns to host, you see. Only we'd never have taken the liberty, had we known you were home. We were expecting you later, Sir.'

He clasped his hands together. 'Do you have everything you need? Tea? A small sherry perhaps?'

'It's only ten o'clock,' someone pointed out.

'Ah yes, a little early. But then again, why not? I have my evening whisky earlier and earlier these days. We're not living in normal times, so why be normal?'

'We shall have tea later, in the kitchen,' Mrs Mason said firmly, when the laughter had finally died down.

'Right, good. Fine.' Joseph nodded. 'Marvellous work, ladies. I will leave you but if you change your mind about the sherry, do help yourselves.' He pointed at the drinks cabinet on the far wall. 'It's not locked!'

The women were still laughing as he stepped backwards out of the room, closing the door behind him. He saved the last glance for Gwen, who'd lifted her face now. She was watching him closely, with soft eyes.

Chapter 5

The horse and cart swung sharply off the lane and onto a gravelled drive.

Maggie, sitting up high next to the driver, grabbed the rail as they went through a pair of metal gates and past a lodge on the left. She was feeling a queer mixture of dread and excitement.

There it was, at the end of a long avenue of trees: Snowden Hall. The cart rattled and shook as the men in the back stood up.

One of them gave a low whistle. 'Now, that's what you call a house!'

'Mansion, more like!'

'Surprised those iron gates haven't gone for tanks!'

They sounded thrilled and eager to get there. Was she the only one who was a bag of nerves?

The horse started to speed up. Every few strides, his steady walk turned into a more purposeful trot and then back to a walk again.

''E knows he's nearly home,' the driver said, still staring straight ahead. He was an old chap, with a grey beard and flat cap. Those were the first words he'd spoken since Maggie and the men had climbed aboard at the station. 'Wants 'is dinner,' he added, with a gap-toothed grin.

He wasn't the only one. Maggie's stomach was rumbling. She

hadn't eaten a thing since a rushed piece of toast that morning. She'd eaten it so fast that she'd got indigestion as she tried to run for a cab, with Kath Deacon's coins gripped firmly in her hand.

She hoped there'd be something to eat when they arrived. A sandwich would do, or a piece of bread and dripping. Anything.

Maggie hadn't minded the driver's silence on the slow journey from the station. It had given her chance to look about and breathe in the fresh – and sometimes whiffy – air. The horse's rhythmic clip-clopping was soothing after the busy morning she'd just had.

They'd travelled along empty lanes, past rolling green meadows and fields of crops. In the distance, she'd spotted the tiny white dots of sheep on the hillsides. Everything looked so lush and healthy. Such a contrast to grey, sick London. It was as though Maggie had been dropped into another world.

She'd expected to see farmers, or perhaps a shepherd with a crook, but they hadn't seen another soul the whole way. Nor a cart, carriage or even anyone on a bicycle.

Where was everyone? How would she ever get used to all this space?

'There's a kestrel!' one of the men yelled from the back of the cart. It sounded like Ray Maguire.

Maggie jumped, thinking for a moment they meant a plane. A Spitfire, a Hurricane or – God help them – enemy aircraft. But no, it was a beautiful brown bird, hovering in the air, wings fluttering. She exhaled, remembering she was safe now.

The Hall was looming ever larger. How many two-up and two-downs could fit into that? It reminded Maggie of Buck House, or Buckingham Palace as Mutti preferred them to say. Mutti had taken her and Vi to see the palace once. They'd stood on the pavement and peered through the railings.

'Ain't the windows mucky!' Vi had said, which made them laugh. But Mutti had told them the palace had over six hundred rooms, which was a lot of windows to clean.

Apart from that trip out, the nearest Maggie had ever come

to a posh place like this was one winter's day before Violet was born. Mutti had been doing some tailoring for a lady and had to deliver the finished garment to her house on the other side of town. They had to take the Tube and two buses and even then, there was a long walk but when they got there, it was worth it.

The house was tall, with iron railings and a gate and stone steps up to the front door, which was dark blue, with a shiny letter box and knocker.

Mutti had lifted Maggie up, so she could lift the knocker and make the rat-a-tat-tat on the door. It made her giggle.

The lady of the house invited them in. It was so warm after the chill of outside, and the drawing room, as it was called, was full of so many lovely things that Maggie almost went cross-eyed, staring at them all.

Mutti told her firmly to sit in her seat and not to move.

The floor was covered in Persian rugs and little tables bearing photographs and ornaments. There were paintings on the walls and little treasures everywhere. It was like being in a shop. A coal fire burned in the grate and the room smelled of pine wood and polish.

Maggie would have liked to have stayed in that room forever but once they'd had a cup of tea – served in a fine china tea set, with a plate of biscuits – they had to leave. It was dark outside by then and even colder than when they'd arrived.

'*Komm*, walk fast and you will get warm,' Mutti said, reaching for Maggie's hand.

Maggie hadn't been able to resist turning her head for one last glimpse of the house. The drawing-room window was glowing orange and as she watched, someone pulled the curtains closed.

'*Was ist los, Liebchen?*' Mutti asked. 'What's the matter? Didn't you have a nice time?'

All the joy she'd had from the rare treat of a day out had melted away.

It wasn't fair, Maggie said to her mother, how rich people

lived in big houses like that, while other people were poor and had nothing.

But Mutti said she should be quiet and count her blessings.

'There is always someone in a worse place than you, Maggie. Always.'

Mutti had been right. The whole of London was in a worse place than Maggie now. She'd left the bombing and the destruction behind and although she was glad – and grateful – she felt horribly guilty too.

She gazed at Snowden Hall. With its golden stone and rows of windows, it really was like a palace. Surely, they wouldn't be lodging there? More likely, she'd be sharing a room in one of the outbuildings or somewhere in the grounds.

It would all be much easier if Maggie knew her colleagues a little better. They hadn't made much effort with her after she'd told Miss Sharp she wouldn't be moving to the country with the bank; she could hardly blame them. By the time Vi's postcard came and Maggie changed her mind about leaving London, it was too late to make pals.

And now they probably thought she was standoffish as well as flighty, as she'd spent the whole train journey loitering in the corridor with soldiers, playing hide-and-seek with the cat.

As well as the horse and cart, a sleek motor car with running boards and a uniformed driver had been sent to meet them from the train. Maggie didn't think the other women, in their smart wool suits and overcoats, would take too kindly to sharing the car with a cat, so she'd opted to ride in the cart.

'We know our place, Tabby, don't we, eh?' Maggie whispered into the carpet bag on her lap.

It had been a queer journey from Paddington. Maggie had planned to hide with Tabby in the WC, well out of everyone's way, but she hadn't reckoned on the train being so full, or the cat making that sudden bid for freedom.

What a difference from the last time she'd been on a train, the summer before war broke out. That had been a glorious day: the last time she'd been truly happy.

Maggie, Mutti and Violet had gone to the seaside on a Sunday School trip that had been planned, and saved for on a penny-a-week savings scheme, for months. Mutti handed a penny to Violet each Sunday morning and she ran all the way to the church, without stopping, to deliver it to Mrs Bottomley and have the card ticked off.

By the time the day of the trip arrived, they were all paid up.

At the last minute, it looked as though Mutti wouldn't be able to go. Dad was moaning and she pulled a face at the girls and said she should probably stay at home. Dad was poorly. He was always poorly, when he didn't like the thought of her going out. In the end, though, Maggie and Vi had persuaded her to come.

'Very well,' she agreed. 'I'll face the consequences later!'

Maggie loved the way Mutti said 'conse-qvences'. It was a word she could never quite master but still insisted on using. Probably because she knew it made Maggie and Violet laugh.

They took a knapsack of sandwiches wrapped in greaseproof paper and chatted excitedly on the train, all the way to the coast. The gas masks on their laps were the only hint of what might be to come but, on that day, they couldn't even imagine it. The world, with its bright sunshine reflected in everyone's happy smiles, seemed like a perfect place that nothing could ever spoil.

It had been good to get away for a day, to escape the tension-filled house and the news on the wireless. Dad listened to it constantly, shaking his head and forecasting the end of the world.

When they arrived at the little seaside station, they climbed down onto the platform, waved goodbye to the others and walked quickly down to the beach. They didn't want to be lumbered with anyone else.

The sun beat down, they were grateful for their hats and they cooled their feet with a paddle in the sea. The water was freezing and when a particularly large wave caught them out and soaked the hems of their dresses, they ran screaming and laughing back up the beach.

They flopped down on the hot sand, put their faces up to the sun and basked in the warmth. In no time, their cotton dresses were dry again. They folded up their cardigans, put them under their heads for pillows and lay back, listening to the rhythmic swish and pull of the waves on the shore.

Mutti loved the beach; it reminded her of home. She didn't speak much about where she'd grown up, in North Germany, but Maggie knew it was on the coast, with miles of golden sand. No wonder an occasional flash of sadness passed across Mutti's face that day; she'd given up a lot to marry their father.

After a while, Violet could lie still no longer. She started to do handstands and cartwheels on the sand. Then something caught her eye.

'Look!' she called out. 'Donkeys!'

She knew better than to ask if she could have a donkey ride but Maggie and Mutti saw the yearning in her eyes and exchanged smiles. She'd always been horse mad. Goodness only knew where she got it from, because apart from on the big screen, on rare trips to the cinema, the only horses Vi had ever seen were the rag-and-bone man's skinny nag and the coalman's dray horse. The coalman's horse had long hair on his feet, which Violet told them was called feathering.

'Ach, Violet. You must have been a grand *Dame* in another life,' Mutti said. 'A lady who rode to hounds. Side-saddle!'

They picked themselves up off the sand. Mutti gave Violet a sixpence and nodded in the direction of the donkeys. '*Komm!*' she said. '*Wir gehen mal gucken.*'

Maggie shot her a warning glance. Although war still seemed a remote possibility, they couldn't risk anyone hearing her speak.

'English, Mutti,' she said. 'Always English, now. Remember?'

Meanwhile, Violet had raced down the beach ahead of them

and when they caught her up, she was patting the donkeys' woolly necks and reading out their names from the browbands.

'There's Neddy, that one's Ted and this is Samson. Oh look, there's even one called Winston!'

Violet chose Dandy, the prettiest of them all. She gave the man her sixpence and he swung her up into the saddle as though she weighed no more than a pound of sugar.

He tapped the metal bar that stood up from the saddle. ''Old on to that.'

As soon as he moved away, Violet took her hands off the bar and folded her arms across her chest. 'That's for babies,' she told Maggie.

They had to wait until a few more customers arrived before the donkey procession down the beach could start.

'Let's wait here,' Mutti said. 'They will soon be back.'

They watched the retreating donkeys for a minute and then Mutti turned to Maggie and stroked her fingers gently over her cheeks. Her eyes were filled with tears. She started to say something but a woman nearby suddenly screamed blue murder as a seagull flew too close, aiming for her ice cream. By the time the commotion was over, Violet and the donkeys were back and so was Mutti's smile. The moment had passed.

Maggie shook herself back to the present; they'd almost reached Snowden's front door. This must be what it felt like to be a lady of the manor, arriving home, even if she were in a cart pulled by a blinkered old horse rather than a carriage.

If only Mutti could see her! Maggie imagined her clapping her hands in delight. 'Clever girl! Look at you! Going up in the world!'

Against all the odds, against her dad's wishes and her own doubts, Maggie was here. She'd escaped or she'd arrived, depending on which way you looked at it.

Oh, but her head was in a spin. On the one hand, she thought Mutti would approve. She could imagine her saying, 'Maggie, you did the right thing.' As she'd been dragged away, hadn't her mother's last words been, 'Look after Violet!'?

But another voice inside her head was saying, 'Maggie Corbett, you're a disgrace. You don't deserve this. So much for wanting to do your bit. You've simply left the war behind and run away.'

Then, there was the small matter of Dad. He'd be going barmy. She wouldn't put it past him to track her down and take her home. The thought of it made her heart race.

No doubt, as soon as he got in from work today, Kath Deacon would run round from next door to tell him Maggie had gone. They were thick as thieves, those two. Maggie couldn't stand the woman and yet, it was odd, the way things had turned out. If it hadn't been for Kath Deacon, she wouldn't have got away at all.

This morning, Dad had gone off to work early and Maggie had resolved to leave. She simply had to pack a bag and go. It was easy. Except, she couldn't leave Tabby behind.

'If you go,' Dad had said, on the night she'd announced the bank was moving, 'there's no telling what'll 'appen to that bloody cat.'

Maggie knew what that meant. It was worse than forgetting to feed her; he'd have the cat put down.

He'd tried once before when war broke out and that stupid leaflet came round and everyone was doing it – queuing up to have their pets put to sleep. It was for 'the best' he'd argued but Maggie, Mutti and Vi had bravely ganged together and managed to talk him round. But if Maggie left, there'd be no one to stick up for the cat.

There was nothing else for it. If Maggie was leaving, Tabby had to come too. But five minutes before she was due to go, she still couldn't find her.

She'd raced up and down the alleyways, calling, 'Here, Puss Puss!' She'd checked the tops of walls, behind dustbins and stuck her head into yards where sheets and shirts and pillowcases billowed on washing lines.

There was no trace of Tabby. Maggie felt rotten but she was going to have to leave the cat behind. If she didn't run now, she'd miss the bus and the train and the chance of another life.

But when she let herself back into the house, dejected and worn out, and glanced at the kitchen clock, she realised the game was up. It was too late.

She slumped at the table. It wasn't meant to be. She could have put her head in her hands and wept.

'This what you're looking for?'

Kath Deacon was standing in the doorway, Tabby curled up against her chest. 'Found 'er in me yard, sitting in a puddle of sunshine.'

Maggie didn't know whether to be pleased or cross. Of all the people to find her!

'Ta, Kath, but it's too late. I've missed the bus and the train now.'

She hadn't intended to blurt out quite so much information but as a wave of tiredness washed over her, she suddenly didn't care anymore.

Kath glanced down at the small case, standing by the door. 'Off on your 'olidays? No, course not. Tell me to mind me own, eh? You could still catch a cab, couldn't you? Leg it up to the High Street and flag down one of them black cabs. Provided they can get through, would you make it to the station then?'

Maggie pursed her lips. It was an idea. As long as the roads weren't blocked, a taxi would probably get her there in time. But that would cost a small fortune. She didn't have it. No, she couldn't do it.

''Ere.' Kath put Tabby down and placed some coins on the kitchen table.

Maggie looked at the money. 'I can't.'

'You can. Give it me back, one day. We'll call it a loan.'

There wasn't time to argue. Maggie put the coins in a pocket, muttered a thank you and picked up the cat. Then, to the obvious surprise of both her neighbour and Tabby, she placed the cat in a carpet bag and closed it up. Tabby let out an indignant miaow.

Maggie didn't look back, or leave a note; she simply left.

* * *

'Whoa up!' the driver called now, pulling on the reins.

The horse came to a juddering halt in front of Snowden Hall. The car that had brought the others from the station, was already there.

The cart creaked as the men jumped out and landed with a crunch on the gravelled drive.

'Cor, look! Cabbages!' the red-headed chap exclaimed. The borders around the drive had been turned into a giant vegetable patch, with neat rows of cabbages, beetroot and long green stems of brussels sprouts visible in the dark soil. The war effort had even reached the countryside.

Tabby popped her head out of the carpet bag and Maggie gave her a reassuring stroke.

The men were in high spirits, joking and shoving one another, as they heaved the bags off the cart. They seemed oblivious to her, sitting up at the front, waiting for someone to give her a hand down.

Maggie envied them their easy repartee and confidence. She was full of doubts. What was she doing here? She glanced at the gas mask in her lap. Did she even need this anymore?

'What did you do in the war?' she imagined someone asking her one day and her answer would be so shameful she didn't know if she'd dare admit it. What could she say, after all? 'Oh, I did my bit, all right. I ran away to the countryside and I saved the life of a cat.'

Chapter 6

'And this'll be your room,' Mrs Mason, the housekeeper, said.

Maggie could hardly believe her luck; she was bunking down in the house after all! She was sharing a room at the back of the house, but it was still the closest she'd ever get to the life of a royal princess.

Her roommates were Miss Fry and Miss Barbour. They were a little older than her – early twenties, she guessed – and their clothes were very up-to-the-minute but they seemed nice enough. They'd already told her to call them 'Nancy and Pam'.

'You're to keep the room tidy yourselves,' Mrs Mason said. She sniffed. 'There's no one here to clean up after you, do you hear?'

After the butler – an *actual* butler – had opened Snowden's front door to the bank staff, it was Mrs Mason who'd welcomed them.

If you could call it a welcome.

She'd stood in the hall as they came in and shaken their hands without enthusiasm. 'Dakin'll show you around down here before I take you up to your rooms. And I'll be needing your ration books. Don't forget, mind,' she'd said.

She was a dour woman in her sixties, with a neat bun of grey hair, ruddy cheeks and an unmistakeable black eye. She reminded Maggie of the no-nonsense women from the street back home.

Now, on the landing, the girls peered into the room. There were two sash windows on the far wall, three neatly made narrow beds with hardly a gap between them, a wooden chest, mirror and wardrobe.

'Tonks'll bring your bags up,' Mrs Mason said. 'We'll be serving a late lunch in half an hour. Bathroom's down the corridor.'

An indoor lav! What a treat! No chamber pot or trekking out to the privy at night. Maggie almost squealed at the thought but the other two were taking it all in their stride, so she kept quiet.

'Thank you!' she called down the corridor, as the housekeeper took her leave. 'I'm sure we'll be very comfortable!'

By the time she'd turned around, the others had shot into the room. Pam was stretched out on the bed against the far wall, Nancy on the middle one, leaving the bed closest to the door for Maggie. It would be draughty, no doubt, and there wasn't a lock, so if an intruder came, she'd be first to get it. But, on the bright side, if she needed to get up in the night, at least she wouldn't have to scramble over anyone.

Through the huge windows, the view outside was like a painting: the sky, a mottled grey and below it were vast curves of rolling green hills.

Maggie squeezed through the gap between the end of her bed and the wardrobe, to get a better look. She leaned on the windowsill and gazed out.

So, this was the Cotswolds. Odd name. Odd place.

'Can you see the swimming pool?' Nancy called over. 'The chaps say they're going to swim every morning!'

Maggie looked down at the bright green square of lawn and spotted a perfect rectangle of azure blue.

'Rather them than me,' Pam said. She was lying on her back, gazing up at the ceiling.

Maggie gazed wistfully at the pool. She'd never swum in an outdoor pool; she'd rather like to, even if it were cold. She could swim rather well. Her dad had taught her in the public pool, a bus ride away. They'd go on Saturday afternoons and he was surprisingly patient, as they splashed around in the water. They were some of the few happy times she'd spent with him.

Imagine swimming in that pool during the glorious hot summer they'd just had! Heaven. And even now, the air was still warm. She could have taken a dip, if only she'd brought her swimming costume. But packing for Snowden had been such a rush and she'd been packing to come to work, not for a holiday.

'Yikes!' Nancy said suddenly. 'Good springs in this one!' She was bouncing on the bed, her blonde curls bobbing. 'This is like a dorm! Like the good old days, back at school!'

'Minus midnight feasts or pillow fights,' Pam said.

Nancy grinned. 'Oh, I don't know. We might manage one or two of those. I say, Maggie, which school did you go to?'

'I … I didn't go away to school,' she admitted. 'I went to grammar school, though.'

'Ooh, clever clogs!'

'Not really.' She wouldn't tell them she'd won a scholarship. 'I didn't like it much,' she added.

'Gosh, didn't you? I *loved* school!' Nancy said. 'Best days of your life! I'm hoping this is going to be rather like school, aren't you, Pam?'

'Abso-blinking-lutely!'

The other two had been to boarding school; no wonder they found this all so easy. Maggie had never even been away from home before and as for school … her stomach churned at the memory of the grammar school, where scholarship girls like her from the East End were looked down on. She'd only stuck it out because Mutti had been so proud. She'd scrimped and saved to buy the uniform, despite Dad's moaning. He thought it was a waste of money, couldn't see the point in educating a girl.

Pam sat up with a sigh and gazed around. 'It's rather cramped but at least none of us has to bunk up with Miss Sharp. Poor Elsie. Bet Sharpy snores like a trooper!'

Nancy looked worried. 'I think perhaps I might snore.'

Pam shook her head. 'I bet Miss Sharp snores like a rhinoceros!'

'Or a warthog!' Nancy added.

They collapsed into hysterics. Nancy had a raucous, braying laugh which made Maggie wince.

Pam flopped back down on the bed. 'I wonder where the chaps are?' She yawned. 'We can't even unpack until the boy brings our bags up.'

'I know. Bore-dom,' Nancy agreed.

'We could have brought up our own bags really, couldn't we?' Maggie said. Her voice sounded small. She wanted to add 'It wouldn't have killed us', but thought better of it.

'Speak for yourself,' Pam said. 'I've brought tons. I'll need half that wardrobe, I'm warning you both now. Heaven only knows how long we're going to be here.'

'Till the war ends,' Nancy said. 'It was supposed to be over by Christmas but crikey, it might go on for another ten years!' She sighed and thumped the pillow. 'Why did the war have to happen now and spoil the best years of our lives? I wish I could wake up to find it's all simply been a bad dream.'

Pam rolled her eyes. 'Oh, do buck up, Nancy! We have to face facts that it's probably going to be rather dull, out here in the sticks. No cinemas, no theatres and definitely no opera. And where am I going to get my hair permed?'

Nancy patted her curls. 'Thank goodness I managed to fit in one more decent cut and set before we left.'

Maggie wouldn't miss any of those. She'd never been to the opera and since that time she'd got lost coming home in the blackout from the pictures, she hadn't dared go again. As for visiting a hairdressing salon, luckily her hair had a natural curl because she never had the money for it.

She pressed her cheek against the cool windowpane.

Blimey, it looked so vast and open; it didn't look real. But Violet was out there somewhere. And hopefully not too far away.

'Oh, I say! Tidings of great joy!' Nancy shrieked. 'Look what I found on top of the chest!' She was waving a piece of paper in the air. 'An invitation! A "Welcome Reception" at seven o'clock tonight!'

Pam shot up and jiggled her hand. 'Give it here!'

A 'welcome reception'? Maggie's heart sank. What did that mean? It sounded serious. And posh.

Pam read the note and grinned. 'Super! This is more like it!' She tilted her head to one side, put her hand on her hip and struck a pose. 'Drinks on the terrace, darling?'

Maggie's heart and mind were racing. She'd have to talk to strange, new people. What would she say? And she had nothing to wear, or at least, nothing that didn't look like she was off to work. But unless she pretended to be ill, or hid under the bed, how on earth could she get out of it?

'What's the matter?' Pam asked, suddenly noticing Maggie's silence. 'Cat got your tongue?'

They burst out laughing again. Pam finally stopped and cast her eyes around the room. 'Where is that cat of yours, anyway? Don't get any ideas about it sleeping in here, will you?'

'Oh no,' Nancy agreed. 'Cat hair makes me sneeze something rotten.'

Maggie shook her head. 'Course not. She's outside.'

When they'd arrived at Snowden Hall and the others had gone with the butler on a tour of the ground floor, Maggie had followed the housekeeper into the vast kitchen. There was a strong smell of cabbage and gravy and her stomach had growled. She hoped that was a meal for them.

Two women in aprons and headscarves were bustling around, chopping veg at a large wooden table in the centre and filling pans with water at the double sink.

They turned in surprise when Maggie came in. Her arms were aching from clutching the carpet bag to her chest. She asked if she might have a bowl of water.

Mrs Mason frowned. 'A *bowl*? This might not be fancy London town but we do have cups, you know.'

'It's for my cat,' Maggie said. She put the bag down and braced herself for another ticking off, but Mrs Mason seemed unconcerned.

'Got it in there, have you? Best let it out then.'

When Tabby emerged, stretching, and sat on the stone floor and cleaned herself, apparently quite unperturbed by her adventures, the housekeeper smiled for the first time. 'Aw, it's a poppet. Best put some butter on its paws, Cook, what d'you say? So's it doesn't stray too far.'

They had butter. Enough to put on a cat's paws! Maggie's heart lifted; perhaps it was going to be all right here, after all.

'Is it a good mouser?' Cook asked.

'Ever so good,' Maggie said. In truth, she'd never seen Tabby catch anything but her words had the desired effect.

'Good. It can't stay in the house – her Ladyship would have forty fits – but there's plenty of mice around the stable yard and the barns. And there's warm straw to bed down in.'

Maggie's chest flooded with relief. Tabby was going to be allowed to stay. She'd be fine as long as she learned to catch her own food. Maggie would save her some scraps from her own plate at mealtimes, until the cat got the hang of it.

Right, that was one problem solved. And now the next: how was she going to manage to see Violet?

'Can you tell me where the nearest bus stop is, please?' she asked.

The women laughed.

'There's no buses round these parts,' the housekeeper said. 'Your choices are: hitch a lift, jump on a bicycle or Shanks' pony!'

The women were still laughing and shaking their heads when Maggie thanked them and took Tabby out through the back door, to introduce her to her new home.

* * *

'Oh, where is that silly fellow with our bags?' Pam asked now. 'I want to get changed before lunch. Public transport makes one feel so dirty. Then, Nancy, we need to decide on our outfits for tonight.'

Oh, honestly! Maggie's chest tightened. There were still hours to go before the drinks reception. Were these two really going to talk about nothing else until then?

Pam glanced across the room. 'Looking forward to it, Maggie? Chance to get dressed up, put your face on, have a drink?'

'Perhaps,' Nancy said archly, 'she's TT.'

Maggie flushed. She wasn't quite teetotal but she certainly wasn't used to drink. A port and lemon or half a stout on special occasions was about her limit. But it wasn't the drink she was worried about; it was the clothes. She hadn't brought anything suitable for a party. What in heaven's name was she going to wear?

'I say, Maggie, are you courting?' Nancy asked suddenly. 'We both are. Pam's chap, Jim, is in the RAF. He's so much better than the last one, who threw her over for a WREN.' She laughed. 'And we don't even talk about the one before that!'

Pam rolled her eyes, presumably at the thought of all the useless boyfriends before dreamy Jim. 'He's training overseas,' she said. 'All very hush-hush. And he's not my *boyfriend*—' she gave Nancy a mock glare '—he's my fiancé.'

She extended her left hand and Maggie politely stepped forward to admire her diamond ring.

'We got engaged in July. We'd only known one another six weeks. But everyone's doing it, aren't they?'

Maggie nodded. Were they?

'And my Ken's a soldier,' Nancy said. 'He looks so handsome in his uniform. Of course, we miss our chaps dreadfully but there's no point moping around. We have to keep our spirits up as best we can. What about you, Maggie? Stepping out with anyone?'

They were both sitting upright on their beds now, waiting for her response.

They were going to be disappointed. Maggie had never wished so much for a boyfriend in her life but, although the idea flashed through her mind, she couldn't simply make one up. Not on the spot like that.

'I'm not, no,' she said, retreating back to her position at the window.

'Ooh!' Nancy rubbed her hands together and her eyes widened. 'Perhaps you'll fall for one of the chaps here! "Courting in the Cotswolds"!' She laughed. 'Could be the title of a romance! Now, let's see ...'

Pam was pulling a face. 'The men are hardly anything to write home about, Nance. Don't want to raise a girl's hopes, do we?'

But there was no stopping Nancy. 'There's someone for everyone, as the saying goes,' she said.

Pam yawned.

'Let's go through them one at a time,' Nancy said.

'No, really—' Maggie said but she was cut off.

'Right, first off: Mr Braithwaite. Geoff,' Nancy said.

'Oh no!' Pam said. 'Of course, he's sweet but ... shy. He never looks you in the eye and if you so much as speak to the poor chap—'

'—or even glance at him!' Nancy added.

'—he shrinks! Looks like he wants to curl up and die.' Pam lowered her voice. 'He's got the most terrible stammer.'

There was no time for Maggie to feel sorry for poor, stuttering Geoff because they'd already moved on to the next candidate.

'Mr Dunn? Big Bill?' Nancy suggested.

'Hm ...' Pam gave this prospective candidate a little more thought. She gazed into the distance, as though picturing him. 'He's nice, Bill. And I must say, I've always had a thing for red hair. If he lost his *Billy Bunter* belly, he'd be quite handsome. But, putting all that aside ...' She raised a manicured finger. 'The question is, as a boyfriend, does he really cut the mustard?'

'Too immature?' Nancy suggested, her head cocked.

'Exactly!'

Maggie sighed. Would they even notice if she slipped out of the room? They seemed to have completely forgotten she was there.

'Mr Keeling – Norman – is, of course, married,' Nancy said. She sounded most put out, as though he'd deliberately walked down the aisle in order to spite her matchmaking endeavours.

'Is he?' Maggie asked. She wasn't the slightest interested but felt she ought to show willing. They were going to quite a lot of effort, after all, and perhaps this was their way of trying to be chummy.

Nancy sighed. 'His wife didn't want to come. I think everyone else's were grateful for the offer. She's taken the kiddies and gone to her parents in Cornwall. And then of course …' She slowed down her voice, as though she'd left the best for last. 'There's Ray Maguire!'

Was it Maggie's imagination or did Nancy shoot Pam an odd look as she pronounced Ray's name? Pam was lying back, staring at the ceiling again. There was no telling what she was thinking.

'Mr Maguire? Oh no!' Maggie said. 'That's to say, I suppose he's nice and everything but—'

'Too bossy?' Nancy asked.

'Well, yes.' Was she being indiscreet? Maggie hoped the girls wouldn't tell him. She didn't entirely trust them.

'He's not usually like that,' Nancy said. 'He's gone uppity since he got his promotion. We used to be able to rely on Ray to fix a stuck drawer or swivel chair—'

'—or a sticky typewriter key,' Pam said.

'Yes, awfully good with his hands. But he won't touch anything like that now,' Nancy said. 'Ray used to be good fun. And he's the most terrible flirt!'

'But take no notice,' Pam added, with what sounded like a touch of bitterness, 'of the flirting. It doesn't signify anything.'

Maggie frowned. 'Good fun' and 'a flirt'? That didn't sound like the man she'd met. She wondered, for a moment, if there were another Ray who worked at the bank.

Nancy sighed. 'And that's it. All the other men are married.'

'And ancient,' Pam added. 'No one's under forty.'

'Don't—' Maggie was about to say 'Don't worry yourself about me'. But Nancy didn't let her get a word in edgeways.

'Perhaps,' Nancy said, brightening at the thought, 'there'll be someone here who'll catch your eye! A stable hand or a butler? You never know your luck. Perhaps this chap who's bringing up our bags? He might be a total dish!'

'If he ever turns up,' Pam said. 'Oh, wait! That's him now, by the sound of it.' She sat up in anticipation, pressed her legs together and swivelled neatly off the bed.

The girls exchanged glances and frowns as the noises – grunting and rasping breaths – got nearer. Maggie wondered whether she should see if he needed help. This was the Snowden employee that Nancy thought might be a match for Maggie? He certainly didn't sound like love's young dream; more like someone on the verge of a seizure.

Moments later, he appeared in the doorway: a grizzled old man, not unlike the one who'd driven the cart from the station. He was loaded up like a packhorse, with bags under each arm and a case in each hand. Another bag hung from its strap around his neck.

''Ere's your fings!' he announced, as he dropped everything onto the floor in a succession of loud thumps.

When the old man had left, rubbing his arms and ignoring Maggie's 'Thank you!', and the girls had finally stopped laughing at the thought of him as Maggie's beau, Nancy suggested they should unpack.

Pam shook her head. 'Come on, I'm tired of hanging around. Let's take a look at the bathroom and then find out where the chaps are hiding themselves!'

Moments later, they left the room. Maggie was glad they hadn't invited her along. She wasn't quite sure what she thought about Pam and Nancy and it had been quite exhausting, trying not to say the wrong thing. She put her head around the door and watched as they waltzed down the corridor with linked arms, chattering nineteen to the dozen.

Oh! What was that? She turned her head, just in time to see a small figure with dark hair race across the landing at the other end of the corridor. He was gone in a flash. Maggie stared at the place where he'd been. A child, a little boy, she was sure of it. Or was she seeing things? Had he been real?

She swallowed. She didn't believe in ghosts. Not really. But then, she'd never been anywhere like Snowden Hall before. It must be centuries old. If anywhere was haunted, it was here. She glanced back the other way but Pam and Nancy had disappeared too. She was quite alone.

Oh, she was being fanciful. She'd seen someone's child, that was all. He probably belonged to someone who worked here, or the Ashfords themselves. She knew so little about the couple that were hosting them. As much as she was dreading it, at least she might find out more at this drinks party tonight.

She turned back into the room, glad to have some time to herself and to unpack the few things she'd brought.

She hoped Nancy wasn't going to make it her mission to find her a chap. None of the men from the bank that she'd met so far had set her heart a-flutter and besides, romance was the last thing on Maggie's mind.

All she wanted to do was to concentrate on her work, make sure Vi was happy and well cared for and find out, somehow, where they'd taken Mutti.

Nothing else mattered.

Chapter 7

Just before seven o'clock that evening, Maggie and the others gathered on the first-floor landing, in readiness for the welcome reception.

They'd all scrubbed up rather well. The chaps – Ray Maguire and Big Bill and two others whose names Maggie had forgotten – looked dapper in crisp shirts, flannels and Fair Isle pullovers. Even middle-aged Miss Sharp looked surprisingly glamorous, sporting a bright slick of scarlet lipstick and without her spectacles.

Laughter and chatter filled the air and drifted up from the hallway, where bank workers and their wives, who'd driven up from London earlier that day, were arriving for the party.

Pam and Nancy were hanging over the balustrade, calling out and waving to colleagues below. They were dolled up in pretty dresses, high heels and plenty of what Maggie's dad would've called 'war paint'.

In comparison, Maggie felt rather drab in her navy skirt and the cream blouse she'd only finished sewing last week. She should have packed the couple of dresses that Mutti had left behind. She'd thought about it. She'd got as far as opening the wardrobe in her parents' room this morning. But as well as the smell of mothballs, there'd been a waft of her mother's sweet lavender scent. She'd quickly shut the wardrobe doors again and turned the key. She'd swallowed hard, determined not to cry. She couldn't take anything. It was like saying Mutti didn't need them; that she wouldn't be coming back.

Nancy suddenly appeared at Maggie's side. She was frowning.

'Say, aren't you going to get ready, Maggie?' she asked. 'Chop, chop! We've got to go down any minute!'

Maggie blushed and stepped back, as though she'd been punched in the stomach. She *was* ready, for goodness' sake! She'd changed, washed her face, applied Pond's cream and a dab of precious lipstick and told herself that would have to do. But it wasn't good enough.

It was mortifying but at least no one else seemed to have heard. The chaps were gathered nearby, teasing each other and larking around. Nancy's words had almost certainly been drowned out by the babble of voices.

The next moment, someone yelled, 'Let's go!' and Nancy dashed off without another word. She jostled her way past the others, the first to head downstairs and join the throng below.

Still smarting, Maggie leaned back on the wood-panelled wall behind her, between two large oil paintings. An old building like Snowden Hall was bound to have secret panels and passages. Oh, if only she could accidentally touch one and disappear!

The thought of joining the party downstairs was making her feel quite ill. Rosman's staff were all so pally with each other and, unlike her, everyone looked the part. She didn't belong. Why had she ever agreed to come to this stupid place with all these strangers? It was turning into the worst decision she'd ever made.

She took a deep breath and forced herself to take a few paces to the top of the stairs. In the hall below, everyone was filing through a doorway, their excited chatter getting increasingly fainter. In a moment, they'd all be gone.

Maggie's fingers grazed the cool oak of the carved banister.

Did she dare slip away, back to her room and spend the evening there? Surely, she wouldn't be missed?

But as the last of the crowd disappeared from view, one person remained: Ray Maguire. He turned one way, then the other, as though searching for something. Then he glanced up the stairs and spotted her.

Was it her imagination, or did his face soften? Was that a look of sympathy or – more likely – exasperation? She was most definitely in his bad books after that ridiculous business with the cat on the train.

He'd been looking for her. Heaven only knew why. It certainly wasn't to flirt with her. Pam and Nancy had said he was a terrible flirt but she'd not seen any evidence of it. Perhaps they'd got him confused with someone else. Or perhaps – and this was more likely – Maggie just wasn't his type.

She felt a thud of disappointment. Ray Maguire wasn't going to allow her to escape. He took the stairs two at a time, his long legs making short work of the distance to the top.

'Anything the matter, Miss Corbett?'

It wasn't her place to suggest that away from the office, they might use first names. She'd already started to think of him as 'Ray' but clearly that wasn't right.

She forced a smile. 'No! Thank you, Mr Maguire. Everything's tickety-boo.'

Tickety-boo? Maggie winced. She'd never used that expression before in her life.

He was smiling at her now. Laughing, probably. He held out the crook of his arm. 'Shall we?'

Had he guessed she'd felt like running away? More likely, he remembered how she'd almost somersaulted her way into Rosman's that first morning and he didn't trust her to navigate the stairs.

Maggie took his arm awkwardly, resting her hand so it was barely touching his shirt sleeve. It was easier than offending him by saying she could manage.

Ray Maguire had now rescued her twice. If he hadn't waited on the platform and heaved her onto the train at Paddington, she wouldn't have made it to Snowden Hall. And now, without his shepherding, she'd probably have missed the welcome drinks altogether. Which mightn't have been a bad thing. She wasn't sure whether to be grateful to him or not.

As they reached the last step and a passing waitress directed them through the Long Gallery, Maggie removed her hand from Ray's arm. She wondered if she was going to have to spend the whole evening with him.

The Gallery was long and narrow, with an aisle down the middle and, unexpectedly, it was laid out with rows of desks. Some of the desks had covered typewriters on them.

Maggie gasped. 'Is this ...?'

'Impressive, isn't it? Yes, this is our banking hall,' Ray said, standing a little taller. 'Rosman's will be run from here.'

Imagine working in such a place! It was more like a beautiful, treasure-filled museum than an office. At the far end stood two cabinets, filled with plates, glasses and ornaments.

'Cor! You'd think they'd take the pictures down and hide the best china,' Maggie said, in an undertone. 'Not because we might nick anything, of course,' she added quickly, 'but in case something gets damaged. All this must be worth a fortune.'

For a moment, as she pictured herself sitting here, surrounded by sparkling chandeliers and paintings, like a Lady dealing with her correspondence, Maggie forgot to be worried about the evening ahead.

But then they made their way to the French doors which opened out onto the terrace and her stomach flipped over.

Before they went through, Ray tapped Maggie's arm, so that she stopped and turned towards him.

He cleared his throat and spoke quietly. 'I should ... erm ... take no notice of anything Nancy Fry says, Miss Corbett.' He looked down at the carpet and then back at Maggie. She could hardly meet his eye. He'd heard Nancy! Oh, this was too embarrassing.

'She blurts out whatever comes into her head. You … er … you look …' he seemed to be searching for the right word. '… Most presentable.'

Presentable? Was that all? Maggie thought she might laugh. Or cry.

Before she could reply, he stepped outside and took two glasses of wine from a waiter with a tray.

Maggie followed him. A few people standing nearby glanced around and then, clearly not finding them particularly interesting, returned to their conversations.

'Wine?' He was holding out a glass.

There didn't seem to be anything else on offer, so she took it.

'Don't get tight, will you? Best sip it,' he said.

Maggie pulled a face at him, but Ray was too busy gazing around to notice.

It was dusk and the air was still warm. Small groups of men and women – drinking, smoking, laughing and greeting friends – were dotted around the terrace and on the lawn beyond. A gramophone, set up near the open French doors, was playing big band music and from somewhere nearby, came Nancy's unmistakeable hee-haw laugh.

Lord Ashford, dressed in slacks and a patterned waistcoat, was standing on the terrace, talking to a semicircle of guests. He looked relaxed and younger, somehow, out of his business suit.

'I knew my troops here wouldn't let me down,' he was saying. 'I sent a telegram to Dakin and got one straight back. Two words: SNOWDEN READY.'

As she scanned the crowd, looking for familiar faces, Maggie spotted a pretty blonde, standing alone. She was about her age, with a pageboy hairstyle and wearing a red floral party frock, with a tasselled lace shawl draped around her shoulders. She was smoking a cigarette from an elegant holder and blowing smoke rings into the evening air. She was alone but she didn't look lonely. Rather, she looked perfectly at home. Perhaps this was her home? She might even be a member of the Ashford family.

In her other hand, the girl was holding a glass and as Maggie watched, she threw her head back and drained it. A waiter immediately appeared at her side and swapped the empty glass for a full one.

'How's the wine?' Ray asked Maggie.

She took a sip and tried not to grimace.

He laughed. 'That good?'

It was horrible. Velvety and almost dry; it had the oddest texture. 'It's not too bad, I suppose,' Maggie said. 'It's … erm, very nice.'

'Liar,' he said, laughing.

'Who's that?' Maggie asked Ray, nodding towards the blonde girl.

'I don't have the foggiest but shall we go and find out?'

She was even prettier close up. Her name was Charity Richmond.

'And yes,' she said, 'there *are* three of us: Faith, Hope and yours truly. My mother collects things. She's a …' She laughed. 'Now, let me get this right, she's a philatelist and a plangonologist. Stamps and dolls. And daughters, it turned out. She collects daughters, too. Tell me I'm not the only one with a mad mother!'

She was looking straight at Maggie.

'I … no. My mother's gone,' she said. Her stomach plunged. Blimey, why had she said that? She'd panicked.

Charity pulled a sympathetic face. 'I'm so dreadfully sorry. That damned Jerry's got a lot to answer for, hasn't he?'

'There are three girls in my family too,' Ray said and Maggie was grateful to him for deflecting attention away from her.

'Well, I don't wish to be a topper, Mr Maguire,' Charity said, 'but there are actually four girls in mine. Gracie came along two years after me. An accident, by all accounts. Oh, but a lovely one. I adore my little sister.'

'Oh, so do I!' Maggie blurted out. 'That is, I adore mine.'

She felt herself redden. She'd never gushed like that over Violet before but the others didn't seem to find it odd. In any case, why shouldn't she say she adored Violet? She did, after all.

She forced down the lump in her throat. She wouldn't cry. But heavens, she did love her sister. She wouldn't be here, putting herself through all this, otherwise.

'I'm Land Army,' Charity was saying. 'There are two of us working on the estate. Gillian's not here tonight. Not her scene. We're billeted with an old dear in the village, we have a ten o'clock curfew and we have to share a bed, which was—' she rolled her eyes '—unexpected!'

They laughed.

'Hullo, there. What's so funny?' a voice said from behind. It was Pam, with Nancy. Ray stepped to one side to make room for them to join the circle. They introduced themselves to Charity and Pam asked again, why they'd all been laughing.

'I was just saying,' Charity started to explain, 'that I'm billeted with—'

But she was cut off as Pam gasped and held up a hand as though stopping traffic. 'Oh! It's "Till the Lights of London Shine Again"!' she said, tilting her head towards the gramophone, as a new record started to play.

'So it is!' Nancy agreed.

'That's our song. Mine and Jim's,' Pam said, darting a look at Ray.

They all listened politely to the music. Maggie twirled the glass of wine in her hands. Ray fidgeted and looked over the top of their heads, as though he'd rather be somewhere else.

'Oh, I say,' Pam said suddenly, all thoughts of 'their song' apparently forgotten. 'Dreamboat at three o'clock, Nancy!'

Maggie frowned, unsure where she was supposed to look, but

Nancy, judging from her widening eyes, had understood immediately. They all followed her gaze.

The 'dreamboat' – a young airman in RAF uniform, his right arm in a sling – was marching towards them from the direction of the lawn. As he got nearer – and stopped for a moment to talk to someone – they all quickly averted their gaze. He was rather dashing. It was the uniform, of course. Men couldn't help but look dashing in uniform.

'He's injured, poor thing,' Nancy murmured, smothering a giggle. 'I'd kiss it better! Although, up close he might be all burned or pimply. We've been disappointed like that before.'

Ray rolled his eyes. Maggie wanted to beg him not to leave her with Pam and Nancy but it was too late.

'I'll leave you girls in peace,' he said, backing away. 'You've clearly got important matters to discuss.' He raised his glass of wine at them and Maggie imagined his relief, as he joined a group of chaps standing nearby. He slapped one of them on the back, making him jump and the other men roared with laughter.

Now, the airman was heading their way again. He was within touching distance. Maggie held her breath and cast her eyes at her feet, expecting him to walk straight past, but she felt him looking at her and glanced up. Nancy needn't have worried; his skin was perfect. He was perfect. For a moment, their eyes locked.

'Good evening, ladies,' he said, tipping his cap and smiling.

'Good evening!' they chimed.

He had high cheekbones and the whitest teeth. Gosh, Pam was right, he was a dreamboat. And to think, if Maggie had missed this party, she'd have missed him too.

He barely broke his stride. Almost as soon as he'd appeared, he was gone again, through the French doors and into the house.

Nancy fanned herself with her hand as though she might faint. She frowned. 'Did a gorgeous airman just wish us a good evening or were we all dreaming?'

She said it with such a puzzled air, that Charity and Maggie caught each other's eye and grinned and the next moment, all four of them were laughing. The airman had sent them quite giddy. Nancy's donkey laugh was drawing glances from the other guests, but none of them cared.

Oh, this was fun. Despite the horrid start to the evening, Maggie was actually enjoying herself. Maybe tonight wasn't turning out so bad after all.

'Excuse me, Miss.' A balding middle-aged man in a dogtooth checked jacket was tapping Maggie on the shoulder.

Still laughing, she turned to face him. She covered her mouth with her hand. 'Yes?'

'Is there any chance,' he asked pleasantly, nodding at the woman by his side, 'that my wife could have a glass of water, please?'

Maggie's hand dropped. Goodness. A waitress! Even without a frilly white apron, one of the guests thought she was a waitress. It was too humiliating.

Pam and Nancy were nudging one another and trying – unsuccessfully – not to giggle.

Charity glared at them until they stopped and immediately accosted a passing waiter. 'I'm sure this chap can help you, Sir,' she said to the man in the checked jacket.

She took Maggie's arm and steered her away. 'Silly old duffer,' she muttered. 'Here, take this.' She pulled the cream lace shawl from her shoulders with a flick of her wrist and held it out to Maggie between two fingers.

'No, I couldn't possibly—'

Charity shoved her wine glass into Pam's free hand, her cigarette holder into Nancy's and arranged the shawl around Maggie's shoulders.

'There! I know how it is when you don't have time to get ready, press a frock or find the right thing,' she said.

'But Maggie had lots of—' Nancy started. She stopped as Charity shot her a dirty look.

There was a moment's awkward silence.

Nancy bit her lip and looked remorseful. 'That shawl does look well on you, Maggie,' she said.

'Yes,' Pam said. 'It suits you, I must say.'

Charity gave them both an approving nod. She took back her glass and cigarette holder and looked appraisingly at Maggie. 'It looks perfect. To be honest, I was wondering whether a shawl was rather *de trop* with this frock, so you've done me a favour.'

Maggie blushed. They were all staring at her.

Charity raised her glass to her lips and her attention was caught by something. She gave a little start of recognition. 'Oh, I say, there's Esther!' She stood on tiptoe and waved to someone on the lawn behind them. 'ESTHER!'

They all turned to look at a woman twenty yards away, wearing a long crimson gown and matching turban.

'Oh! Do you know Lady Ashford?' Pam asked, sounding impressed.

Charity gave a small nod and smiled. 'Do excuse me, won't you? If I don't catch her now, I'll miss my chance. It was very nice to meet you all.'

And then she was gone and Maggie felt flat. She didn't care to know too much about the airman. He'd been a lovely distraction but whoever he was, he didn't belong to the bank or the house staff. He'd soon be heading back to his squadron, for certain; they weren't likely to see him again.

She'd much rather that Charity had stayed.

Charity skipped across the terrace and greeted Lady Ashford with a cry of delight and a kiss on each cheek. Maggie crossed her left arm over her chest and touched the tassels of Charity's lace shawl. She'd met someone nice, a possible pal. But if Charity mixed in those kind of social circles – with the actual Lady Ashford – she'd hardly want to be friends with her.

A little while later, a bell rang to call for order. The gramophone was switched off and the volume of chatter gradually decreased until, eventually, there was silence.

Lord Ashford had stepped up onto the low wall that skirted the terrace and now he reached down and took Lady Ashford's hand, so she could join him.

She wobbled slightly and laughed as she found her balance and he asked her softly, 'All right, my darling?'

It almost made Maggie ache to look at them. They were like film stars standing on a stage. She – and everyone else – were the audience.

As Lady Ashford raised her hand to tuck a loose strand of dark hair into her turban, the bangles on her wrist clinked gently together and glinted in the evening sun.

Lord Ashford cleared his throat and his steely gaze swept over them all. Maggie felt her shoulders drop. She'd been like a coiled spring for most of the evening but his Lordship made her feel calm. Even if the *Luftwaffe* suddenly flew over that ridge straight towards them, she didn't think she'd be scared. Not with him here, in charge.

'Good evening, ladies and gentlemen,' he said, in his clear, deep voice. 'I'll keep this short and sweet as I expect you're tired after the journey up from London and of course—' he pretended to glare '—work starts with a vengeance in the morning!'

There were a few groans, followed by laughter.

'War, or no war,' he continued, 'our motto must be "business as usual"! But, enough of that, for a moment. This is, after all, a special occasion! Esther and I …' He paused as they exchanged fond glances. 'Esther and I want to welcome you to our home, in the hope that, in the coming weeks, it will become *your* home. And that includes those of you who are billeted in the village. Please, do, think of Snowden Hall as your home too.'

He paused for a second and raised a finger to a nearby waiter, who swiftly brought him a glass of whisky on a tray.

He took a sip before resuming his speech. 'I've brought you here because you are our most important assets. Yes, you.'

Everyone grew silent and serious.

'We have important work to do. We're not on the front line, it's true; we don't wear uniforms—' he raised his glass to the airman who had reappeared and was standing alone, at the back '—or carry rifles and, yet, the work of the bank is vital to the war effort. More vital than perhaps you know.'

He paused. 'When war comes, it asks questions of us all. Are we strong or weak? Capable or chaotic? Will we crumple or cope? Sometimes the answers aren't what we hoped but one thing is certain: none of us will be the same when this war is over, as we were when it began.'

There were murmurs of agreement.

He smiled. 'But it's my fervent wish that you'll be happy here. Thank you for agreeing to come and to leave your families and friends behind. It won't be forever. This war will be over, one day. It will be won—'

'Hear, hear!' a man's voice called out.

'—and you will be reunited with those you love. But in the meantime, I hope you'll find friends and a kind of family here, at Snowden.' Lord Ashford raised his glass. 'To us. And to victory!'

Everyone joined him in lifting their glasses. 'To victory!'

Tears sprang into Maggie's eyes. That word, *family*, was a reminder of all she'd lost. Mutti was goodness only knew where and little Violet was living among strangers. Please God, let them be kind to her.

Now Lord Ashford's speech was over, people were moving away and reforming in little clusters around the lawn and terrace.

Maggie glanced around. She couldn't see anyone she knew; none of the gang from the train, as she was starting to think of them. She wondered where Charity had got to and whether she might find her again.

The glass of horrible wine in her hand was still almost completely full. She couldn't bear to take another sip. Perhaps she could put it down somewhere, or tip it into one of those stone urns, without being seen.

Oh! Suddenly the lace shawl started to slip from her shoulders and Maggie twisted to catch it before it fell.

It happened in a flash.

Someone pushed past, nudging her elbow hard and Maggie screamed as the whole, almost-full glass of red wine tipped down her front, soaking her right through to the skin.

Chapter 8

'Here!' Lady Ashford – a picture of elegance in her red evening gown and turban – stood in front of Maggie, holding out her slender hand.

Maggie, shocked and dripping and all too aware of gasps and giggles around her, gave the now-empty glass to her Ladyship, who immediately passed it to someone behind her. Then, with a light hand on Maggie's arm, Lady Ashford guided her across the lawn, dodging clusters of party guests, and through a side door into the Hall. 'Come along,' she said, kindly, 'we'll soon get you fixed up. I can't abide that Beaujolais either. Good riddance, eh?'

Immediately, in the silence of Snowden's interior and away from everyone's curious stares, Maggie felt a little less wretched.

'I'm so clumsy,' she said, as they skirted the Long Gallery, where the blackouts were being put up. She glanced down at her chest. 'Blimey. It looks like I've been stabbed.'

Oh, she wished she could take that back. But Lady Ashford didn't seem to mind.

'Quite,' she said simply, quickening her pace so that Maggie almost had to run to keep up.

The housekeeper was sitting at the table in the kitchen, ticking items off a long list. She looked up as they bustled in and shot up out of her seat. 'Your Ladyship?'

'Now, I'm sure Mrs Mason and her good ladies know all the tricks for removing stains,' Lady Ashford said. 'It's no good asking me, I can't even make a cup of tea!' She laughed. 'You must run upstairs at once, change out of this wet blouse and bring it back for Mrs Mason to work her magic.'

The housekeeper raised her eyebrows at the state of Maggie.

'Oh, no really, it's no trouble. I can do it myself,' Maggie said.

'Sort it out between yourselves, won't you?' Lady Ashford said, moving towards the door. 'I'll leave you now, then, er …'

'Maggie. Maggie Corbett.' Should she add 'Ma'am'? Or curtsey?

'Lovely.' With a smile and a nod, Lady Ashford glided from the room.

Mrs Mason ran a critical eye over Maggie. 'Upset someone, did you? And not used to wine, I dare say.' She pointed to a door on the far side of the kitchen. 'Scullery's that way, when you're ready. Soak it in the dolly tub. There's Rinso. Be quick, mind, or you'll never get that stain out.'

* * *

Maggie placed her blouse on the washing board and started to rub at the purple stains. Oh, it was ruined! She didn't even like wine, that was the stupid part. She'd never touch it again, no matter who was offering it.

Snowden's scullery was huge – as big as their whole downstairs back home – but the contents weren't any different: a mangle, a dolly tub and posser, a couple of washboards, a wicker basket and a bag of pegs. Through the window, Maggie could see the washing line strung up in the yard.

It had been a Monday – a washday – when they'd come for Mutti. Maggie had been working a late shift at the factory that day, so she was at home, pegging out sheets, when the police car drew up. Two uniformed coppers got out.

'What do you want?' Maggie asked but they marched straight past her, through the yard and into the house. They had papers and no time to spare. Mutti had five minutes to pack and say goodbye.

'Do not worry, Maggie,' she said. 'It is all a mistake.' She was trying to sound calm but there was a fearful look in her eyes.

Why was no one helping them? Why wasn't Dad here when he was needed?

Maggie glanced out through the back door. Women from the street – neighbours – were standing in a line, with crossed arms and steely faces, not even pretending to scrub their steps. They watched as Mutti was marched out of the house. One or two – including Kath Deacon – nodded, as though they approved of what was happening. Maggie's chest tightened. She'd never forgive them.

'Noooo!' she yelled, grabbing Mutti's arm and trying to pull her back.

Mutti shook her head and gently pushed Maggie's hands away. 'I must,' she said.

'Where're you taking her?' Maggie demanded.

'Holloway prison, Miss. Now, if you'll stand out the way and let us do our job—'

Holloway? Maggie's legs almost gave way.

'Look after Violet, *ja*?' Mutti called.

She was bundled into the back of the car. The last Maggie saw of her mother was a small white face like a petal, turning towards her. The car bounced over the cobbled street and away.

At the memory, Maggie started to cry. She could still hardly fathom how kind and gentle Mutti, who never even swore, had ended up in Holloway alongside murderers, thieves and vagabonds.

They hadn't even been allowed to visit; they could only write and the last letter had been returned. If Mutti wasn't at the prison any longer, where, in heaven's name, was she?

There'd been a vain hope that the authorities had finally realised their mistake and released her but as the days went by and Mutti didn't come home, all they could do was wait.

Oh, this was silly. Crying wouldn't help one bit. Maggie blew her nose, dried her eyes and pulled herself together.

She heard a noise out in the corridor. She held her breath and listened. Nothing for a moment but then, it came again. A voice, a murmur. A child, giggling. Thank goodness it wasn't dark down here else she might have had a seizure. As it was, her heart was hammering like an ack-ack gun. Perhaps the Hall really was haunted?

Maggie tiptoed towards the door, wiping her hands on her skirt. She put her head out into the corridor.

There was a little boy a few feet away, kneeling on the floor with his back to her and softly singing as he played with a toy. She glimpsed his socks, short trousers and little leather boots before she pulled her head back inside the scullery.

Not a ghost then, after all. He was tiny, like a doll, with a mop of dark curls. Maggie's heart lifted as his sweet voice grew louder. German! He was singing in German and it was a song she knew well.

'*Bunt sind schon die Wälder*
gelb die Stoppelfelder
und der Herbst beginnt
Rote Blätter fallen
Graue Nebel wallen
Kühler weht der Wind …'

She pressed her back against the wall and smiled as she mouthed the words. She'd known this nursery rhyme since she was a child. It was about autumn: fields of stubble, red leaves falling and the cool wind.

Mutti used to sing it to her and Vi.

Smiling now and laughing at herself for being frightened by a child, Maggie swung her arms out in time with the song and – oh blast! She'd caught a mop with her finger and sent it crashing to the ground.

Instantly, the singing stopped.

Maggie put her head around the door again. The boy was staring back at her with troubled dark eyes. She'd never seen a child with such a pale, pinched face.

'Hallo,' she said, as gently as she could. What was he doing here? A *German* child?

She stepped slowly out into the corridor. '*Ich bin Maggie*,' she said, gently, pointing to herself. What else could she do but tell him her name? She crouched down and held out her hand. '*Und du? Wie heisst du?*'

The child's face crumpled. 'I must no German speak,' he said, so quietly she had to lean forward to catch the words. 'It is ...' He was clearly struggling for the word. He finally resorted to '*verboten*.'

Who had forbidden him to speak German? Before Maggie could ask, he jumped up and raced down the corridor, his leather shoes slapping on the floor.

He'd left his toy behind: a little brown teddy bear. She picked it up. The fur was worn around its nose and paws, as though it had been held, and loved, for many years. It smelled, oddly, of tobacco.

What was a German child doing here and who did he belong to? She had to find out more. Perhaps his parents were here too. But why?

Maggie grasped the teddy tightly and set off after him down the passageway. It was dimly lit and there were other passages and doors leading off at regular intervals. The only sound was the echoing clickety click of her heels on the stone floor. There was no sign of the child.

After a minute or two, Maggie's resolve started to weaken. She was on the verge of giving up and turning back, when she reached the end of the corridor – a stone wall – and, on the right-hand side, a flight of steps, twisting upwards, identical to those at the other end of the house.

A movement caught her eye. There he was! The little boy was standing a few steps up, gripping the banister and gazing at her coyly from beneath his curls. Perhaps he'd realised he'd dropped the toy and had been about to retrace his steps.

'*Du hast deinen Teddybär vergessen*,' Maggie said gently, making the bear's arm wave at him.

The child almost smiled.

'*Wie heisst du*?' she asked again and this time he told her his name.

'Rudi.'

'*Rudi? Das ist aber ein guter Name*,' she said.

She wanted to ask him so many questions but he was only about four years old. First, she had to earn his trust.

She stepped forward to give him the bear and he stretched out a hand and took it, gripping it tightly in his fist.

'*Wie heisst der Bär*?' She pointed to the teddy.

'*Er gehört mir nicht*.'

The bear wasn't his. So, there must be at least one other child, unless—

'Oh, *there* you are, you little scamp!'

Maggie jumped at the sound of a man's voice coming from the stairwell above them. It was a plummy, confident voice but it didn't sound like Lord Ashford. It was someone younger. The boy's father, perhaps?

She oughtn't to be here, in this part of the house, talking to this child, she was sure. She was going to be in trouble. Maggie glanced back down the corridor, the way she'd come, but there wasn't time to move.

A pair of shiny black shoes appeared first on the steps, followed by navy trousers with a sharp crease – an RAF uniform – and a right arm held up in a sling.

It was the airman.

Maggie swallowed. Heat was rising in her face and her legs felt weak. She stepped nearer to the child and held onto the banister for support.

He stopped a few steps above them and smiled. He seemed quite unconcerned to find her there. Oh, fiddlesticks! Her face was scorching now. It always gave her away.

'We've been looking all over for you, young man,' the airman said to the child. He sounded amused rather than cross. 'It's past your bedtime. And you've got Sebastian, too, you little rascal!'

Rudi looked up and surrendered the teddy, which the airman used to tap him lightly on the head. The child giggled.

'It's my uncle's,' he said to Maggie. 'This bear. A kind of mascot. Very precious.' He gazed at the teddy for a moment then looked back at her. 'Don't think we've been introduced, have we, Miss?' He tucked the bear under his arm and came towards her down the steps, holding out his left hand. 'Sorry, can't shake properly. John Rosman. Jack to my friends. I'm the errant nephew. Pleased to meet you!'

Maggie swallowed. Rosman. He was part of the family, then. He seemed to fill the whole space in front of her, so that for a moment she couldn't think straight. If he'd been a regular Tommy or someone from down her street, she'd have had no trouble talking to him. But he was so handsome, with the most piercing blue eyes, it was putting her in a tizz.

She quickly stretched out her hand. His was warm to the touch.

He seemed amused. 'And you are?'

'Oh! I'm just Maggie. Maggie Corbett.'

'Hullo, "just Maggie". Here with the bank? Yes, of course you are. I saw you earlier. Lucky devils, aren't you? Got out of London at exactly the right time. Heaven only knows when the bombing's going to stop. It's relentless.'

She didn't want to talk about the bombing.

'Is he German?' she blurted out, nodding at the child standing next to her.

Jack Rosman pursed his lips. 'Yes. No, he's Austrian. My uncle got him out before it all started. The only English he knew when he arrived was "I'm hungry. May I have a piece of bread?"'. He laughed. 'His parents taught him before they packed him off!'

Poor little mite. He seemed awfully young to be travelling around Europe alone. And they probably oughtn't to talk about his parents in front of him like this; he might get upset.

'His English is still rather ropey but it's getting better, isn't it, Rudes?'

The little boy stared up at the airman trustingly but didn't reply. There was no telling if he'd understood.

'He … he said he was forbidden to speak German,' Maggie said.

Jack Rosman waved his hand, dismissively. 'Oh, he's not forbidden. It's simply that if he speaks German, none of us can understand a word! But you, on the other hand …'

Her stomach flipped over.

He turned his blue eyes – and his charm – on her. 'Tell me, "just Maggie", how come you speak German? Are you—'

'No!' she said quickly. 'I'm not.' Her face was burning. Could she make it any more obvious that she was lying?

But he merely laughed and held up his left hand in a gesture of surrender. 'Steady on! Look, I couldn't help but overhear your little tête-à-tête with Rudi. Or should that be "*Kopf und Kopf*" or whatever the hell it is in German? In any case—' he laughed again '—your secret's safe with me, Maggie. I shall call you Poppy if it's all the same to you. On account of that delightful way you have of blushing. Hey, I'm serious. Don't take on so!' He tapped his mouth. 'Mum's the word! Believe me, I'm an excellent secret-keeper. Top notch! Come along, Rudi, old chap. There's a young lady upstairs waiting to put you to bed.'

He took the child's hand and they mounted the stairs slowly, one at a time. Maggie watched them go with a hollow feeling in the pit of her stomach.

Jack Rosman was handsome and charming but he was a total stranger. Could she trust him?

Oh, what did she think she was doing, speaking German here? You never knew who was listening. 'Careless talk costs lives.' She knew that saying as much as anyone.

She'd done the very thing she'd warned Mutti about. Stupid, so stupid! She could have banged her head against the rough basement wall.

Chapter 9

'Did you sort it out?' Mrs Mason asked, as Maggie came into the kitchen, slamming the scullery door behind her. 'You've been a while.'

She was tying her headscarf under her chin and putting on her coat.

'Yes, ta,' Maggie said.

She was out of breath. Once Jack Rosman and Rudi had gone, she'd hurried back down the corridor, given her blouse a quick prod with the posser, left it to soak and climbed the stairs to the kitchen.

Perhaps Mrs Mason knew more about the little boy and why he was here? But on second thoughts, it might be difficult to describe meeting him without admitting she'd heard him speak German and that she'd spoken it herself.

Mrs Mason was tutting. 'Oh, would you look at that!' She'd put a finger through a hole in her worsted overcoat. 'It's worn right through here and here. You can see daylight. I shall have to darn it.'

'Or put a patch on,' Maggie said.

The housekeeper sighed.

'You could always turn it.' Maggie knew about turning

overcoats; she'd seen Mutti do it often enough. 'You undo all the seams—'

'Yes, I know what it is. It's a question of time—'

'I could do it for you,' Maggie offered.

Mrs Mason raised her eyebrows. She really did have a corker of a black eye. 'And,' the older woman added firmly, 'not having another coat to wear while it's being done.' She sniffed, put her coat back on and picked up her bag from the table.

'Cripes, I almost forgot,' she said, holding something out to Maggie, bunched in her hand. 'One of the waiters brought this in. Yours, ain't it?'

It was Charity's lace shawl. It must have been left on the lawn when Maggie was propelled into the Hall by Lady Ashford.

She took it, hardly daring to look but, miraculously, the shawl seemed to have escaped any damage. The cream lace was still pristine.

'Nice,' Mrs Mason said, nodding approvingly. She raised her eyebrows. 'Family heirloom, is it?'

Maggie laughed and shook her head. 'No. At least, not my family. We don't have any heirlooms.'

The housekeeper's face softened. 'No, love. You and me both.' She put her coat on with a sigh. 'I'll be off then.'

'Oh, don't you live here?'

Mrs Mason shook her head. 'I might as well, eh? No, dear, I have a husband to look after. Besides, where would I sleep, with all you cockneys taking up the rooms?' She gave Maggie a curt nod. 'See you in the morning. Night, night. God bless.'

* * *

It was gone midnight before Pam and Nancy got into bed.

Maggie was curled up in a ball under the eiderdown, which smelled faintly of camphor, pretending to be asleep and trying not to sneeze. The girls had spent ages putting their rollers in and the smell of setting lotion had gone up her nose.

'Where did you disappear to, Maggie?' Pam asked. The beds creaked as she and Nancy climbed into them.

'Yes, we didn't see hide nor hair of you after you poured that wine over yourself,' Nancy said, with a giggle. 'And we'd asked around and got the lowdown on the handsome airman, too. We were dying to tell you.'

Maggie had to stuff her fist into her mouth, to stop herself laughing. If only they knew!

'Well, his name is John Rosman.'

Jack, actually, Maggie thought. *Jack to his friends.*

Nancy continued, 'And he's Lord Ashford's nephew! Which explains the good looks. And, here's the best part: he's not married!'

Maggie wasn't interested, of course she wasn't and yet, why had her heart missed a beat when Nancy said he wasn't married?

'Yet,' Pam said, firmly. 'He'll be snapped up any day, mark my words. Especially as—'

'But that might not be true!' Nancy interrupted. 'It's probably just village gossip.'

Especially as what? Maggie held her breath, straining to hear through the thick eiderdown and trying desperately to think what 'especially as' might be referring to.

But, to her frustration, Pam said no more on the subject.

The girls were silent, as though waiting for Maggie's reaction but she stayed still under the eiderdown.

'Oh, she's not taking the bait,' Nancy said. 'Never mind. Perhaps she really is asleep. Anyway, we had a lovely time tonight, didn't we, Pam? I think we're going to have a jolly good war here!'

'Yes,' Pam agreed. 'I say, did you see Lady Ashford's pendant? Wasn't it divine?'

'And that exquisite turquoise ring?'

'What about the gold bangles? I counted at least six. She positively chimed—'

'And he charmed!'

They laughed.

'I wonder why the Ashfords don't have children?' Pam mused. 'Perhaps he can't, you know, do it? War wound or something from the last one? He's such a dish, though, I've always thought that. I'd find it hard to say no, wouldn't you, Nance?'

They laughed. Nancy had such a raucous laugh the chaps could probably hear her all the way down the corridor.

'He's ten years older than her, you know,' Pam said.

'But he's not ancient, is he? He can't be past it,' Nancy said.

The girls' conversation moved away from the Ashfords and they started to talk about places and people and parties that Maggie neither knew nor cared about.

It had been like that at the munitions factory. The only saving grace there was that it was too noisy to speak during the shifts, so at least she didn't have to try to join in with the gossip. It was only during the tea breaks, when the girls talked about sweethearts and nights out, that Maggie simply didn't know what to say.

She'd almost had a boyfriend, once. There'd been a nice chap a few months back, a fireman she'd met on fire-watching duty at the factory. He'd wanted to take her out and even came to the house once to pick her up, but when Dad got wind of it, he'd gone barmy. He'd yelled at Mutti. What in hell's name was she doing, letting Maggie out with strange men? So, Maggie had to make an excuse and put an end to things before they'd even started.

'She's glad now that she did it, you know,' Pam was saying, about someone or other. 'Went all the way with him, I mean. I don't blame her one jot. Her chap might not make it. He's being posted out to goodness only knows where next week. She said it was a kind of goodbye present.'

Maggie turned over. Honestly, she couldn't bear it. She pushed her fingers into her ears and instantly the girls' voices were reduced to indecipherable murmurs. A few minutes later, even the murmuring had stopped. They were breathing heavily. They'd finally fallen asleep.

Lucky them. Maggie's head was whirling like a windmill and even though she was tired beyond belief, she couldn't drop off. The day's events were running through her mind like a film. There'd never been a day like it.

To think, this morning, she'd still been in London. Since then, she'd raced to Paddington, almost missed the train, lost the cat, found it again, been insulted – twice – at the drinks reception, tipped wine all over herself, been rescued by an actual Lady, spoken German – she grimaced at the thought – and finally, she'd met a dashing airman in RAF uniform. A real hero.

She wished she could tell Mutti and Violet all about it. They'd be enraptured. They'd laugh and gasp and protest in all the right places.

'Dear God …' she started to pray, in a whisper. She didn't really believe in God, of course. How could you? The last war was supposed to be the war to end all wars and here they were, in the middle of another. No, she didn't believe but there wasn't anyone else to talk to and it couldn't do any harm.

'Dear God, please take care of Mutti and Violet, wherever they are and please let me hear from them soon. Amen.'

She wasn't going to waste any prayers on Dad. She pictured him getting home from work today and finding her gone. No note, no dinner on the stove. Kath Deacon would have gone running in to spill the beans, patting down her hair and simpering, like she did.

He'd have blown a fuse. And he didn't even have a cat to kick anymore.

Oh, blimey, the cat! Maggie sat up. She'd completely forgotten about Tabby, since taking her out of the back door hours ago and leaving her to explore.

She threw off the eiderdown and slipped out of bed. She'd smuggled a crust of bread up her sleeve at lunchtime. She'd try to find Tabby now and give it to her and then she might, finally, be able to fall asleep.

She pulled her cardigan on over her nightdress and grabbed

her shoes from under the bed. Her torch was under the pillow; she took that too. Nancy and Pam didn't stir.

Maggie made her way carefully down the grand staircase, into the hall and through the Long Gallery to reach the French doors, retracing the journey she'd made earlier that evening. She half expected the doors to be locked but they opened easily and she stepped outside, relieved to breathe in the fresh cold air.

The moon was huge in the black sky. It wasn't quite a full moon, there was a sliver missing but it hung in the sky like a floodlight, turning the whole terrace into a kind of stage.

Maggie gazed up. Maybe Mutti and Violet, wherever they were, were looking up at that same moon too. It was a comforting thought.

As she stepped onto the terrace she whispered, 'Tabby! Tabs!'

There was barely a sound. No distant gunfire or the drone of enemy bombers. Nothing, except the breeze rustling through the trees and the wavering 'woo woo' of an owl. How queer to be able to walk outside in the dead of night, without worrying about raids or falling off the kerb or tripping over sandbags in the street. Maggie exhaled. Standing here, you could easily imagine there was no war on at all.

Behind her, the Hall was in complete darkness but in one of the outbuildings, a light was shining from a first-floor window.

According to Pam and Nancy, the Ashfords had moved out of their rooms to make way for bank staff and were now living in a flat over the stable block. Perhaps the light was coming from their apartment.

'Oh!' Something soft had just brushed against Maggie's leg. Tabby! Thank goodness. 'Clever girl,' she said, bending to stroke the cat. She gave her the scraps of bread and the cat took them greedily.

As Maggie moved her hand through Tabby's soft fur, her gaze was drawn in the direction of the light. She shouldn't really, she felt like a Peeping Tom, but Maggie couldn't help herself.

There she was, Lady Ashford silhouetted against the window. She was brushing out her long hair. Maggie held her breath and ducked down below a stone plinth. Her heart was hammering in her chest.

What must it feel like, to be her? Beautiful and rich, married to handsome Lord Ashford, who clearly adored her, and to live here, in this mansion?

Maggie sighed. Lady Ashford. *Esther*. Even her name was magical, like a whisper. Maggie thought she'd never admired anyone so much in all her life.

Chapter 10

Joseph sat on the edge of the bed, unfastening his cufflinks and shirt collar.

The deed was done; he'd moved the bank to Snowden.

Other businesses had evacuated at the outbreak of war – the Bank of England for one – but he'd held back. His sources had assured him the war would be fought offshore for a while and so it had proved. But it was here now, with a vengeance. London was under attack. His judgement had been right.

'I do hope you haven't set the wrong tone tonight, Jay,' Esther said. She was sitting at the dressing table next to the window. He watched as she unwound her turban, shook out her dark hair and reached around her neck to undo the pendant.

When he stepped forward to help, she ducked, with a shake of her head, undid the necklace herself and tossed it onto the dressing table. It clattered on the glass top and made him jump.

He sat back down on the bed and sighed. 'I think everyone understood it was simply a welcome, my dear. A small gesture. It's done now.'

'It's asking an awful lot of the house staff.'

Joseph looked up, surprised. Esther didn't normally concern herself with the staff or their workload. Their employees only had to exert themselves when he and Esther brought hunting and shooting parties up from London for holidays or weekends.

Bringing the bank here changed everything, of course, but he had every confidence in his staff.

Esther glanced around the room, at the two single beds and sighed. Before she started to complain again about their lack of spacious, separate rooms, he said firmly, 'There's a war on. Sacrifices have to be made.'

She pulled out her bottom lip in a gesture that he used to find endearing. 'How long will it be for?'

'What a ridiculous question! I don't have a crystal ball, Esther.'

She was in a foul mood, although she'd disguised it well enough at the party tonight. She'd been the life and soul. If he couldn't get her to buck up, she wouldn't talk to him for days, or longer. She'd disappear off to The Dorchester and still be in a sulk when she returned.

She'd played her part, tonight, admittedly. She'd been in her element, dressed up to the nines, attracting admiring glances from men and women alike. Esther came alive when she was appreciated like that, basking in the glow of other people's regard. The worst thing in the world for Esther was to be ignored.

She had disappeared for a while though, taking that girl into the house.

Joseph had looked for her a few times but when she hadn't reappeared, he'd interrupted the chap who was holding forth, lecturing them all on how America would, eventually, have to join the war, by holding up his hand. 'Would you excuse me please, for one minute?'

He strode across the terrace, acknowledging his guests with nods and smiles. As he entered the house, Dakin stepped forward. 'Is everything to your satisfaction, Sir?'

'Absolutely,' Joseph said, patting him on the shoulder absent-mindedly and looking around. There was no sign of Esther. 'No, actually. I rather seem to have mislaid my wife.'

'I think you'll find she's in your study, Sir.'

Joseph marched through the Long Gallery and flung open the office door. What was he trying to do? Catch her in the act? Sure enough, there she was, as slim as a pencil, standing at his desk with her back to him, speaking into the telephone. She turned as he burst in and gazed at him with those limpid eyes. She was like a Vermeer portrait.

'Jay's here,' she said, calmly, into the receiver. She was holding it in her right hand and cupping the end nearest her mouth with her left. Almost tenderly.

Joseph's chest was tight. He rubbed his forehead and forced himself to lean against the doorframe and wait.

There was a pause, as she listened to whoever was speaking, then she said, 'Very well. Goodbye,' in a voice so devoid of emotion, that she might have been talking to an employee.

She carefully replaced the receiver. All her movements were precise and unhurried.

Joseph gave her a questioning look as she sauntered towards him. She wrinkled her nose. 'Only wanted to hear a friendly voice,' she said, reaching up to give him a peck on the cheek.

Now, she half turned towards him, as she sat at the dressing table. 'Who on earth was that creature tonight with the donkey laugh? And the girl who covered herself in Beaujolais? I must say, Jay, they're something of a motley crew. Are you sure you've done the right thing?'

Joseph frowned. It was true, they were only a skeleton staff and perhaps they wouldn't all have been his first choice. Some chaps had resigned rather than move out of London; others had enlisted. He'd expected that. Casualties. But they'd manage. At least they were away from the beastly bombs.

Esther was gazing thoughtfully at her reflection in the mirror. 'I shouldn't be at all surprised if another girl hadn't knocked her glass deliberately. Honestly, Jay, girls can be quite horrid.'

He looked up. 'I know.'

'She did look rather petrified. She'll be heading back to London before you can say Jack Robinson. She won't stick it out.' She examined her front teeth in the mirror, pulled back and gave a satisfied nod. 'Petty jealousies. I've known them all my life. She's actually quite a pretty girl.'

'Who?'

'Mary, Martha or whatever her name is. The one who spilled the wine.' Esther raised a finger. 'Say, if she decides banking's not for her, I've got just the job. I need a new maid.'

Joseph gritted his teeth and reached for his pyjamas, which were folded neatly on the pillow. 'Please don't start requisitioning my workers. I need everyone. I'm worried enough that they'll tire of the country and want to head back to the bright lights. Bombs or no bombs.'

'Only an idea,' Esther said, waving her hand airily. 'It's impossible to get domestics these days, you know. Everyone's off doing war work!' She said it as though it were a bad thing.

'Well, if that's all you've got to worry about,' he murmured, but she didn't reply.

Esther had that dreamy look in her eyes again as though she was somewhere else entirely.

She snapped out of her reverie with a shake of the head and looked at his reflection in the mirror. 'Good, so that's the last of it? I've played my part. The dutiful wife. Smiled and welcomed everyone. You're not expecting anything more?'

He sighed and finished undressing. It was enough. They'd put on a good show.

Esther was brushing out her long dark hair now. It was like a skein of silk. He used to brush that for her, once.

When they'd first met, introduced by their mothers, Joseph couldn't do a thing wrong in Esther Jewell's eyes. But they'd married too soon; they'd been little more than acquaintances. And now they were stuck with each other. *Till death do us part* and all that.

'I'm heading back to The Dorchester on Monday,' Esther said. 'Safest place in London! Reinforced concrete, you know.'

'So you keep telling me.'

He wondered what other attractions The Dorchester offered, because safety wasn't usually one of Esther's concerns. She was fearless. She drove like a maniac and, on the hunting field, she tackled fences that men on bigger horses baulked at. No, there was something – or, more specifically, *someone* – calling her back to London.

'What's going to happen to Rudi if you disappear off to The Dorchester?' he asked.

She shrugged. 'I could take him with me.'

'You can't! To London, with bombs raining down every night? Don't be ridiculous, Esther. We're supposed to be keeping him safe. I won't allow it. Did you get in touch with Sarah?'

'Hmm?'

'Sarah. Your niece. You thought she might be game?'

'Oh yes, I've written. Let's see.'

Flighty Sarah. As far as Joseph knew, she had no experience of nannying. What had she done, up to now, apart from shine as a debutante? Before the war, Sarah had been in Germany of all places, for the season, looking for a husband. Thank goodness she hadn't found one.

No, Sarah Jewell was not ideal but Esther had assured him there were no governesses or nannies to be had. They couldn't expect house staff to look after Rudi in between their other tasks. Sarah would have to do.

'What else are you mixed up in, Jay?' Esther asked, suddenly.

He was pulling back the covers, getting into bed. 'I don't know what you mean.'

'Before the war, it was the children. I know you. Banking isn't enough. There's bound to be something.'

Joseph shook his head. He couldn't tell her. Heaven only knew who she was associating with these days.

'Oh, I know you don't trust me with anything,' she said. 'Loose lips and all that. But be careful, won't you, Jay? Whatever it is?'

There was a moment's silence.

'I'm having the pools drained,' he said.

'Oh no! Must you? Not the Mirror Pool?'

He nodded. 'Both of them. They shine like glass in the moonlight.'

'But what about skating, in the winter?'

'They're like beacons, showing the enemy exactly where they are, helping them find their targets. Coventry, Oxford, Birmingham.'

'Oh, Jay!'

'It's our duty. Talking of which, don't you think you should pull down the blackout?'

'I want to see the moon. It's a waning moon, Jay. Do you know what that means?'

He sighed. 'It's practically a Bomber's Moon. And you know what that means.'

She made no move to block out the light. Joseph climbed of bed, marched to the window and yanked the blind down.

'Oh Jay, always spoiling my fun,' she murmured.

He got back into bed, snapped off his lamp and turned his back on her. Oblivion, that's what he wanted. Not those awful dreams. No more of those, please God.

As he drifted off to sleep, an image flashed through his mind and for once, it was something good. A heart-shaped face, brown, intelligent eyes, a steady smile. He'd seen her this morning for the first time in almost thirty years.

Gwen.

Chapter 11

Snowden Hall
Snowden
Gloucestershire

Dear Vi

Got the P.C. saying where you've ended up and you'll never guess – I'm not that far away!

The place I'm working has moved us all to the countryside! You could say, we're vackies too and I've even brought the cat! Yes, Tabby's a country bumpkin now. So, you needn't worry about her. She's quite safe, here with me.

Course, Dad wasn't best pleased at first, at the thought of being all on his tod but when we found out you were in Gloucestershire, he gave me his blessing to go.

We only arrived yesterday and we've been hard at it this morning, sorting out all the boxes and papers and getting everything in the office shipshape.

I'm on my tea break now, so I've snatched five minutes to drop you a line and give you my address. Do write back quick as you can, Vi, and tell me everything. What's it like on the farm (when I saw they'd sent you to a farm I knew you'd be over the moon!), what kind of animals do they have and what is the family like that you're boarding with? Don't forget to mind your Ps and Qs and say please and thank you, will you?

I'm sure it won't be long before we hear from Mutti, Mum, so don't worry.

Can't promise anything because I haven't worked out how far away you are but, with a bit of luck, I'll be able to come and visit.

In any case, I thought it might cheer you up to know I'm nearer than you thought.

Better go! I can hear the clink of cups, which means tea break's over!

Can't wait to hear from you, Vi, so don't dilly-dally!

Toodle pip

Lots of love,

Maggie

XXX

Maggie sat at her new desk and read the letter through. Did it sound cheery enough? It had been quite exhausting, summoning up that amount of cheerfulness.

There were a couple of white lies, of course. Dad had hardly given his blessing and as for Mutti and hearing from her soon, that wasn't true either.

In truth, Maggie had no idea how to track Mutti down. The last letter she'd written to Holloway had been returned. Mutti wasn't there; they'd moved her. She hadn't had a chance to find out any more. Perhaps Dad knew by now. Surely, they couldn't drag someone off and not inform next of kin? But if she wrote to Dad to find out, she'd have to give him her address here at Snowden and she didn't dare.

She frowned at the crossing out on the page. It had seemed best not to use 'Mutti'. You couldn't be too careful.

The big kisses at the bottom of the page would, hopefully, remind Violet of what they'd agreed before she left.

Maggie bit her lip. The worry was there, constantly, like a twisting worm in her stomach. She hated this separation, this not knowing. The only small consolation was that everyone was missing someone. You didn't talk about it. No one liked a moaner. You simply had to grin and bear it.

Maggie gazed out of the windows in the Long Gallery at the huge expanse of lawn, as green and neat as a park and beyond that, the rolling Cotswold hills.

It had been queer, waking up here this morning. She supposed she'd get used to it: the scramble for the bathroom (Miss Sharp took precedence and the others had to queue on the landing, their towels rolled up under their arms) and then breakfasting together at a round table set up at the end of the Long Gallery.

Instead of catching the bus to work, having been up half the night going to and from the shelters (on her own, because Dad always refused to leave the house), now she didn't even need to put a coat on. There were no wailing sirens, or shaking ground or deafening explosions. All she had to do was walk down the stairs.

'Wasn't that a relief,' Norm had said, over breakfast, 'to get a solid night's sleep last night?'

Most people agreed but Maggie had put her head down. She wondered how bad the raids were in London. Because they wouldn't have been spared, that was a certainty. She couldn't enjoy being away from it all, being safe. She felt too guilty.

Ray Maguire had suddenly glanced at his pocket watch and declared, 'It's one minute to. Time for work!'

'Not quite, Mr Maguire,' Miss Sharp said, setting the strainer on her cup and pouring out another cup of tea. 'I make it three minutes to.'

They'd all had to wait until Miss Sharp agreed with Mr Maguire, that the working day could begin. From the glances around the table, Maggie knew the others were thinking the same as her; it was queer how both Miss Sharp and Mr Maguire seemed to think they were in charge.

It was a relief to settle at her desk with a pile of letters and memos for typing and have something to concentrate on. But her eyes kept drifting to the windows and the view outside.

It was all such a far cry from the city, like a dream from which she'd wake any minute and find herself in the shelter, shivering and cuddled up next to a stranger.

Now, Maggie glanced at the clock on the wall, behind Miss Sharp's desk. She'd missed her cuppa but never mind. It had been more important to write to Vi as soon as she could.

She reached into the desk drawer, took out a brown envelope and carefully folded her letter inside it. Then she sealed the envelope and started to copy down Vi's address on the front. She'd made a note of Vi's address before she left home. She'd left the postcard behind, for Dad.

Someone coughed nearby, then a man's voice said, 'Is that a private letter, Miss Corbett?'

Ray Maguire was standing over her. His shadow had fallen across her desk a moment before he spoke, making her jump.

Was he making polite conversation or was she in trouble?

Everyone was filing back to their desks. Elsie Davenport, the feisty redhead that Maggie remembered from her first day at Rosman's, was taking her seat in front of Maggie's desk. 'Take no notice,' she said. 'He's gone queer since they put him in charge.'

Ray opened his mouth but before he could reply, another voice rang out.

'*Actually* ...' It was Miss Sharp, who'd swivelled around and was now marching down the aisle towards them. 'I think you'll find that I'm still in charge of this office!'

Ray crossed his arms and faced her. 'She's using company stationery,' he said but his voice faltered. Miss Sharp was almost as tall as him and she was stern.

'I'm sorry—' Maggie started.

Miss Sharp put her hand out, all pointed nails and slender fingers.

'Don't apologise, Miss Corbett.' She looked around and addressed everyone. 'You're all allowed to write one letter home each week, using company paper and an envelope.'

'Says who?' Ray asked.

'Says me!' Miss Sharp said. She frowned slightly and then added, in a quieter voice, 'Say I. Anyone wishing to write more often will need to purchase their own supplies, of course.'

Maggie watched as her colleagues exchanged surprised glances and then pretended to resume work. Typewriters were silent, no one picked up a telephone. They were all listening.

'Satisfied, Mr Maguire?' Miss Sharp asked.

Maggie watched as Ray unfolded his arms and gave a curt nod. He'd been acting strangely all morning. He'd ordered everyone to change the address on their ID cards to 'Snowden Hall' *straight-away* and sent two of the chaps to fetch their gas masks because, 'Hitler won't send a warning.'

Which had prompted Miss Sharp – who had been getting crosser and crosser every time Ray issued an order – to send Miss Davenport and Miss Fry up to their rooms to put stockings on.

'Bare legs,' she'd announced, 'won't be tolerated. Even in this warm weather.'

Now, she was sweeping back to her desk in undisguised triumph. It was clear she'd been building up to that outburst for a while.

Maggie felt rotten, she hadn't meant to cause a row. She'd only been writing a letter to her little sister, in her tea break. Who'd have thought it would cause such a to-do? From now on she'd keep her head down.

A minute before lunch, Ray appeared at Maggie's desk again. Blimey, now what? Was he coming to tick her off again?

He held his right hand out, palm upwards. It was a large, square hand with soft skin and ink-stained fingers. A bank clerk's hand. She was ever so tempted to give it a slap.

He was biting his lip. He actually looked rather sheepish. He swallowed. 'Miss Corbett, would you like me to post your letter?'

'I wouldn't trust 'im with that as far as I could throw 'im,' Elsie muttered from the desk in front.

Ray's stern voice and steely look of earlier had gone. It was as though he'd been playing a part. And not very well, at that.

'I'm cycling down to the village,' he said, tilting his chin. 'Put a stamp on it and I'll drop it in the post box for you, if you like.' He seemed to sense her reluctance and added, 'Unless you want to ride down there yourself, of course?'

He was having a laugh, wasn't he? Maggie could no more ride a bicycle than fly to the moon.

'There's no need to glare at me like that,' he said. 'I shan't steam it open and read it, I promise.'

'Well, it's written in invisible ink anyway, so you'd have a job,' Maggie said.

Elsie laughed and even Ray gave a wry smile. Perhaps he wasn't such a chump, after all. He was probably trying to make amends.

'Very well,' she said. 'Thank you. If you don't mind. It's to my little sister. She's a vackie round here. Gawd knows exactly where. Could be a mile away, could be ten. The sooner it gets there, the better.'

Chapter 12

Charity was mucking out the pigsty. 'Oh, hello you!' she said, as she spotted Maggie. She straightened up, leaned on her pitchfork and shielded her eyes from the sun. 'Escaped the clutches of the typewriter? Good for you. It's Maggie, isn't it?'

Maggie nodded, pleased to have been remembered. Charity looked so different from last night. Gone was the red party dress, high heels and make-up. Today she was dressed for work, in breeches, a headscarf, a green jersey with a shirt underneath, long socks and lace-ups.

'Say, aren't you missing lunch?' Charity asked, frowning.

Maggie wrinkled her nose. 'Didn't fancy it. It's rook pie or something with squirrels in it.'

Charity laughed. 'Who on earth told you that? I think they might have been pulling your leg. They eat pretty well in the house, I hear.'

In truth, Maggie had decided to skip lunch and find Charity instead. It was a sunny day and it was a relief to stand up, stretch and get some fresh air. She hadn't moved from her desk all morning and her hands were aching from pounding the stiff typewriter keys.

Before they went in for lunch, her colleagues had made the

most of the September sunshine and spilled out onto the lawn, to smoke, chat and stroll over the grass to take a look at the swimming pool.

Maggie had spotted the old chap who'd brought their bags up yesterday, pushing a wheelbarrow and had asked him where she might find the Land Girls. He'd pointed her in the direction of the small farm behind the stable block, where the girls were working.

'This all used to be flower borders,' Charity said now. 'That's my pal Gill over there, cleaning out the chickens.'

The pig – gosh, it was enormous – was feeding noisily from a bucket of slops, while Charity used a pitchfork to lift dirty straw from around it and pile it up in a barrow.

'Don't mind if I carry on, do you?' Charity said. 'Nearly finished and then it'll be time for lunch.'

Maggie stepped back as the stench from the pig hit her nostrils.

Charity laughed. 'Stinks, doesn't he? Breathe through your mouth, that's best.'

There was a smudge of mud on her chin.

'Look at the size of it!' Maggie said. 'I didn't realise pigs were so big. What on earth do you feed it?'

Charity laughed. 'He's called Bing. He's part of the village pig club. Everyone collects scraps for him and he has acorns and conkers too. They'll all get a share … well, you know …' She lowered her voice. 'When the time comes. But in the meantime, he's happy enough.'

She must have noticed Maggie gazing at her clothes because she glanced down at her breeches. 'Like the outfit? I only joined the Land Army for the uniform. And to meet a handsome farmer!'

'And have you?' Maggie asked. 'Met one?'

Charity rolled her eyes. 'What do you think? You don't have a choice, you know, they can send you anywhere. I ended up here, helping out old Tonks. All we do is grow veg and herbs, keep chickens and fatten up the pig. Have to step it up a bit now there are more mouths to feed.' She paused and became suddenly more serious. 'I wanted to do my bit as well.'

'Of course,' Maggie agreed.

'It's been frightfully dull,' Charity said. Her eyes lit up. 'So, I'm delighted the Bank's come to Snowden!'

Maggie smiled. At least someone was. She got the impression – from the housekeeper and the grumpy gardener, at least – that as far as the house staff were concerned, it just meant more work for them.

'Actually, I do like the uniform,' Charity admitted, cheerfully. 'This shirt's a bugger though, pardon my French. It itches like mad!' She pulled at the shirt's collar.

'What's it like?' Maggie asked. 'Wearing trousers?'

Charity pulled a face. 'Never seen a girl in slacks before?'

Maggie shook her head. Some of the women in the munitions factory had worn dungarees but Maggie's line had only been issued with overalls.

Charity looked down and grinned. 'Oh, but they're the best! You don't have to worry about knicker elastic fail, for starters.'

Maggie giggled and looked around to check no one was within earshot.

'That happened to me, once, you know,' Charity said. 'Ping! I felt it go and then my unmentionables worked their way down my legs until they reached the point of no return.'

Maggie gasped. 'You mean they ...?'

'Yes! But we'd been taught what to do "in case of an emergency" in "Deportment". Step out of them, kick them to the side with a deft flick, keep walking and never look back.'

'And did that work?'

'Perfectly. Until a chap a few yards behind picked them up and ran up to me calling, "Miss, Miss, you've dropped something!"'

They laughed.

'Oh here,' Maggie said, suddenly remembering her reason for seeking Charity out. 'Your shawl. Thanks for lending it to me.'

She held it up, bundled in her hand. 'I've checked all over and I can't see any stains.'

Charity frowned and shook her head.

'Oh, perhaps you didn't see …' Maggie said. Charity must have been the only one who hadn't. 'I had an accident with a glass of wine last night. Poured it all over myself. Lady Ashford came to my rescue.'

'Ah, I see.' Charity nodded. 'Could you put it on the bale of straw over there, behind the fence and out of harm's way? Bing'll eat it if he gets the chance. Thank you. No, I didn't see any of that commotion! Poor you.'

Maggie wondered if that was true or whether Charity was simply being kind. Either way, she was grateful.

'But that sounds like Esther. She's a good egg,' Charity said.

'Have you known her long?'

'Oh yes, since forever!'

Maggie's heart sank but lifted again as Charity added. 'She's more a friend of the family than my particular pal though. My eldest sister, Faith, and Esther go back yonks.'

'Well, thanks again, for the loan of the shawl.'

'My pleasure. Say, are those other girls being spiteful to you?'

'No!' Maggie said, a little too quickly and Charity narrowed her eyes, as though not quite believing her.

'I can't abide bullies,' Charity went on. 'You have to face up to them, or they carry on. Hitler's bullying the whole of Europe, of course. But we're standing up to him.'

Maggie nodded. She supposed that was true; she'd never thought of it like that.

Charity swapped the pitchfork for a broom, swept up the last of the straw and muck, pushed the barrow to the side of the stall and wiped the back of her hand across her brow.

'Phew, there, done! Come and sit down. You can share my sandwiches.' She looked over towards the hen house and called, 'Gill! Lunchtime!'

They sat on a bale of straw and Gill – a strong-looking girl with dark hair plaited down her back – joined them. They watched as the pig jerked its head out of the now-empty bucket and snuffled around the stall, grunting contentedly.

Charity pulled a gas mask carton out of her knapsack and opened it. 'Help yourself to a jam sandwich,' she said but Maggie shook her head. She couldn't take the girls' lunch. Goodness, they needed it, the amount of energy they were using up.

Charity stretched her legs out and winced. 'I'm aching all over. We're permanently aching, aren't we, Gill?'

'Yes, but it could be worse. At least we don't have to kill rats.'

'Rats?' Maggie thought of Tabby in the barn and wondered if she'd made her first kill yet.

'It's a real job!' Gillian said. 'A girlfriend of mine is down in the West Country and it's all they do all day: kill rats!'

Charity nodded. 'Anti-vermin squad. They kill thousands of the blighters.'

Maggie shuddered. She didn't dare ask how they did it. Surely not with their bare hands? It didn't bear thinking about. It made her job – sitting at a desk, in a room with a view and drinking tea at regular intervals – seem awfully tame.

'Speaking of rats,' Maggie said. 'I brought my cat, so she might catch a few, if she gets the hang of it. A little tabby.'

Charity's eyes were wide. 'You brought your cat? From London?'

Maggie nodded. 'If I'd left her behind, my dad … well, there was no saying what he'd do.' She tugged on a piece of straw from the bale and shrugged. 'He didn't want me to come here but I did it anyway.'

Charity wiped a crumb from her lips. 'Good for you! Quite the little rebel, aren't you? So, you're getting along with the other girls then?'

Maggie winced, not quite sure what to say. 'They're pals, so I'm a bit surplus to requirements. But I'm not complaining. I haven't come here to make friends, after all. I've come to find my sister and work hard and—'

'Oh well, if you don't want to be friends ...' Charity said, pretending to be upset.

'I didn't mean you! I mean—'

'Only teasing,' Charity said, waving her sandwich dismissively. 'Say, I know a fabulous watering hole not a million miles away.'

Maggie's face must have been blank.

Charity laughed. 'A pub, dear girl! The pub in the village! Let's have a night out there soon, shall we?'

Chapter 13

'Morale, Maguire, I'm putting you in charge of morale.'

The lad standing in front of Joseph, his arms respectfully behind his back, was pale and gauche in his too-big jacket.

He nodded. 'Morale, Sir? As you wish, Sir.'

Yes, Sir, No, Sir, Three bags full, Sir. Oh, how Joseph hated 'yes men'.

'Do sit,' he said. 'Don't stand on ceremony.' He reached across his desk for the cigar box and picked out a panatela. He lit it and sucked on it until it glowed and then sat back and enjoyed it for a moment.

He couldn't help regretting the loss of Wilcock, Middleton and Grainger. Good men, all of them. But, of course, they'd joined up immediately, or in Grainger's case, retired. He'd have to make the best of what he had.

'What age are you, Maguire?'

'Twenty-five next birthday, Sir.'

Joseph drew on his cigar and nodded. They both knew what he was driving at. The role of bank clerk was only reserved from twenty-five and above. There was still time for Maguire to enlist.

Before Bob Grainger had retired, Joseph had asked him for a recommendation – he hoped that hadn't been a mistake – and

Grainger had suggested Maguire, sitting here now, twisting his hands in his lap.

The boy was keen but was he a leader? Could he take charge? Clearly, he'd already put Cynthia Sharp's nose out of joint.

Joseph had badly misjudged that business with Miss Sharp.

He'd spotted an engagement ring on her hand a while ago. He didn't notice jewellery, as a rule, but every time Miss Sharp brought papers to be signed, the glinting diamond on her left hand seemed to be in his eyeline.

He remembered hearing that Miss Sharp had lost the chap she was supposed to marry in the Great War, so he'd felt vaguely pleased that she'd found someone else.

He'd assumed a wedding was on the cards. There'd been no announcement but Miss Sharp, he was sure, would inform him in her own good time.

Weddings, according to Esther, were arranged quickly these days, so Joseph assumed that Miss Sharp, as a soon-to-be married woman, wouldn't move with the bank to Snowden Hall, and before his announcement to the staff, he'd taken steps to replace her. With Ray Maguire.

But as quickly as it had appeared, the ring had gone. It was a delicate matter but, clearly, she'd been let down. Perhaps the chap in question was missing in action. Or worse.

And when Miss Sharp confirmed that she would be coming to Snowden, after all – a relief in one way because she was an absolute treasure – it left Joseph with Maguire. And a tiresome situation.

Today after lunch, Miss Sharp had – most unusually – asked to see him.

'Is your room quite in order?' Joseph had asked her. 'I did give instructions that you should have—'

But it was nothing like that.

'It's Mr Maguire,' she said. She cast around for the right words. 'To be perfectly honest, your Lordship, it's proving rather difficult.

I understood Ray Maguire was in charge of the move of personnel to Snowden—'

'Correct. And he seems to have carried that out adequately. All the office furniture has arrived intact, ditto the staff and they have all found somewhere to lay their heads at night, correct?'

'Yes. But now he's sticking his oar in, trying to run my office and quite frankly, I won't have it.' The colour on Miss Sharp's face heightened quite alarmingly. Two bright spots of red appeared, one on each cheekbone. 'It's him or me!'

When he'd managed to calm her with a large sweet sherry and she'd left his office much placated, Joseph reflected that he hadn't really thought this through.

He'd have to come up with something else for Maguire.

It hadn't taken him more than two puffs on a cigar to think of one.

'Yes, morale, Maguire,' Joseph said now. 'It's vital. Once the novelty of this place wears off, boredom may set in. The countryside isn't for everyone. Happy folk will stay put, they won't dash home for the weekend or decide that life would be a darn sight more exciting if they joined up.'

It would, of course, but that wasn't the point. Joseph needed workers and preferably people who knew the ropes. He couldn't afford to lose more staff to the war effort.

'You don't want them to go home at weekends, Sir?'

Joseph waved a hand. 'Of course, they're entirely at liberty to do so. This isn't a prison camp!' He gave a grim laugh. 'But I'd prefer them to stay. And that's where you come in, Maguire.' He pointed his cigar at the lad. 'Big responsibility. "Heavy is the head that wears a crown" and all that. Think you're up for the challenge?'

Joseph sat back and waited. Sometimes silence was your best weapon. Most people couldn't stand it; they'd say anything, simply to fill it.

'I think I can do that, Sir.'

'Keep them entertained, happy, that kind of thing.'

Maguire pursed his lips. He looked as though he was already thinking. Good. Joseph was trying not to think badly of the men from the bank who hadn't seen fit to enlist. If he'd been their age, hell or high water wouldn't have stopped him. But he supposed he should be grateful. What would he have done if every bank clerk had resigned?

Maguire's gaze was focused over Joseph's head now, at the painting on the wall behind his desk.

'Canaletto,' Joseph said, turning in his seat to admire it himself. It was a particular favourite of his. 'Venice,' he said. 'From St Mark's basin, looking towards the Doge's Palace. Oil, obviously.'

When he turned back, Maguire was nodding, thoughtfully.

'Do you like art, Maguire?'

'Art, Sir?'

'Paintings? Pictures, like this one?'

Maguire gave a shrug. 'I suppose it cheers up a plain wall, Sir.'

Joseph laughed. 'That's certainly one way of looking at it!' He'd been about to say something pompous, about 'art being the perfect distraction from the miseries of life' but actually, he preferred Maguire's line.

'Excellent. Well, I shall leave staff morale in your capable hands.'

He turned back to the report he'd been ploughing through. Maguire hesitated before understanding he'd been dismissed.

Joseph raised his eyes and watched him leave. Poor posture: rounded shoulders, hunched back. He was padding across the carpet as though he thought a mine might go off.

Joseph had to fight the urge to yell, 'Shoulders back, stand up straight!' At the door, Maguire turned. 'Wellingtons!' he said.

Joseph raised his eyebrows.

'Boots might encourage the staff to stroll around the grounds? Take in the air?'

'Yes! That's exactly the kind of thing. We do have a boot room; there will be some in there. But speak to Dakin – bald chap, my butler. He'll tell you how to order more. There's a shortage of rubber, of course, so there are no guarantees but see what you can do.'

'Thank you, Sir. That's super.'

Joseph tried not to smile. 'Super,' he repeated. He took a drag on his cigar and turned back to the papers on his desk. 'Thank you, Maguire,' he murmured. 'Dismissed.'

Five minutes later, there was another knock on the door. Oh, for goodness' sake. He'd never get anything done at this rate.

'Come!' he yelled.

It was Mrs Mason. 'I see you found your watch then, Sir?'

Joseph glanced at his wrist. 'Ah, yes. Turned up in the nursery. Rudi the magpie had it.'

He flipped his cigar box open and then closed it again. Bad habit, starting a cigar whenever he was interrupted. It only made the interruption even longer.

Mrs Mason was clearing her throat. 'I wondered if I might ask you something, Sir?'

'Go ahead.'

'I could do with more help in the house. You did say, Sir, I should let you know if I thought it would be too much and what with young Rudi and now all the bank folk …' She shrugged and looked at him.

Domestic business. Not his department.

'Of course. But this is her Ladyship's area. Please, if you could speak to her?'

In anticipation of Mrs Mason's departure, he started to gather up some of the papers on his desk.

'With respect, your Lordship, her Ladyship said to ask you. I only want another pair of hands in the kitchen.'

He sighed and put the papers down. 'Very well. My wife informs me it's difficult to find domestic staff these days but if you can find someone, go ahead. No Nazi sympathisers or Blackshirts, obviously!'

Mrs Mason didn't laugh. 'Mrs Nicholls is looking for work,' she said.

Joseph scratched his head. Clearly, he was meant to know who Mrs Nicholls was. He was usually pretty competent at that sort of thing; he took pride in never forgetting a name or a face. But Mrs Nicholls? No, he was stumped.

Oh, blast. If he said yes and Esther didn't like this woman, or she turned out to be a liability, his life would be hell.

'I think perhaps—' he started.

'That's Miss Tapper, as was,' Mrs Mason interrupted, in a quiet voice. 'Gwen Tapper.'

Joseph reached for the glass paperweight that sat on his desk between Sebastian and the telephone. It had been his mother's and had held a fascination for him since he was a boy. He often toyed with it when he wanted to think.

Inside the glass globe was a perfect white dandelion clock, frozen in time. It fitted snugly into the palm of his hand. There was something soothing about its weight and its cool, smooth surface.

'Gwen Tapper. I see,' he said. 'But I thought she'd come back to the village to nurse her sick mother?'

'She did, Sir, but her mother's passed on. She was eighty-two, Sir. We all has to go at some point.'

'True. And eighty-two is a good innings.'

Joseph remembered Gwen's mother; a bright, astute lady, who'd welcomed him into their little flat above the village shop. She never stood on ceremony; she'd always treated him like any other boy.

He felt a wave of gratitude towards the old woman for having the good grace to die now. It felt, somehow, as though it were meant to be. Because, of course, he was going to say yes.

He cleared his throat. 'That puts a different slant on it,' he said. 'Mrs Nicholls will, I'm sure, be an excellent and … very helpful addition to the staff.' He waved his hand in the air. 'Please, go ahead, Mrs Mason.'

'Thank you, Sir.'

Joseph kept his head down and focused on the paperweight, until the door closed with a gentle click.

Gwen Tapper. Whatever her married name, he could never think of her as anything but Gwen Tapper. Here, at Snowden, after all this time.

Joseph put the paperweight down and reached instead for Sebastian. He'd had the little bear since he was a baby; a gift from a doting uncle long since gone. Sebastian had been a constant presence through everything: Eton, Oxford, France, his marriage to Esther. And now this, another war.

Sebastian was like a charm. Joseph wasn't superstitious, except when it came to the bear. If he ever lost him, he thought his luck would almost certainly run out.

'Remember Gwen?' he asked the bear. 'She's coming to help us out. Gwen at Snowden again. Like the old days. If you're very good, old chum, I might even let you see her.'

Was he being sentimental? No. It was a practical solution to a problem. Gwen was looking for employment; they needed staff.

He was simply helping out an old friend. Anyone would have done the same. There was absolutely nothing more to it than that.

Chapter 14

Two days after they arrived at Snowden Hall, it was Saturday, a half day. At breakfast there was a holiday atmosphere, as everyone looked forward to the weekend and Miss Sharp had to remind them all, more than once, that there was still a morning's work to get through.

Norm and Big Bill appeared fresh from their first swim in the pool, with rosy cheeks and sopping wet hair.

'The water's like ice!' Bill confirmed cheerfully, dropping heavily into the chair next to Maggie.

'Crikey!' Nancy mimed a shiver. 'You wouldn't get me in there for all the tea in China.'

'Speaking of which,' Ray said, with an uncharacteristically cheeky grin, 'would you mind passing me the teapot, Pam? Or better still, if I give you my cup, would you be mother?'

Pam stuck her tongue out at him but took his cup and saucer.

Meanwhile, Norm and Bill were bragging about the arctic temperatures they'd overcome and the number of lengths they'd managed. They had, they assured everyone, definitely got the edge on their colleagues Mr Gill and Mr Whitehouse, who'd cycled up from the village for a dip.

'That's hardly surprising,' Ray said, stretching across the table to take his cup from Pam. 'You're about half their age!'

'You should try it, Raymondo,' Bill said. 'It means getting up extra early but we'll give you a shove.'

'Not allowed,' Ray said. 'Doctor's orders. I've had rheumatic fever.'

'What about you, Geoff?' Bill asked.

Geoff jumped, as though he hadn't expected anyone to speak to him. 'I c-c-can't swim,' he admitted.

Maggie thought one of the chaps might offer to teach him. Everyone should have the chance to learn to swim, after all. Blimey, if she only had a swimsuit – and the nerve – she'd get in that bloomin' water and teach him herself.

'All that splashing around doesn't half build an appetite,' Norm said. 'I say, Maggie, are you going to eat that other piece of toast or …?'

She looked down at her plate. She'd been about to eat the toast with a dollop of carrot jam, which wasn't too bad if you spread it thickly. But she felt sorry for him. A big chap like Norm needed food more than her.

'You have it,' she said and was rewarded with a smile.

'So, what's everyone doing with their half day?' Elsie asked. She peered around Big Bill and looked out of the window. 'Sun's shining out there. Let's hope it lasts until this afternoon.'

'We're going to take the bicycles out and see how far we can get, aren't we, chaps?' Bill said.

'First I've heard of it,' Ray said, sounding put out.

'Oh, yes. Do you want to tag along?' Bill asked.

Maggie winced and looked down at the tablecloth. Bill couldn't have made it more obvious if he'd tried that Ray had been left out of their plans. She felt a momentary pang for him but he was braving it out.

'No,' he said, shaking his head. 'I've got something else to do, thank you very much.'

Miss Sharp got out of her seat and made a show of looking at her watch. 'Time to start work, everyone! We women know exactly how we're going to spend this afternoon, don't we?'

* * *

Later that day, Miss Sharp's shrill voice filled the air, as Maggie strolled back towards the house from the stable yard.

'And a one and a two and a one, two, three – KICK!'

The much-anticipated 'Keep Fit' session had started. The other girls had talked about nothing else since Miss Sharp had announced it at breakfast.

'Cynth – I mean – Miss Sharp's awfully good,' Pam had said, ignoring the supervisor's coy attempts to shush her. 'She could have been an instructor for the League. She's done displays in the Albert Hall and all sorts.'

Maggie had been to check up on Tabby and take her a few scraps of food from lunch. Now, she quickened her step. This, she had to see.

Elsie, Pam and Nancy were lined up on the lawn with their backs to her and facing Miss Sharp. All the women had bare legs and feet and were wearing identical white satin leotards and black shorts.

This morning, Nancy had stood in her underwear with her rollers in, pushing out her elbows as she chanted, 'I must, I must, improve my bust!' The first sign that her colleagues were serious about the body beautiful.

Now, they were touching their toes, with straight legs – first the left and then the right and all perfectly in time, while Miss Sharp shouted out instructions in a voice that any sergeant major would be proud of.

'Not joining in, Poppy?'

Maggie jumped. She recognised that smooth deep voice and her stomach did a somersault. It was him again; the airman, Jack

Rosman. There'd been no sign of him since their first encounter in the basement the other night and Maggie had begun to think he must have left Snowden. But he was still here! It was ridiculous how pleased she felt.

He was out of uniform this time but still looked dapper in his flannels, a collarless shirt and pullover. His right arm was held up in the sling across his chest. He was standing close, towering above her, and he smelled rather nice, of spicy cologne.

Maggie swallowed. It almost seemed – but no, she was imagining it – why would someone like him be interested in her? But she had the impression that he'd been looking for her.

'Not for you, eh?' he asked with a smile, nodding towards the girls on the lawn but not taking his eyes off her.

The girls were now lying down, cycling their legs in the air. Maggie was glad Jack wasn't gawping at them; in fact, he was hardly paying them any attention. All his focus seemed to be on her. It was making her blush.

She shook her head. 'I'm not in The League.'

He laughed. 'The League of Nations?'

'The League of Health and Beauty. They did ask me but …' Maggie wrinkled her nose.

'Don't blame you. All looks rather virtuous and energetic, doesn't it?'

She'd declined the girls' invitation. She hadn't admitted it but not only had she never done 'Keep Fit', she didn't have any idea what it entailed. And besides, what would she wear?

'Say, Poppy,' Jack said smoothly, tilting his head in the direction of the distant hills. 'I'm about to take a stroll around the grounds. There are a couple of pretty pools on the far side that are worth a look. Would you care to keep me company?'

Chapter 15

That evening after dinner, the girls sat in the drawing room, listening to the wireless and flicking through magazines.

Maggie was knitting, although she could hardly concentrate on the stitches. She sat quietly in a dimly lit corner, her legs tucked up on the armchair, minding her own business.

She'd been given the wool and needles as she was taking cover in a department store basement in town a couple of weeks earlier.

'Care to knit for the troops?' the shop assistant had asked cheerfully, holding out a basket of wool and then, as Maggie hesitated, she'd added, 'There's no charge.'

Maggie had thanked her and taken a ball of blue twine and two needles. The RAF was doing a sterling job, after all; she'd knit for those boys. The girl tried to press a pattern on her too but she didn't need it. She'd make a scarf. That'd be warm and easy, too.

At that point, she'd never met anyone serving in the RAF, or in any of the forces, for that matter. And now, she'd met an airman! A dashing, handsome airman who seemed to have taken a shine to her.

She let the other girls' conversation drift around her, lost in another world and hugging to herself the time she'd spent that afternoon with Jack.

She'd worried, at first, that he had only asked her to walk with him so that he could grill her on why she spoke such good German. She waited for the conversation to turn in that direction, but it never did and after a few minutes, she started to relax.

He walked rather fast. She'd had to ask him if he wouldn't mind please slowing down, and then they'd strolled as far as a large stretch of water, which Jack told her was called the Mirror Pool. There were tall reeds around the edges and a rowing boat tied up to a wooden pontoon. The sun was shining on the water, and insects – even a dragonfly – were swirling around. If only Jack wasn't injured, they might have gone out in the boat. She imagined gliding across the water, trailing her hands, as he rowed them across to the other side.

'It's beautiful,' Maggie said, looking at the pool.

'Yes, well my uncle's about to have it drained. Jolly good idea. That way it can't be used as a marker.'

'A marker?'

'By enemy planes.'

As he said the words 'enemy planes' his smile faltered. Maggie wondered how much action he'd seen and how terrible it had been and how many of his fellow airmen hadn't made it back. But she couldn't ask him. He'd tell her, if he wanted to.

'When you see those dots in the sky – the enemy planes – coming towards you, it's pretty damn frightening, Poppy, I don't mind telling you. And anyone who tells you they're not terrified is – well, he's a liar. We prayed for bad weather the whole summer but you know what it's been like: clear blue skies and sunshine. Just when you don't want it.'

He bent to pick up a stone and she wondered whether it was to hide the emotion on his face. She was a little shocked. She hadn't expected him to be like this: thoughtful and sensitive. It made her warm to him even more.

Jack took his left arm back and skimmed the stone across the water. It skipped a couple of times and then sank, sending ripples across the surface of the pool.

'Pah, can't do it properly with this hand,' he complained.

The throw had looked fine to Maggie; it was better than she'd have managed, even without a broken wrist, but Jack tutted and chose another stone to skim. It missed a duck, bobbing about in the middle of the water, by about an inch. Maggie's hands flew to her face. 'Careful!'

The duck gave an indignant squawk and flew off, feathers decidedly ruffled.

Jack laughed. 'Missed! Shame! We could have taken it back to Cook for dinner!'

They walked on.

'I've kept my promise, Poppy,' he said, turning to look at her. Maggie knew what he meant and as no one had breathed a word to her about speaking German, he must be telling the truth.

'Thank you,' she said, praying he wouldn't ask her any more about it.

'And I'll let you into a little secret of my own. My uncle doesn't like me to bandy it about, in case people treat me differently, so keep it under your hat but one day, Pops, all this—' he stretched out his left arm and gazed out over the water '—will be mine!'

Maggie shook her head. Could that really be true?

He shrugged. 'My uncle and Esther don't have children. "Without issue" is the legal term. So, I'm the heir. Of this whole place!' He grinned. 'Isn't it mad?'

It must be true. He wouldn't make up something like that.

She realised, in a flash, that must have been what Pam meant when she'd said Jack Rosman would be snapped up 'especially as …' Was this the 'especially as' she'd been referring to?

Now, in the drawing room, the other girls were laughing and chattering away. No one had asked Maggie how she'd spent the afternoon, neither had anyone mentioned seeing her with Jack Rosman. She appeared to have got away with it. She hoped so. She wanted to keep it – whatever 'it' was – to herself for a little longer.

When Miss Sharp got up from her seat and went upstairs to fetch her *Vogue*, the others took the chance to talk about her.

'Say, Miss Sharp's awfully keen on The League, isn't she?' Nancy said.

'*Cynthia*,' Pam corrected. 'Out of working hours, we're to call her Cynthia.'

'The League? Oh, you can say that again!' Elsie said. 'I'm bloomin' freezing in that room at night because *Cynthia* insists on having the window open. Fresh air's good for you, she says.'

'Gosh, you knit awfully strangely,' Nancy said suddenly breaking off from the conversation and frowning at Maggie from the sofa. 'Look, you two. No, don't stop, Maggie. Show them. See how she puts the needle in underneath there, and then hooks the wool round, the wrong way? You're not left-handed, are you?'

Maggie shrugged and looked down at the six-inch square of knitting in her hands. She'd never thought about it before.

'Left-handed? No. I've always knitted this way. It's the way my mother taught me. Perhaps it's the Ger—' she stopped herself. She felt suddenly breathless.

'Perhaps it's the what?' Nancy asked, shuffling forward in her seat.

Miss Sharp had reappeared. 'What?' she asked, seeing them all staring at Maggie. 'What's happening?'

Maggie reddened. 'It's *just* the way I've always done it,' she said, grateful for the low lighting in the room.

Nancy sniffed and crossed her legs. 'Well, I think it looks jolly awkward. I'll show you the proper way some time.'

Maggie exhaled. She peered down at her handiwork, pretending to concentrate on the next stitch. That had been a close shave.

Even in the evenings, when they were supposed to be relaxing, she had to watch what she said. She couldn't tell her colleagues she was half-German; it was hard enough fitting in as it was. No, that had to remain a secret, for as long as she was here.

Chapter 16

When the library door burst open, Ray was ten feet up a rolling ladder. The book he'd just found, after an hour's search, was propped between the shelf and his knee and he'd been carefully turning the pages. Blast! He'd jumped as the door opened and the page had ripped.

He'd found the library after dinner. Shelves packed with books lined the walls from floor to ceiling and there was a musty smell that reminded him of his nan's.

He'd peered at dozens of spines of what had turned out to be novels, arranged alphabetically by the author's surname. He didn't know much about books but he'd heard of some of the writers: Jane Austen and Charles Dickens and, a little further along, that chap George Eliot.

But he wasn't searching for that kind of book. Perhaps the library didn't have what he was looking for. In the same way that station names and signposts had been removed, maps and atlases might have been destroyed, in case of invasion.

He suddenly had a horrid image of being gagged and tied to a chair, while a snarling Nazi in grey uniform aimed a pointy finger at him. 'Tell us the vey to Oxford, now!' Ray was shaking his head and yelling – as much as he could, given the gag – 'Never! I'll never tell you!'

His stomach twisted at the thought of what they might do next. Let's face it, as soon as he was pushed into the chair, he'd blab. He went hot at the thought.

Five minutes ago, when he'd finally found what he'd been looking for, he'd been jubilant. Geronimo! If the book hadn't been so dusty – and the ladder so wobbly – he'd have raised it to his lips and kissed it.

Other, braver chaps would laugh at the idea – it was hardly derring-do, after all – but facing his fear of heights like this was quite a trial.

He wasn't even sure if he was allowed in here. On arrival, they'd been given a tour of the rooms allocated to them and it hadn't included the library. Ray hadn't asked, in case the answer was no, he'd simply taken himself off after dinner and found it.

He still felt guilty about the way he'd snapped at Maggie Corbett yesterday. He'd thought she was being frivolous, spending her break writing to a sweetheart. At least, that had been his first thought. He hadn't meant to sound so cross. Blimey, her bottom lip had actually wobbled and then, it turned out, she was only writing to her little sister, an evacuee. Maggie had come to the countryside to be nearer to her. He'd have done the same. Family was everything, after all.

Once he'd found the library, he'd scoured the lower shelves first, without luck, so had no choice but to ignore his churning stomach and the sweat forming on his brow and climb up onto the rolling ladder, a strange contraption that rattled along the shelves on runners. He couldn't imagine this place got an awful lot of use and he hoped the ladder was still in working order. If it suddenly broke free and he fell back, pulling the shelf down on top of him, he'd be crushed by about a hundredweight of books.

What a way to go. Mind you, it would save him a lot of bother, if he were dead.

He should be on top of the world. He was away from the bombing, he'd finally been given some real responsibility and he was living like a toff.

But it was no use; he still felt glum.

Everyone seemed to hate him. Miss Sharp – Cynthia – definitely hated him. He was 'officious' and he'd 'got beyond his station'. Those had been her actual words, before she'd stormed off to Lord Ashford's office, yesterday, to make her complaint.

He wasn't entirely sure what 'officious' meant but it was definitely an insult. He could tell by the way she'd spat it out.

The other chaps weren't entirely on his side now either. When he said he wouldn't be joining them at the pub this evening, no one had tried to persuade him otherwise.

The girls were listening to the wireless in the drawing room. Ray had no interest in that these days. The news was bleak; it brought him down.

Now, if *It's That Man Again!*, his absolute favourite, had been broadcasting, wild horses wouldn't have kept him away. Tommy Handley hardly had to open his mouth to have Ray in stitches. But *ITMA* had been off the air for a while now, so that was that.

He didn't think he'd be that welcome in the drawing room, in any case. He didn't seem able to cheer the girls up these days. Over dinner, Nancy had complained about being bored and she hadn't taken too kindly to his suggestion that she should put on a pair of boots and go for a walk.

'Walk? I never walk anywhere!' she'd said, looking down at her feet and pulling a face that made everyone laugh. 'Look, my shoes are already muddy. As for boots, no thanks. I'd look like a baby elephant!'

On top of everything, the promotion that Ray had been so proud of had turned out to be temporary, merely to move all the staff and office equipment here. Perhaps this new position, in charge of 'morale' was merely something his Lordship had invented to make him feel better. It was all too clear that Lord

Ashford, the one person he really wanted to impress, doubted his ability.

Oh, what did it matter? He should give it his best shot. If he could prove himself, he might be trusted with something else.

'Whooaaa!' The ladder shook as the library door swung open and Ray tore the page he'd been studying.

It was the girls. Pam first, followed, as always, by Nancy. Then, Elsie stomped in, arms folded, looking as though she was there under duress and finally, bringing up the rear, Maggie Corbett. Miss Sharp, he was relieved to see, wasn't with them.

'Crikey!' Nancy exclaimed, looking around. 'Books, everywhere! They've got more than Foyles!'

'Oh hullo, Ray,' Pam said, craning her neck to look up at him. 'We wondered where you'd got to.'

The girls spread out, stepping between the shelves and pulling out books with barely a glance at the titles or covers.

'We got rather bored of magazines and the wireless,' Pam said, by way of explanation. 'Cynthia's had a much better idea.'

Looking down at them, Ray started to feel queasy. The patterns in the parquet flooring were getting bigger and then smaller, swirling around, making him dizzy. He quickly pulled his head up again.

'Found anything good?' Pam asked from somewhere to the left of him.

Ray had spotted something earlier that would be just up her street: *The Complete Opera Book* by someone called Gustave Kobbe. He could remember which shelf it was on, too; the one to the right of the fireplace. But he wouldn't tell her. No doubt, if he mentioned the word 'opera', she – or Nancy, who was bound to have heard the whole sorry tale – would only make some sarky comment.

His trip with Pam to the opera – a 'date' he supposed he should call it – had been a few months back, before the bombing closed the theatres. He wished he could erase it from his memory but something was always cropping up to remind him.

Why had he even agreed to go? Pam had said she had a spare ticket because a pal had let her down, but he'd doubted that was true. He'd been flirting with Pam for a while, wondering if a well-to-do girl like her was really interested or just toying with him. Finally, before he'd plucked up the courage to ask her out, she'd got fed up and asked him herself. Fair enough, he supposed, although it really ought to have been him doing the asking.

But as for that bloomin' opera! He couldn't even remember the name of it. He should have guessed it wouldn't be his sort of thing. Call that a night out? Give him a variety show and a laugh and a sing-song over that, any day. But he'd been flattered to be asked and he'd rather hoped something might come of it. Courting a girl like Pam, well, it would be a feather in his cap. He'd definitely have been punching above his weight.

But, honest to goodness, the opera had been so dull. Who could possibly enjoy that?

Pam might have warned him about the singing (caterwauling more like). He'd half expected the window panes to start shattering.

'What are they saying, for Pete's sake?' he'd asked, as the shrieking went on. Pam had shushed him and whispered, 'It's Italian!'

Italian? What on earth was the point of that? No wonder he hadn't a clue what it was all about.

He'd tried, for about ten minutes. Then, lulled by the plush seat and the warm hall, he'd dropped off and Pam had kicked him hard on his shin to wake him.

She'd turned back to watch the performance, mouth set, arms folded and not looking half as pretty. She'd barely spoken to him for the rest of the night.

Things had been a bit prickly between him and Pam for a few weeks after that. He was sure Pam had spread the word that he was uncouth. He'd fallen asleep in the opera, after all.

It had probably been a mistake to think about dating someone from the bank. Lesson learned; he wouldn't do that again in a hurry.

'Would this one do, Pam?' Nancy was asking, holding up a book.

'Needs to be bigger,' Pam said. 'And heavier.'

'What are you looking for? A doorstop?' Ray asked, keeping his eyes on the shelf in front. He was feeling more chipper since he'd stopped looking down.

'Books!' Nancy said. 'It's for deportment. We'll start with one on our heads and build up to a whole stack.'

Ray frowned. 'Now why,' he muttered, 'would you want to do that?'

He tucked his find under his arm, took a deep breath and stepped carefully down the ladder.

Maggie was standing nearby. 'Because,' she said quietly, 'Miss Sharp says it'll teach us to walk gracefully, as though we're gliding across the floor. And apparently—' her voice dropped to a whisper '—Elsie walks like a man.'

Ray laughed.

The other girls were marching past, each with a stack of books in their arms.

'Let's see what Cynthia has to say about this lot!' Nancy said, as they filed through the door.

Maggie paused. 'What have you got there?' she asked, nodding at the book he'd brought down with him.

He held it up. *Gloucestershire: A Shell Guide.* It was full of maps of the county in beautiful bright colours. It was exactly what he'd been hoping to find.

'I came to find an atlas,' Ray said. 'I thought it might help. See, I've looked up that village, where your sister's living. I saw the address when I posted your letter and it's in here.' He tapped the book's cover. 'I reckon it's about twenty miles away.'

Maggie's face fell. '*Twenty miles*?'

'Not too shabby, is it?' he said encouragingly. 'You could bicycle there. Set off early on a Sunday morning and you'd be back before dark.'

She shook her head. 'That ain't – no, I don't think so!'

She picked up the pile of books she'd collected and hurried from the room.

'Hey!' he called after her. 'Don't shoot the bloody messenger, will you?' And then, to himself, 'Thanks very much Ray, for going to all that trouble.'

He kicked the wooden ladder. Ouch. Then he placed the atlas in a gap on one of the lower shelves. Should he need it again – unlikely as that now seemed – he'd know where to find it.

He wondered whether, before he left, he oughtn't to search for a dictionary and look up that word that Miss Sharp had used about him. What was it again? 'Officious'?

No, on second thoughts, he'd leave it. Perhaps it was better not to know.

Chapter 17

'Anyone else coming to church?' Elsie asked, that first Sunday, over breakfast. She, Miss Sharp and Bill were going to the nine o'clock service in the village.

Maggie sipped her tea and eyed the others around the table over the rim of her cup. No one else seemed keen.

'Chance to take a gander at Snowden village,' Elsie added. She and Pam had walked the mile down to Snowden yesterday and Elsie was now an authority on the place. 'Honest, it's like something out of a fairy story!' she said. 'Golden stone and thatched roofs, made completely of hay!'

'Straw, Elsie, I think you'll find,' Ray said, from across the table. He took a bite of his toast.

'I stayed in a cottage with a thatched roof once,' Pam said, 'and in the middle of the night, a mouse fell on my head.'

Nancy squealed. 'Never! I'd have died on the spot!'

Elsie was still in raptures over Snowden. 'There's a shop and a post office, a pub—'

'The Royal Oak,' Norm interrupted. 'They serve a jolly nice ale in there.'

'Of course,' Elsie continued, darkly, 'you'll hear no church bells ringing this morning. They've been SILENCED!' She made a chopping motion with her knife. 'Only to be rung, in the event of INVASION!'

There were groans and exasperated sighs around the table. 'Oh, don't bring us all down,' Pam said. 'Not on our day off.'

'No,' Nancy agreed. 'The sun's shining and we want to enjoy ourselves. Less of the doom and gloom, please.'

Miss Sharp glanced at her watch and wiped her mouth with her napkin. 'Come along, Elsie, Bill, or we'll be late.'

Norm announced that he and Geoff would be spending the day hiking around the lanes.

Elsie pouted. 'Have you noticed, how it's a "hike" if the men do it but a "walk" if us girls do the very same thing?'

'Not taking the bicycles out again, chaps?' Pam asked archly.

Norm coughed. 'No. We went a fair distance yesterday and …' He shuffled in his seat. 'Well, it was a long time since I'd ridden a bicycle.'

Everyone laughed.

'I can tell. You walked into breakfast like a couple of cowboys,' Pam said. 'And, Geoff, you got far too much sun. Your face was as red as rhubarb. Did you get some calamine lotion on it?'

As everyone's gaze turned to Geoff, he squirmed in his seat. Maggie's heart went out to him. Geoff Braithwaite was the one person in Snowden Hall who was even shyer than her.

It was such a waste, Nancy had said this morning, continuing her assessment of the chaps, because he was rather handsome but if a fellow didn't have the personality to go with the looks, it was a non-starter.

Poor Geoff did have an awful stutter. Like a couple of the keys on Maggie's typewriter, he sometimes got stuck on certain letters. 'S' and 'R' were particularly troublesome. Ray, for example, came out as 'Way'.

A couple of times he'd tried to speak and then gave up, turning red with shame and clenching his fists and his teeth in frustration.

'Come on, spit it out, old boy,' Bill said once, which only made matters worse. Geoff's tongue got in even more of a tangle.

Maggie had wanted to tell Bill that he really wasn't helping. But girls didn't stand up for boys, she'd only embarrass Geoff. The other chaps would tease him something rotten. They might even decide that Maggie had taken a shine to him. So, she'd kept quiet.

Of course, the King had a stammer. And it was worse for him because the whole Commonwealth knew, on account of the speeches he had to make to rally the nations. At least Geoff could sit at his desk and get on with his work, he didn't have to speak much.

Pam and Nancy said they wanted to do nothing more than relax in the garden, knitting and reading. So after breakfast, Maggie dutifully helped carry out tartan rugs and magazines and spread them out on the lawn.

She wondered whether she ought to have gone to church with the others, after all. She could have sat quietly in the pew, letting the sermon drift over her, thinking about Jack. Instead, she was lumbered with Pam and Nancy and – oh, salvation! Within a few minutes she heard a cheery, 'Hello, the house!'

The Land Army girls had arrived.

'We're absolutely fagged out,' Charity announced, throwing herself to the ground. 'All we're fit for is sleep.'

'Yes, sorry to be dull,' Gillian said. 'All this fresh air has worn us out.' She held up her right hand. 'Guess what? I've found a cure for blisters! Last night I had five on my hand and this morning I popped them, washed my hand under the cold tap and look, good as new!'

Nancy was curled up asleep on one of the rugs, while Pam was sitting further back in the shade, propped up against the trunk of one of the huge cedars.

Gillian looked up, caught sight of her and called, 'Hey, Pam, what are you doing back there in the dark?'

Pam looked up from her knitting. Her sunglasses were perched on top of her head. 'Staying out of the sun. Don't want to get a tan, thank you very much.'

Charity and Gillian, who were as brown as berries, exchanged amused glances.

'I think it's rather common,' Pam continued. 'No offence!'

Gillian shook her head. 'None taken, I'm sure.'

Almost as soon as they settled themselves down on the tartan rugs, in the warmth of the morning sun, Charity and Gillian fell asleep.

Maggie decided to head for the outbuildings and check on Tabby.

There was no sign of life in the cobbled yard or stables, apart from the brown horse that had pulled the cart from the station. Its head was hanging over a stable door. But then Tabby came running over the yard to meet her, meowing softly, and lay down on the cobbles in the sunshine.

'There you are, Tabs!' Maggie ran her hands down the cat's soft fur. She looked well enough. Leaving the cat to her sunbathing, Maggie headed for the house to fetch a magazine for herself. On her way through the back door, she bumped straight into Lady Ashford.

'Ah! Mary!'

'Yes?' Maggie said. Blimey, why had she said that? It was too late to correct her Ladyship now.

Lady Ashford was as glamorous as ever, dressed for riding, in a tweed jacket with velvet lapels, cream breeches and long leather boots.

She stepped back and narrowed her eyes at Maggie. 'How strong are you?'

'Me? Oh, no, not very strong at—'

'Would you do me an immense favour?'

Maggie hesitated. She could hardly say no. She gave a brief nod and followed Lady Ashford back towards the stable yard.

'Terrible about John Lewis, isn't it?' Lady Ashford murmured. 'Oh, haven't you heard? Bombed out. Completely flattened.'

'Goodness. Was anyone hurt?'

'Oh, heavens, I don't know. Other shops on Oxford Street have gone too. Isn't the war a frightful bore?'

They were marching over the cobbled yard now.

'It won't take a sec,' Lady Ashford said. 'The lad normally gives me a leg up but it's his day off. It's everyone's day off!' She laughed. 'Luckily, I can still tack up! Pony Club. You never forget.'

She slapped a whip into the gloved palm of her left hand. 'It's such a beautiful day. I simply had to go for a ride, you know?'

Maggie didn't know. She couldn't imagine how it even felt to have that much freedom. Her head was spinning. It was something to do with a horse, this favour, and her experience with horses was precisely nil.

And – oh gosh – there it was. A beast of a horse, tied to a rail, was snorting and swinging out its enormous back end, one way and then the other. As it skittered and danced, its hooves hammered on the cobbles and echoed around the yard.

Maggie swallowed. She wasn't expected to get anywhere near that, was she?

'Here she is!' Lady Ashford said. Maggie wasn't sure which of them – her or the horse – Lady Ashford was referring to.

She hung back.

'Fresh as a daisy! Needs a good day's hunting but that's a few weeks off.'

The horse was jet-black with a white stripe down its face. As it moved, the huge muscles in its legs and chest rippled. Blimey, those legs were almost as big as her. It was like standing close to a dragon.

'We usually have mounting blocks around the place but my husband donated them to the Home Guard, for road blocks.'

Maggie couldn't take her eyes off the horse's rolling eyes, huge teeth and swishing tail. The stirrup was swinging wildly from the saddle. Get too near to that and you'd be knocked clean out.

Surely, she wasn't expected to get any closer than this? Maggie had to suppress a sudden, terrible urge to scream.

Lady Ashford had untied the horse and was tutting as it skittered about. She pulled the reins in tight. 'Oh, do calm down. Making such a fuss!' She looked at Maggie and rolled her eyes. 'Too many oats and not enough exercise! I can't leap on while she's like this.'

Leap on? Why on earth would you do such a thing? Running away would be a far more sensible option. Maggie stepped back, as the horse wheeled around, threw up its head and gave a high-pitched neigh.

'Pre-war,' Lady Ashford said, raising her voice over the ear-piercing neighs and clattering hooves, 'the Boxing Day meet always started here at the Hall. Quite a spectacle. The whole village turned out. You'd have enjoyed it, Mary!' Lady Ashford gazed into the distance, as though remembering, as the horse yanked at her arm. 'But my husband doesn't believe in enjoying oneself too much in wartime, so we'll have to find somewhere else.'

She turned, looked at the horse and bounced up on her toes. 'Right,' she said, 'could you hold her, while I jump aboard? Hold her head?'

Maggie gawped. Hold her head? That dragon's head? She wouldn't be able to reach it, even if she had the nerve. She bit her lip. 'I don't think—'

'Here!'

The reins were thrust into her hands and Maggie had no choice but to grab them and hold tight. The horse immediately jerked her hard but she managed to keep her balance. She gritted her teeth with the effort of staying upright.

The horse stood still for a second – perhaps surprised by Maggie suddenly holding its reins – and Lady Ashford put both hands on the saddle, deftly hoisted herself up and swung her right leg over, in a swift and rather impressive move. She was on board.

'Gosh, well done,' Maggie muttered.

She released the reins and jumped clear, as Lady Ashford gathered them up. The horse was still terrifying, but with a rider on its back it seemed rather more under control.

Maggie was breathless. She wiped her brow. She was actually sweating!

Even Lady Ashford was panting. 'That's the ticket,' she said, turning the horse in a circle and looking down at Maggie from what seemed like ten feet above her. 'I say, do you ride? I'm going to town tomorrow but when I'm back, you must come out one day. I've got a mare that might suit you. Quiet, not like this one. Bomb proof! Ha! Thanks, Mary, you're a brick!'

Her Ladyship's black boot kicked the horse's flank, she waved her stick in the air and trotted out of the yard.

They were gone.

Maggie leaned against the rail. She was in shock. Her heart was hammering in her chest. Had that really just happened? And now – she almost laughed – she had an invitation to go riding with Lady Ashford herself. The idea of getting on a bicycle was bad enough, let alone a horse. She'd never been on either and she wasn't about to start now.

Chapter 18

Ray jerked his head back inside the barn as Lady Ashford clattered past him on her black horse.

What a performance! It would have been comical, if Maggie hadn't looked so pale and unsmiling, flinching every time the horse moved or came too near. But, hats off to her, she'd done it; she'd held on long enough for her Ladyship to hop aboard. He'd underestimated Maggie Corbett, that was certain. She was definitely braver than him.

He'd wanted to help the women, truly he had, but his feet had stuck to the ground as firmly as if they were glued there.

He'd been scared of horses ever since his Uncle Fred (or had it been Larry? There'd been so many uncles, he'd lost track) had hoisted him up onto the back of the milkman's black-and-white nag.

Fred or Larry had stepped away to take a photograph with his Brownie and a sudden noise – a car backfiring or some such thing – had spooked the horse. It had set off, careering down the street, milk churns clanging like church bells, while the milkman and the uncle raced after them, like a scene from *Laurel and Hardy*.

Ray was shaken like dice in a cup, sliding this way and that, his arms flailing around, trying to grab the harness or mane until eventually he'd fallen off and landed with a smack on the cobbles. He'd knocked out a tooth into the bargain.

It was lucky, Ma said, as she tucked him into bed with a cocoa, that the whole cart hadn't rolled over and crushed him.

Ray didn't feel too rotten, apart from the gap in his mouth that his tongue kept finding, the graze on his face and a few bruises. He wanted to go out to play but Ma insisted he stayed in bed for the shock. He wasn't strong, she said, not like other boys.

He'd watched from the window as his cousins played football and hopscotch in the street. Damn that stupid horse for making him miss out on all the fun.

Now, the mere whiff of a horse could send him lightheaded. Imagine if he'd fainted while he was trying to help her Ladyship? No, he'd done the right thing, keeping well out of it.

He was helping Maggie in other ways. She'd been so disappointed when she found out her sister was billeted so far away. But he was about to put the smile back on her face.

'Maggie!' he called, stepping out of the barn and wiping his hands on an oily rag.

She turned and frowned at him. 'Ray? Is that you? Have you been there the whole time?'

He swallowed. 'Yes. No. Not exactly. I've been working … in the barn. Come and see.'

But she wasn't going to be put off that easily.

'Didn't you hear us out here? Me and her Ladyship? We were having a right game. I was …' She stopped to catch her breath. 'I was almost killed!'

Ray started to laugh but he saw Maggie's face and thought better of it. She looked pale and out of sorts. But he'd soon put the roses back in her cheeks. She was going to love this.

'Come and see what I've found!' he said, beckoning her closer.

She scowled and followed him reluctantly into the barn.

'Now, stop there and close your eyes,' he said.

She pulled a face but did as he asked.

Ray took hold of each of her wrists and, stepping backwards, pulled her gently towards him. He guided her carefully around a stack of hay bales. 'Keep 'em closed!' he said.

After a few more steps, he let go of her arms. 'You can open them now.'

He'd found it at the back of the barn. Tonks the gardener had tipped him off. It had been here for years, apparently, gathering dust. It had belonged to Lord Ashford and his brother when they were boys.

'Course, it would have been more impressive if he could have wheeled it forward but both the Dunlop tyres were flat and he hadn't got as far as fixing those yet.'

Maggie opened her eyes, blinked a couple of times and then frowned. 'What's that?'

Ray grinned. 'It's a tandem, of course! The gears are clogged up and the chain's completely rusted but I've been working on it since yesterday and it's looking better. Surprising what you can do with a bit of wire wool.'

Maggie shrugged. She couldn't have looked less interested if she'd tried. 'I see,' she said. 'When you said you'd been working, I thought it was something important. So, you were in here all the while, tinkering with this, while I was almost trampled to death?'

He would ignore that. She was still upset from wrestling with that horse. She'd come round, any minute now.

Ray patted the tandem's front saddle. 'If I spruce it up, oil it and mend the tyres, it'll be as good as new.' He gave a mock bow. 'Cinders, you shall go to the ball!'

She gazed at him blankly.

'You and me! Captain and stoker! We'll cover those twenty miles to your sister in no time!'

She spluttered, hardly managing to speak. 'What're you talking about? You and me? On this … this contraption?'

Ray winced. *Contraption?* He held out his hands. 'To tell the truth, I'm not good with horses.'

'*You're* not? You let me—' she started but he cut her off.

'Oi!' he said. Who did she think she was, talking to him like this? 'I didn't *let* you do anything!'

He couldn't believe how wrong this had gone. They were rowing, properly rowing. She thought he was a coward, she despised him.

What about the times he *had* been brave? Did they count for nothing? Running alongside the train, heaving her aboard and hurting his arm in the process. Climbing the ladder in the library to find a map, despite being sweaty and shaky, and worried that if he fell it might be the morning before anyone found him.

The horse, though, had been a step too far.

His chest felt tight; he didn't trust himself to speak. He shrugged. 'I thought you'd be pleased.'

Maggie turned to go. She was calmer now, colder. 'Well,' she said, 'you bloomin' well thought wrong!'

Chapter 19

Dakin the butler had brought in the mail on a silver tray. The arrival of the first post was the highlight of every morning.

Nancy had a letter from someone in the crew of the warship she'd adopted, there was one for Miss Sharp, another for Ray, which he barely glanced at before tucking it into his jacket pocket. Maggie wondered, fleetingly, if he had a sweetheart but no, surely he'd have looked more pleased.

There was an airmail letter for Pam.

'That'll be from Jim!' she announced. She propped the blue envelope against her cup and continued buttering her toast and talking to Nancy, sat next to her.

Maggie couldn't believe her eyes. If she'd received a letter from her fiancé overseas, she'd have ripped open the envelope that very second.

Dakin was frowning at the last envelope in his hand and Maggie sent up a silent prayer. It had been five days since Ray had taken her letter to the post box. There might be word by now, from Vi.

Dakin was struggling to read the addressee. Maggie had often told Vi that her handwriting looked like an inky spider had crawled over the page, so, perhaps …

'Might that one be for me?' It was hard not to fling out her hand and insist on looking herself.

Dakin looked up. 'Miss Corbett? Ah, yes. I do believe it is.'

Maggie's heart soared as she recognised the handwriting on the envelope. Vi! At last!

'Crikey, someone's excited!' Nancy said.

Pam glanced across the table. 'What's the matter with you, Maggie? You're grinning like a Cheshire cat.'

'Sorry,' she said.

'Don't apologise,' Miss Sharp said, shooting Pam a look. 'Goodness knows, we need all the smiles we can muster, given the state of the world. I don't see why you should say sorry simply for looking happy, Miss Corbett.'

Maggie put her finger inside the flap and tore the envelope open. She stopped. Everyone was watching.

'Go on then,' Elsie urged. 'Who's it from?'

'What is it? A letter from her sweetheart?' Big Bill asked.

'Can't be,' Nancy replied. 'She told us she wasn't courting.'

Honestly, they were talking as though she wasn't there.

'It's from my little sister,' Maggie said, firmly. 'She's an evacuee.'

She felt Ray's eyes on her from across the table. Since their tiff at the weekend, they'd only spoken to each other out of necessity, when they were working in the banking hall and, even then, their exchanges had been stiff and formal.

No doubt, he thought she was silly for turning down his offer of the tandem. He was probably right. She shouldn't have been so impulsive. But it was too late now, she'd burned her bridges there.

Elsie sighed loudly. 'A vackie, you say? I do hope she's getting on all right. You hear some shocking stories. My sister's neighbour's boy was sent away with the school to Devon and the poor mite was half starved. His foster family didn't want him there, by all accounts, and hardly fed him.'

Maggie stood up and pushed back her chair. 'Excuse me.'

'Yes, go on,' Miss Sharp said, glaring at Elsie. 'Read it somewhere more private.'

Maggie hesitated. Where should she go? There were bound to be people milling around in the hall or the drawing room. The other bank staff, coming in from the houses in the village and on the estate, would be arriving now. Work started in half an hour and they often came early for a smoke or a chat with the kitchen staff.

'Morning all! I say, any tea left in that pot?' It was Mr Richards. He always helped himself to a cuppa before he started work. Maggie could hear voices and footsteps now as other workers arrived. There was nowhere she could be alone.

She glanced out through the windows. The whole Snowden estate and, beyond it, the hills of Gloucestershire, lay there. It was drizzling but that didn't matter. She'd go outside.

She ran for the shelter of an oak tree on the edge of the lawn. Blast, it was raining harder than she'd thought but the fresh air was welcoming. It was nice to be away from everyone.

Under the tree, as the rain made a steady pitter-patter on the leaves above, Maggie pulled the letter out – just a single, thin sheet of paper – and read:

Dear Maggie

Ta for the letter. I am having a very nice time here at the farm. There is another girl my age, so I have a fiend.

Is Tabby all right?

'Ow!' A raindrop fell onto the paper and smudged the ink, threatening to wash Violet's precious words away. Maggie stepped nearer to the trunk and covered the sheet with her arm.

There are horses, pigs, cows and sheep and hens. We mustn't get too fond of them because they'll all be going for meat. (Not the horses, though).

Have you heard from Mutti? Send her my love pleese.

And let me know when youre able to come and see me. I cant wait.

Love from Vi

It was only a short note and Maggie re-read it, looking for clues that her sister was unhappy. At least she'd got a friend (hopefully not a 'fiend'), which was something.

Maggie quickly turned the piece of paper over and felt a thud of disappointment; there was nothing on the back.

It was such a relief. Vi was safe and she sounded cheerful. Some of the butterflies in Maggie's stomach had settled now but her mind still wasn't at rest. It was a frustratingly brief note and then, there were—

'Oh!' Someone was coming along the path. A man, judging from the heavy tread.

Two big dogs – one black, one golden – raced joyfully across the lawn, barking as they chased a squirrel.

Perhaps it was Jack Rosman? Her stomach did a loop-the-loop at the thought. She hadn't seen him since their walk to the Mirror Pool last Saturday. He'd told her then that he'd be unable to re-join his squadron for at least a few weeks, until his wrist mended and that he came and went from Snowden Hall. She would, he'd assured her with that steady smile, see him again.

She'd seen little Rudi, though, a few times. He was usually scampering around the house or across the lawn with a harassed housemaid or Dakin the butler in hot pursuit. As much as she'd wanted to speak to the little boy, Maggie had always ducked out of sight. She didn't dare let him see her; if he spoke to her in German, the game would be up.

The footsteps on the path were getting nearer. It wasn't Jack. It was Lord Ashford. Unlike her, he was dressed for the wet weather: in boots, a long mac and hat. Maggie pushed her back against the tree trunk and held her breath, but he'd spotted her.

He smiled and tipped his hat. 'Good morning! Miss Corbett, isn't it?'

He'd never spoken to her before. How did he even know her name? It flashed through her mind that perhaps Jack Rosman had told him about her – 'the girl who spoke German' – and her stomach fell.

'Aren't you getting rather wet under there? Would you care to borrow an umbrella from the house?'

'No. Thank you. It's quite dry.' A raindrop landed on her nose. She hoped his Lordship would walk on but he seemed in no rush. He ducked under the branches and stepped closer.

'Say, how are you settling in, Miss Corbett?' He was near enough that Maggie could see how his eyes crinkled at the sides in tiny smile lines.

'Well, Sir. Thank you.'

He was only being polite, he probably asked everyone the same question.

'It must be very different from home. Where is home, by the way?'

'The East End, Sir.'

'Ouch. They've had it bad there, haven't they?'

Maggie nodded, not trusting herself to speak. Vi's letter had already left her feeling close to tears.

He peered at her more closely. 'My dear young lady, you're shivering! We can't have you catching double pneumonia. What would I tell your mother?'

At the mention of the word 'mother', Maggie's eyes filled and her lips started to tremble.

'Oh, you're upset. I do beg your pardon. Your letter … it wasn't bad news, I hope?'

Maggie shook her head. 'No. It's … there aren't any …' This was going to sound daft but she'd started now. 'There aren't any kisses.'

He frowned. 'No kisses?'

'It's from my sister, Sir, you see,' Maggie said quickly, blushing in case he thought the letter was from a chap. 'She's a vackie, twenty miles from here. We worked out a code before she left home.' She was gabbling. She stopped to catch her breath.

'Go on.'

'On her letters, I mean, Sir. Three kisses or more meant that everything was fine and I wasn't to worry. But one kiss meant it was awful and I promised, if I saw one kiss, to move heaven and earth to get her out of there.'

'Goodness. Well, that's frightfully clever. You're wasted here, Miss Corbett, I should think the Intelligence Service could use your skills! Ah, but I can see you're worried. Mightn't she have simply forgotten? How old is your sister?'

Maggie bit her lip. 'She's twelve.'

She wouldn't put it past Vi to forget. Especially if she was having a nice time. The code would've gone clean out of her head. But there was another alternative, perhaps her billet was so bad, it didn't even merit one kiss.

'Twenty miles, did you say? That's not too far. Couldn't you visit? Petrol's rationed, of course, otherwise …' He shook his head. 'Or perhaps you could bicycle there?'

'Perhaps,' she said politely.

His Lordship turned away to whistle for his dogs, who were nowhere to be seen. After a few seconds, they emerged – bedraggled – from bushes on the other side of the lawn and bounded back towards them.

'Rabbits,' he said. 'Oh, don't worry, they never catch them. Now, how are the rest of your family? Are they coping with the raids?'

Maggie wrinkled her nose. 'I … dunno. I'm not … I haven't heard from my dad and my mother's … not there. She was taken away, Sir. By the police.'

Now she'd started, it seemed like she couldn't stop.

Lord Ashford frowned. 'Is she …?'

He had kind eyes, he'd be sympathetic – and she couldn't hold it in any more in any case. 'She's German, yes, Sir,' Maggie said. She held her breath, waiting for his reaction but his face didn't change. 'I suppose I should have mentioned it before.'

He smiled. 'Why? Is your mother a member of the National Socialist Party?'

Maggie frowned. 'Is she ...?'

'Is she a Nazi?'

'Gosh, no!'

'Good! And where is she now? Has she been interned? As an enemy alien?' he asked.

'Yes.' That was it, that was the horrid expression. 'And I don't know where they've taken her. But it's not true. She's not an enemy. She's lived in this country for years and ... it's all been a terrible mistake.'

Lord Ashford sighed. 'There have been a lot of terrible mistakes made. Try not to worry, Miss Corbett. She's not an enemy of this country; she won't come to any harm.'

That was the first time anyone had said anything remotely reassuring. A flicker of hope lit in Maggie's chest.

He looked as though he was about to call his dogs and walk away but something made him stop. 'I expect you speak the language, do you?'

'Yes, Sir.' Mutti had spoken German to her and Vi since they were little. Dad flew into a rage if they spoke it when he was around but between themselves, they often did. She hoped that wasn't a bad thing or that she wasn't going to be in trouble.

But Lord Ashford simply smiled. Oh, he did have a lovely smile. His eyes twinkled. 'Excellent,' he said. 'Do you think you could teach me?'

Chapter 20

That evening, Maggie and Charity were sitting side by side in The Royal Oak, making a pint of shandy last all night.

Charity had suggested sitting up at the bar but Maggie didn't want anyone to overhear their conversation, so they'd bought their drinks and headed for a table far away from anyone else.

Charity looked at Maggie curiously. 'You have been in a pub before, haven't you?'

'Of course!' Maggie said, but, in truth, only a few times and never like this, with a girlfriend.

Back home, Maggie had to account for everything: where she was going, who she was going with and what time she'd be home. Now – it was a kind of miracle – she was absolutely free. Free to go for a walk with an airman, free to go to the pub with a friend and roll home whenever she liked.

'So, what's new?' Charity asked. 'I've nothing thrilling to report, I'm afraid. Oh, except that Molly's started laying double yolkers.'

They laughed.

It was a few days since the girls had seen one another and Maggie had so much to tell Charity, she barely knew where to begin.

'The good news is that I've finally had a letter from my sister,'

Maggie said. 'But the bad news is that her billet is twenty miles away. Ray Maguire found a map and looked it up for me.'

'Twenty miles? Oh, rotten luck. Couldn't you hitchhike? No, on second thoughts, you could wait all day for one car to come by—'

'—and then it might not even be heading in the right direction,' Maggie agreed. 'Ray did make another suggestion.' She wrinkled her nose. 'Oh, but it's too stupid to even contemplate.'

'Go on.'

'He said – oh, it's silly – he's found an old tandem in the barn. It's a complete wreck but Ray says he can fix it and once it's ready, he's offered to take me to my sister's.'

Charity laughed and slapped her thigh. 'On the tandem? What a lark! And what did you say?'

Maggie frowned, suddenly doubting herself. 'I said no, of course. I don't think I can even ride a bicycle, for a start.'

'But you could learn! Look at me. D'you honestly think I knew how to dig and sow and muck out before I came here? Finishing school to farming, in the blink of an eye!' Charity took a gulp of her shandy and licked her lips. 'Anything else? You look as though you're bursting!'

Maggie swallowed. She should have come straight out with it but she was jittery. Charity was her only real friend here. What if she didn't want to be pals anymore, once she knew the truth?

'There is something I want to tell you,' Maggie said slowly.

'I say, this sounds serious!' Charity pulled her chair closer to the table and leaned in. 'Out with it, then.'

Maggie took a deep breath. 'Well, my mother's not dead.'

Charity pulled her head back and frowned. 'Isn't she? Well, I'm jolly pleased. Good for her!'

'No, you don't understand. The first time we met, I think I probably gave you the impression that she was. But she's not dead, she's interned.' Maggie glanced over at the bar before lowering her voice to a whisper, 'My mother's German. So that makes me half-German.'

Charity's eyes lit up. 'Gosh, how exciting. There are no dark secrets like that in my family, more's the pity.' She laughed.

Relief flooded through Maggie. 'You don't mind?'

'I don't care a fig! You could come from the moon and I wouldn't mind.' Charity twisted her mouth thoughtfully. 'But some of the others might.'

'That's what I'm worried about.'

'I'd keep Mum if I were you,' Charity said. 'Pardon the pun.'

It was a relief, a weight off her mind, although there were still other weights. Lord Ashford's request, for one. Maggie still hadn't given him her answer.

'This morning, when Lord Ashford found out about me—' she lowered her voice '—being you-know-what, he asked me to teach him Ger … the language. But I can't! Then everyone will know I'm half an enemy, won't they? But how can I say no?'

'Did you say no?' Charity asked, wide-eyed.

'Not yet. He said, "Always buy yourself time, Miss Corbett. If someone asks you to do something you'd rather not, say, 'I'd like some time to think about that, if I may'".'

Her eyes met Charity's. 'I can't possibly do it. But how shall I turn him down?'

Charity smiled. 'Heavens! Do you always say no to everything? Life's a lot more fun if you say yes occasionally!'

Maggie pulled back, surprised. 'Do you think I should say yes to Lord Ashford? And to Ray and the tandem, too?'

Charity pursed her lips. 'Well, it sounds as though Ray's gone to an awful lot of trouble. He's looked up your sister's billet, he's fixing a bicycle. Goodness! If I didn't know better, I'd say he was sweet on you!'

Maggie shook her head. 'He's not!'

Charity raised her eyebrows. 'Chaps don't generally go out of their way to help a girl, you know, unless there's something in it for them.'

Maggie lifted a finger. 'Ah, but there is! Ray's in charge of morale, so if I decide to throw the towel in, he'll have blotted his copy book. He's helping me to see my sister, so I'll stay at Snowden Hall.' She took a breath and glanced at her pint of shandy. She'd drunk almost half of it, it was making her chatty.

Charity was looking thoughtful. 'It's up to you, of course, but why not give the tandem a go? He'll do most of the work, won't he? You'll practically be a passenger.'

Maggie shook her head. She simply couldn't.

'How much do you want to see your sister?' Charity asked.

'Oh, more than anything! I'm so worried about her!'

'Then, there's your answer.' Charity nodded. 'Besides, it might be fun! "Be good, be kind, have fun!" That's my motto.'

Maggie wished she could be more like Charity; game for any challenge.

'It'll take ages to learn, even if I do manage it. You know, I'm not entirely sure I can bear to spend that much time with Ray Maguire!'

Charity waved her hand dismissively. 'You don't have to talk to him while you're riding the tandem. You'll be behind. Say, you won't even have to look at him!'

She couldn't do it. Maggie changed the subject. 'Remember the airman we saw on the first night?'

Charity nodded. Of all of them, she'd been the least excited by Jack Rosman's presence. But perhaps she knew lots of chaps in the forces and he was nothing out of the ordinary to her.

'I went for a walk with him on Saturday,' Maggie said, as matter-of-factly as she could.

'Did you?' Charity almost choked on her pint. 'Oh, you kept that quiet. What's he like?'

Maggie didn't want to gush. Charity would probably laugh at her or warn her off him, so she tried to sound casual. 'He's at a loose end, I think. I expect he just wanted some company and I was the only person around.'

Charity offered a packet of Players to Maggie, who shook her head. 'Yes, but what's he like?' she repeated. She struck a match and lit a cigarette.

Maggie shrugged. 'He walks fast. It's like he's marching everywhere.'

Charity laughed. 'That's it? He walks fast? Ten out of ten for observation! But he's probably not only a fast *walker*. Airmen, eh? Best avoided!'

Maggie frowned. Was that right? Was Jack Rosman 'best avoided'?

She opened her mouth to say something and closed it again with a thud of disappointment. She didn't want to sound like a giddy schoolgirl and if Charity disapproved of airmen, then Maggie wouldn't say any more about him. Not, at least, until there was something more to tell.

Charity slammed her hand down on the table, making Maggie jump. 'There's your answer! Does your pal the airman have access to a vehicle? He looks like the kind of chap that could pull a few strings.'

'He goes back and forth to London with Lord Ashford's driver,' Maggie said, 'but that's bank business. They're taking important documents. He doesn't have his own and even if he did, petrol's rationed. No joy riding allowed.'

Her heart skipped a beat. It would certainly be a joy, such a joy, to see Violet.

'Horse, then?' Charity joked. She didn't yet know about Maggie's encounter with Lady Ashford and the wild black horse on Sunday. Maggie would make Charity laugh with that story before they left the pub.

Charity shrugged. 'That's it, then. You've no other option, Mags.' She nudged her and clinked her glass against Maggie's. 'The tandem it is! Good luck! I'd say, he's actually the answer to your prayers! Ray Maguire is your man!'

Chapter 21

'Are you quite sure that's absolutely necessary, Mr Maguire?' Miss Sharp exclaimed, making everyone look up from their work.

It was Thursday morning, the bank had been at Snowden for a week and Ray had gone to Miss Sharp with his idea as soon as they'd all settled at their desks after breakfast. He had to get his Nibs' permission but he was sure Miss Sharp would approve; she was such a stickler for protocol. But he'd forgotten that, in Miss Sharp's eyes, he couldn't do a thing right.

'Don't you think you're being somewhat over-zealous?' she continued, loudly, peering up at him over her spectacles.

Oh, why didn't the stupid woman shut up? Her voice echoed up through the high ceiling and down the Long Gallery and, once again, it was as though they were putting on a show.

Ray gazed out at the rows of desks and the curious faces of his colleagues. Pam was hiding a smile ineffectually behind her hand.

'It's not like we're in a city,' Elsie piped up. Trust her to put in her two pennies' worth. This was a private conversation he'd have her know: a Management Decision. 'It's not like the sirens are going to go off.'

Ray coughed. 'True. But say there is an incident?' He put his hand up to silence the few who tried to interrupt him. 'I don't want to cause alarm but …' he had their attention now. Even Big Bill had stopped sifting papers and was reclining in his chair, arms folded, listening.

'Say the worst happens and the Nazis do invade.' There were a few sharp intakes of breath. The usually steely Miss Sharp put her hand to her chest and gave a little gasp.

'Look at France and the Channel Islands,' he said. 'We could be next.'

'Yes, thank you Mr Maguire,' Miss Sharp said, raising her eyebrows at him, as though he'd suggested something quite improper.

'And,' he continued, 'what if the Nazis march on Snowden? Backed up by bombers? We'd have to do something, wouldn't we? We couldn't sit here, like this—' he spread his hands 'like—'

'Sittin' ducks?' Elsie offered.

The mood in the room was sober now. Some of the older chaps were muttering to each other and nodding.

'Precisely. Like sitting ducks.' They were actually listening to him and they had to admit he was making sense.

'So, where're we going to go then?' Norm asked. 'For this air raid drill?'

'Good question!' Ray raised a finger. 'I'll let you know.'

They all groaned. Some of the men shook their heads and got back to work.

'Blimey! Talk about getting us all worked up for nothing!' Elsie said.

Ray pulled his shirt collar away from his neck. It was hot in here. He needed some air.

'I wanted your agreement that it was something we should consider and, erm … in fact, do. Right, fine. Good.' He put his hand up and then down again. 'I'll report back. Very soon. Carry on!'

As he sidled out of the room, he could have sworn Elsie muttered, 'Pompous twerp!'

That had gone well, then.

'You're twirly,' Cook snapped, as he entered the kitchen. He wasn't sure why he'd headed there; perhaps in the hope of finding a sympathetic ear. Sometimes the driver was in there, drinking tea. But Cook and another woman, in white caps and pinnies, were peeling veg at a rate of knots and clearly had no time for him.

'You're twirly!' she said again.

What on earth did she mean? Was that some kind of dialect? First Miss Sharp and now Cook. Everyone was talking to him like he was nobody.

Cook rolled her eyes in an exaggerated motion toward the clock on the wall. 'I said you're *too early*. Lunch ain't 'til one. Now scoot! Out of my kitchen!'

The back door that led out onto the cobbled yard was open and Ray sat on the step in the late morning sunshine. He patted his jacket pockets. Too bad, he'd left his ciggies in the boys' dorm. It was a bore, having to share a room. It was difficult to command respect when the other chaps saw you in your socks and underpants and with your hair at half-mast before you'd taken the Brylcreem to it.

He pulled out the letter he'd received from his old lady yesterday and sighed as he re-read it.

He'd been dreading hearing from her because he knew it'd make him wince with guilt. At least her scrawly handwriting on the envelope meant she was safe and sound. Or, at least, she had been when she'd put pen to paper. Anything could have happened in the meantime but he couldn't let himself think about that.

He felt rotten; he should be there, sitting it out with them all.

Course, whatever she said to the contrary, he knew Ma hadn't been happy about him going off to the country, leaving her on her tod. His sisters only lived down the street but it wasn't the same. Since Dad had gone, Ray was the man of the house.

He'd never had the chance to tell Ma about the flat above the bank that he'd been offered – him and Big Bill – at a token rent, as long as they opened up in the mornings and generally kept an eye on the place. Ma wouldn't have been over the moon about that either but at least he'd have been nearer to her than here.

Once the bombing started and his Lordship decided to move the bank, that had been the end of Ray's plans for a bachelor life.

Ma's letter was full of news about neighbours, aunts and uncles and people he hardly knew, who'd been killed or caught out or bombed out.

I'm missin' you, son, and your jokes. There ain't much laughter round here no more although we do our best to grin and bear it.

Its mekin' me so happy thinking of you in that big posh house, Raymond. Don't you worry about us, we'll get thru it. I'm glad you ain't enlisted. Remember how your Uncle Don signed up last time and he was never the same agen?

Ray grimaced at the spelling and grammar and then felt bad for being ashamed of his own mother.

His sister's baby was due any day now and Ma was knitting a matinee jacket, which, she wrote, *meks a nice change from gloves for the troops.*

Ma was pleased he worked at Rosman's. She'd always wanted him to have an office job. It was a good job, too and, usually, before all this promotion lark started, he could manage it without much bother. But sometimes, lately, the collar around his neck felt awful tight. As though he was wearing someone else's clothes.

A woman was coming across the yard towards him, picking her way over the cobbles. He tucked the letter away. He'd keep it in his jacket pocket until he had a chance to write back and then he'd put it on the fire. He'd die of shame if anyone else read it.

The woman was silhouetted against the sun. Ray put his hand up to his eyes to try to make her out.

It wasn't anyone he recognised. She was slender and in her mid-forties, he guessed. She was dressed in an overcoat and headscarf. Visitors or guests wouldn't come through the back door; he wondered who she was.

She was nearly upon him now. He knew he must look rather sorry for himself and he tried to perk up. The last thing he wanted to hear was, 'Cheer up, it might never happen!'

But the woman merely thanked him with a tight smile as he shifted along the step, to let her past.

'Well, here goes nothing,' she said quietly, as though bracing herself and then she walked through into the kitchen.

There was a moment's silence, then exclamations of surprise and delight.

'Oh, 'ere she is!'

'Well, as I live and breathe!'

Whoever she was, she was getting a better welcome than him. You'd think Queen Elizabeth herself had arrived.

'Now then, Gwen,' someone said from inside the house. It sounded like the housekeeper's gravelly voice. 'I've got just the errand for you.'

A little cat padded across the cobbled yard towards Ray, meowing softly, asking to be stroked. He wondered what had happened to the cat Maggie had brought on the train. Perhaps this was it, it looked similar. At least the cat seemed to like him, even if no one else did. He rubbed the soft fur on its head.

Was he really 'pompous', like Elsie had said? He wasn't one of the gang anymore, that was for sure. He was above them all now. Above his station, they probably thought.

His gut twisted. Giving orders and being in charge wasn't all it was cracked up to be. Uncle Bob had urged him to aim high but what if he wasn't cut out for management, for something better?

He definitely couldn't face joining up.

'It's your nerves, love,' Ma said, whenever the subject arose. 'And you're chesty. You take after your father, God rest his soul. You like your home comforts, Raymond. You wouldn't be any good out there in the desert, trying to be a soldier.'

He exhaled and the little cat twirled itself through his hands, tail held high. There was no point in getting fed up, he would simply have to rise above it.

But the thought wouldn't go away. If he wasn't cut out for management or joining up, what in heaven's name was he cut out for?

Chapter 22

There was a rap on the door of Joseph's office.

Perhaps it was Miss Corbett, with the answer to his request? When he'd asked her to teach him German yesterday, she'd looked bemused. And most unwilling. So, he'd allowed her to buy herself some time. The situation had been something of a novelty. When he made a request, people tended not to say no.

Before the war, he'd asked friends and business acquaintances to help fund the refugee children – the Kindertransport, as they'd called it – and not a single person had refused. He'd been to America to garner support and asked everyone he knew for sponsorship or to act as host to a child. They'd all agreed.

His requests were always reasonable and sensible, after all. He rewarded loyalty; he cared for his employees. He was housing bank staff in his own home. He'd even incurred the wrath of his wife – something lesser men wouldn't dare – and vacated rooms to make way for employees.

Of course, he couldn't offer the same level of care and protection to those other, mostly nameless, people who were working on his behalf on the continent, putting themselves in mortal danger. That was regretful but there was little he could do about that.

But now – he wasn't sure whether it was irksome or admirable

– this diffident young woman, who looked like a puff of wind would blow her down, had said no to him. Or at least, she hadn't – yet – said yes.

'Come!' he barked, without looking up.

The door opened, there was a clink of a cup and saucer. A soft woman's voice said, 'Sorry, Sir. I can come back later …'

Joseph's head snapped up. There, in the doorway, was Gwen, with his morning coffee. She was gazing at him, her head slightly tilted. It was the look he remembered from all those years ago.

He leapt to his feet, dropping his fountain pen on the rug. Half a dozen sheets of paper almost went flying but he grabbed them, shoving them onto the desk, not caring how much they creased.

'No, no! Do come in!' He stepped forward to take the cup from her. 'Please …' He indicated the armchair next to the fireplace. 'Sit down for a moment, won't you?'

He felt strangely ill at ease. He'd been taken by surprise, half expecting to see Gwen around the Hall any day – he'd agreed to her appointment, after all – but not now, not like this.

'What should I call you?' he blurted out. She wasn't 'Miss Tapper' any longer, he couldn't remember her married name and didn't want to presume anything by calling her 'Gwen'.

She didn't answer.

Joseph placed the cup carefully on a shelf of the bookcase and turned to her, spreading his hands. 'I was so sorry to hear about your mother.'

She thanked him but didn't move towards the chair. 'I have to get back, Sir,' she said politely. 'It's my first day.'

'Ah. The new girl, eh?'

They smiled at one another. Of course, she wasn't the new girl, not really. She knew this place – Snowden Hall – very well.

She turned to go.

'I always envied you your mother, you know,' he said, quickly, before she could disappear.

Gwen turned back and looked at him curiously.

'Yes and your father too, of course.' He swallowed. 'Your happy home. Your family.'

Gwen gave the faintest of nods. 'Thank you, Sir.'

He couldn't stand this. 'Please, no. Don't call me "Sir".'

She was slipping out of the door now, closing it gently behind her and by the time Joseph remembered to say thank you for the coffee, she'd gone.

Chapter 23

On Friday, a few minutes before morning break, Miss Sharp rapped her knuckles on her desk and looked particularly stern. Pam was standing next to her, unusually pale and fiddling with the locket around her neck.

'Ladies and gentlemen,' Miss Sharp announced, 'we have a situation.'

'Oh blimey. Jerry's invaded!' Elsie cried, sitting bolt upright.

'No, Miss Davenport. Calm yourself. This country is, for the time being at least, still at liberty. It's nothing like that but I'm afraid it is rather serious.' Miss Sharp took a deep breath. 'Some money has gone missing.'

Elsie gasped and put her hand to her mouth.

'Miss Barbour here,' Miss Sharp gestured to Pam, 'has lost a one-pound note from her handbag.'

Pam bit her lip. Nancy turned in her seat and nodded at everyone gravely, to show that she was in the know.

'She can't pinpoint exactly when the money … er, disappeared, but she definitely had it when she arrived at Snowden Hall.'

Everyone gazed at each other, wide-eyed.

'But who would do such a thing?' Elsie said, looking around the room. 'We all know each other. We're chums, aren't we?'

There was silence. Maggie felt sick. Except me, she thought, I'm the new girl. She'd only known them for a short time. She wasn't anyone's chum. She wouldn't have been surprised if someone had started pointing the finger at her there and then.

She clasped her hands tightly on her lap, not daring to look up. If she caught anyone's eye, she'd blush. And that would be it; she'd look guilty.

It was ridiculous. She knew she hadn't taken the money but she also knew she was bound to be the prime suspect.

All the women left their handbags lying around the Hall, either in their bedrooms or underneath their desks when they went for a break. Those that smoked tucked their cigarettes and matches in their pockets or simply held them.

'First time anything like this has ever happened,' one of the older chaps, Mr Richards, said from the back of the room.

And what was different, Maggie thought. You didn't have to be Sherlock Holmes to work it out.

'Let me say,' Miss Sharp added, speaking over the mutters of disbelief and outrage that were spreading through the banking hall, 'that I'm prepared to offer an amnesty to the petty thief. Perhaps he, or she, is down at heel or has a problem. That doesn't excuse it, of course. Stealing from a colleague will never be tolerated. His Lordship has been notified.'

She peered at them over the top of her glasses. 'I will give the person responsible the weekend to consider their actions. If the money reappears, in my desk—' she slowly opened and closed the top drawer and her eyes moved slowly across everyone's faces '—by eleven o'clock on Monday morning, we'll say no more about it. And please, can everyone ensure they take better care of their valuables from now on.'

She directed this last comment towards Pam, who looked suitably chastened. Miss Sharp glanced up at the clock on the wall. 'Jolly good. And now it's time for tea.' She marched down the aisle between the desks, head held high.

No one moved or spoke until Ray piped up. 'Blimey, that was all very Neville Chamberlain, wasn't it? "By eleven o'clock tomorrow morning …"' Ray mimed Miss Sharp's dramatic opening of the desk drawer and, Maggie had to admit, he did rather a good impersonation of her husky voice. But nobody laughed.

As everyone left their desks, Maggie stayed in her seat. She gazed at the paintings in the Gallery, avoiding her colleague's faces. If they were looking at her with suspicion, she didn't think she could stand it.

Even the fine ladies in the portraits on the walls looked unfriendly now. How had she not noticed the sneers on their faces before? They were looking down on her, with curled lips and cold stares. She suddenly felt very alone. She wanted to go home.

'Hey, Maggie! Coming for a cup of char?' Ray called cheerfully from the end of the Gallery.

It was the first time he'd spoken to her in a friendly tone since their stupid row about the tandem.

Maggie shook her head, without turning round. She knew her voice would crack if she tried to speak.

She expected Ray to carry on without her but, the next moment, he appeared in front of her desk. He leaned on it, with his arms spread and bent, to speak to her.

'Not fretting, are you?' he murmured. 'There are dozens of people in and out of this place every day. Anyone could have taken that money.' He leaned closer. 'It mightn't even be anyone from the bank. Could be Snowden staff.'

Maggie nodded. That was true. There was a hard lump in her throat. She managed a small smile.

'That's the ticket,' he said, straightening up and smiling back 'Coming for that cuppa, then? Come on, before it gets cold.'

'I will,' she said. 'You carry on. I'll be there in a minute.'

The girls were sitting in silence around the table at the far end of the Gallery. As Maggie took a cup and saucer from the tray on the side and joined them, Miss Sharp drained her cup and stood up. 'Here, Miss Corbett. I have to take some papers in to his Lordship, so do have my seat.'

Everyone looked glum. The men had taken their tea outside, onto the sunny terrace; Maggie could see them through the French doors, sitting on the low wall or standing in small groups, smoking. She wished they were in here. One of them could usually be relied on to crack a joke and lighten the mood.

Nancy gave a dramatic sigh and leaned across the table for the teapot. 'Shall I be mother?' she asked and poured some tea for Maggie. 'Anyone else?' Pam and Elsie shook their heads.

Maggie's chest was tight and her fingertips were tingling. Her hand trembled as she held her teacup. She couldn't bear it a moment longer. Her mind was swirling; the right words wouldn't come. Finally, she blurted out, 'I'm sorry about your money, Pam. But it wasn't me. I didn't take it, cross my heart. I just wanted to say that, in case …' Her voice trailed off.

'Sorry, what?' Pam obviously hadn't been listening. Either that or she simply wanted Maggie to say it all over again.

Maggie flushed. 'I said—'

'Oh, don't worry yourself on that score, Maggie,' Nancy interrupted. 'We never dreamed it was you!'

Maggie shot her a grateful glance. Someone was on her side, for once. What a relief!

'No,' Elsie joined in from across the table, 'you wouldn't dare!' They laughed. 'Maggie the mouse!' Elsie added for good measure.

Maggie felt stung. Is that how they all saw her? A little scaredy-cat who wouldn't say boo to a goose?

'Oh, don't be upset,' Nancy said. 'It's absolutely a term of endearment, really it is.'

Maggie dropped her cup onto its saucer, stood up and pushed back her chair. Ignoring the others' surprised looks and Nancy's shriek of, 'Well, really!' she marched outside, through the French doors, to where Ray was standing with some other chaps.

'Might I have a word, Mr Maguire?' she asked.

'Oi, oi!' Big Bill said. He looked as though he was going to say more but Ray glared at him.

Ray put his cup down on the wall and silently led the way, until they were standing outside the windows of the Long Gallery, out of everyone's earshot.

Maggie's head had started to pound. The girls had made her so angry and anger, she realised, was good. It pushed you into doing things you might not otherwise do. She had to say it now, while she had that fire in her belly.

Ray was looking at her, waiting.

Maggie swallowed. 'I wouldn't blame you,' she said, 'I wouldn't blame you if you told me to take a running jump after the way, well, after Sunday and the barn and everything but I've been thinking about your offer, Mr Maguire, your very … very kind offer. The tandem?'

Ray nodded. His dark eyes were fixed on her, he was listening intently.

'If you're still willing to teach me, I'd like to say yes.'

His eyes narrowed. He looked as though he didn't quite believe her. 'It's not ready yet,' he said evenly.

'No, no … there's no rush. Or rather, there is, but …'

His mouth was twitching. 'I should have it finished by next weekend,' he said. 'We'll need to practise. Forty miles in one day is quite a trek. Do you think you're up to it?'

A stab of doubt hit her. Forty miles? But she lifted her chin. 'I think I can, yes.'

'Miss Corbett!' It was Miss Sharp, calling from the terrace. 'His Lordship would like a word. In his office. Now!'

Chapter 24

'Ah, Miss Corbett. Please, do come in and close the door.'

Maggie's heart was thrumming. Why had she been singled out like this so suddenly? Perhaps she was about to be dismissed, after all, for being half-German and therefore half-an-enemy? Or, maybe Dad had discovered her whereabouts and was demanding she come home? Oh, please not that. For all the ups and downs of this place, she'd still rather be at Snowden Hall than back in the East End with him.

No, more likely, it was to do with Pam's missing pound note. She glanced around the room, expecting to see a copper, notebook in hand, ready to question her. But there was only Lord Ashford, in a white shirt and a smart brown suit and tie. He was perched on the windowsill, his legs crossed at the ankle.

'I've been selfish, Miss Corbett,' he said, indicating that she should take the chair in front of his desk.

On the blotting pad in front of her, a small brown teddy bear was propped up against an inkwell. It looked like the one little Rudi had been playing with, down in the basement. He got everywhere, that child. Even, it seemed, into his Lordship's office.

She'd missed some of what he was saying.

'I beg your pardon?' Maggie asked.

'I said I've been selfish, Miss Corbett. If you're going to teach me German, I should offer you something in return.'

Of course. How could she have forgotten about his request?

'I'll do it!' she said, relief making her forget herself for a moment. 'Sir,' she added, more quietly.

He smiled and raised his eyebrows. 'Excellent!' Then his voice became more teasing. 'But you haven't heard my side of the bargain yet, Miss Corbett.'

He moved over to his desk, sat down and fixed her with a steady gaze. 'I can't make any promises,' he said, firmly, 'but I could do my best to find out your mother's whereabouts. What do you say?'

Maggie's heart lifted. 'Could you?'

'I could make a few telephone calls, call in a few favours.' He picked up a pen and started to scribble some notes.

Maggie thought she might burst with hope and happiness. He'd do it, she had no doubt; he was a marvel.

He stopped writing and looked up at her, pen poised over the sheet of paper. 'Did your mother have to go before a tribunal?'

Maggie nodded. A letter had come, summoning Mutti to a meeting. When she'd returned, she wouldn't speak about it. All she would say was that there was nothing to worry about.

Then the coppers had arrived and taken her away.

Lord Ashford made a few notes. 'I should warn you, Miss Corbett,' he said, 'that some internees are being sent overseas. To Canada and Australia, places like that.'

Maggie felt the blood drain from her face. But that was the other side of the world! No, that couldn't be true. She might never see Mutti again.

'I know, it's a blow,' he said, gently. 'But I wanted to be honest with you. Here, write down your mother's details. Name, date of birth, date she was taken. Then I'll tell you why I want your help.'

When she'd finished writing, Lord Ashford leaned back in his chair and made a steeple with his hands. 'If the Nazis invade,

Miss Corbett, it wouldn't do any harm to know a little German. I might be able to negotiate or at least understand something of what they were saying. I'd be on their hit list, that's a certainty.'

Maggie frowned. She couldn't think for a moment why he might be of interest to the Nazis but the moment had passed. In any case, it wasn't her place to ask him.

'In the Home Guard,' he continued, 'I believe they're taught a few simple German phrases but I want to learn more than "*Hände hoch!*"' He smiled. 'And, if we win the war – much more likely, please don't look so vexed – then I might be asked to go to Germany. I could do some good. But none of this can happen unless I speak the language. Do you see?'

She nodded.

'But I'll warn you, languages are not my forte. The only French I can remember from school is "*Où est la gare*?"' His face clouded. 'There wasn't much opportunity to speak the language when I was out in France, last time. And the few phrases of Latin still in here—' he tapped his head '—are about preparing for battles. Which would be useful, I suppose, if we were waging war with ancient Rome!' He spread his hands. 'I am, Miss Corbett, someone who likes to be prepared. So, will you do it? Do we have a deal?'

How could anyone refuse him? Charity would be proud of her. She'd agreed to try riding the tandem and now this. She was turning into someone who said yes.

'I'll have a stab at it, Sir,' she said.

'Excellent!' He smiled and rubbed his hands together. 'Shall we make a start?' He glanced at his watch. 'Do you have a few minutes? No time like the present, eh? Where do you suggest we begin? How about "Hello" and "How do you do?" That kind of thing?'

Maggie's head was spinning.

'With respect, Sir, if the Nazis commandeered the Hall, would you really want to pass the time of day?'

He held up his finger and smiled. 'Good point, Miss Corbett. But I would need to build rapport. I definitely need to know the niceties. Just a moment …' He opened a drawer in his desk, took out a notebook and opened it at the first blank page.

And so, they began.

Maggie had never taught anyone anything in her life. Being thrown in at the deep end was probably for the best. She'd have lost sleep over it, if she'd had time to think.

She taught him *Guten Tag* and *Gute Nacht*. Those words weren't unfamiliar to him. But he struggled with 'How are you?' – *Wie geht es Ihnen*? – and the response – *Es geht mir gut, danke und Ihnen*?

He asked her to spell the words out and he wrote them down, phonetically, too, so he had half a chance of being able to say them.

'Is that right?' he asked her once, frowning. 'It didn't sound anything like how you said it. Way off the mark. Why, it didn't sound like German at all!'

She tried to be encouraging but once, he looked up from his notebook and caught her biting her lip.

'What's the matter?'

'Nothing, Sir.'

'No, do come on. You're smiling. There must be something.'

'It's only … you sound very English, Sir, that's all.'

'That's probably because I am English!'

He was only pretending to be upset, she could tell. He threw his head back and laughed.

Finally, he glanced at his watch and said, 'We'd better stop or Miss Sharp will be on the warpath. Shall we start properly on Monday at 9 a.m.? An hour will do. My old brain can't manage much more.'

He was writing it in his diary. 'I'll clear it with Miss Sharp.'

'Might I …? There is something.' Maggie had to force herself to say it. She couldn't bear it if her secret got out. 'If it's all the same to you, I'd rather we kept this between ourselves, Sir.'

He thought for a moment. 'Very well. Let's say, you're helping me out with some private correspondence.' He snapped the diary shut and smiled at her. 'That should do it!'

Chapter 25

At breakfast time the next day – Saturday – Ray tapped a knife handle on the table. 'Right, who's game for blackberrying this afternoon?'

Everyone looked at him in surprise. Maggie supposed this must be part of his 'morale-boosting' endeavours. She hoped he hadn't forgotten about fixing the tandem. Now that she'd agreed to try it out, she was keen to get started. She'd written to Vi again and told her she might be able to come and visit in a little while.

Pam looked put out. 'Blackberries? But I thought we were going to do Keep Fit?'

Miss Sharp frowned. 'I suppose it might be an idea to do something together, *en masse*, as it were. We can do Keep Fit another time. But are you sure there'll be fruit this late in the season, Mr Maguire? It's already October, after all.'

Ray sat a little taller in his seat. 'There are lots. I did a recce before breakfast.'

They looked at him blankly.

'A reconnaissance,' he said. When they still didn't catch on, he sighed. 'I've checked! There are plenty of brambles, full of fruit, on the other side of the Mirror Pool.'

The other chaps were exchanging conspiratorial glances around the table.

'If it's all the same to you, we'll duck out, Raymondo,' Bill said.

'But we're game, aren't we, girls?' Elsie said. 'It might be fun!'

They had a morning's work to get through, but after lunch Ray led the women across the garden. He was twirling a folded black umbrella, throwing it in the air and doing tricks like a drum majorette. Every time he failed to catch it, Elsie and Nancy yelled.

'Oi, watch it!' Elsie said. 'You'll have someone's eye out!'

'Why on earth have you brought a brolly anyway, Ray?' Pam asked. She and Nancy had linked arms. 'You're hardly likely to need it. Unless you've been doing a rain dance!'

Maggie looked up. Pam had a point. It was a bright sunny day and the sky was Air Force blue, with hardly a cloud.

'You'll see,' Ray said.

On the way through the grounds, they passed Charity pushing a loaded wheelbarrow. Her face was pink and glowing with exertion. Maggie couldn't help but admire her friend; she still looked impossibly glamorous.

Charity set the barrow down and blew a strand of blonde hair off her face. 'Hey, where are you going? Following Ray like he's the Pied Piper of Hamelin?'

Maggie told her. 'When do you finish work? Why don't you come too, if it's not too much of a busman's holiday?'

Charity's face lit up. 'A scramble in the brambles, eh? Yes, please! I've got to chuck this manure on the turnips, then I'll see you over there!'

The brambles stretched for yards along a grassy ridge and as they approached, Maggie spotted dozens of glossy blackberries. She felt her spirits lift. Good old Ray for organising this little excursion. He wasn't half bad, really.

'Right, everyone!' he yelled at that moment. 'Spread out and take a few feet each.' He was directing them with his umbrella.

'Pam, there; Maggie, there. There's plenty for everyone. No need to bunch up!'

Maggie sighed. Bossy as ever. She'd spoken too soon.

Nancy was still puffing. She threw herself down on the grass. 'One second, Sergeant Major, let me catch my breath!'

Ray gazed out over the fields and made a big show of breathing in the fresh air. 'Not half bad, is it? The countryside?'

Elsie pulled a face. 'It's fine when you're hop-picking in Kent but I'm not sure about livin' out in the sticks for ever. Bet there's not a Woolies for miles!'

Everyone laughed.

'Did you go hop-picking, Ray?' Elsie continued. 'You must've done. You're from Bromley, aren't you?'

Maggie looked around. Bromley wasn't far from where she lived, in the East End. But Ray didn't answer. He looked uncomfortable. 'Hop-picking?' he said vaguely. 'Yes, I think we might have done. Once or twice. When I was very young.'

Pam frowned. 'What's hop-picking when it's at home?'

'It's how us East Enders get our 'olidays,' Elsie said. 'Isn't that right, Ray? It's a bit like being here. It's like an 'oliday but you're working too. And you make your own entertainment in the evenings.'

Maggie had been hop-picking once, with Vi and Mutti and Dad. It had been a disaster. Dad wasn't exactly the life and soul of the party and after supper, when all the families gathered together for a drink and a sing-song, he didn't want to join in. He'd rowed with Mutti when she'd stayed late one evening, daring to enjoy herself.

They never went again.

'Ah, very clever, Raymondo,' Nancy said as they watched him use the handle of his umbrella to hook down brambles that were too high to reach.

He smiled. 'I'm not just a pretty face.'

'Hallooo!'

Charity and Gillian had arrived and took a patch of brambles next to Maggie.

Cook had been persuaded to equip everyone with bowls from the kitchen. Pam had grabbed the only wicker basket and was wandering around with it over her arm, gazing into the distance.

'Like Marie Antoinette, going to visit the peasants,' Charity whispered to Maggie and they giggled.

Suddenly, Pam started to sing. 'Do, Re, Mi, Fa, So, La, Ti, Do!' she trilled and then, 'Do, Ti, La, So, Fa, Mi, Re, Do!'

Maggie winced and she and Charity exchanged looks of horror, as Pam repeated it several times. Maggie didn't know anything about singing but the high notes, in particular, sounded screechy.

'Scales,' Pam announced, when she finally stopped. 'Every day, followed by thirty minutes of singing practice.' She shook her head. 'It's the only way.'

'She's awfully good,' Nancy said. 'But Pam, don't overdo it. Don't strain your vocal cords.'

Maggie smothered a giggle and reached for a ripe blackberry, which came away easily in her fingers. She tossed it into her bowl and was immediately reminded of home. There were plenty of blackberries down by the canal at this time of year, among the buddleia and weeds on the towpath. In blackberry season, she and Vi would pick them and before the war, as a special treat, Mutti would make Black Forest gateau, using blackberries instead of cherries.

Pam was standing a few feet away. 'I think picking blackberries is rather like choosing a chap,' she declared.

Charity pulled a face at Maggie, who tried not to laugh. Oh, it was fun to be out here in the fresh air, forgetting all her worries for a while.

'Do you mean,' Charity asked, 'because there are an awful lot of pr—'

'*Problems*!' Gillian yelled.

Pam and Nancy were staring at them in confusion.

Maggie turned away to hide her smile. Charity was such a

breath of fresh air. She looked like an angel but she had the vocabulary of a navvy. As Maggie watched, her friend picked a blackberry – a big juicy-looking one, as big as her thumb – and popped it into her mouth.

'Oh … shhh … sugar,' she said as she bit into it. Her face contorted like a gargoyle.

'Tart?' Nancy asked.

Charity nodded, still wincing. 'I've been called worse.'

Finally, she managed to swallow the fruit. She exhaled with relief. Her smooth skin and wrinkle-free face reappeared. There, she was beautiful again.

Pam was still musing on how choosing a chap was like blackberry-picking.

'There seem to be so many to choose from,' she said, 'when you first look. But there's something wrong with lots of them. For instance, this one here is too red and that one's damaged goods – it's been eaten by birds or flies.'

'Yuck!' Nancy said, nodding at Pam encouragingly.

'Or you can't reach them because they're too high—' Pam said.

'You need an umbrella!' Ray said.

'—or there are nettles or thorns in the way. Sometimes you have to lift up a leaf and look carefully and then you find a perfect one: a treasure.'

'Which is exactly what you've found in Jim,' Nancy said. 'A treasure!' She turned to the others. 'Pam's getting married before the year's out, you know.'

Charity shook her head. 'That's jolly good advice, Pam, I'm sure, and I wish you all the best but unless I can find a handsome farmer, I'm never getting married.'

There were gasps all round. Even Miss Sharp, who'd been quiet up to now, turned to listen, holding her bowl aloft.

'Why ever not?' Elsie asked.

Maggie was sure everyone was thinking the same; that beautiful Charity must surely have her pick of men.

Charity laughed and flexed a bicep. 'Who'd have me, for a start? Look at these muscles! I'm positively ruined!'

When the laughter died down, she grew more serious. 'It strikes me that all wives do is sit around drinking tea and having babies. I want to do something more than that with my life. Why chain yourself to someone who might turn out to be a complete rotter?'

Elsie sniffed. 'You'll change your mind. You simply haven't met the right chap yet.'

'What kind of fella would you like, Elsie?' Pam asked.

Elsie bucked up, clearly pleased to be asked. 'Now, let me think,' she mused. She gazed over the hills, as though imagining her future husband. 'I don't mind how ugly he is, as long as he doesn't have false teeth.'

They all shrieked.

'Imagine them,' Elsie went on, 'smiling at you in a glass on the bedstand at night!'

'Anything else?' Pam asked.

Elsie pursed her lips. 'Someone like my old dad. Down to earth and handy round the house. Provided he has a good heart and is sincere, I don't mind what he looks like.'

'What about you, Maggie?' Pam asked. 'What kind of chap do you go for?'

Everyone was looking at her. Oh, blast Pam and Nancy and their stupid questions about men. Couldn't they talk about anything else?

'This is like being with your aunties at a wedding,' Ray said. 'Are you courting, dear?' He did a fairly convincing impression of an old lady and everyone laughed.

Maggie was so grateful to him for distracting everyone that, for a split second, she could have kissed Ray Maguire.

'Whenever I'm at a wedding,' he continued, 'old people poke me and say, "You'll be next!". I've started to do the same to them at funerals.'

'Oh Ray, you're a card!' Nancy said, shaking her head.

'Anyway,' Pam said, 'at the risk of sounding like one of Ray's nosy aunties, we were asking Maggie what kind of chap she goes for.'

She was going to have to answer. Who would she like? Not someone like her dad, that was for sure. She envied Elsie her nice, kind dad. But, unlike Elsie, she couldn't put up with anyone ugly. Not when you thought about the facts of life. She shuddered. She couldn't even think of doing anything like that with someone who wasn't at least the tiniest bit gorgeous.

There was Jack, of course. She'd like someone like him, but she couldn't say it. If she was being honest with herself, could she even dream it? He was, like Pam said, rather like a blackberry that was out of her reach.

Everyone was waiting.

Maggie sighed. 'I dunno. Cary Grant would do.'

The girls laughed then, agreeing with her.

'A man in uniform, for certain,' she continued. 'Someone in the services, doing his bit. Someone I can have respect for.'

She hadn't expected to say so much. She blushed, feeling everyone's eyes on her. They looked uncomfortable. Everyone was silent. Nancy pulled a face and Miss Sharp coughed.

What was the matter? Oh, blow. Ray! Ray, who wasn't in uniform. She'd forgotten about him. He was probably offended.

She'd answered without thinking. She didn't dare look over and catch his eye. Just when they'd made up again, too. She quickly plucked some blackberries from the brambles, not caring about the thorns or the nettles that stung her hand.

'I SAY!' Pam yelled. 'Look at this! It's a queer kind of blackberry. Anyone know what it is?'

She was holding something between her thumb and forefinger.

'What colour?' Charity called. 'Hold on, I'll come and take a look.'

'It's black,' Pam said. 'Like a bead of jet.'

The others gathered round and Pam held the berry out for inspection in the palm of her hand.

'That's deadly nightshade,' Charity said, after a quick glance. 'You'd better wash your hands when you get back. It's awfully poisonous.'

Everyone gasped and Nancy screamed.

'Steady on, Nancy,' Pam said. 'You're not even within two feet of it!'

Nancy bit her lip. 'Sorry. Nervous disposition. When France fell, I got hysterical, didn't I, Pam?' She turned to the others. 'Pam had to slap me round the face.' She touched her cheek, as though remembering.

'How many of these would it take to kill a person?' Pam asked.

Charity shrugged. 'A handful, maybe. Not many. Don't mix them up with the blackberries, will you? Look, here's where the plant's growing. Let's steer clear of this patch and pick from the brambles over there.'

'Quite right,' Ray said. 'I was going to suggest that myself.'

Pam was like a dog with a bone, she couldn't stop her questions. 'Do you think it's a very painful death?' she asked.

Charity frowned. 'Why, who are you hoping to bump off?'

'If the Nazis come,' Pam said, lifting her chin defiantly, 'I'd eat the berries. I'd rather die than let Jerry get his hands on me.'

'You sound like our landlady,' Gillian said. 'She's told us she's got the rat poison ready. It's in the shed and she'll take it, if they come.'

Everyone fell silent. The sun went behind a cloud and for the rest of the afternoon, they picked the fruit in subdued near silence. Finally, they laid their bowls – and Pam's wicker basket – on the ground and admired their handiwork.

'What in heaven's name will Cook do with all these?' Nancy asked. 'We've picked tons!'

Miss Sharp raised a finger. 'I know. She's going to bottle them for Christmas.'

Christmas! It was over two months away – a lifetime, and, yet, it would be here in a flash. Where would she be at Christmas, Maggie wondered, and what on earth would have happened by then?

Chapter 26

Ray wheeled the tandem out of the barn and over the cobbles in the yard.

'Ta dah!' he said. 'Your carriage awaits!'

Oh, he wished he hadn't made so much of it. Maggie looked pale and serious. He should have acted more casual, as though going out on a tandem was nothing out of the ordinary.

Her hair was pulled back in a ponytail and she was wearing slacks that were too big and sagged around the knees. He pretended not to notice as she hitched them up.

'Gosh, you have done a good job on it,' she said.

It was true. The tandem looked brand new, with its bright green paintwork and plump black tyres. His fingers were still sore from the hours he'd spent rubbing away at the rust with wire wool and then giving it a lick of paint.

He had remembered what his dad had taught him as a boy, when they used to spend Sundays in the shed, tinkering with an old sit-up-and-beg bicycle. His old man had been able to make or repair anything.

Ray shrugged. 'I haven't minded it, to tell the truth. Made a change from putting figures in ledgers.'

For those hours, as he'd worked, he'd forgotten about the war and morale and being responsible.

It had irked him, when he'd had that silly tiff with Maggie and she hadn't wanted anything to do with the tandem. He couldn't quite put his finger on why, but he'd wanted her to be as excited about the bicycle as him. At least, finally – and probably because she had no other choice – she'd agreed to give it a go. And now here they were, about to ride it for the first time.

'Come on,' he said encouragingly, 'let's find a patch of lawn. Grass, for a softer landing!'

'Do you think I might manage it?' Maggie asked, as they set off, Ray wheeling the tandem between them. She sounded doubtful. 'I haven't been on a bicycle since I was a nipper.'

'Well, you know what they say. Riding a bicycle is like … riding a bicycle! One of those things you never forget. But you'll be sitting here, remember,' he tapped the saddle at the back. 'Don't get any ideas about being captain!'

He was trying to make a joke but she was too anxious to notice.

'Have you tried it out yourself?' she asked.

'I had a practice yesterday on the drive, to make sure I could steer and brake. It all went well until I lost control and rode right over Mr Tonks' cabbage patch. He wasn't too pleased!'

Maggie managed a small laugh. 'And that's supposed to fill me with confidence?'

Once they'd chosen their spot on a flat stretch of lawn, hidden from the house and any prying eyes by a beech hedge, Ray straddled the tandem and planted his feet wide on either side of the frame. 'Right, hop on the back. We need to check your saddle's the right height. Hold on to me if that helps you balance.'

Maggie took a deep breath, placed one hand lightly on his shoulder and swung her leg over the saddle at the back. Ray felt the tandem sink a little as she sat down.

'How's that? Can your feet touch the ground?'

'Yes,' she said. Her voice was lighter. 'It's not too bad.'

'Now, put your feet up on the pedals and your hands on the handlebars.' When she hesitated, he added, 'I'm holding it. You're quite safe.'

Once Maggie had lifted her feet off the ground, Ray turned the pedals into the right position and placed his right foot on the top one. All he had to do was lean into it and press down, the wheels would start to move and they'd be off.

Suddenly, he had the jitters. If it all went wrong and they overbalanced, she'd never trust him again. She might even refuse to get back on. He wanted to make a success of this so much. How wonderful would it feel, to make it, eventually, all the way to Maggie's sister's billet. For the first time since he'd arrived at Snowden Hall, he had something to look forward to.

Maggie was awfully still in the seat behind him.

Ray turned his head. He couldn't quite see her but he could feel her there and hear her breathing, coming a little fast. 'Ready for the off?'

'Yes,' she said in a quiet voice.

'See the weeping willow at the edge of the pool over there? A hundred yards away?' The tandem moved slightly as she shifted in the seat to look. 'We'll head towards that. Don't worry, I'll brake before we get to the water!'

'Oh blimey,' she muttered. 'I'm not sure about this.'

'Just pedal as much as you're able,' Ray said firmly. 'Don't wriggle. Keep everything, apart from your legs, as still as you can.'

Before she could change her mind, Ray pushed his foot down on the pedal. The chain creaked and clanked – blimey, it needed more oil – but they were moving.

'Wayyyyy heeeeyyyy!' Maggie yelled.

He was sitting in the saddle now. The grass was bumpier than he'd expected and, at first, it was hard going. Blimey, they were hardly moving. He pressed down harder.

'Pedal!' he yelled and felt Maggie start to push down too, behind him.

That was it, this was better. They'd straightened out now, and they were picking up speed. They were doing it. They were riding the tandem!

Chapter 27

The following Wednesday evening, Maggie, Pam and Nancy piled into Miss Sharp and Elsie's room, along the corridor. It was the same size as theirs but much tidier. Maggie always made her bed – something drilled into her by Dad since she was small – but Pam and Nancy's were regularly a crumpled mess, covered in discarded clothes, rollers, stockings and hairpins.

There was an armchair near the window, which Elsie had commandeered. Miss Sharp was pinning up her hair in front of the mirror. Maggie and Nancy sat on one of the beds, Pam was stretched out on the other.

'You were awfully hard on us on Saturday, Cynthia,' Pam said, prodding her stomach gingerly. 'Ouch! I'm still paying for it!'

Nancy pursed her lips. 'Well, you know what they say: "No gains, without pains"! Pam, to be fair, you did say you wanted a washboard stomach rather than—'

'—a blancmange, I know! I'm only saying it was jolly hard!'

Miss Sharp took the last hairgrip out of her mouth, stuck it into the back of her bun and then answered Pam's reflection. 'It'll have done you the world of good. It's like deportment once you've mastered it; an upright spine can lead to better moods and overall health. Even in wartime, one mustn't lose interest in one's personal appearance.'

'Oh no,' agreed Nancy. 'We simply must, "Stay beautiful!"' She sighed. 'You're so knowledgeable, Cynthia.'

Miss Sharp looked pleased, as she swivelled around from the mirror to face them. 'Actually,' she said, looking around the room until she found her handbag, 'something else I can recommend is "skin airing".'

The others exchanged puzzled looks.

'Swimming,' she announced, 'in the nude!'

Elsie started to cough and had to be slapped on the back.

Pam sat up, eyes wide. 'You wouldn't, would you, Cynthia?'

'There is a swimming pool out there,' Nancy added, with a grin. It sounded like a challenge.

'You'd be surprised how freeing it is, to swim without a bathing suit. There's quite a sense of liberation,' Miss Sharp said.

'You mean, you've actually done it?' Nancy asked, in a hushed tone.

'You'd be astonished, the difference even a small layer of wool makes.'

Maggie laughed. She could hardly imagine prim and proper Miss Sharp taking off her clothes and jumping into the pool.

'You wouldn't though, would you, Cynthia?' Pam asked again.

But despite their badgering, Miss Sharp wouldn't give them that assurance. 'It's rather too chilly at the moment.' She held up an elegant finger. 'But in the spring, who knows?'

'Heavens, what's that din?' Pam asked, when they'd all finally stopped giggling.

'Sounds like a horn,' Elsie said. 'Oh blimey!' She jumped up. 'I know what it is! It's Ray's bloomin' air raid drill!'

* * *

‘Give it ’ere, Raymondo,’ Bill said, heaving his bulk out of the armchair and holding out his hand. ‘That wouldn’t summon a mouse.’

Ray had waited until after dinner, when everyone had made themselves scarce, then he’d tilted the hunting horn towards the ceiling, taken a deep breath and blown into it as hard as he could.

It was useless; he’d only managed a pathetic ‘Parp!’

Thank goodness only his chum Bill was here to witness his paltry attempt. Norm and Geoff had disappeared; they were probably outside having a ciggie. The women had filed upstairs to freshen up before they came down to spend the evening listening to the wireless or playing records.

Ray was grateful now that he’d enlisted Bill’s help. Bill played tuba for the Salvation Army; he lifted the horn to his mouth and blew. His cheeks turned redder and rounder – he looked like an overgrown Cupid – and then a loud trumpeting filled the room.

‘Goodo!’ Ray slapped Bill on the shoulder. ‘Walk around! Go on! Out into the hallway, so everyone can hear!’

Ray was checking his pocket watch as the girls filed downstairs, exclaiming crossly and pulling on cardigans. Snowden staff were emerging from the kitchen, wiping hands on aprons. Ray recognised Lord Ashford’s driver striding along the corridor, buttoning his jacket and patting down his hair.

Everyone looked out of sorts, which was exactly the way he’d planned it.

‘Remember where you’re supposed to go?’ he asked. ‘Have you got *everything*?’

Cripes, if this was the real thing, there wouldn’t be time to stand like this.

He ushered everyone down to the basement, waving his clipboard, ignoring Pam and Nancy’s rolling eyes and Elsie’s resentful expression. Only Maggie managed to give him a smile. They were pals now, since Saturday’s successful attempt to ride the tandem.

He'd have suggested another practice on Sunday too, if it hadn't poured with rain.

The wooden cellar door, sunk into the wall, was so battered and ancient-looking, it might have been the entrance to the Ark. Ray pushed it open and stood to one side, shouting, 'Mind your head!' and 'DUCK!' as everyone went through and then, 'Watch your step! Let your eyes adjust!' as they descended the flight of rickety stairs, into the gloom of the cellar.

It took several minutes. Some people had run back for their gas masks but Pam point-blank refused. 'Ghastly things,' she said. 'I never have mine. If they gas us, they'll get me for sure.'

Brummie, his Lordship's driver, didn't have one either. 'Don't believe in 'em,' he said, gruffly. 'I'll put a wet towel over my face, if it comes to it.'

Oh blimey, here was his Nibs. He was carrying something. No, *someone*: a small, sleeping child wearing striped pyjamas. Lord Ashford had his own gas mask and a child's Mickey Mouse mask hanging from straps over his shoulder.

Ray felt suddenly like a maître d' at one of those posh restaurants up West. He tried to assume the air of someone in control. He gave a little bow from the waist. 'Good evening, Sir.'

'You got the hang of the hunting horn then, Maguire? It can be the very devil to sound, so well done.'

Ray swallowed. 'Thank you, Sir. Will, er … will her Ladyship be joining us? No? Very good, Sir. Do mind your head as you go through.'

His Lordship paused at the door. 'Any news on Miss Barbour's money?'

Ray's stomach fell. He'd hoped his Lordship wouldn't ask about that. The whole sorry business was making his head ache. Why had he been lumbered with investigating the matter?

'No, Sir, afraid not.'

'Not good for morale, Maguire, a thief among the staff.'

'No, Sir.'

'The last thing I want is to have to involve the police.' He nodded at the list in Ray's hands. 'Is that the lot now, Maguire?'

'Yes, Sir. I mean, no, Sir.'

There it was again: that unmistakeable flash of irritation on Lord Ashford's face.

'If anyone's missing now, we'll take it they're not coming,' his Nibs said. 'Assume the worst, as though this were a real raid.' He placed a protective hand over the crown of the child's head and bent to go through the cellar door.

After one final glance down the empty corridor, Ray followed him, shutting the door firmly behind them.

The cold hit him immediately, along with a musty, earthy smell. There were a few lights in the ceiling, which cast shadows onto the stone walls. Ray braced himself. There were bound to be grumbles from the staff.

Rows of wooden benches had been set up in the cellar. Snowden employees were seated on one side, bank workers on the other.

Elsie, unsurprisingly, was the first to complain. 'Cor!' she said. 'It doesn't half smell of mushrooms down here!'

Laughter echoed around the cellar.

Bill must have spotted the racks of bottles and huge oak barrels behind them. He suddenly piped up, 'Perfect place for a party!'

'It's certainly the perfect place for my wine,' Lord Ashford said. He was sitting on a bench at the front, facing everyone, the sleeping child on his lap. 'Some of it's laid up specially for when we win the war. We'll have the party to end all parties then!'

That was greeted with murmurs of approval.

Ray stood to one side and peered at his list. He'd crossed off most names as people arrived at the cellar door. There were only one or two of the Snowden staff that he didn't know.

Elsie was still sniffing and complaining about mushrooms. 'It's ever so damp in here,' she said.

'You're right, Miss Davenport,' Lord Ashford said. 'Originally, I'd planned to put all my artwork down here, for safety. We actually moved some of the paintings but blue mould started to appear on the frames, so I had them all brought up again. And unless anything changes, there they will stay for the duration.'

'And aren't we the lucky ones?' Ray said, looking up and glaring at Elsie. 'Surrounded by all those pictures while we work.'

Miss Sharp picked up one of the blankets that had been laid out on the benches and wrapped it around herself. 'Someone's been very thoughtful,' she murmured.

'It's chilly down here,' Lord Ashford said. 'I had them brought down. Here, Gw— Mrs Nicholls, why don't you take this one?'

Ah, that was the woman's name. Ray crossed her off his list. 'Mrs Nicholls'. He recognised her from last week. She was the woman he'd seen arrive at the back door.

He gazed up the stairs, tapping his foot, willing Geoff and Norm to appear.

'All present and correct, Maguire?' his Nibs asked.

'Mr Keeling and Mr Braithwaite aren't here yet, Sir. I'm, ah … not sure where they could have got to.'

Ray gritted his teeth. He could swing for Geoff and Norm. Clearly, they'd gone further than the terrace for a ciggie. He tried to catch Bill's eye, to ask if he'd seen them but Bill was too busy entertaining the women. Even Miss Sharp was giggling. That used to be Ray's job, making the girls laugh. He felt a twist of envy, watching Bill holding court.

'Have a word, will you, Maguire, when you track them down? It's rather a poor show,' Lord Ashford said, and Ray nodded, smarting at the ticking off. With everyone else on his list crossed off now, Ray sat down on the bench next to Maggie.

That moment, the door at the top of the stairs opened with a creak and a bang.

At last! Ray stood up but it wasn't the chaps. It was an airman, in RAF uniform. He looked vaguely familiar.

Just in case the new arrival had any ideas about taking his seat, Ray quickly sat back down. 'Evening all! Better late than never!'

the airman called cheerfully. He trotted down the stairs with a confident swagger.

Now Ray remembered. They'd seen him on the first night, at the drinks reception out on the lawn. He'd sent the girls into a tizzy. Ray noticed Nancy give Pam a hefty nudge and on the bench beside him, Maggie gave a little start of recognition.

Lord Ashford glanced up. 'Ah, there you are. Can I introduce my nephew? John Rosman. Air Bomber Command.'

The airman's arm was still in a sling, so he saluted them with his left hand. 'Call me Jack!' he said. 'All my friends do.'

A pilot, an actual fighter pilot and if that wasn't enough, Lord Ashford's relative too. He probably flew Spitfires. There were gasps and giggles from the girls. No doubt they were thinking, *here comes a proper man, a man in uniform.*

Call-me-Jack's eyes darted around and landed on Maggie. She cleared her throat and looked down at her hands, clasped in her lap.

'Hello there, Poppy!' he said. 'Room for a little one?'

'I think you'll find her name is Maggie,' Ray muttered, wondering how on earth they knew each other. This clearly wasn't the first time they'd met.

'Shift along there, fella, would you mind?'

Ray moved ungraciously to his right, while Maggie shuffled along to make room the other way. The airman dropped into the gap between them, making the bench shake.

So much for 'room for a little one'. This chap was over six feet tall and bulky. His not insubstantial rear end had landed on the edge of Ray's jacket, which was now tugging at his neck. Ray pulled the jacket out from under the airman with a grimace. Not that the fellow noticed – he was too busy making eyes at Maggie.

Pam leaned over from the bench behind. 'Excuse me, do you mind me asking what you did to your arm?'

The airman looked down at the sling. 'Bit of a prang, broke my wrist. It's such a nuisance, not being able to fly.'

'There was an altercation between his car and an oak tree,' Lord Ashford called over. 'The tree came off best.'

His nephew put his left hand up in a gesture of surrender. 'Guilty, as charged.' He looked down at Maggie. 'Warm enough, Pops? There's a blanket, put it on your lap. It's chilly as an ice store in here.'

Conceited ass, Ray thought. At least the broken wrist was a result of recklessness; driving too fast, most likely. If his injury had been caused by some act of derring-do, Ray didn't think he could have stood it.

Neither Maggie nor the airman seemed to notice as he got up and moved away to an empty bench. He'd had quite enough of being a gooseberry to those two.

'We don't often see our nephew here at Snowden,' Lord Ashford announced, 'but as soon as he heard we had young ladies in the house, it was surprising how quickly he decided to visit!'

'And I haven't been disappointed!' Jack said, looking directly at Maggie.

* * *

Joseph watched as Jack squeezed in beside Miss Corbett. There was plenty of room elsewhere in the cellar – but he only had eyes for her.

Leonard, Jack's father, had been the same: a ladies' man. But Jack's choice was surprising. Miss Corbett was pretty and dainty – far too clever for him, of course – and a delightful young lady. Young being the operative word. She seemed awfully naive and unworldly. There were other women among the bank staff that, he was certain, were more Jack's type.

He turned slightly and caught Gwen's eye. Mrs Nicholls, he should say. A look passed between them. He sensed she'd been watching Jack too.

Gwen was still rather wary of him but each morning, when she brought Joseph his coffee, she lingered a little longer.

He'd managed to eke out of her where she'd been for all these years: Coventry. Not a million miles away. She'd had a husband and when he died, as war broke out – Joseph had thought it indelicate to ask what had happened to him – she'd got work in a uniform factory.

She'd returned to Snowden to care for her widowed mother.

'I never go into the village,' Joseph told her. 'Not been there for years. Too many …' He stopped himself.

There were too many memories, good and bad. Men he'd served with in France, the village hall, the cricket team, parts of his life that were too painful to recall.

'Do they still have that thing on the blacksmith's door?' he'd asked Gwen one day, as she turned to leave.

'Oh yes,' she'd said. 'They do.'

Another morning, she'd gasped in surprise when she saw Sebastian on Joseph's desk.

'Do you remember him?'

'Of course. That's Sebastian. I can't believe you've still got him after all these years. He's looking a little rough round the edges, mind.'

Joseph gave a wry smile. 'Aren't we all?' And then, realising how ungentlemanly that sounded, quickly added, 'Present company excepted, of course.'

Gwen tucked a strand of hair behind one ear, self-consciously. Her hair had streaks of grey now, her face was thinner. But she was still the same Gwen.

'Isn't it queer to be this old, Joey?' she asked. 'You can never imagine it when you're young.'

He shrugged. 'Oh, I've had a good innings.'

She laughed. 'You're not even fifty! You're not out yet.'

Cricket. It made his heart lift to think that Gwen remembered those days, too. He'd played for the village team. He'd been a fast bowler, a pretty decent batter and he could throw a ball a country mile.

To his surprise, his mother had encouraged him to play. 'Your grandfather was a wonderful cricketer,' she'd told him. 'He knew W.G. Grace. Could have played for the county.'

It wasn't just the game he'd enjoyed. There were the teas, made by the women of the village. Egg sandwiches and Victoria sponges, light as air. And the camaraderie, the gentle ribbing, being one of the boys, not treated any differently from the other chaps.

Later, on the Western Front, he'd had some of the same feelings. Only the cricket had, at times, seemed even more important than the war.

Gwen hadn't been impressed by the Big House. She'd only been impressed by his batting, running and fielding. On the odd occasion that she wasn't there for a match, the whole day was ruined.

When he thought back to his youth, the best times were those long summer holidays and being with Gwen.

Joseph was brought back to the present as little Rudi on his lap stirred and sat up.

On the opposite bench, Miss Corbett was blushing and laughing softly at something Jack had said to her *sotto voce*. She was going to be horribly upset when his arm was A1 again and he disappeared off back to his squadron.

Perhaps he should have a quiet word and advise Jack to rein it in? Or better still, ask Esther to, when she eventually favoured them with her presence. She and Jack were awfully chummy, he might take more notice of her.

Joseph sighed. There was no doubting Jack's courage. Half the valiant souls engaged in those dog fights with the *Luftwaffe* weren't making it home. Terrible business. When he wasn't writing off cars, Jack was doing his bit, most admirably. But Joseph still found it hard to warm to the boy. Even his choice of clothes was irritating. When he wasn't in uniform, Jack was a proper dandy with his Savile Row suits and Italian leather shoes.

'He's always so beautifully turned out,' Esther often said, as though he were a pony in a show ring.

Jack was a particular favourite of Esther's. Not in that way. Joseph had observed them often enough and although they flirted, it was clearly done in jest. He wasn't a threat. But he was hardly what Joseph would have chosen for Snowden. He had no interest in the place, other than as a party venue. Once it was his, he'd probably sell the land off to the railways, chop down the trees and lay off half the villagers who worked here.

In the dim and distant past, Joseph had harboured hopes of a son and heir but that longed-for coy announcement had never come. And never would, now. So that was it; Jack would inherit Snowden.

Jack wouldn't be here for much longer. He'd be back with his squadron in Lincolnshire as soon as that arm was mended. Joseph should make the most of having him here. *Carpe diem*. He'd show him around the estate, introduce him to the tenant farmers and try, as much as he could – heaven help him – to *interest* Jack in the place.

Joseph looked around him. Hall and bank staff were sitting separately, one group on either side of the cellar. It was understandable. It was barely three weeks since the bank had relocated here and they hardly knew each other.

He hoped the division between the two camps would become less marked as the weeks went by. Perhaps, in spring, he'd organise a cricket match. House versus bank or, better still, mixed teams (Gwen would approve of that).

* * *

The kiddie on Lord Ashford's lap was getting bored. Any minute now he'd want to be off, careering around the cellar and he, Ray, couldn't allow it; this place wasn't a playground.

'Cooeee!' The new woman – Mrs Nicholls – was leaning forward and waving at the boy. He covered his face with his hand, shyly for a moment and then waved back.

'And who is this little chap?' she asked.

His Lordship jiggled him on his knee, pulling faces and making him laugh. 'This is Rudi. Say hello to everyone, Rudi!'

The boy put his head down and didn't respond as some of the women waved and called his name.

'Rudi's come all the way from Austria, for … a holiday, let's say. Until things at home calm down.'

An evacuee, then, Ray thought. Of a kind. He'd heard of other children from the continent being sent over to England for the duration, although it made no sense to him. Surely, the children were simply swapping one war-torn country for another?

'Here, Rudi!' When Ray had the child's attention, he faced the cellar wall, put up his hand and made a shadow puppet – a rabbit's head – with his fist and two fingers for the ears. Rudi giggled and Ray added a twitching nose, using his thumb.

Immediately, other people in the cellar joined in and the air filled with laughter, jeers and cries of delight, as the wall was covered firstly with shadow rabbits and then, following Ray's lead, birds with flapping wings, dogs and cats.

Oh, blast! He'd been so busy with the shadow puppets, that he'd forgotten something – a vital part of the drill.

'Gas masks on, everyone!' Ray shouted, standing up so fast that the bench he'd been sitting on tipped back. He ignored the groans and those who were continuing to meow and bark and, finally, the shadow play stopped. 'Chin first, then pull them on. Come on! We're supposed to practise this every day!'

'Don't you hate that 'orrible rubbery smell,' Elsie said, sniffing her mask. 'Makes me feel quite Moby Dick.'

The airman didn't have his gas mask with him. It looked as though he were about to help Maggie with hers.

'Excuse me,' Ray said, stepping towards them, 'if there's a gas attack, she needs to be able to do it herself. Best if you don't help her.'

The airman put his left hand up in mock surrender and exchanged rueful glances with Maggie.

A huge raspberry sound reverberated through the cellar, as Bill blew on the rubber of his mask, making everyone laugh.

Ray smiled, despite himself. Perhaps it was good for morale. He was in charge of morale, so perhaps he was in charge of laughter too. Even his Nibs' broad shoulders were quivering, as he put on the child's Mickey Mouse mask and he was shaking his head, as though laughing at raspberries was against his better nature.

'I'm all misted up. Can't see a bloomin' thing!' someone said, in a muffled voice.

It was queer, seeing everyone in their masks, suddenly anonymous and looking like mutant beetles.

Ray made them wait a minute or two and then gave the order to take them off. Instantly the cellar was full of sighs and exaggerated gasps for air. Nancy fished around in her handbag and started applying lipstick; Miss Sharp and Elsie fussed with their hair. Honestly, what a to-do. Anyone would think that he, Ray, had personally come up with the rules.

Nancy snapped her mirror shut. 'Is that it? Can we go now?'

'You need to sound the "all-clear", Ray!' Elsie said.

He frowned. 'Oh, no. I don't think that'll be necessary.'

'I'll do it,' Bill said, holding up the horn. Ray winced and stole a glance at Lord Ashford. He was talking to Mrs Nicholls, so, with a bit of luck, he wouldn't notice that it was Bill who sounded the horn.

'It needs to be a different sound though,' Bill said. 'One long note for "air raid" and then something else for "all-clear". How about this?'

He took a deep breath and sounded a long note, followed by three short ones.

The girls cowered, covering their ears.

'You're deafening us!'

'Stop! For heaven's sake!'

'Enough, enough!' Ray waved his arms at Bill. 'We've got the message.'

That was it. The drill was over.

Ray looked around for Maggie, thinking they might perhaps leave the cellar together but she was already halfway up the stairs, following closely behind the airman. Ray's shoulders slumped. The drill had gone to plan, more or less, but he felt disappointed and vaguely unsettled. It was all to do with Maggie. He had a sense that he didn't know her very well at all.

The other girls were laughing at something Jack had said. Pam cooed, 'Come and listen to some music in the drawing room, if you like.'

Ray's chest tightened. The girls never spoke to him like that. Now he really did feel down.

He waited until everyone had trooped up the stairs and out of the cellar. He should be the last to leave, like the captain of a sinking ship. Besides checking that everyone was safely out, he wanted to be sure that no one (he was thinking of Bill, in particular) had decided to help themselves to a bottle.

The last person to leave – one of the kitchen staff – had reached the top of the stairs, slipped through the door and closed it behind her.

Ray swung his gas mask over his shoulder, suddenly feeling very weary. As he mounted the first step, the door creaked open again.

It was him, 'Call-me-Jack'. He looked down at Ray. 'Last one out, turn off the lights, won't you, old chap?'

The door slammed behind him, leaving Ray standing in the dimly lit cellar, quite alone.

Chapter 28

It was difficult to see in the dark but as Bill flashed his torch across the village green, Ray could make it out: The Royal Oak.

The building was small and square, like a house and if it hadn't been for the sign outside, creaking as it swayed in the wind, Ray would never have guessed it was a pub.

There was a chink of light seeping from one of the windows. Ray nudged Bill. 'Look! Don't suppose they've got any wardens round here. I'll mention it, shall I, when we get inside?'

But when they pushed open the door and a hush fell in the bar, as a dozen heads turned to stare, Ray thought better of it. He dropped his hand, which had been half-raised towards the blackout blind, and smothered his intended words with a cough.

There was a log fire roaring in the grate; it was warm. Shame the same couldn't be said for the welcome.

Two old chaps were leaning on the polished bar, smoking pipes. They gazed impassively at Bill and Ray. The landlord stood behind white-handled bar pumps, drying a pint glass with a towel. He gave them a curt nod. In the far corner, in a blue-ish haze of cigarette smoke, a group of men were playing darts.

'Eh up. The cavalry's arrived!' one of the darts players said.

He was a large old fellow, with a black patch over one eye. The others laughed.

He stepped up to the board, retrieved his darts and turned to Ray and Bill, who were still standing in the doorway. 'Come in, if you're coming. You're letting all the heat out. You're too late, mind, if you've come for that pair of scoundrels. They fell out that door ten minutes ago.'

'But we'd have passed them on the way, if they've only just left,' Bill said.

The man with the eye patch slurped his pint and wiped his mouth with the back of his hand. 'True. Unless, of course, they went in the wrong direction.'

His pals roared with laughter again and Ray sighed. This was getting worse by the minute. He and Bill were on a mission to find Geoff and Norm. No one had seen them since dinner and Ray was furious they'd missed the air raid drill and made him look incompetent.

The driver, Brummie, had tipped Ray off. He'd spotted Geoff and Norm heading for the village and, by the way they were striding out, guessed they were going to the pub.

And they had been here, by the sounds of it, until a few minutes ago.

Ray turned to leave.

'Hey, where're you rushing off to, Raymondo?' Bill asked. He was already taking off his hat and unbuttoning his coat. 'Might as well have a drink while we're here. We'll never find them out there. It's pitch black. Besides, I'm parched.'

Bill had a point. They didn't know the village, after all. And in the unfamiliar darkness, they might fall into a ditch or stumble into the field of a vicious bull. The countryside was full of dangers.

'Mine's a pint, Raymondo, thank you very much.'

They stood at the bar and exchanged nods with the old chaps who sucked their pipes and regarded them silently.

The darts players seemed to have lost interest in them. Judging by the heavy thudding as darts hit the board, they'd resumed their game, along with their wisecracks and raucous laughter.

'I swear, on me old lady's life,' one of them said in a gruff voice, 'Bob Tandy's painted white stripes on all 'is cattle, to stop 'em getting run over in the dark.'

The rhythmic thump of the darts took Ray back. It was a long time since he'd been in a pub. Since the blackout, going out at night was a risky business. Aside from the risk of raids, or breaking your neck tripping over in the dark, he'd heard of people getting killed as they stepped out of pubs, run over by cars and buses with their lights covered up.

Of course, there weren't many vehicles out here in the country. Not a single one had passed them the whole way here. Ray had been glad of Bill's company though; the pub had been a devil to find, even with torches.

It was a blow that they'd missed Geoff and Norm. Ray had rehearsed exactly what he was going to say and now he'd have to wait, by which time he'd have cooled off and it wouldn't be half as satisfying. But the ale tasted good, there was no denying it, and the next thing he knew, Bill was asking, 'Same again, Raymondo?'

He opened his mouth to object, to say they ought to get back to the Hall but his heart wasn't in it. The pub was warm, the crackling log fire was comforting and the beer was making him feel quite mellow. It was only a couple of pints. He deserved it after the aggravation of this evening and that sour taste he got in his mouth when he thought about Maggie and that blasted airman.

'All right, mate?' Bill asked, bringing back the pints. 'You've got a face on you like a slapped kipper! Come on, cheer up! We're in the pub, remember! Away from London town! Life doesn't get much better than this!' He clinked his glass with Ray's. 'Bottoms up!' They each took a long slurp of ale.

By the time they'd started their third pint, Ray was finding himself agreeing with Bill, that Norm and Geoff weren't bad chaps, on the whole.

'They're bored,' Bill said. 'There's not much else to do in the evenings, except go on the beer.'

The door behind them opened. It was the Land Army girl, Charity, marching in as bold as brass, still wearing her work trousers.

'Hullo, you two,' she said. Her blonde ponytail swung as she pulled up a stool at the bar and hoisted herself onto it. Before Ray could ask if she'd like a drink, she'd placed her order. 'The usual, please, Derek.'

She pulled a packet of Players from her trouser pocket and lit a cigarette. 'Not seen you here before, Ray,' she said.

Ray explained they were on the trail of Geoff and Norm.

'Ah, nanny duties.' She tilted her head and blew smoke up towards the wooden beams. 'They're big boys, you know, I'm sure they can look after themselves.'

That was all very well, Ray thought, but if they got into trouble or were in no fit state for work in the morning, he'd feel responsible.

The bartender placed a pint of ale in front of Charity and she paid him. Ray and Bill watched as she took a gulp of beer, then licked the foam moustache from her top lip with a giggle. 'Look at you two! Never seen a girl with a pint before? I was a rum and lime girl before I came here, but this is good.'

Bill looked puzzled. 'Don't you feel out of place, coming here alone?'

Charity shrugged. 'Should I?'

'Back home, the only women who go into pubs on their own,' Bill said, 'are tarts. OWWW!'

Ray had given him a deft nudge in the ribs.

Charity laughed. 'You know, women are doing as much as men in this war,' she said, looking at Bill but raising her voice, so the darts players in the far corner could hear. 'So why should anyone turn up their nose because we wear slacks and order beer?'

The man with the eye patch looked round. 'We don't have any quarrel with you, sweetheart, you're doing your bit!'

Ray swallowed and kept his eyes firmly fixed on the row of glass optics at the back of the bar. He knew what was coming next.

'What's your excuse then, fella?'

There it was.

'Oh, shut up, Ted! Not that again!' Charity yelled. She shook her head at Ray. 'They gave your two chums the third degree the other night in here, too. Called them army dodgers, duckers, idlers and all sorts. No wonder there was almost a fight.'

'Banking's an essential industry!' Ray called back. It sounded lame and uppity. He should have stayed quiet. Why had he let himself rise to the bait?

'What's that you say, fella? Bean counting's more important than doing your bit for King and Country?' the man threw back.

'Leave it,' Bill muttered. 'You can't win, chum.'

Ray wanted to curl up in a corner. Called out on why he wasn't in khaki, yet again and, to his shame, he'd been defended by a woman. And what was this about a *fight*? Ray didn't want a fight, not one little bit. The men in the corner might be getting on a bit – and the chap who was heckling him only had one eye – but they were as tough as old boots. He reckoned they could still give him and Bill a good walloping.

Bill was obviously thinking the same. He'd raised his eyebrows at Ray and nodded at the door.

He was right. They should go.

Ray went to pick up his glass but missed and his hand hit the bar instead. He felt quite woozy all of a sudden. There were two blurry Bills standing next to him.

Charity was still barracking the darts players across the pub. 'Give it a rest, now, Ted, or else I won't play again!'

'You play darts?' Ray asked. His words had come out rather slurred. But honestly, was there nothing this girl couldn't do?

She laughed, throwing her head back. 'Not darts, silly!' She jumped neatly off the bar stool and pointed to a dark corner of the pub. 'That!'

'Oh yes!' Bill said, rubbing his hands together, all thoughts of leaving apparently gone. 'They've got an Aunt Joanna!'

One of the silent pipe smokers at the bar came to life. 'Play for us now, will you, love?' he asked Charity. 'Go on! You're ever so good.' He gave her a gummy smile. 'Remind me of Deanna Durbin, you do.'

She glanced at her watch. 'Go on, then, seeing as you asked so nicely, Fred. But not for long, mind! I have a ten o'clock curfew and an early start.'

The eyes of every man in the pub were on Charity as she settled herself on the piano stool. The darts players emerged from the smoky end and came closer, clutching their pints. Ray looked at them warily.

'It needs a good tune, I'll warn you now,' she said.

Ray didn't know anything about music. He wasn't sure what he was expecting but whatever it was, it had to be better than opera. He arranged his face in what he hoped was a thoughtful expression, which wasn't easy because his lips had gone numb.

Charity looked up and grinned at them and then her long fingers struck the piano keys, deftly, assuredly, as good as anything Ray had ever heard. She thumped out the chords and belted out the song for all she was worth and in moments, all the men in the pub had joined in too.

'There's a garden, what a garden
Only happy faces bloom there
And there's never any room there
For a worry or a gloom there …'

By the time they were on the final chorus of 'Roll out the barrel, we'll have a barrel of fun …' and Bill – smirking and singing his heart out – had nodded at him encouragingly at least a dozen times, Ray was singing along too. Well, if you couldn't beat them, you might as well join them, as his old man used to say.

It wasn't any different from a night in an East End pub or a ding-dong down in the Underground. In fact, it was better.

Perhaps it was the beer turning him soft but Ray felt a sudden swell of fondness for good old Bill and for Charity too. It wasn't a bad life, if you could forget about the war for a while. When the men from the village were singing and smiling like this, they didn't seem so bad, after all. He could almost imagine he was among friends.

'You could tell 'em some of your jokes, Ray,' Bill said, when the song ended. He was slurring his words and nudging Ray. 'Go on – make 'em laugh!'

Ray pushed him off, grateful to Charity for going straight into the next number, 'Knees Up Mother Brown'.

As they reached the final line, everyone clapped and cheered. Charity beamed as she accepted their applause and the offer of a drink on the house from the landlord. She stood up and bowed to the left and right, with an extravagant gesture of her hand, making them all laugh.

Then there was a rush for the bar, as pints were ordered and requests rang out for other tunes. It looked as though they were in for the night.

'When are you Land Girls gonna do another one of them shows?' one of the pipe smokers asked Charity. 'We enjoyed that last one, didn't we, Howard?'

She smiled. 'The recital, you mean? Yes, it was jolly fun, wasn't it?' She caught Ray's eye. 'We joined up with some other local Land Girls and put on a show in the village hall. Singing, tap dancing, someone recited poetry, I banged out a few tunes. We raised a pile of money for the Spitfire Fund. Maybe we'll do it again one day!'

Ray wanted to ask her more about the recital but, at that moment, a pint of ale arrived for her. Charity took it gratefully in both hands and started to knock it back.

As the noise in the bar finally quietened down, in readiness for the next song, the unmistakeable sound of men singing – loudly and out of tune – drifted in from outside.

'Shush!' Charity ordered. Everyone stood, heads cocked and listened.

The song was, of all things, 'Old Macdonald Had a Farm', complete with animal noises – moos and baas and cluck clucks – and rather a lot of giggling.

'Blimey, that's them!' Bill said, throwing back the dregs of his pint. 'They're absolutely pickled, Raymondo. Quick!'

Ray frowned and listened again. Yes, that was them. They must've realised they were heading in the wrong direction and doubled back. It was strange how, when Geoff sang, there wasn't a trace of his stammer. Or perhaps it was because he was completely blotto.

'Come on!' Bill urged. 'Or we'll miss 'em again!' The singing outside was growing fainter. Geoff and Norm had obviously passed the pub now and were making their way up the lane.

Ray looked wistfully at his beer on the bar. He'd still got half a pint left. Charity appeared at his side and cupped her hand around the pint glass.

'Don't worry, Ray, I'll finish this off for you.'

But they weren't quite out of the woods. The chap with the eye patch – Ted – couldn't resist having one final go.

As they reached the pub door, he called out. 'My grandson's fighting in France! I don't know if I shall ever see him again.'

Ray hesitated, his hand on the door handle.

'Ignore him,' Bill said.

'Swim in the pool every morning, don't you?' Ted added and a few of the men jeered.

Ray felt a surge of heat in his chest. He'd just about had enough. He turned quickly and staggered a few steps towards Ted, jabbing his finger at him. 'What the hell do you want me to do?'

He wasn't expecting an answer and sure enough, none came. He seemed to have stunned them. Bill had opened the door now and an icy blast blew in from outside.

'Come on!' Bill urged.

In the blackness, somewhere down the road, Geoff and Norm were singing, 'Ee-i-ee-i-o ...!'

'There is summat you can do!' Ted yelled, as they were stepping outside. 'All you so-called men up at the Big House!'

Bill and Ray looked at each other.

'Seven o'clock tomorrow in the village hall!' Ted said. 'Be there! And don't be late!'

Chapter 29

'He's awfully nice, Jack, isn't he?' Pam mused at breakfast, the morning after the air raid drill. 'So debonair.'

She stretched out a hand and admired her nails. 'You know, if I wasn't already spoken for …' She let the words hang in the air and when no one chipped in with encouragement or surprise, she looked up and frowned.

'Yes, I saw you making glad eyes at him, Pam,' Elsie said, 'but you don't stand a chance!' She covered her mouth with her hand, as she chewed her toast. 'Not while a certain someone's around. I'd say he's got his eye on Maggie here!'

Maggie blushed.

It had been mortifying, the way Jack had made a beeline for her at the air raid drill. Even in the gloom of the cellar, everyone had seen it. Ray had definitely noticed; she'd seen the surprise on his face. Lord Ashford had even watched them, for a while. What was going through their minds? She hoped no one thought she'd encouraged him.

Jack had sat so close on the bench she'd felt the heat from his thigh on hers. Someone like him couldn't possibly be interested in her, could he? It was as though someone was playing a trick on her. She wouldn't have been surprised to hear someone yell, 'Fooled ya!'

When Bill had sounded the 'all-clear' and they'd all trooped out of the cellar, Pam had invited Jack to join the girls in the drawing room.

Maggie's heart was in her mouth when he accepted. What if he found it dull? Or flirted with the others? Or – worst of all – let slip that Maggie spoke German?

But she needn't have worried, the evening had been jolly good fun and apart from a few minutes when he'd tried to help Pam and Nancy with their dancing, Jack had barely left her side.

Pam and Nancy were trying to learn the tango from a dance book. Their efforts mostly consisted of standing on one another's toes and getting cross, while Maggie and Jack tried not to laugh.

'I wish it were Jim here, instead of you!' Pam said.

'Charmed, I'm sure!'

Nancy turned to Jack and sighed. 'Oh, it's hopeless. I've had to be the man for so long now, I'll never remember the lady's part.'

Jack took the hint and tried to lend a hand, although Maggie was sure he was only being polite and it was almost impossible with one arm in a sling. He wasn't much better than the girls at the tango. 'I'm more of a foxtrot man,' he assured them. He'd looked straight at Maggie and added, 'I'll show you, one of these days.'

By the end of the evening, she was sure Jack liked her. And now Elsie had just confirmed it. Maggie couldn't help feeling pleased. She wasn't imagining it; other people had noticed Jack's fondness for her, too.

Pam seemed to be considering Elsie's words and she looked most unimpressed. She pursed her lips. 'Everyone's little favourite these days, aren't you, Maggie?' she said.

Not that again. There'd already been a few snide remarks about how Maggie was helping Lord Ashford with 'private correspondence'. The other girls couldn't understand why Maggie had been singled out and she couldn't tell them the truth.

After their first German lesson on Monday, Maggie had returned to the banking hall, expecting to slip in without any fuss, sit down at her desk and resume her work, but at least a dozen faces had turned to stare at her. Even Miss Sharp asked, 'Is everything all right, Miss Corbett?'

'Perfectly, thank you,' Maggie said. She sat down at her desk.

Elsie turned to face her. 'What were you laughing about so much in there? We could all hear you.'

Oh, fiddlesticks! Lord Ashford's office was near to the Long Gallery but she hadn't realised how much the sound carried. Had they heard her speaking German? What must they think of her?

'Yes,' Nancy said. 'You were giggling so much we thought he must be tickling you!'

'Miss Fry, really!' Miss Sharp said crossly.

Elsie had turned to Maggie, her bottom lip pulled out 'Our shorthand's as good as yours,' she said. 'He might, at least, let us take it in turns.'

Chapter 30

Before breakfast the next day, Maggie stood at the window of the bedroom she shared with Pam and Nancy.

On the lawn below, Miss Sharp and the others were doing Keep Fit. They'd missed out on Sunday's session, just as she and Ray had missed out on riding the tandem, due to rain and Miss Sharp had suggested doing it this morning, instead.

Although it had finally stopped raining, there was dew on the grass and a low mist over the distant ridge of hills. Conditions weren't ideal. No doubt, Elsie would complain about being chilled for the rest of the day.

'Did you not fancy it, then?' a voice asked through the open bedroom door. It was Mrs Mason. Another woman was standing behind her in the corridor. They were holding armfuls of laundry.

'No,' Mrs Mason added, stepping into the room, 'I dare say you've got too much sense.'

Maggie blinked. That was as close to a compliment as she'd ever had from the older woman.

They joined Maggie at the window and peered down. The women were dressed in their Keep Fit outfits of white satin leotards and black shorts. Their feet and legs were bare.

Mrs Mason tutted. 'They're practically naked! They'll catch

their death!' She placed the washing down on Pam's unmade bed and Maggie glimpsed a bandage around Mrs Mason's wrist.

The girls were performing a backstroke motion with their arms. Maggie wasn't sure which was funnier, the girls' movements or the housekeeper's outrage. She had to stifle a giggle.

'Where's their shoes? I ask you! There was a frost out there this morning!' The housekeeper shook her head.

'Oh, that won't trouble Miss Sharp,' Maggie said. 'She likes the cold!'

It was a wonder their supervisor didn't insist on opening all the windows while they were working. They were only spared on account of his Lordship's precious artwork, which, fortunately, had to be preserved from extreme temperatures.

Now the women were lying on their backs on blankets, pedalling their legs.

'They've got very nice pins,' Maggie murmured.

'That's just what was going through my mind,' said the woman next to Mrs Mason, with a smile. 'Perhaps there's something in it. We shall have to try it! I'm Gwen, by the way. I'm helping Maureen out.'

Gwen shifted the pile of linen in her arms and shook Maggie's hand. 'You must be one of the bank girls.' She laughed. 'Maureen begged me to take the job here. She said Snowden was "overrun with cockneys"!'

Mrs Mason grunted and rolled her eyes.

It was strange to think of Mrs Mason as 'Maureen' and even stranger to find that she had a pal, Gwen, who knew her well enough to use her first name and to tease her.

'I'm Maggie,' she said. 'Very pleased to meet you.'

Gwen's eyes lit up. 'Are you the same Maggie that's offered to turn Maureen's overcoat? I've got another to lend her, while you do it.'

'Then I definitely shall, whenever you can let me have it, Mrs Mason.'

The housekeeper gave a distracted nod, she was still watching the spectacle down on the lawn.

Maggie turned to Gwen. 'Do you live in the village?'

Before she could answer, Mrs Mason said, 'She grew up in the village, ain't that right, Gwen? We go back a long way. Gwen used to play with his Lordship when they were nippers and I was kitchen maid here. She hadn't seen him for nigh on thirty years, when, heaven preserve us, he turned up at the knitting circle!'

'You used to play with Lord Ashford?' Maggie asked. It was hard to imagine him as a boy. She wanted to add, 'What was he like?' but thought better of it.

'Yes. In the holidays, when he came back from school. None of the village boys would play with him, so I took pity on him.' She laughed. 'Of course, later, when they found out he could play cricket, he was welcomed with open arms.'

Mrs Mason gave the girls on the lawn one last glare and gathered up the laundry from the bed. 'Come on, Gwen. This lot won't iron itself. And as for those men—' she called back from the doorway '—it shouldn't be allowed! We shall have to put bromide in their tea!'

Men? Maggie cupped her hands and peered out of the window. There! Lurking under the cedar trees at the edge of the lawn, she could just make out two male figures. They looked suspiciously like Norm and Bill. They were probably on their way back from the swimming pool and they'd decided to spy on the girls.

Maggie glanced down at the women but they were too busy touching their toes to notice. Miss Sharp would go barmy if she spotted them. It was lucky for Ray, she thought, that he wasn't among them. Miss Sharp already had him earmarked as a troublemaker.

Chapter 31

A week later, Maggie and Charity were sitting on the wall around the dung heap, which was a haven of warmth on wintery days like today. Steam rose from the heaps of straw mixed with animal droppings. Maggie didn't even mind the smell anymore, although she was careful not to sit downwind of it.

'Say, I like your wellingtons!' Charity said, looking down. 'You do look the part!'

Ray had ordered boots for all staff and Mrs Mason was already complaining at the number of pairs piling up at the back door.

'Can't you put 'em away?' she moaned. 'One inside the other and then chuck 'em in the boot store? It's not difficult!'

Maggie had never heard of a boot store until she came to Snowden. Overcoats and jackets were kept there too and it was as big as their whole kitchen back home.

Charity held out a corned beef sandwich and when Maggie hesitated, she said, 'Go on. I've got heaps today.'

They sat and ate for a minute in companionable silence, then Charity asked, 'So, how's the tandem? Making progress?'

Maggie pulled a face. 'It's bloomin' hard work!'

Charity winced. 'Oh dear. Is Ray rather dull, after all?'

'No, I meant the tandem. It weighs a ton! I shall end up with enormous calf muscles and have to wear slacks for the rest of my life to cover them up.' She shifted her position cautiously on the wall and winced. 'Ouch! I don't half ache.'

Charity nodded. 'Welcome to the club. So, you're getting on with Ray, then?'

Maggie nodded. They'd practised a few times now around the estate, sometimes changing and dashing out in their lunchbreaks for a quick half-hour. He was actually rather nice, once you got him away from the banking hall. She needn't have worried about him being overbearing or cross with her if she couldn't manage to ride the bloomin' thing. He was nicer, away from work.

It had been a shock, when she first straddled the tandem, how close they had to sit. Ray's broad back was just inches away. But once they started moving, she felt the wind in her hair and realised that it was rather good fun, it didn't seem so strange, to be sitting so close.

She couldn't see ahead unless she stuck her head out to the side and then the whole tandem shook and Ray yelled, 'Don't lean!'

So, she'd had to stop trying to look ahead and simply had to trust him.

'Thanks for lending me the breeches, by the way,' Maggie said. 'They've been a godsend.'

'Not too big, are they?'

Maggie shook her head. 'A little but I'm very glad of them. At least, if the worst happens and I end up headfirst in a ditch, I'll keep some dignity! You know, the other girls have christened the tandem "Daisy"? Pam and Nancy can't stop singing the song. You know the one?'

Charity rolled her eyes. 'Oh, yes. "You'll look sweet, upon the seat of a bicycle made for two." Gosh, I bet Pam murders that, doesn't she? Whoever told her she could sing wants locking up!'

They laughed.

'Are they behaving themselves otherwise, those roommates of

yours?' Charity asked. She leaned to one side to fish a packet of cigarettes and matches out of her breeches' pocket.

Maggie thought for a moment. No one liked a moaner so she didn't want to complain. 'Yes, everything's fine,' she said. 'Mind you, Pam's money still hasn't appeared and even though Elsie said no one thought it was me, I'm sure I'm suspect number one.'

'But why?'

'Because I'm the last one in! They've all known each other for ages.'

It was also probably obvious to everyone that she was hard up. Perhaps they thought the temptation would be greater for her.

'It's horrid,' Maggie said, 'knowing that people I live and work with, might think I'm a thief.'

Charity tutted. 'I've a good mind to box their ears for them! What's Pam doing with that much money in her purse, anyway? A whole pound! After board and lodgings, that's more than I earn in a week! You'll simply have to face it with a brave heart, Maggie. Hold your head up and wait for the truth to come out. It usually does.'

They discussed their plans for the weekend.

'Gill and I are cycling over to see some friends,' Charity said. 'Land Army girls, on a farm about five miles from here. They'll put us up in the barn on Saturday night. What are you up to? Suppose you're out on the tandem again?'

They were. Yet another letter had arrived from Violet without any kisses and Maggie was desperate now to get to Vi's billet and set her mind at rest.

Charity's eyes widened. 'Glutton for punishment, aren't you?'

'It's a forty-mile round trip and it's too dark now to practise after work, so Ray says we have to pack as much into weekends as we can. He says riding a tandem's like dancing; someone has to lead and on a tandem it's the captain. That's him. I'm the stoker.'

Charity laughed, took a drag of her cigarette and swung out her legs. 'Ray this, Ray that! Getting rather chummy, aren't you?'

'Oh, leave it out!' Maggie gave Charity a gentle thump on the arm.

Charity blew a ring of smoke into the air. 'Are you quite sure he hasn't got a soft spot for you?'

'Don't be daft! I'm not his type.'

'What makes you say that?'

Maggie pursed her lips. 'He thinks I'm a clumsy oaf, I'm sure. And besides, Ray Maguire wants to make something of himself.'

'Nothing wrong with that,' Charity pointed out. 'Some would say good for him.'

'What I mean is, I'm not a step up for him. We're both cockneys. Sound of Bow Bells and all that. And he's trying to leave that behind. I know he is.'

'Here,' Charity said, opening her gas mask box. 'I've got one corned beef sandwich left. Split it?'

Maggie waited while Charity ripped it in two and held the larger piece out to Maggie. She took the smaller piece instead and thanked her.

'You're probably right,' Charity said. 'About Ray, I mean. Gill was talking to Nancy the other night and apparently …' Maggie shuffled closer to Charity, to hear the gossip more clearly. 'Apparently, Ray used to be sweet on Pam!'

Maggie almost fell backwards off the wall.

'What d'you mean, sweet?' With a mouth full of corned beef sandwich, it had come out like gobbledygook and Charity laughed.

'Yes, they were courting last summer. Fancy! No accounting for taste, eh? I wonder who threw whom over? Perhaps Pam threw him and he still holds a torch for her.'

Maggie's mind started spinning. It was the strangest thing. Posh Pam and that way she had of looking down on most people – and Ray Maguire? No, she wouldn't have put those two together at all. It was strange but she felt rather let down. Suddenly she was seeing Ray in a very different light.

Charity was still talking about Ray. 'Of course, you know better than me but I do think he's a good egg. Did I tell you he was in the pub the other week and he's not half as stuffy as I thought, especially when he's had a drink.'

'Ray?' Maggie asked. 'Tall, thin—'

'—the one who took us blackberrying that time? Yes, it was definitely him. He's all right! And …' Charity opened her eyes wide. 'I'll tell you something else: he knows every single word to "Knees Up Mother Brown"!'

Chapter 32

Ray saw him first. They were cycling up the drive towards the gatehouse on a Saturday afternoon, about to take the tandem on the road for the first time. His stomach was full of butterflies and he wasn't sure why. It was hardly Piccadilly Circus out there.

It was him – that blasted airman again. The proverbial bad penny. In his uniform, arm still in a sling, leaning casually against the wall in front of the gatehouse. He was chatting to a smart young woman wearing a camel coat and a wide-brimmed hat. She and the airman seemed to know each other rather well. They were having a right old laugh. Any second now Maggie would hear them and—

'Hey!' Ray called back, as the tandem swerved. 'What have I told you about leaning out?'

Maggie had seen them, he could tell. She'd stopped pedalling.

'Now,' he said, determined to act unconcerned, 'once we're on the road, I'll shout if I spot a pothole or change down a gear, because it might throw you off balance.'

She didn't answer and by now, they'd reached the couple.

The airman saw them and stopped mid-sentence, then laughed. 'Gosh, look at you two!' He put out his thumb as though hitching a ride. Ray gave them a wide berth and a curt nod. He heard

Maggie utter a small, 'Hello,' then he pushed down hard on the pedals, to get past as fast as possible.

What was going on? Call-Me-Jack had been all over Maggie like a rash at the air raid drill and now he was acting as though he hardly knew her. It would put anyone out, to be treated like that. Poor Maggie. If only they hadn't come this way, or had gone past half an hour later and not seen them at all.

Ray applied the brake as they reached the lane. 'Better check first,' he said. 'Don't want to get knocked down by a haycart or a flock of sheep!'

Behind them, he heard the door of the gatehouse open and then close. They'd gone inside.

'Right,' he said, 'remember, don't try to steer. Keep straight, else we'll crash. Keep in line with the tandem and lean if we go round a bend.'

'Anything else?' Maggie said, speaking at last.

'You could do a bit of back rubbing now and then if you fancied it, or sing encouraging songs, that kind of thing.'

Oh blimey, he wished he could take that back. Maggie was silent behind him. He was trying to cheer her up but he'd missed the mark completely. Sometimes, he simply couldn't help himself; the old Ray came out.

'Sorry,' he muttered under his breath and then, 'Off we go, then!'

It took a little while to get the spin right. At first, he was turning the pedals too fast.

'Hey, slow down, I can't keep up!' Maggie called out.

But once they got into a rhythm, it was better. It was surprisingly easy to talk too and that uncomfortable moment seemed to be forgotten.

'Don't coast,' Ray said. 'Even if you're tired. It's better to keep your legs moving. You don't have to press down hard and it'll stop your legs stiffening up.'

The air smelled fresh after all the recent rain and it was fun, splashing through the puddles. It felt good to be out of Snowden

Hall and away from the others. As long as he could cheer Maggie up, they were in for a good time.

As they cycled down the lane towards the village, Ray called back, 'Hey, I've got news. I've joined up!'

'You haven't!' Maggie thumped him lightly on the back.

'Both hands on the handlebar at all times please, Miss Corbett!' He hoped she could tell he was teasing.

Of course, she didn't believe him. Was it that obvious – the unlikelihood of him enlisting?

'No, you're right,' he admitted, cheerfully. 'Not quite. But me and the other chaps have joined the LDV. The Home Guard, they call it now.'

There was a moment while she registered the news, then she gave a little shriek. 'Oh! Good for you. What made you do that?'

'We thought it only right to do our bit for the village, in case of invasion! Nah, I'm fibbing! Truth is, we were shamed into joining by a one-eyed veteran from the last one. We met him in the pub and he ordered us to report for duty. We didn't dare say no!'

'Have you got uniforms?' Maggie asked.

'No!'

'Weapons?'

'Not yet.'

Maggie was giggling now; it sounded nice.

'Whoa up a minute,' Ray said. They'd reached the bottom of a steep hill and the tandem had already slowed right down. 'Come on, I think we'll have to get off.'

He pushed the tandem up the slope and Maggie walked on the other side. Within a few yards, they were both panting.

'How, exactly,' she asked, catching her breath, 'do you qualify for the Home Guard?'

'Ah. I was hoping you wouldn't ask that.'

When he explained, she laughed again. 'Oh, Ray, that's a scream. You must tell the others. Tell them tonight, at dinner!'

* * *

'... and then we had to say we'd fired a rifle and we had to be "capable of free movement",' Ray said.

Miss Sharp, sitting on the other side of the table, inclined her head. 'Free movement? Interesting. How did you demonstrate that?'

He shrugged. 'We had to run around the village hall.'

'And is that true?' Nancy asked, glancing around at the men. 'Have you all fired a rifle?'

Norm waved his fork in the air. 'No, we bloody well haven't! But it doesn't matter because they don't have any! There's one Lee-Enfield rifle from the last war and a load of pitchforks.'

Bill quickly swallowed a mouthful of food. 'Don't forget the golf club, Norm! The Boche won't stand a chance, if they ever make it this far!'

Ray had embellished the story of how they'd joined the Home Guard, so that even the other chaps, who, he could tell from their red faces and hard stares, were furious at first that their secret was out, were soon laughing and chipping in with their own anecdotes.

'To think,' Pam said, 'when you kept disappearing in the evenings, we thought you were in the pub!'

The men exchanged guilty glances. Sometimes – quite often, in fact – they had been in the pub. Best not admit that now, though.

Even Miss Sharp was wiping her eyes and shaking her head. 'Oh, I haven't laughed so much in ages. You're wasted, Ray,' she said. 'You should be on the stage.'

'Yeah, scrubbing it!' Bill said.

'What else goes on in this Home Guard?' Nancy asked. 'Sounds a hoot. Are ladies allowed?'

'Don't be daft,' Norm said.

'There's nothing daft about it,' Miss Sharp said. 'We're perfectly capable. The only thing I've been asked to do so far for the war effort is "bandaging practice" with the vicar's wife. Perhaps we women should start our own branch of the Home Guard, if we're not allowed in yours.'

'We could arm ourselves with knitting needles!' Nancy said.

'And crochet hooks!' Elsie added.

Miss Sharp looked unimpressed. 'I was thinking more along the lines of carving knives from the kitchen.'

'It's nothing to write home about, the Home Guard,' Norm said. 'It's mostly old gaffers who saw action last time. Reckon they know their way round a rifle, mind.'

'If they can lay their hands on one,' Bill said.

Ray explained how, when they were on duty, they'd be on the lookout for German parachutists.

'Well, I could do that,' Pam said. 'I've got my opera glasses with me.'

'Apparently,' Norm said, 'they're dropping in from Holland, dressed as nuns.'

Ray described the bayonet practice they'd had last night in the village hall and was rewarded with a few 'oohs' and grimaces from Nancy and Elsie.

The bayonet practice had consisted of running at a sack filled with straw and stabbing it, using a knife strapped to a broom handle, while yelling. And then, pulling back. The yelling, Ray had assumed, was as much to frighten them into doing it as to terrify the potential enemy.

'And do you think you could actually do that – with the bayonet – to a real person, if it came to it?' Maggie asked, wide-eyed. 'Could you actually stab someone?'

Everyone stopped eating and waited for Ray's response.

He looked down at his hands, twisting in his lap. 'No. I know I couldn't.'

Let's face it, he couldn't even kill a spider. They got huge ones in the privy at home – black and leggy, big as tarantulas, so enormous they sent his old lady running out before she had a chance to pull her drawers down. If she ever spotted one, she'd come screaming for Ray to get rid of it. He'd march outside to sort it out, give it a prod with a rolled-up newspaper to make it move and then tell her it had gone.

''Ave you definitely killed it?' she'd ask. 'Made a proper job of it?'

'Course, Ma,' he said. But he never did. He couldn't hurt a fly.

A fine soldier he'd have made.

Chapter 33

'Do you mind?' Joseph asked Miss Corbett when she arrived in his study for their German lesson on Monday morning. 'It's a little less formal.'

Rather than sit across the desk from one another, as they had for their first few meetings, he'd arranged two armchairs in front of the fireplace, with a low table between them. The fire had been lit earlier and the logs were glowing, crackling and sending a comforting warmth into the room.

He lit his cigar and sat back, not quite ready to start work yet. 'You know,' he said, 'in the last war, the Hall was used as a hospital. What's German for hospital, by the way?'

'*Das Krankenhaus.*'

'*Krankenhaus.*' He tried it out. 'Sick house. Yes, makes sense. I thought the same might happen this time and the government would want to requisition the place. Fortunately, they didn't. It was pure luck that enabled me to move the bank here. Otherwise—' he grimaced '—we'd still be taking our chances with the raids in London. Awful business. Are you following the news, Miss Corbett? No let up now for fifty nights.' He stared into the flames. 'Poor sods. They're being truly blitz-ed.'

'Is that so?' she answered, faintly. 'I never listen to the news,

Sir. When the others huddle around the wireless at nine o'clock, I slip out. I can't bear it.' She shrugged. 'Being so far away, I don't feel as though I have the right to listen.'

It was an interesting topic but before Joseph could respond, there was a loud thud on the door which made them jump. The door swung open. Rudi. He was breathless and wide-eyed, hanging from the door handle, gazing at them.

'Hello, there, young man!' Joseph said. 'Now, what—'

'I'm *so* sorry, Uncle Jay!' Sarah came dashing in after the boy. Her hair pins had come loose. Joseph had never seen her so dishevelled.

'Miss Corbett, this is my niece, Miss Jewell. She's helping us out with Rudi.' The girls smiled briefly at one another. 'Not proving too much of a handful, is he, Sarah?' he asked.

Red-faced and flustered, she shook her head and tried in vain to catch another hair pin as it dropped out. Joseph pretended not to notice.

'No, no,' Sarah said. 'He's rather lively in the mornings but …' She took a deep breath and painted on a smile. 'Nothing I can't manage!'

She was attempting to prise the child's hand from the handle. 'Come along, Rudi, this is naughty. You're not allowed here! You're disturbing Uncle Jay. Let's go and find you something nice in the kitchen. Quickly, now!'

Finally, Rudi released his grip on the door and allowed Sarah to lead him away.

The door closed softly behind them. Had he imagined that note of impatience in Sarah's voice? Already? He really had his doubts about that arrangement.

He looked up. Miss Corbett was watching him.

'Good little chap, Rudi, but full of beans!' he said.

'He misses his parents, I suppose.'

Joseph sighed. 'Yes.' He stretched his legs towards the flickering flames in the grate. 'You know, I was involved in something, before the war. We got as many children out as we could. They were in danger. Jewish children, mostly.'

'Danger? What kind?'

He hesitated. How much could he burden her with?

'There were – are – things happening …' He shook his head. He was regretting starting this conversation.

'In Poland?'

'In – oh, everywhere. Dark days, Miss Corbett, dark days. I wanted to bring more children out, but the war started and … it wasn't possible. If I'd had my way, the parents would have come too. But the authorities wouldn't allow it. Only the children. Rudi was initially staying with friends of ours but when they couldn't look after him any longer, my wife brought him here.'

He didn't mention that Rudi had become something of a plaything for Esther. Which had been fine, while it lasted. But Esther, as Joseph knew to his cost, was easily bored.

He picked up his notebook and pen and glanced at his watch. 'I suppose we'd better crack on, Miss Corbett. It's almost twenty past and as my Irish nanny used to say, "Not a child in the house washed"!'

* * *

Sarah Jewell. So, that was the girl's name. And she was Lord Ashford's niece. No wonder she'd been talking to Jack at the gatehouse so comfortably – she was part of the family. She and Jack might even be cousins. It had made Maggie's insides twist to see them at the time, but she had nothing to be worried about, after all.

Oh, but it had all been so uncomfortable. Maggie had tried to smile at Jack but she'd felt silly, perched on the back of that tandem. She'd wished she wasn't wearing breeches and had put some powder or lipstick on, so that she looked more ladylike, more like the glamorous girl he was with. Mind you, she hadn't looked quite so sophisticated a few minutes ago, haring around after young Rudi.

Sarah Jewell clearly hadn't recognised Maggie from the other day but then, she'd been so engrossed in her conversation with Jack, that she'd barely glanced around.

His Lordship coughed politely. 'Miss Corbett?'

He was waiting, head inclined towards her, smiling.

Maggie snapped out of her daydream. 'Oh, sorry, Sir!' she said, shuffling her pages of notes. 'Yes, of course. Let's make a start.'

They had a good lesson although, once Mrs Nicholls – Gwen, as she'd insisted Maggie should call her – interrupted them to deliver his Lordship's coffee, he couldn't seem to concentrate. He rubbed his head and suggested they call it a day.

As Maggie gathered up her things, the telephone on Lord Ashford's desk rang and he strode over and snatched it up. 'Ashford?'

She'd got as far as the door when he called her back. 'Miss Corbett!'

Maggie turned. He had moved slightly, so that he was standing in front of the window, the autumn sun making a halo around his head.

He was holding up his hand and still listening into the receiver. His eyes were shining.

When he finally spoke, Maggie knew she'd never forget that moment, not as long as she lived.

'We've found her, Miss Corbett!' he said, his voice trembling. 'We've found your mother!'

Chapter 34

A few days later, Bill, Norm and Geoff were standing at the table in the kitchen, staring at an orange.

'Is it real, do you think?' Bill asked. 'Or a phoney one?'

Maggie looked up from her sewing and laughed. She was sitting at the end of the table, Mrs Mason's unpicked overcoat spread out in front of her.

Tabby was laid out on the stone floor in front of the range. If Cook had been around, she'd have shooed the cat out, but it was her day off, so Tabby was safe.

Norm picked up the orange and held it up to his nose. 'Smells real enough. D'you think they'll let us have a piece?'

Mrs Mason came up from behind and snatched the orange out of Norm's hand. 'Oi! You should be ashamed, stealing from the mouth of babes! His Lordship's got this for Rudi. I have no idea how he managed it but it's certainly not meant for any of us. Now, where is the little rascal? Hiding, I expect, in case it's time for his cod liver oil!'

She chased the chaps out of the kitchen. 'Off with you! Find summat useful to do!'

Maggie had almost finished turning the coat. She'd unstitched it, turned it inside out and was stitching it all back together. The kitchen, with its warm range and row of windows through which the light streamed, was her favourite place to work. She'd be sorry when she'd finished.

Thanks to Lord Ashford, she now knew that Mutti was on the Isle of Man, in a women's camp, with other internees.

'Not some faraway colony, then,' he'd added. 'That's something.'

Maggie was flooded with relief. But where exactly was the Isle of Man?

His Lordship took an atlas down from the shelf in his study, flicked through the index and then held out the map to her. 'There. It's a rugged little island in the middle of the Irish Sea.' He smiled. 'Hard to escape from a place like that, unless you're a very good swimmer indeed. But I have it on good authority that your mother's in good health and being well treated. Here, I've written down her address.'

Maggie had written to Mutti straight away and sent Violet a letter too, telling her the good news.

'Here he is!' Gwen interrupted Maggie's thoughts as she led Rudi into the kitchen by the hand. 'Look,' she said, taking the orange from the table. 'Here's a treat for you, lucky boy!'

There was no telling if Rudi understood the words but he certainly understood the gesture. He took the orange from her solemnly and turned it over.

'I found him wandering round the basement,' Gwen said. 'On his own, again.'

Mrs Mason grumbled under her breath. 'No sign of her, then?' she asked, passing Gwen a knife so she could peel the orange. 'Once I've made this pastry, we're done. All the veg is prepped for tomorrow and Cook'll be here to make something tasty for your dinner.'

Maggie hoped she was right. The food at Snowden was queer, at times. Last week, Cook's 'something tasty' had turned out to be mock sausage, made with oats and herbs. Maggie had eaten it, of course ('Hunger is a good sauce!' Cook was fond of saying) but it had been rather bland.

'Hello, ladies! Say, Mrs M, any chance of a cup of char?'

Maggie dropped her needle into the fabric of the coat at the sound of his voice. It was Jack Rosman, storming into the kitchen. He did everything at high speed, as though he didn't have a moment to lose. 'I'm positively gagging!' He held his throat and made choking noises, which made Maggie laugh.

Mrs Mason looked down at her hands, coated in flour up to the wrists.

'I'll do it,' Maggie said. She stood up and put her sewing down on the chair. She set the kettle on the range and hunted for the tea pot and cups in the cupboards. She couldn't think straight. Every time Jack appeared – always when she was least expecting it – he had this effect on her.

By the time she'd turned around to ask who else wanted tea, Gwen, Mrs Mason and Rudi had disappeared. She was alone with Jack.

She set everything down on the table and busied herself making the tea, conscious that Jack was leaning back in his seat, watching her and smiling.

'You're back, then?' she said and could have kicked herself. Could she have made it any more obvious that she'd been watching out for him? She knew, from listening to Pam and Nancy's chatter, that it put men right off if you appeared too eager. Men liked to do the chasing.

'Yes, got back last night.' He yanked the sling further up his shoulder. 'Where were you? We were all in the drawing room playing games. It was a hoot!'

Maggie had been in the pub with Charity. She'd enjoyed herself but now that she knew Jack had been here at Snowden, she wished she'd never gone.

He gave a loud yawn and looked down mournfully at his arm. 'Bah, I feel rotten, Poppy, I don't mind telling you, not doing my bit. The chaps are all carrying on without me and I'm …' He cast around for the right words. 'I'm next to useless. I need to be back up there, in the air.'

Maggie's stomach flipped at the thought of him in the sky, fighting the *Luftwaffe*. 'Aren't you ever scared?' she asked.

Jack drained his cup in three large gulps and then stared down into it, at the tea leaves on the bottom. 'Can you read my fortune, Pops? Tell me my fate? No, best not, eh? Best not to know. What did you say? Am I scared?' He thought for a moment. 'Not scared for myself. But for my pals, I am.'

He twisted the tea cup on the saucer and a cloud crossed his face. 'Lost a few, since this whole business started. Not only because they bought it, you understand. Sometimes really good chums get transferred, posted overseas. My mate Mike, for instance.' He smiled in a resigned kind of way. 'He's A1, is Mike. A jolly decent sort, a good chap. I miss him.' He rubbed his face and looked thoughtful for a moment. Then he picked up his cup. 'Say, any chance of another?'

Maggie set the strainer on the cup and poured the tea. It wasn't the first time Jack had mentioned this Mike. She sat down opposite him. 'Does he have a sweetheart, this pal of yours, Mike?' she asked. 'Someone special, waiting for him?'

She hoped Jack didn't have a sweetheart. He didn't give her that impression; he'd certainly never mentioned anyone.

Jack nodded slowly. 'Mike? Yes, he does have someone special.'

'Poor thing. She must worry terribly.'

'Say, come for a drink sometime, will you, Poppy?' Jack said suddenly, leaning towards her across the table. 'I'm heading off again tomorrow and hopefully I'll be getting shot of this—' He held up his arm in the sling. 'But I'll be back, next week. Come over to my place one evening, won't you?'

Maggie frowned. 'Your place?'

He laughed. 'It's not grand, I'll warn you. They've put me up in the gatehouse. There's no room in the inn here, of course but the gatehouse suits me fine. Bring a pal along, if you like.' He gazed into Maggie's eyes.

She could feel his warm breath on her face. She looked at his lips and thought for one terrifying moment, that he was going to lean right over and kiss her. She wanted it and she didn't, all at the same time.

'But I'd prefer it,' he added softly, 'if it were just the two of us.'

Chapter 35

'I'm coming with you!' Charity said firmly. 'No, don't look at me like that, Maggie. He's an airman. Everyone knows what they're like.'

It was the following evening and they were sitting up at the bar in The Royal Oak. Pam, Nancy and Norm were there too, playing darts at the back of the pub. Bill and Ray were sitting by the fire. Ray had already been over to buy drinks and to speak to Charity but he hadn't stayed long.

Maggie laughed at Charity's outrage. 'It's only a drink!'

Charity pulled a face. 'It's never "only a drink".'

'Actually, he did say I could bring someone.'

'That's it, then. Decided. In any case, I'm looking forward to meeting him!'

Maggie sipped her shandy. She hadn't been entirely honest with Charity about how much time she'd spent with Jack over the past few weeks or how much she'd grown to like him. But perhaps, if Charity could meet him – and approve – Maggie might confide in her a little more.

'He calls me Poppy, by the way,' she said. 'It's just a nickname.'

Charity gave her a look. 'Nicknames? Very cosy.'

Of course, there was one obvious drawback to introducing Charity to Jack; he might take one look at her, with her creamy skin and blonde mane, and fall madly in love. It was a risk she'd have to take.

* * *

'What were you talking to Miss Hoity Toity about?' Bill asked as Ray brought two pints back to the table. They usually propped up the bar, but the girls were there tonight, perched on stools, so Ray had suggested Bill grab the table nearest the fire while he got the beers in.

Ray took a long gulp of ale and wiped the foam from his top lip. 'Come on, Bill. She might be a deb' but Charity's not uppity. Actually, I was talking to her about the concert. His Nibs has agreed we can do it and as she's arranged one before, she's going to help.'

Ray had asked Lord Ashford if he might organise a morale-raising concert in the village hall. There'd be singing, dancing and all kinds of acts. Everyone could get involved and they'd charge sixpence a ticket, in aid of the 'Spitfire Fund'.

In case his Lordship wasn't aware, Ray had added, a Spitfire wing cost £2000, a gun £200, a spark plug eight shillings and a rivet sixpence.

'Enough!' his Nibs said, laughing and holding up his hand. 'I'm convinced. In fact, you had me at "morale-raising". When were you thinking of holding it?'

'I thought after Christmas, Sir. January's always a bleak month.'

'Yes, we'll be in need of cheering up by then. Jolly good. Go ahead, on condition that all rehearsals are done in everyone's own free time.'

'Of course, Sir.'

'And—' Lord Ashford raised a finger '—provided that you don't expect me to get on stage and make a fool of myself.'

Ray smiled. 'Certainly not.'

As he turned to leave, his Lordship stopped him. 'You know,

Maguire, I sometimes think the whole of one's life is like a performance. People come and go, there are moments of excitement, comedy and tragedy and if you're lucky, happy times and people to love. And when the curtain finally comes down, you just hope it's all been worthwhile and …'

'… that you've put on a good show, Sir?' Ray finished.

His Lordship looked at him and something flashed between them, an understanding. 'Exactly,' he said.

Bill looked disappointed now, facing Ray. 'Oh, the concert,' he said. 'I thought you were getting to know her. I've always thought you liked Miss Hoity Toity.'

'I do not like Miss Hoi—' Ray stopped himself and put his glass down. Why did everyone think he had a soft spot for Charity? Maggie had teased him once or twice about her too. 'Bill, listen to me, Charity—' he said her name quietly '—is a very nice girl. But she's not for me.'

He glanced at the bar to check the girls hadn't overheard. Maggie was saying something to Charity which made them both roar. It made him smile too.

'It's 'er then, isn't it?' Bill said. 'Maggie?'

'Sshhh.'

'Don't think I haven't noticed, Raymondo, old chum. I know you moved your desk six inches to the left so you could see her chair better from yours.'

Ray's face went hot. 'You're imagining things, pal,' he said. But the truth was, he *had* done that. Blimey, if Bill had guessed, it must be obvious to everyone. As plain as the nose on your face, as his old ma would say.

'I say, Bill,' he said, rapidly changing the subject, 'here's a joke for you. A man walks into the records office and asks to change his name. The clerk isn't keen to help but he asks his name and the man replies, "My name is Adolf Stinkfoot …"'

An hour and two pints later, they were still at the table. The fire in the grate had gone out and Ray was daydreaming.

‘Penny for ’em?’ Bill asked. ‘Come on, tell your Uncle Bill all about it.’

‘I was only thinking that I still haven’t got any further with the mysterious case of Miss Barbour’s stolen money.’

‘What?’ Bill cupped his hand around his ear.

Honestly, Bill could be dense – and deaf – sometimes.

Ray leaned across the table and yelled into his ear. ‘I said, isn’t it a shame about Pam’s lost nicker?’

Bill spluttered, sending beer all over the table and Ray’s shirt. ‘What? Pam’s lost knickers?’

In spite of himself – and his wet shirt – Ray laughed. He was still laughing when he leapt up out of his seat to slap Bill on the back. Bill’s beer had gone down the wrong way and he was doubled up and coughing hard.

Ray whacked him once, twice and then three times, for luck. ‘No, you daft sod,’ he said into Bill’s ear, when the spluttering finally stopped. ‘Her lost nicker! The pound note!’

It was funny though, he had to admit. They laughed with abandon then, not caring when everyone in the pub turned to look. When Maggie and Charity twisted round on their bar stools, Ray raised his pint to them and the girls raised their glasses back. Maggie’s was almost empty, he noticed. He stood up. He’d have to do something about that.

Chapter 36

The following Thursday evening, the girls walked briskly up from the Hall, shining their torches ahead of them on the gravelled drive. Charity wheeled her bicycle with one hand and held her torch in the other.

It was chilly and their breath made plumes like smoke in the air.

When they arrived at the end of the drive, the gatehouse was silent and dark, as though no one was at home. Maggie felt deflated. She'd been so excited about seeing Jack again.

She knocked three times on the door and they were on the verge of giving up and heading down to the pub in the village instead, when the door swung open.

Jack stood in front of them, looking tall and elegant, without a tie and, finally, without his sling. His shirt was open at the neck. He seemed a little out of breath.

'Surprise!' Maggie said, sounding more confident than she felt.

Was that a look of disappointment, flashing across his face? Maggie felt like she could cry. And in front of Charity, too. It was too bad.

'Is this all right?' Maggie asked. 'You did say …'

But then her doubts vanished. Jack's blue eyes sparkled and his face lit up with a delighted grin.

'Poppy!' he cried. 'This is too much! A dream! Is it really you?' He stood back and raised a hand, as though blinded by her beauty. 'So, what's the occasion?'

Her heart fell again. She tried to smile. 'What? No, there is none. You said to come for a drink and bring a friend, so here we are! This is Charity Richmond.'

Maggie watched his face for any unwelcome reaction but it didn't change. He nodded politely at Charity and shook her hand. 'Delighted. Any friend of Poppy's and all that. Do come on in out of the cold. I'm celebrating my fixed wrist! We can make a little party of it.'

A party? So, there was someone else here. She knew it! Please, don't let it be another woman. It was probably Sarah, the one who'd arrived to help look after Rudi. It was bound to be her. She was pretty and jolly and probably exactly Jack's type. Oh, this was awful. She wished they'd never come.

Jack stood back from the door and ushered them in. He seemed somehow flustered and not quite himself.

They walked through into the drawing room, as Charity exclaimed how charming the place was. Maggie was grateful to her for talking and filling the uneasy silence – and yes, it was true, Jack did have another guest.

It was Geoff.

Oh, the relief. Just Geoff, standing near the fireplace. Nothing to worry about. Maggie looked around the room, wondering if perhaps the other chaps were here too but there was no sign of anyone else.

Jack and Geoff had been drinking, that was clear. The decanter on the sideboard, its crystal stopper laid carelessly on the side, was half-empty and there were two glasses next to it, half-filled with red wine.

It all made sense now. Jack had been drinking, that's why he looked rather bashful. He was tipsy! And he'd completely forgotten about his invitation to her last week. Oh well, never mind, easily done.

'So, your wrist is mended?' Maggie asked.

Jack smiled and cautiously waved his right arm, as though trying it out. 'Yes, isn't it marvellous? I've been signed off, so I'm off to my squadron in the early hours. Goodness knows when I'll be back. But whenever I get leave, even if it's only a day or two, I'll try to come back.'

Maggie felt so disappointed. If she and Charity hadn't appeared like this tonight, would he just have left, without seeing her again? And without saying goodbye?

'Geoff and I have been putting the world to rights, isn't that right, old chum?' Jack said, picking up his glass of wine.

Geoff smiled. 'Hello,' he said to Maggie and, 'Nice to see you, Miss Richmond.' The words were a little hesitant but it was strange, there was no sign of his usual stammer.

'Now,' Jack asked, 'what can I get you girls to drink?'

* * *

As they left the gatehouse a couple of hours later and stepped out into the dark, Jack gently closed the door behind them. Charity seemed unusually quiet.

'What did you think?' Maggie asked, as soon as she was sure he'd gone.

'He seems nice.'

'Nice?' Was that all?

Charity seemed to be choosing her words carefully. 'I'm not sure whether—'

Maggie turned towards her. 'Oh, I know exactly what you're thinking! He's a toff and I'm ordinary and how can that work out?'

Charity put her hand up. 'No, it's not that at all!'

'And you're too kind to say it and I understand but don't you see? This war is turning everything on its head! Look at me, living in a mansion and we're friends, you and me, aren't we, and who'd have thought it?'

Charity laughed and grasped Maggie's hands which were flying about. She held them tight. 'Oh, Maggie, you dear thing, shush a minute. I shouldn't have let you have that last sherry, I do believe you're tight. Come on, let's get my bicycle and I'll walk you back up to the house. And yes, of course, you're right, in any other time, our paths would most likely never have crossed. So at least we have the war to thank for something.'

As they walked back up the drive towards the Hall, Charity glanced back at the gatehouse. 'Funny that Geoff didn't leave at the same time as us,' she said.

Maggie shook her head. 'Oh, Geoff's nervous around women. I wasn't surprised at all.'

'Oh, Maggie, don't go falling for him, will you?' Charity said. 'He'll break your heart.'

But it was too late; she *had* fallen for him. Oh, she loved him! She knew Charity was only trying to be kind and wanted to stop her from getting hurt but she was wrong. Jack would never hurt her. Other people had seen it too; Jack liked her, he liked her a lot. He made her feel warm and happy and who knew what the future held?

Chapter 37

Lord Ashford was holding up a book as Maggie stepped into his office on Monday morning: *A Skeleton German Grammar*.

'I thought it might help,' he said, 'but it's actually confusing me even more. It's preposterous!' He flicked through the pages and tossed the book onto his desk. 'The nouns have genders *and* plurals. Quite insane! My dear young lady, how on earth do you remember it all?'

'*Guten Morgen, Herr Ashford*.'

'Oh, yes … I beg your pardon. *Guten Morgen*,' he mumbled.

Maggie took her seat at the fireplace, took pity on him and spoke in English. 'I dunno, Sir. How do any of us remember words? How do you know that the plural of box is boxes? Or that goose becomes geese? That it's two sheep, not sheeps?'

'Good point.'

'It's what you get used to,' she said with a shrug. 'It sounds right.'

His Lordship took his seat beside her and frowned. 'And if I don't know if it "sounds right" because I've never heard it before?'

'*Dann müssen Sie es auswendig lernen*.' She smiled. 'You have to learn it off by heart.'

They were learning words for people: mother, father, wife, colleague.

'What's the word for "friend"?' Lord Ashford asked.

'It depends. A male friend or female?'

He frowned. 'There's a word for each? Very good, well, let's say female friend.'

'*Die Freundin.*'

'And male friend?'

'*Der Freund.*'

'*Freundin* and *Freund*,' he repeated. He wrote them in his book.

'They can mean boyfriend and girlfriend, too,' Maggie added.

When he concentrated hard like this, frowning and grimacing, his handsome face was quite spoiled. He opened his mouth again. Any second now … he was going to …

'Miss—'

'*Nein*!' Maggie snapped. It came out rather louder than she'd intended. She mouthed, 'Sorry!' The banking hall wasn't far away; someone might have heard.

'*Nein*,' she repeated, more quietly. '*Wir müssen Deutsch reden.*'

'*Deutsch*?' he repeated. 'German?' He'd understood that much at least.

'*Wir*,' Maggie said, pointing to herself and then to him. Wasn't it obvious that she was saying 'we'? But his face was blank.

She had to look away so he didn't see her smiling. This was going to be another of those lessons when his Lordship was too distracted to take anything in.

Suddenly, he stood up, unlocked a drawer in his desk, took out an envelope and handed it to her.

'I hadn't been planning on asking you this, Miss Corbett. Or, at least, not yet. But time is of the essence. Would you mind? There's a letter in there. In German. Would you mind? Could you read it and tell me what it says?'

* * *

As she left his Lordship's office an hour later, Maggie felt happier than she'd felt for ages, since she'd come to Snowden, in fact.

She almost skipped the few yards back to the banking hall.

She was of use, at last! She understood now, why, all those weeks ago, Mrs Leibervich had told her this would be 'essential work'. Her old teacher was a friend of the family; she must have had an idea of what Lord Ashford was trying to do. He was bringing endangered people – adult Jews – out of Nazi Germany and smuggling them into Britain.

* * *

No one looked up when she entered the Long Gallery. It was oddly silent, as though everyone were holding their breath. Miss Sharp was concentrating, head down. Pam's desk at the front – and Nancy's too – were empty. Something didn't feel right.

Maggie slid into her seat. 'What's the matter?' she whispered to Elsie.

Elsie's back stiffened. She half turned in her seat. Her eyes were red. She whispered back, 'Jim's in the drink. Pam's had a letter from his mother.'

In the drink! Gosh, that was bad news. He must have been shot down, over the Channel or the North Sea. She wanted to ask more but Elsie had already turned back to her work and the room was as quiet as a church. No telephones rang, no typewriters clattered, no drawers squeaked or slammed. Everyone was working or, at least, they were pretending to.

Ray came over to Maggie's desk, on the pretext of bringing her a stack of papers. On the top page he'd written, *Pam's fiancé MIA. Shot down over France.*

Maggie's stomach lurched. It wasn't hopeless, of course, but everyone knew what 'missing in action' meant. It was almost the very worst news Pam could have had.

What would she say to her later? Words were useless at a time like this. What was the point in saying, 'He'll be all right, Pam, you wait and see; he'll be back,' because everyone knew, the chances of her ever seeing him again were slim.

She and Pam would never be chums but Maggie felt a deep pang of pity for her. How would she feel if something like that happened to Jack? If she ever got a message to say he was 'missing in action'? Her stomach swooped away at the thought of it. She simply wouldn't be able to bear it.

Chapter 38

Maggie put a final double stitch into the hem, pulled the thread taut and bit it off between her teeth. There! Mrs Mason's overcoat was finished. She held it out and examined at it. Even if she did say so herself, it didn't look half bad.

Maggie couldn't wait to give it to her and see her smile, for once.

It would be nice to see someone smile because the mood in the banking hall was gloomy. Within a few days of Pam's Jim being reported as 'MIA', she'd had news from his parents, confirming the worst.

Pam had sobbed into her pillow for a few nights, appeared pale-faced at breakfast, dressed in black and was excused work.

Maggie had summoned up the courage to say, 'I'm so sorry about Jim. So sorry for your loss, Pam.'

Pam had thanked her. 'You know, you're the only one, Maggie, apart from Norm, who's said that. Everyone else is pussyfooting around me, acting as though nothing's happened.'

There was no sign of Mrs Mason at breakfast and at lunchtime, when Maggie came into the kitchen to find her. Cook said she still hadn't turned up.

'Which ain't like her at all.'

Gwen was heaving a stack of plates from the cupboard onto the table. She and Maggie exchanged worried glances.

'Do you think something might have happened? Might she be ill?' Maggie asked.

Gwen looked as though she was going to say something and then thought better of it.

'Should we go and check on her? She lives in the village, doesn't she?' Maggie said.

Gwen nodded and started to undo her apron strings. 'I know where she lives,' she said, giving Cook a questioning look.

'Go on then, but be quick, mind,' Cook said.

Mrs Mason lived in a row of narrow golden-stoned terraced houses that had, Gwen told Maggie, once been the home of workers at a nearby mill.

They opened the rickety gate and walked up to the front door. There was no answer when they rapped on it and nothing to be seen when they peered in through the window. No one seemed to be at home.

'Is there a back door? Shall we try that?' Maggie asked.

Gwen shook her head. ''Spect so. I've never been here before.'

Maggie frowned. 'But I thought you were friends?'

'We never held the knitting circle here. Maureen always made an excuse. She blamed it on her husband. I assumed he wasn't well and that a houseful of gossiping women would be too much.'

Round the back, Maggie tried the door handle and it opened. They called Mrs Mason's name and walked through to the kitchen.

'Oh, my word!' Gwen cried out.

The housekeeper was lying on her side on the stone-flagged floor, her limbs at strange angles.

'Is she … is she …?' Maggie asked, as Gwen rushed forwards and touched her wrist.

'No, there's a pulse, but she's out cold. There, she's coming round. Get me a glass of water from the sink there, would you, Maggie?'

Mrs Mason tried to get up but she couldn't manage it. She collapsed back with a cry of anguish. 'I must've fallen,' she said. Her voice was muffled. Gwen bent down and touched her face. When she lifted her hand, it was covered in blood.

'We'll have to fetch a doctor.'

Mrs Mason shook her head and pushed Gwen's hand away. 'No, no, there's no need. I'm fine. Help me up into that chair.'

'Where's your husband, Mrs Mason?' Maggie asked. Surely, they should let him know?

Another voice – a woman standing in the open doorway – answered, 'He's at the pub, most like. I live next door. He ain't done it again, has he?'

Mrs Mason was groaning now and between them they managed to lift her onto an armchair next to the empty fire grate. She held her head in her hands.

While Gwen soothed her, Maggie put the kettle on. A nice cup of tea always made things a bit better.

'Knocks her about,' the woman said, lowering her voice until it was almost a whisper. 'Ain't you ever noticed, all the cuts and bruises?'

* * *

A little while later, after she'd had a cup of tea and Gwen had bathed the wound on her head, Mrs Mason was sitting in her armchair, with rather more colour in her cheeks.

'I should come with you, back to the Hall,' she said, trying to stand, but Gwen pushed her gently back down.

'Oh no. If you won't see a doctor then at least you need to rest. Snowden can manage without you for a day or so.'

'I'll be there tomorrow, you can be sure,' Mrs Mason said. There was a pause. She sighed and toyed with the material of her skirt.

'He wasn't always like this,' she said. 'He was a good man until he went off to war.'

'Do you want to come and stay with me for a bit?' Gwen asked. 'Give him a shock? He'll think you've left.'

Maggie shook her head. 'That'll only make it—'

'—worse,' Mrs Mason finished. The two women exchanged rueful glances. 'When he comes back,' the housekeeper continued and then she jumped and cocked her head, listening. 'Oh, my good God, that's him!' She flapped her arms at them, shooing them out like flies. 'Quick!' she said, 'Out the front! He can't find you here!'

* * *

They walked silently back to Snowden through the village, subdued by what they'd seen. Maggie felt horribly guilty about leaving Mrs Mason with that man. Would she be safe?

'How do you know all this, Maggie?' Gwen asked. 'That if Maureen pretended to leave him, it would only make things worse?'

'Because,' Maggie said, 'my dad's the same.'

She'd never admitted that to anyone before; that her dad was a bully. It was easier to say it to Gwen, someone she didn't know very well.

Maybe that explained why her dad was bad-tempered and snappy, why they could never do right for doing wrong, why all of them – Maggie, Violet and Mutti – were scared of him. Perhaps it was because he'd fought in the Great War. Like Mrs Mason's husband, it had sent him barmy.

They were passing the village green now and The Royal Oak and Maggie glanced over, wondering how often Mrs Mason's husband drank in there.

'We carry our own guilt here, you know,' Gwen said.

Maggie looked at her. 'What do you mean?'

Gwen waved her hand over the green. 'Have you ever noticed how there's no monument to the war dead, from the last one? Most villages have one but Snowden is a "Thankful Village", which means we lost no men in the Great War. There's a sign up in the church, if you care to look. It says, "All men who went to fight for King and Country in the Great War, came back again."'

Maggie didn't understand. 'But … but that's a good thing, isn't it?'

Gwen wrinkled her nose. 'In a way. All the men came back, they survived, but that doesn't mean they were the same. And Snowden was surrounded by villages where men weren't returning, so there was a mix of shame and guilt here. As though we hadn't paid the price for peace. A couple in the next village lost all four of their sons.

'Every Snowden man who went to fight in the Great War gave the blacksmith a penny and he nailed it to his door, under a horseshoe, for luck. Joey – Lord Ashford – was one of them. They all came back. Ted March lost an eye, another fella, a leg, so the smithy took a chink out of two coins. They're all there, on the blacksmith's door. Still there.'

'But they all came back?' Maggie insisted.

'That time, they did. Not this time. Two boys are missing in action, one is definitely … gone.'

'And Mrs Mason's husband?' Maggie prompted. 'I did notice she had a black eye once. And she often has bruises but—'

'Yes, it's him. He does it. It's like she said; he's not the same man who went off to war.'

'And there's nothing we can do,' Maggie said. Her dad had fought last time and she wondered, suddenly, what he'd been through. She'd never asked him; he'd never said.

'No,' Gwen agreed. 'There's nothing we can do. I asked Maureen once, if everything was all right at home. She's proud; I didn't expect her to tell me but she did say that she married him "in sickness and in health" and she'll stand by that vow. I know she will, until the day she dies.'

Chapter 39

Joseph sat at his desk, tapping a pen into his palm, waiting for a telephone call.

He felt calmer than he'd done for some time. The bank staff had settled in and Rosman's was operating as efficiently as ever. He'd tracked down Miss Corbett's mother on the Isle of Man and that had assuaged some of the guilt he felt in asking her to help him with his 'correspondence'.

Progress was being made.

He pursed his lips and the thought crossed his idling mind that Sebastian was nowhere to be seen. He hadn't seen the bear for a couple of days. Rudi again, no doubt. He'd have to start locking his office.

There was a knock on the door and Gwen came in with his coffee. Was it that time already? As he stood and smiled at her, the telephone on his desk started to ring.

Damn.

'Beg your pardon, I have to take this,' he said, snatching up the receiver. 'Ashford!' He turned to face the window. It was overseas, a bad line. He had to cover his left ear in order to hear anything.

He was vaguely aware of Gwen approaching his desk and then, a moment or two later, closing the door, as she left.

'Yes, yes, I can hear you,' he said to the caller. 'Go ahead.'

It was twenty minutes before he put the receiver down. His coffee was cold and he'd missed the highlight of his day: speaking to Gwen.

He sat down heavily at his desk, picked up the dandelion paperweight and allowed himself to remember.

Gwen Tapper was his childhood sweetheart and the first girl he'd ever kissed. They were fifteen or sixteen. He could still remember those long summer days, the feel of her soft lips on his and her sweet scent.

He thought it would last forever but everything changed when he went up to Oxford and his mother forbade him to 'fraternise' with the villagers.

'It was fine while you were a boy,' she said, 'but one day, you'll be the master of this house. I'm only thinking of you and your future.'

You didn't argue with Mother but it didn't stop him feeling rotten about how easily he'd given up his pals in the cricket team. And Gwen.

The last time he'd seen her was when he'd brought some of the chaps home for a shooting weekend. While they were out near Bunker's Field, on the edge of the copse, suddenly there was Gwen.

She was one of the beaters. The dogs had recognised her and, wagging their tails, rushed up, greeting her joyfully. He should have done the same but, instead, he was aloof and distant. He felt a stab of self-loathing when he remembered how he'd treated her.

'Hello, Joey!' she'd said, all smiles.

He'd winced. No one called him Joey anymore.

'Hullo,' he'd said, hardly looking at her, and then turned and fired at a bird that had just been flushed. And missed.

His friends had hooted with laughter. 'Bad luck, chap.' Someone slapped him on the back. 'Try again.'

When he looked around, Gwen was gone.

Someone asked, 'Who was that girl?'

'No one,' he'd answered. 'Someone from the village.'

Perhaps she'd heard him, perhaps not. Either way, he'd felt like a complete rotter.

He sighed now and placed the paperweight back down on the desk.

Then he spotted him; Sebastian, propped up against the cup of cold coffee. But he looked different. He was dressed. His patchy brown fur was covered in a khaki knitted pullover.

* * *

The next day, when Gwen arrived with his coffee and he held the bear up to her, she shrugged. 'I've got spare wool. I've been unravelling pullovers.' She smiled at him. 'I thought he looked cold, poor lamb.'

Chapter 40

They were going downhill and the tandem was gathering pace. She should be used to this by now but Maggie still had to bite her lip and fight the urge to scream, as bare trees and brown hedges flashed past in a blur.

'Bump!' Ray yelled and then 'Granny!' as he moved down into a low gear.

Once on the flat, they pedalled in silence, the only sound the swish of the tyres on the road and the spinning chain.

It was a bright, chilly afternoon in mid-November. Maggie looked up at the cloudless sky. It was as blue as forget-me-nots. How could the world be in such turmoil, when, here, there was perfect peace and perfect weather?

If you didn't listen to the wireless or Norm and the older chaps from the bank, who talked endlessly about invasions, pacts and bombings, you'd never guess there was anything amiss.

'Hey!' Ray had obviously sensed her shifting in the saddle and taking pressure off the pedals. 'Have you gone to sleep back there?'

'Sorry!' Maggie called back. 'I've had another letter from Vi, by the way.'

'And?'

'There's a kiss, on the bottom of the page. A small one.'

'That's good, isn't it?'

'No!' Maggie said. 'One kiss means it's terrible and I'm supposed to move heaven and earth to get her out!'

She gave a shriek as something ran out from the hedgerow. 'Goodness! What was that?'

A huge bird, bigger than a hen and as brightly coloured as a painting, had strutted out into the lane, thought better of it and scurried back again, letting out a loud 'cuck-cuck-cuck!'

'Cor, was it a peacock?' she asked. 'Or a cuckoo?'

Ray's back and shoulders were shaking.

'What's so funny?' Maggie asked. 'It sounded like a cuckoo!'

'That was a pheasant,' Ray called back. 'A cock pheasant. The females are brown; not so pretty.'

Maggie only knew two types of birds: sparrows and pigeons. She'd been to Trafalgar Square once and the place had swarmed with horrible pigeons. 'Rats with wings', her dad called them. They strutted along the ground and then flew up in a big burst of flapping feathers. If that was birds, you could keep them.

On their early rides, when they'd seen pigeons pecking the ground, barely summoning the energy to fly off as the tandem approached and leaving it until the very last second to take off, Ray had told her, 'They're wood pigeons. They eat them round here.'

'Yuck. I won't.'

'Bet you will.'

In contrast to the dull pigeons, the pheasant had been gorgeous, with bright copper feathers and a white collar, like a vicar. It looked like it belonged in a zoo, not roaming free in the countryside.

'Could we eat it?' Maggie asked and Ray laughed again.

'So it's just pigeons you don't like? You're happy to eat everything else in sight!'

They hit a hole in the road with a hard bang.

'Ow!' Maggie yelled.

'Sorry! No time to warn you! Shall we have a break here?'

They'd reached a village that they often passed through on

their rides. It had a pretty green in the middle. They dismounted, propped Daisy up against a rickety wooden bench and sat down.

'Not for too long, though,' Maggie said, 'Or we'll freeze.'

'Here, sit close to me, it's warmer.' Ray produced two apples. 'Red or green?' he asked, holding them out.

Maggie shook her head. 'I don't mind.'

Ray sighed. 'You have to choose.'

Maggie looked at them. 'But if I choose the green one, the red one will feel left out. I'll feel sorry for it.'

Ray laughed and gave her the red one. 'There. I'll choose for you.'

They bit into the apples and crunched in silence for a few minutes.

'How does Pam seem to you?' Ray asked, suddenly. 'Have you noticed Norm being very … kind, shall we say?'

Since her fiancé had died, all the men had all been very solicitous of Pam and Maggie had wondered whether Ray might get close to her again. He and Pam had once been sweethearts, after all, if Nancy were to be believed. She'd watched them carefully but there'd been no sign of anything. It was a relief; they weren't suited, of that Maggie was quite sure. Rather, it was Norm who'd become close to Pam. They sat together every mealtime, smoked cigarettes on the terrace and they laughed. They laughed an awful lot.

Now, Maggie nodded. 'Charity says Norm's "consoling her" and although he's married, she's probably not the first and she won't be the last.'

'Not shocked, are you?' Ray asked. He shrugged. 'It's the war, Maggie. It does strange things to people. Look,' he said, 'someone's coming over.'

An old woman with grey hair and leaning heavily on a wooden stick, was making her way across the green towards them. They watched her slow progress.

'Blimey,' Ray said, under his breath. 'I hope she's not bringing me a white feather.'

He stood up to offer her his place on the bench but she shook her head and stood, leaning on her stick.

'I like to watch you two young'uns on that bicycle,' she said. 'I've seen you before, see.' She gazed at Ray with rheumy eyes. 'You remind me of my son. I lost him in the Great War.' She nodded at the tandem. 'What's it called?'

'It's a tandem,' Ray said. 'It's a bicycle made for two.'

The woman's face broke into a gummy smile. 'That's the one. A tandem. I like to think of him, up there—' she glanced skywards '—riding around, like you, with his girl on the back.'

They watched her totter back across the village green and return to her cottage.

'Poor old dear,' Maggie said. 'She came out in the cold specially to tell us that.' She took a deep breath and added, 'I wonder if she'd think so well of us if she knew I was half-German.'

Ray stopped mid-bite and stared at her, holding the apple aloft.

'That's why I'm always with his Lordship,' Maggie said. 'I'm teaching him the language.'

Ray frowned.

'Do you hate me now?' she asked, only half joking.

'Don't be daft. I dunno why you've kept it a secret, though. From me, I mean. I don't hold a grudge against the Germans. They're bombing us but we're bombing them right back. They've been dragged into this war too.' He toyed with the apple in his hands. 'Imagine being able to speak another language though! I have enough trouble with the King's English! You're bilingual and Charity plays piano like a professional. And then, there's me. What am I good at?' He put his hand out. 'No, don't answer that. Playing the fool, I know.'

Maggie laughed. 'No, it's more than that, Ray. You've got a real talent. When you make people laugh, you make them feel better.'

She stretched out her legs, regretting for the first time that she was wearing slacks. Once you were cycling, it wasn't cold. It would have been nice to feel the fresh air and the sun – weak though it was – on her bare legs.

She considered rolling up the legs of her trousers but thought better of it. It probably wasn't the done thing.

If no one else had been around, she wouldn't have minded showing off her white pins. Ray wouldn't care about her milk bottle legs, just as he didn't care that she was half-German. She leaned back on the bench, closed her eyes and lifted her face to the sun.

That was the good thing about Ray, with him, she could be herself.

Chapter 41

There was a loud bang as the drawing-room door burst open and slammed against the wall. Maggie looked up from the armchair by the fire, where she was knitting. Gwen had been unravelling her late husband's old pullovers and had given Maggie some yarn. She was making presents for Christmas.

It was Geoff. He flew into the room, looking pale and agitated, so different from the confident, calm Geoff at the gatehouse the other week.

'Crikey! Watch out!' Nancy cried. 'Aw, look! They're all over the place!' She and Elsie had been playing rummy. Cards had been blown off the table and onto the rug. They tutted at Geoff and set about picking them up.

At the far end of the room, the gramophone was playing, furniture had been pushed against the walls and amid much laughter and toe-treading, Miss Sharp was trying to teach Bill to foxtrot. Pam was cuddled up close to Norm on the sofa.

Maggie stood up and peered at Geoff. Was he drunk? She put a hand on his arm. 'What's the matter?'

She had to raise her voice over the music. His breath smelled of cigarettes and cold air clung to his shirt.

'W-w-w …'

'Ray?' Maggie prompted. Ray was out, on a Home Guard drill. He wouldn't be back until later.

Geoff shook his head and jabbed his finger urgently at the door, pointing and gesturing urgently for Maggie to come with him. Finally, he resorted to pulling her arm.

'Come on, then!' Should she fetch a coat? Oh, there was no time.

As they hurried from the room, Norm whistled after them and one of the girls called, 'Say, where are you two going?'

The music faded away as they raced through the brightly lit Long Gallery.

'Have you got a torch?' Maggie asked and in reply Geoff flashed the beam up at the ceiling.

'It's W … W-WUDI!' he managed at last. Maggie's legs almost buckled beneath her. Rudi? Something had happened to Rudi! It was late, way past his bedtime. What on earth could it be?

The French doors onto the terrace were open, allowing light from the room to spill out. Dozens of moths were flying around. It wasn't like Geoff to jeopardise the blackout. He must have run in from the garden in a complete panic.

They stepped out into the cold night and Maggie pushed the doors to behind them. For a second, she could see nothing. There was no moon and no sign of Geoff.

Then he was back at her side, pulling on her sleeve. 'H-hurry,' he said. 'W … w … in the w-water.'

Water? Rudi was in the water? In the swimming pool!

It was too dark to see without the torch, so Maggie grabbed Geoff's arm and urged him forward. The terrace – and then the grass – were iced with frost and slippy. If he'd been walking along the edge of the pool, Rudi could easily have slipped in.

Maggie strained her ears but there were no cries for help. Perhaps Geoff was mistaken? But if Rudi really was in the water, then – she felt sick at the thought – maybe they were already too late.

They reached the edge of the pool. The water was black and

still. Maggie pulled Geoff back. He was frantic now, whimpering. She reached up, pulled him towards her by the lapel and grabbed his face in both hands.

'Listen!' she yelled. 'Shine the torch into the water. Help me! Do you hear?'

She felt him nod. He was shivering hard. She let go, tugged off her cardigan – there was no time to remove anything else – pinched her nose and jumped.

The cold was agony. Like a simultaneous electric shock and a punch in the face. It stunned her.

Then she surfaced, spluttering and coughing, already feeling sharp twinges of cramp in her legs. Geoff was doing his best; there were small circles of torchlight on the water's surface but they only showed waves and ripples. No sign of a child. Maggie trod water. She was already gasping and shaking.

'Rudi? RUDI!' She called his name until she was trembling too much to speak.

She should have taken off Charity's heavy twill trousers, they were dragging her down. It was no good. Geoff must have been mistaken. There was no one here. She was going to drown, in this freezing pool, for nothing.

Unless …? He must be on the bottom. But where was that? She'd lost all sense of direction; she could hardly think straight. She'd lost all feeling in her feet and her hands. How much longer could she stay afloat? Her limbs were lead.

Her lungs were hurting now, fit to bursting and she was close to crying huge, hysterical tears.

She took the biggest breath she could manage and dived, pushing against the walls of water and finally feeling the rough bottom of the pool.

As she was about to kick off with her feet and surface, her hand touched something, and she grabbed it. It was a sleeve or a cuff.

She'd got him! She dragged him up, up, up in a seemingly never-ending struggle to reach air. Then she burst out onto the surface and gasped and gasped, choking, coughing and bobbing down under the water again.

Someone was in the water, pulling her to the shallow end, arms were lifting her out. Her arm hit the hard stone edge of the pool and she was coughing up water.

There were shouts from the Hall and the sounds of people coming over the grass towards them. Maggie lay in a sopping heap on the side of the pool. Had she got him? Was Rudi safe? She didn't know … and then, she didn't care. She was exhausted, she had nothing left to give. She felt like she was waiting to die.

Chapter 42

Joseph stood at the window in the vestibule, watching Brummie load Sarah's suitcases into the car.

'She's been given her marching orders then?' a soft voice said.

It was Gwen. Joseph had been so deep in thought about everything that had happened in the last couple of days, he hadn't heard her approach.

They stood side by side and watched as Brummie opened the door and Sarah slid into the back seat. Joseph had already said goodbye. He wouldn't be waving her off from the front door; it was hardly what she deserved.

'What on earth happened?' Gwen asked. 'There are twenty different versions going around the kitchen.'

Joseph explained how, the night before last, Rudi had woken and wandered out into the garden. Sarah – drinking with Jack in the gatehouse – was completely unaware that her charge was on the loose. Mr Braithwaite, who was smoking out on the terrace, saw Rudi on the lawn, heard the fateful splash, failed to reach him in the pool and ran inside for help.

'In the form of Miss Corbett,' he continued. 'Who, fortunately, can swim and is very brave. She launched herself into the freezing water and Mr Maguire, arriving back from Home Guard duties and presumably feeling very gung ho, leapt in to assist. He managed to pull them both to the shallow end, even though he can barely swim and, he tells me, once had rheumatic fever.'

Gwen patted his arm and left her hand there for a moment or two. 'How awful,' she murmured.

'You know,' Joseph said, 'I should have trusted my instincts about that young woman. A few nights ago, unable to sleep, I came over to the office and I heard the most almighty din coming from the drawing room. Sarah was holding court and a group of them – men and women – were leaping on and off the armchairs. Apparently, every piece of furniture was an "island" and the carpet was "shark-infested waters". Why are you laughing?'

Gwen bit her lip in an attempt to stop. 'Sorry, Joey. It's the way you said it. How do you know about the sharks?'

'I hauled Maguire in the next day to explain and told him morale-boosting had possibly gone rather too far.'

'Oh, Joey.' Gwen's eyes were shining. 'They're young. Remember that?' She became more serious. 'But there was absolutely no excuse for the way she neglected that little boy. Disgraceful. It doesn't bear thinking about – he could have drowned. What'll happen to him now?'

Joseph grimaced. He'd been pondering that ever since the doctor had confirmed that Rudi would make a full recovery. He'd have to find the child another host family. He hated the thought of Rudi being passed around like a parcel but he couldn't see any other option.

Gwen touched his arm again, as though to remind him she was still there. 'I've got an idea, Joey,' she said. 'If you think it would be acceptable …'

* * *

Later that morning, Miss Corbett arrived for Joseph's German lesson.

On his instruction, she'd spent yesterday in bed and had meals brought to her on a tray. Now, she looked pale but otherwise, she, too – thank God – seemed none the worse for her ordeal.

As much as Joseph enjoyed the intellectual challenge of the lessons and Miss Corbett's quiet competence, today there would be no teaching.

'I wanted to inform you,' he told her, 'that Rudi will be lodging with Mrs Nicholls from now on. She's offered to take him and I approve wholeheartedly. He'll get the care and attention that has been sadly lacking in recent times and that, without your brave intervention, Miss Corbett, could have resulted in a terrible tragedy.'

She nodded. 'That's a wonderful idea, Sir. And Sarah? Miss Jewell?'

He grimaced. 'Gone. Let's talk no more about her. More importantly, how are you feeling?'

'I'm fine, Sir. My secret's out though.'

'Which one?'

He'd managed to make her smile, at least.

'The ... er ... the being-half-German secret. When Geoff raised the alarm and the others came running out of the house, as I started to come to on the poolside, I was speaking German, by all accounts or "gibberish", as Elsie – Miss Davenport – put it.'

'And?'

She shrugged. 'They're being perfectly nice.'

'I should jolly well think so! You'd saved a child's life, which is more than any of them did. Maguire excepted. He helped.'

Miss Corbett gave a wan smile. 'That's more or less what they said, Sir.'

'Good, good.' Joseph rubbed his hands together. 'Right, I think you need a few days' convalescence, Miss Corbett, so no work for you for the time being but there is something I want you to consider.'

He cleared his throat. He hoped he wasn't overburdening the

girl, especially given all that she'd just been through. But he was sure that, inside that rather fragile-looking exterior, there was a solid core, a strength to Maggie Corbett that perhaps she didn't even realise she had.

Joseph coughed again. This was ridiculous but he felt suddenly rather sentimental. 'I thank my lucky stars that you walked into Rosman's bank in September,' he said, with a firm nod. 'You are valuable to me, in so many ways and the last thing I want is for you to leave us. But – no, please, let me finish. Sadly, regrettably, I have come to the conclusion that you and your not inconsiderable talents are wasted here, Miss Corbett. It would be selfish of me to keep you all to myself. There's more, much more, you could be doing for the war effort. And I have an inkling you'd like that. Would you? Would you be interested in something rather more challenging?'

Chapter 43

Just before lunch, Miss Sharp sent Maggie on an errand. When she returned to the banking hall, no one was there. Charming! They'd all started lunch without her.

Then she heard a giggle from the far end of the Gallery and looked up. All her colleagues were standing around the table, in front of their seats and staring at her.

'What on earth?' She started to walk towards them.

'Hip, hip—' Ray yelled.

'—hooray!' the others finished.

She walked up to the table and took her seat to a round of applause. And then she noticed everyone was there; not only her bank colleagues but, standing at the back wall, were Gwen and Cook, wiping her hands on her apron and Brummie the driver and Mrs Mason and even, in the doorway, with folded arms and a proud smile on his face, Lord Ashford himself.

'A little celebration, dear Miss Corbett,' Miss Sharp said. She patted Maggie gently on the back. 'Cook's made your favourite mock sausage and if we could give you a medal, we would!'

'You were so brave, Maggie,' Nancy said.

Maggie smiled at her. 'Not Maggie the mouse?'

'No, no!' they chorused.

'Maggie the mighty!' Pam said firmly and Ray, sitting beside her, so quietly that, in the ensuing laughter, only Maggie could hear, squeezed her hand under the table and said, 'Maggie the magnificent.'

* * *

When lunch was finished and her colleagues started to drift away from the table, Dakin the butler brought in the second post.

'A letter for you, Miss Corbett,' he said.

The envelope had a label stuck to the back: Opened by examiner 5,544.

Censored.

Finally, it had come: a letter from Mutti.

Liebe Maggie, she read. Maggie smiled, hearing Mutti's voice in her head.

> *I was so happy to receive your letter and news and knowing that you and little Vi are well and away from the bombing in London.*
>
> *I, too, am lucky. I find myself on a beautiful place called the Island of Man. Which is strange, because there are no men. No soldiers at all but hundreds of women in the town. All internees, like me. We are quite free except for the barbed wire which is to keep us in. And the sea, which keeps us in, also.*
>
> *There are babies here and they are hugged and cuddled so often by all of us women, that the mothers have to pin notices on them asking please, do not kiss them. It is hard. We all miss our children very much.*
>
> *I am staying in a hotel. It is nice and I am able to sew.*

Maggie frowned. A hotel? That couldn't possibly be true, could it? She would be in a prison camp, surely?

When we arrived in September, the weather was very good. We spent all the days on the beach! It was like our trip to Clacton. Happy times. Do you remember? Perfekt.

Some of the women here are so clever. Artists and writers and so forth. They are planning to make a university. Perhaps I will learn something!

Write soon, darling Maggie, and tell me all your news. We do not hear very much of the outside world. Only when someone new arrives.

Missing you so much, hoping and praying you are safe and well and HAPPY!

Mutti xxx

Maggie put the letter down and frowned. While she'd been reading it, everyone had slipped away. She was quite alone at the table.

It was wonderful to hear from Mutti after all this time but what on earth was all this nonsense about beaches, sunshine, a hotel and a university? That sounded like pure fantasy. Was she quite right in the head? Maggie read through the letter again.

No doubt, Mutti had to be careful what she wrote. She probably didn't dare criticise the arrangements because they might take it out on her. She might be put in solitary confinement or flogged or worse. So, when she said she'd been on the beach enjoying the sunshine and some of those other things, they simply couldn't be true.

Perhaps it was code? Rather like the kisses on Violet's letters only more complicated. Yes, that was it: a code. Maggie only wished she had the key to unlock it.

Chapter 44

Over the next few weeks, in the letters that she sent to Vi and Mutti, Maggie made no mention of that night in the swimming pool.

Her letters were meant to cheer them up, after all, and the story of how she and Rudi had almost drowned wasn't something to trouble them with.

Instead, she wrote about the pranks the chaps played on one another – the apple pie beds and alarm clocks under pillows – and the game they played, passing a box of matches in a chain, using only your nose. She told them about Miss Sharp's hilarious Keep Fit classes and all Ray's jokes and one-liners.

Perhaps, one day, when they were back together again, she'd tell them the truth. Just as Violet might reveal she hadn't been happy at first on the farm and Mutti might admit she'd felt lonely and frightened when she arrived on the Isle of Man.

But now, they both seemed happy.

The number of kisses had gradually increased on Violet's letters. The pages were full of them.

As for Mutti, the second letter that arrived was still full of her life in the camp and how she was enjoying it. It wasn't a 'code' at all, her mother really was quite content.

'Marvellous!' Lord Ashford had said, when Maggie heard

from Mutti. 'Now, we'll have to see if we can get your mother released!'

But Maggie wasn't sure if Mutti would want to come home, even if his Lordship could pull some strings. She never mentioned Dad, and Maggie didn't ask if they were in touch. She stuck to her rule, her letters only focused on good things.

Even though she felt reassured that her sister was happy now in her billet, Maggie couldn't wait to see it for herself. And at the start of December, Maggie and Ray were finally ready to cycle to Violet's farm.

'I think this might be it!' Ray said, as they rode the tandem into a hamlet. After miles of nothing but lanes, hedges and fields they'd reached civilisation: a cluster of cottages with black smoke swirling from their chimneys.

Maggie could hardly believe it. Had they really cycled twenty miles from Snowden Hall, setting out at first light, when there was still frost on the ground?

The last few miles had been hard. She'd hardly even had the energy to speak. She'd focused on keeping up with Ray's pedalling as hard as she could, anxious not to leave all the hard work to him. She'd concentrated on the rhythmic swish of the wheels and tried not to cry out when they hit yet another hole with a bang and a bone-shaking thud and cold rainwater had splashed up her legs.

'Sorry!' Ray called back, between what sounded like gritted teeth.

Maggie patted him on the back each time, to say she understood. It saved talking.

A horse and cart was trundling slowly down the lane towards them. At the sound of the steady clip-clop of the shire horse's hooves, Ray slowed Daisy down, called out a warning to Maggie and pulled up onto the grass verge.

The horse veered off to the side as it approached, eyeing them with suspicion. It probably felt the same way about tandems as she did about horses.

The farmer was chewing a straw, the reins held loosely in his hands. When Ray asked if they were anywhere near Jenks' farm, he jerked his head, indicating that the farm lay ahead of them.

They were almost there.

In the farmyard, it smelled of hay and dung, and brown chickens, clucking softly, ran ahead of them. A black-and-white sheepdog slunk out from behind a stack of hay bales and stared with strikingly blue eyes but didn't make a sound. He moved silently behind them.

'He's rounding us up!' Ray said, laughing.

A middle-aged woman had come out of the farmhouse and was walking towards them. She was wearing an overcoat, wellingtons and a headscarf and had a wicker basket looped over her arm.

'Yes?' she asked.

As they stopped the tandem and dismounted, the sheepdog came closer and sniffed the wheels. Maggie introduced herself. 'I'm Violet Corbett's sister. The little girl who's billeted with you?'

The woman frowned and pursed her lips. 'Violet,' she said, absent-mindedly. 'She's not here.'

'Not here?'

'She's out with Joan, the other vackie. They'll be back soon; they've only gone round the fields with Seth.'

Ray and Maggie exchanged relieved glances. Imagine if they'd cycled all this way, only to find that Violet was elsewhere.

'Do you mind if we wait?' Ray asked.

'Not at all, come inside, you look plum wore out, the pair of you.' Mrs Jenks, as she turned out to be, set about making tea. They sat at the kitchen table, which was covered in a gingham checked tablecloth. The place looked clean and homely. There was a perky blue budgie sitting in a cage near the sink.

'That's Charlie,' Mrs Jenks said. 'He's got his own gas mask.'

'Has Vi been getting on all right?' Maggie asked, unable to wait any longer. She wanted to know everything. Had Mrs Jenks been feeding her, keeping her warm, sending her to school, being kind? It was only politeness that was holding her back from a torrent of questions.

'Vi? Oh yes, she's good as gold. Once she settled in, you know. I think she was a bit homesick to start with. We were worried about having a child from the slums, I don't mind telling you. You hear such stories! That cockney children don't know how to behave, never eaten at a table before, wet the bed at night, they're covered in fleas and lice …'

Maggie's chest tightened. Bloomin' cheek! They mightn't have had much money but Vi was clean and well brought up, Maggie would have her know.

Mrs Jenks was oblivious to Maggie's outrage. 'Someone in the village has taken in an expectant mother and two little 'uns and she's had all manner of trouble. As for the other girl I've got – Joan – she's been a bother. She had German measles when she arrived. That's been sent over by the Germans, you know. Right little tearaway. Still swears like a trooper, mind. Turns the air blue. Your Violet's been a good influence.'

Maggie exhaled. Finally, some good news. 'So, she's settled in, then?'

Mrs Jenks looked towards the door. 'Why don't you ask her yourself?'

'MAGGIE!'

She barely had time to stand before Vi was launching herself into her arms, almost sending her flying. They laughed and hugged one another.

'You're here!' Vi said. 'You made it! Did you bring Tabby?'

'Stand back and let me look at you,' Maggie said. 'My, you've grown, haven't you? And no, silly, we didn't bring the cat!'

'There now, how do you think she looks?' Mrs Jenks asked, folding her arms and smiling at them.

Maggie had to admit that Vi looked very well. She had rosy cheeks and a healthy glow. The country must be suiting her.

'I have an egg for breakfast every day!' Violet declared.

'She looks smashing!' Maggie said. Her face was aching, she was smiling so hard. 'Thank you, Mrs Jenks. Vi, this is my friend Ray. We work together. He's organised this whole excursion.'

Vi smiled at Ray. 'Where is it? The tandem?'

'Where's Joan?' Mrs Jenks asked. She and Vi exchanged worried glances. The next moment there was a crash from outside.

'There's Joan!' Vi and Mrs Jenks said, simultaneously.

Vi skipped out to inspect the damage and Ray followed her.

Mrs Jenks poured more tea into Maggie's cup. 'How long have you two been courting?'

Maggie laughed. 'Courting? Oh no, we're not.'

'Are you sure, love?'

Maggie giggled, wondering what Ray would make of that. 'Quite sure,' she said firmly.

'I wish my Seth was courting,' Mrs Jenks said, shaking her head and staring into the distance. 'He's got half the girls in the village in love with him and not one of them's good enough for 'im. I dunno what he's waiting for. A goddess or summat!'

Once Ray had returned and reported that the tandem was, fortunately, undamaged, Vi gave them a tour of the farm.

'I collect the eggs, milk the goats, herd the cows and muck out the pigs,' she told them, proudly.

'And what about school?' Maggie asked.

'Oh yes, there's a school in the village. Me and Joanie ride there on Hercules.' She rode to school on a horse! Maggie couldn't have imagined a better place for Vi. It was clear she was in heaven.

* * *

It was dusk as they reached the last mile of the journey home and the setting sun was a glorious golden orb in the west.

'Shall we stop and watch it for a minute?' Ray suggested, slowing down the tandem. He hoped Maggie wasn't going to laugh at him for being slushy. 'Not for long, though. We must get back before dark or there's no telling where we'll end up.'

They dismounted and watched the flaming sun.

'Cor, it's like egg yolk spilling over the sky,' Maggie said. 'Are those eggs still in one piece, by the way?'

Mrs Jenks had insisted on giving them a couple of eggs. Ray had wrapped them in his handkerchief and tucked them into his coat pocket. If they survived the journey, he'd give them to Cook for Rudi. He tapped the pocket gently now. 'Yes, they're all right.'

'What are you thinking about?' Maggie asked, suddenly.

'I was thinking about that budgie back at the farm,' Ray said, truthfully. 'Charlie. I wish I'd seen its gas mask.'

Maggie laughed and prodded him. 'You daft thing. And there was me thinking you were going to come out with something poetic, looking at that red and gold sky.'

'Did you?'

'Yes, something like, "it's the perfect end to the perfect day". That's what I was thinking, anyway.'

Ray's heart was hammering. If this was a film, this would be the moment when the hero would say something romantic to the girl he was in love with. It was the perfect setting: the sun was a fire in the sky, the trees and hills were black silhouettes and they were completely alone. He swallowed. His mind was blank; he couldn't do it.

'Maggie ...' he started.

'Yes?'

'I expect you're happy that you've seen your sister, then?'

'Oh yes. Thanks for pushing me into it.'

'You were the one who did the pushing,' he said, unable to resist the joke. He didn't need any thanks; he'd enjoyed every minute.

'If it weren't for you, none of this would have happened. I am grateful, Ray, really I am.'

He waved away her thanks. 'You'd have managed, somehow.'

'I wouldn't! I can't ride a bike on my own or read a map or a compass.'

Ray put his finger on his chin and pretended to think. 'No, you're right. You'd never have managed in a million years!'

Maggie laughed.

'I might as well tell you this now,' she said. 'I've been offered the chance to go and do my bit.'

Ray's stomach plunged but, at the same time, he wasn't surprised.

'It was Lord Ashford's idea,' she went on. 'He knows of a unit that needs good German speakers to listen into pilots' radio transmissions and translate them.'

He fixed his mouth in a smile and continued to look out at the sunset. It was starting to disappear over the horizon. It didn't look quite so brilliant anymore.

'Well done, you,' he said. His voice sounded flat; his mind was racing. Did this mean she'd be leaving Snowden?

'I had to speak to someone on the phone in German. It was an interview, I suppose, and anyway …' She shrugged. 'I must have passed the test because, if I want it, the position is mine.'

Ray swallowed. 'And do you think it would suit you?'

She nodded enthusiastically. 'Yes, I do. After all, I don't want to spend the whole war sitting behind a typewriter. I don't know where I'll be posted yet, of course.'

Ray nudged her. 'Well, if you go by train, don't forget to take that carpet bag and the bloomin' cat, will you?'

She giggled. 'Oh, I love you, Ray! You don't half make me laugh.'

His heart missed a beat. He cleared his throat. Of course, she didn't mean it. She didn't love him. Not like that. It was only a turn of phrase.

Imagine if he'd taken her words at face value, grabbed her hands and blurted out, 'Maggie Corbett, I love you too!'

The thought of it made him go hot and then cold.

'When my dad died,' he said, quickly, 'my ma couldn't ever get to sleep. She used to ask me to tell her stories about nice things. So, I did. And I always tried to make her laugh.'

He could hardly see Maggie now; the light was almost gone.

'And did it help?'

Ray nodded, wishing he didn't feel so blue all of a sudden. 'Yes.' His voice was cracking. He coughed and turned away. 'Yes, it did.'

Chapter 45

A few days before Christmas, the girls were playing *Monopoly* in the drawing room.

Nancy twirled the spinner and moved her counter along the board. 'Do you think the bombing will stop for Christmas?' she asked.

Maggie's stomach somersaulted, as it always did whenever anyone mentioned the raids.

Norm was sitting in the armchair nearest to Pam. He looked up from the *Daily Mail*. 'You mean like a ceasefire?'

'I was only surmising,' Nancy said. 'They stopped fighting at Christmas last time, didn't they, and played football? Jerry and our boys?'

Norm pulled a face. 'If you believe that, yes.' He grunted and turned back to his newspaper.

'They might stop, Nancy,' Maggie said, suddenly filled with an urge to stick up for her. Norm could be so condescending at times. As though no one else could have an opinion on the war except him. 'I'm sure the Germans want a nice Christmas, too. Let's hope so, eh?'

Norm stood up, threw his paper down on the chair and marched out of the room.

'Cor, who's rattled his cage?' Elsie asked. 'There's no need to worry about us, Maggie. We'll only be away a couple of days and we're not exactly going to the Front. We'll be back before you know it.'

'Hey, don't wish our Christmas holidays away!' Nancy complained. She picked up a Community Chest card and read, 'You have won second prize in a beauty contest, collect ten pounds.'

'Only second, Nancy?' Pam asked archly.

'I'm happy with that, thank you very much, Banker!' she snatched the white paper note from Pam and giggled.

Everyone was going back to London for Christmas except her and Ray and Maggie was surprised to find that she was, all of a sudden, worried about them.

Since she'd saved Rudi and they'd all heard her speak German on the side of the pool, the girls had been nicer than ever. They understood now why she spent all that time with his Lordship. Of course, they didn't know the whole story; they only knew she was teaching him the language and nothing about the letters and documents she'd been translating. And as Jack was back in Lincolnshire with his squadron, there were no sly comments about him, either.

They weren't merely colleagues anymore, they were pals.

'Yes,' Nancy said, firmly, 'we'll be back before you know it, so don't get any ideas about swiping my bed!'

'Borrow anything you like from my side of the wardrobe, Maggie,' Pam said quietly. 'If you'd like to, that is. We're about the same size.'

She'd never seen Pam look coy before.

'Thank you, Pam, that's kind. I will,' Maggie said.

* * *

On Christmas Eve, Maggie and Ray waved everyone off, after work.

As her colleagues piled excitedly into Lord Ashford's car and the horse and cart which were to take them to the station, Maggie felt a twinge of envy. She didn't have anyone waiting for her in London; no one who'd be pleased to see her.

'Behave yourselves, you two!' Big Bill called back at them as the cart rolled off down the drive.

When Ray had mentioned he might be staying at Snowden for Christmas too, Maggie had teased him. 'Charity won't be here, you know!'

But she'd been pleased. Apart from Charity, Ray was her best friend here. 'It'll be smashing to have you here,' she'd added. 'But won't your mum be upset?'

Ray had wrinkled his nose. 'She's got a new grandchild to make a fuss of. My sister's first. I don't think I'll be missed very much.'

Chapter 46

Joseph ruined Christmas Day within ten minutes of waking up.

Dakin brought breakfast to their room on a tray and as Esther sipped her tea, bleary-eyed, Joseph retrieved the box he'd stashed at the bottom of the wardrobe.

He heaved it across the room and placed it on the floor next to her bed. 'Here's your present, darling. It would've been a devil to wrap, hence the box. Thought we'd do our presents here, just the two of us.'

Esther frowned. 'You know I'm going for a ride this morning?'

Joseph tapped the box and beamed at her.

She didn't smile back. 'It's awfully big.'

'Something different this year. How many earrings can a girl wear, after all?'

Esther sighed, drained her cup, placed it on the bedstand and leaned down to flip open the lid of the box. She peered inside and then looked up at Joseph. 'A saddle,' she said.

'Didn't you say you needed a new one?'

'I daresay I did.'

Joseph wanted to say something about austerity and being practical rather than extravagant but he bit his tongue. The saddle had been surprisingly expensive and he'd gone to a lot of trouble, ensuring it was the right size. It would actually have been easier to give her jewellery as usual but he'd wanted to surprise her.

He kissed her lightly on the forehead, ignoring her flinch. She said thank you quietly.

'I haven't had a chance to wrap your gift yet, Jay. I'll give it to you later.'

He nodded. 'Go and enjoy your ride, have a bath when you get back and by then our guests will have arrived.'

Esther's face brightened. 'Ah yes, Rudi. I've missed him terribly.'

Rudi was coming for Christmas Day. And that meant Gwen was coming too. And for Joseph, that was going to be the best part of Christmas.

* * *

How queer it was, Maggie thought, to wake up alone on Christmas morning in the room she normally shared with Pam and Nancy.

She'd expected to relish the peace and quiet but, in truth, she missed them. She even missed the customary morning rush for the bathroom.

She and Ray had been out for a ride on Daisy the tandem after breakfast. They'd cut some holly and mistletoe to decorate the house and seen some of the villagers coming back from church.

'Merry Christmas!' the locals had called to them and she and Ray had waved and yelled it back.

It would have been perfect if it had snowed. When she'd passed Lord Ashford in the corridor, he'd apologised for the lack of snow.

'You'd have thought we could have magicked some up,' he'd said. 'The house is named for snow, after all. We could have taken the children sledging.'

Some of the vackies from the village were coming later, for tea. Maggie had heard that news with a pang. She'd have liked nothing better than for Violet to be here too, but she consoled herself with the thought that Vi was quite happy where she was, among her beloved animals. They'd see each other again, soon enough. She mustn't be greedy and wish for too much. And then, there was Jack. He'd promised to try to come to Snowden for Christmas. She was bubbling with excitement about seeing him again.

There was an eight-foot Christmas tree in the hall, covered in snakes of glittery tinsel and decorated with glass baubles, that had, according to Mrs Mason, been in the family for years. They were nothing like the decorations that Maggie was used to: paperchains and fringes made from newspaper.

She'd only ever seen anything as beautiful as the tree at Snowden Hall in Harrods, when Mutti took her and Violet up West to gaze at the window displays at Christmas.

And now, before lunch, she was back in her room to change. She smiled to herself. Goodness, she'd become quite gentrified.

She opened the wardrobe and gazed at the array of dresses. She had her pick of any of Pam's. She moved her hands through the rail, feeling like a lady in an expensive dress shop. Jack had told her blue suited her, once, so that was decided, she'd choose a blue one.

* * *

Ray came downstairs, carrying the wooden plane he'd so carefully made and wrapped for Rudi. Damn! That was the unmistakeable booming voice of Jack Rosman. What was *he* doing here? Ray's good mood evaporated in an instant. He hadn't dared ask but he'd prayed Rosman would get a sudden posting, now that he was fit to fly again, and would be elsewhere for Christmas.

That was the day spoiled.

Call-Me-Jack would be all over Maggie, flirting and calling her by that stupid nickname and he, Ray, wouldn't get a look in. This hadn't been the plan at all.

He'd missed his chance now, good and proper. He should have said something to Maggie when they were out on the tandem this morning. But how could he, when he couldn't even look her in the eye? But later, when they'd collected that huge ball of mistletoe, that had been his opportunity. For Gawd's sake, how much more romantic could you get?

'Ah there you are, Maguire, good man, come on through.'

His thoughts were interrupted by his Nibs, welcoming him into the drawing room, where the fire was blazing in the hearth and the gramophone was playing Christmas carols.

Don't be such a miserable Scrooge, Ray told himself. It's Christmas Day, you're spending it in the lap of luxury, while other poor sods are down in the shelters, damp, cold and terrified. Things could be worse.

He could smell the dinner cooking in the kitchen down the hall. 'We're having goose,' Lady Ashford was telling Jack Rosman. 'Of course, it's not a proper Christmas. No plum pudding, although Cook assures me she's made a stack of blackberry mince pies instead.'

Ray had only stayed here for Christmas because of Maggie. At last, they'd have some time together. He was planning to tell her, finally, how he felt and ask if she wanted to be his girl.

Being out on the tandem was all very well but they were usually freezing cold and he couldn't even see her. You couldn't speak properly when the other person – the girl you couldn't get out of your mind – was sitting behind you.

They'd sat with the house staff at breakfast and exchanged presents. She'd knitted him a pair of gloves and a balaclava helmet and he'd given her the box he'd carved from a block of wood he'd found in the barn.

'I was half expecting you to give me a pair of bicycle clips!' she'd said and then, opening it, 'A jewellery box!' In the next breath she'd added, 'I don't have any!'

He'd explained then, that it wasn't necessarily for jewellery. It was for trinkets or anything she wanted to keep safe.

She had seemed pleased, though. 'It's beautiful, Ray,' she'd said. 'Aren't you clever?'

Then they'd been out on the tandem. She hadn't minded when he'd teased her about her red nose. She'd held the ladder for him as he'd climbed up an apple tree in the orchard and cut down some mistletoe. His legs had only wobbled a little.

'Too bad Charity's not here!' she'd said, as they gathered it up. Why did she think he held a torch for Charity? Because they'd spent all that time together, organising the concert? She was pretty enough and she had class, you had to admit, but Charity Richmond wasn't a patch on Maggie.

Here she was, now, coming into the drawing room.

Before Ray could say a word, Jack piped up. 'Hey, Poppy! Merry Christmas! You look a picture. New dress?'

Ray was still clutching the present for Rudi to his chest.

'Here, come and put that down and have a drink,' Lady Ashford said. 'Actually, there's something I'd like to ask you, Ray, if I might. A favour ...'

Maggie caught his eye and raised her eyebrows. He had to smile. They were thinking the same thing: Lady Ashford's 'favours' could be dangerous. As long as it was nothing to do with getting on a horse ...

* * *

A little while later, Mrs Nicholls arrived with Rudi, who, if Ray had understood right, was living with her now. Lady Ashford went into raptures about the child, which was queer, Ray thought. If she loved the little boy that much, why did she spend so much time away from him? But maybe that was how posh folk loved their children, at a distance.

They all sat together in the drawing room.

Lady Ashford seemed out of sorts. If he had to describe it, Ray would have said she was sulking. As she sat on the settee with Lord Ashford, there was a gap between them and her arms were crossed. Perhaps they'd had a row.

When it was time for the presents, her Ladyship cheered up a little as she handed out little parcels for everyone, wrapped in cloth.

'Now, they're only a few tokens!' she said. There was soap and hand cream ('from my stash!') for Maggie and Gwen and for the men, *Reader's Union* books, scarves and calendars.

'Rudi has some presents that he'd like to give out,' Mrs Nicholls said. 'He insisted on wrapping them himself, in secret, so I don't know what any of them are!' She lowered her voice. 'Only little bits and bobs, I expect.'

'How delightful!' Lady Ashford patted the space beside her on the plush sofa. 'Rudi, come and sit with me, up here.'

The first present was for Ray.

He got up from his seat and took the little parcel from Rudi. It was a pencil – a rather blunt pencil, at that – undoubtedly filched from the banking hall or perhaps even his Nibs' office. 'Thank you, Rudi. Most kind,' Ray said with a small bow.

'Some of the gifts are wrapped in newspaper, I'm afraid,' Mrs Nicholls said. 'We ran out of brown paper.'

Lady Ashford's present was an acorn. She gasped and put her hand to her chest. 'It's the sweetest thing! Oh, Rudi! That's my best Christmas present ever!'

'This one?' Mrs Nicholls asked and Rudi whispered in her ear. 'This one he says is for Maggie.'

Ray's heart went out to her, she blushed and looked so self-conscious, as everyone watched her struggle with the string on the tiny package.

'I wonder what it can be?' Maggie said. She shook it and frowned and Rudi laughed, enjoying the game. 'Could it be a feather, maybe? It's ever so light!'

As she pulled it apart, Maggie gasped. She unfolded something and held it up for everyone to see. Ray saw a flash of white paper and then the words *Bank of England*.

It was a creased and rather battered one-pound note.

There was a moment's silence, as everyone looked in astonishment.

'Goodness, where on earth did you get that, Rudi?' Mrs Nicholls asked. 'So much money, I—'

Joseph put his hand up and shook his head reassuringly. 'I'll explain later. A mystery has been solved, today, that's for certain. And I'm sure Miss Corbett knows where that money belongs. Now, where's my present, Rudi, old chap? You haven't forgotten me, have you?'

* * *

Joseph had done the seating plan for Christmas dinner. He'd placed Esther on his right-hand side and on the other, Gwen.

When Esther had bustled out to the kitchen halfway through the main course – most likely to reprimand the staff for something that wasn't quite up to scratch – Gwen glanced up at him.

'I was half expecting to see you dressed in a red suit and a white beard, Joey,' she murmured. 'Didn't your father used to dress up on Christmas Day?'

Joseph smiled, pleased she'd remembered. 'He did indeed. And we still have the outfit. But I've delegated that task this year.'

Gwen nodded across the table towards Maggie and Jack, who were sitting opposite them and laughing. 'She seems rather taken with your nephew.'

He nodded. Perhaps it had been a mistake to sit them next to each other. He'd put Maguire on the other side of Maggie but he was talking to little Rudi, who was between him and Gwen.

'Yes,' Joseph said, keeping his voice low. 'I fear she's going to get her heart broken.'

Gwen sighed. 'Sometimes, I'm glad I'm not that age anymore.' And then, as Esther glided back into the dining room, she raised her voice and said, 'Your Ladyship, this goose is quite delicious!'

* * *

After lunch, when they'd returned to the drawing room and the evacuee children had arrived with their host families, for tea and games, Joseph clapped his hands. A game of charades had just finished. 'What shall we play next? There's *Ludo* or Pontoon or this one …' He picked up a box. '*Monopoly!*'

Esther groaned. 'Heavens, not that, darling! It takes forever! The King's speech is in half an hour and then it'll be time for Father Christmas!' She clapped her hands and the children let out excited squeals. 'Let's play something a bit lively! How about hide-and-seek?'

When it was Joseph's turn to 'seek', he discovered Gwen hiding in the darkness of the boot room. He knew it was her straightaway, by her sweet scent.

He should have called out, 'Found you!' which would have marked the end of the game but instead, he moved carefully through the coats in the pitch black and found her. The next moment, he was kissing her. He'd waited nearly thirty years to do that again and it had been worth the wait. He thought – he hoped – from the way she kissed him back, that she felt the same way.

There was so much to say. 'I—' he started, when they finally drew apart but Gwen stopped him with a finger laid gently on his lips.

'My mother couldn't stand my husband,' she whispered, 'or the one or two sweethearts before him. Oh yes, there were a couple. I think the only man she ever thought good enough for me was you, Joey.'

'JAAAAY!' A voice yelled from the corridor outside. Esther.

He couldn't see Gwen in the dark but she gave a little gasp and he felt her jump. He put his mouth to her ear, smelled her clean hair, let her soft curls touch his cheek.

'Shhh,' he said and he felt more alive in that moment than he could ever remember.

The door was flung open and a shaft of light shone in like a searchlight, making Joseph squint and put his hand up to his eyes. He stepped in front of Gwen, to hide her. Her body was pressed up against his back.

'Oh, goodness. There you are!' Esther said, crossly. 'What on earth are you doing in here? The game's OVER, Jay! What, were you going to stay hidden all night?'

He didn't move and she tapped her foot.

'Do come on, Jay. We're playing parlour games now. Everyone's waiting!'

His heart was racing but his voice, when he spoke, was calm and nonchalant. 'Very well, darling. You go ahead. I'll be right there.'

He didn't quite know what he'd do if Esther insisted he came now but she huffed, turned on her heels and stomped off without another word.

He and Gwen exhaled. The door was half open and the light was shining in from the hall. He could see her now. They waited another minute, not daring to speak until they were sure no one was around.

'You go first,' Joseph whispered. 'I'll wait a respectable interval before I appear.' He held her hand for a moment and then released it, so that she could slip away.

Alone now, he had an overwhelming urge to laugh. He couldn't even blame it on too much whisky because he hadn't touched a drop. Blame it on the war, then. Blame it on wanting to grasp a little happiness, while you still could.

* * *

At three o'clock everyone gathered around the wireless to listen to the Royal Christmas message. They all stood for the national anthem.

His Majesty spoke about the children. 'I am sure we will all do our best to make it a happy one for them,' he said before he went on to talk about 'the sadness of separation' and how 'many family circles are broken'.

Poor devil, Joseph thought. The King sounded slow, his speech laboured. He was struggling but he was doing his best, doing his duty.

When it had finished and they'd all stood once more for the national anthem, the children started running around, impatient for more games. Glasses were refilled and Lady Ashford issued more instructions to the staff.

* * *

Ray walked through the Long Gallery and stepped out onto the terrace for a cigarette. It was late afternoon now and already dark outside.

The evacuee kiddies were a good bunch and they were away from home and their families, so he wanted to give them a good time, but blimey, they were exhausting. He hardly smoked these days but he needed a ciggie now.

Somehow, he'd ended up organising the children's games and they'd only managed to sit still for five minutes when Lord Ashford had asked him to do some shadow puppets on the walls. Lights had been dimmed and lamps turned on and the children had been enchanted by Ray's rabbit and flapping bird and the new animals he'd added to his repertoire: a stag with antlers, a horse and a snail.

He'd left them in the drawing room, still trying, with varying levels of success, to create their own puppets. He'd slipped out for a break. He reckoned he'd earned it.

He'd only taken one or two drags on the ciggie when he heard the French doors opening and first Maggie's voice and then, a moment later, Jack Rosman's. He cursed to himself and stepped back, to take cover in the bushes.

Could today get any worse? They'd obviously come out for some quiet time together. It was the last thing he wanted to witness and he was sure as eggs were eggs that they had no desire to see him either. Playing gooseberry, once again.

But now – oh blast! – he should have made his escape some other way. He was trapped. If he moved in any direction, they'd see him and from his position in the bushes – unless they decided to head out across the lawn – he couldn't help but hear what they were saying.

He felt rotten, like some kind of Peeping Tom or spy. He dropped his ciggie and put it out with the ball of his foot, wafting the smoke away quickly.

It was cold and he could see that Maggie was shivering. The fella could at least give her his jacket. Ah yes, there he was, taking it off and putting it over her shoulders. But that wasn't what he wanted to see either. *Keep your hands off her*, Ray wanted to shout.

If this wasn't so utterly tragic, and bloody freezing cold – he couldn't feel his fingers and he felt like he had frostbite in his nose – then it would actually be funny. The flipside of tragedy was comedy, wasn't it? If you could laugh at your troubles, you were halfway to conquering them. Him stuck out here, hiding behind a bush and likely to get pneumonia, while his girl – that was how he thought of Maggie now – while his girl was there, a few feet away, with another man. Why, it was like one of those French farces. People would pay good money to watch a funny scene like this. They'd laugh their socks off. Yes, very amusing if you weren't the one being made a fool of.

* * *

'We mustn't be too long,' Maggie said. Even with Jack's jacket over her shoulders, her teeth were chattering and it was so dark out here, she could barely see him. 'They're doing the presents for the kiddies next. Father Christmas. I don't want to miss that.'

Did that sound ungrateful? She was pleased he wanted to be with her, of course and she was excited about the present he was about to give her but when he'd asked her to come outside, she'd rather he'd done it more discreetly. She'd seen Gwen and

Lord Ashford's gaze follow them as they'd left the drawing room together.

She was feeling a little weepy after the King's speech. His Majesty had spoken about everyone doing their bit to make Christmas a happy one for the children, 'wherever they may be', and her mind had drifted to Vi and Mutti. She wished they could have all been together.

Now, the sound of the gramophone was a faint noise from the house – 'Hark the Herald Angels Sing' was playing. But otherwise, it was quiet and still out here and so bitter they could see their breath billowing out every time they spoke.

Maggie stamped her feet to try to keep warm. 'Do you think it's right, what the King said?' she asked Jack. 'About our "feet being planted on the path of victory"?'

Jack seemed distracted. He was pacing the terrace, back and forth. Had he even listened to the King's speech?

'I don't know!' he said. It wasn't like him to be snappy. He sighed and said, 'Yes, yes. Try not to worry, little Pops. I'm sure we are.'

He'd stopped pacing now and was standing near her. He took a deep breath and Maggie felt a thrill of anticipation. So, this was the present. She hoped it wasn't going to be something too extravagant. It would be embarrassing. She'd only given him a handknitted scarf, after all.

'We rub along quite well, don't we Pops?' he said suddenly. 'We're good friends, aren't we?'

Maggie frowned. What was he driving at? He was making a speech! She'd hardly expected that. She nodded and then realised he couldn't see her properly so she said, 'Yes, yes of course.'

Was he about to admit something, take her into his confidence? She wasn't sure that she wanted to hear it, whatever he was about to say.

'There's something I wanted to ask you.' It wasn't like Jack to be so serious. Goodness, he wasn't ill, was he? Perhaps it was going to be one of those morbid discussions about what might happen to him. An 'If I don't make it' or 'If the worst happens' chat? He wouldn't do that, not at Christmas, would he?

He took Maggie's hand – ah, that was better – and pressed an object into it. It felt like a small box. Before she could open it or even say anything, Jack seemed to disappear. He'd dropped to the ground.

She gave a little 'Ooh!' Had he fallen? She started to reach out to help him up but then she realised where he was and stopped herself.

Jack Rosman had gone down on one knee.

'Don't you realise what I'm asking you? Pops, let's get married. Will you be my wife?'

Maggie was stunned.

Was he really doing this? Proposing? It wasn't the kind of proposal she'd ever imagined. Not that she'd ever imagined Jack … Goodness, she was still waiting for him to kiss her! And now this. It was too much.

Her head was still reeling as the French doors opened. It was Dakin the butler. If he could make out Jack, kneeling on the icy terrace, he didn't show any surprise.

'Has anyone seen Mr Maguire?' he called out. 'Her Ladyship's looking for him!'

* * *

In the bushes, Ray gasped. Blast, he'd clean forgotten the favour he'd agreed to do for Lady Ashford. His ears still ringing from the disastrous scene he'd just witnessed, he tiptoed away as quietly as he could manage, hoping, if Maggie and Jack heard anything at all, they'd think it was a bird in the bushes.

He'd be spotted if he went through the French doors, so he had to run around the side of the house and go in through the kitchen. How could he have been so stupid as to forget? They'd all be waiting for him and he still had to get changed into his outfit. He was, after all, Father Christmas!

* * *

'You know I'm heir to Snowden,' Jack was saying. He'd stood up now and they were standing in the cold, facing one another. 'You could live here – eventually – would you like that? To be mistress of this house?'

Maggie frowned. What did he mean? 'Mistress of this house'? Was he having a laugh, toying with her?

'Sooner or later, Pops, someone's going to guess the truth. About me, I mean. Chaps like me are supposed to have lots of girls. But I don't want you to think that you're …' He laughed. 'What I'm trying to say, and making a right hash of it, is it's different with you.'

'Is it?' Maggie's heart lifted for a moment. This was what she wanted – expected – to hear but, in the next breath, he disappointed her again.

'Aunt Esther knows. She's met Mike, she approves. But she's worried for me. I could lose everything, you know. "Get yourself a nice girl", she told me. And I've met a nice girl, Poppy. I've met you.'

Maggie swallowed and closed her eyes for a second. How could this have all gone so wrong? She should be over the moon but, instead, she was confused and dreadfully let down. What was he saying? Was that all she was? A 'nice girl'? And this Mike – was he more important to Jack than her?

'Tell me …' She could hardly speak, she was so cold but she had to try to understand. 'Tell me about you and Mike.'

'Ah yes, Mike.' His voice softened, as it always did when he mentioned his pal. 'Look, it will help us, if you and me can marry. But once we're married, we can do what we like. Independently. You can have your own life but you'll have a nice house and – you'll want for nothing, Pops.'

She opened her mouth to reply but before she could speak, Jack had grabbed her hand.

'Oh, you're like a block of ice!' he said. 'Let's go inside, into the warmth and tell everyone we're engaged! They'll be delighted; everyone likes you, Pops. They'll be pleased for us.'

'No!' Maggie tugged her hand away. 'I haven't … well, I haven't given you my answer.'

She wasn't sure whether to laugh or cry, it hadn't even occurred to Jack Rosman that she might turn him down. Why would she? He was a catch and a half, a dreamboat, she'd be the envy of all the girls, she'd never have to work or to worry about money again.

'It'll keep me out of prison,' he murmured.

Maggie's heart lurched. Mutti was in a kind of prison and the thought of someone else that she loved, locked up, oh, it was too much to bear.

Jack's liberty, as well as his happiness, was in her hands.

She pulled herself up tall. 'I'd like some time to think about it, if I may,' she said, remembering the phrase Lord Ashford had taught her. It didn't sound like her at all and for a moment, Jack didn't speak.

Then he cleared his throat. 'Of course. Take as long as you like, Pops. I'm sorry if I'm rushing you. I'm just so … excited!'

She wasn't excited. She was numb and it wasn't only on account of the chilly December air.

'Here, take this back, for now,' she said, pressing the box back into his hands. She hadn't even looked at the ring. Wasn't he supposed to put the ring on her finger, not hand her the box and expect her to do it herself?

'We'd better go back in,' she said. She felt flat now and cross. Cross with him for letting her down. 'Come on. They'll all be wondering where we've gone.'

Chapter 47

After a sleepless night, Maggie was glad of the distraction of the Boxing Day meet.

Jack had left Snowden. He'd had to set off early to return to his squadron. He told her he would wait for her reply.

It was still hard to fathom what had happened, even though she'd been over it all night. Had Jack Rosman really asked her to marry him? It had been so unexpected. She was all mixed up inside.

It was hardly the kind of proposal she'd dreamed of. It had been rushed, in the dark and cold, and instead of feeling happy, she'd felt miserable.

Jack was offering her nothing short of a business deal. She wasn't even sure if he loved her at all.

Oh, if only Charity was here; she'd have something to say about it. But there was only Ray and he was a boy and he didn't even like Jack, she could tell. She could hardly discuss her dilemma with him.

Ray had been unusually quiet at breakfast. Perhaps he had a hangover. He'd drunk rather a lot on Christmas Day.

'Come and watch the meet at the front of the house,' Maggie had said. 'Fresh air will help clear your head.'

When he arrived, he was wearing the balaclava helmet and the gloves she'd given him for Christmas.

'They're the right size then,' she said. 'I thought your head might have got too big for the hat!' She nudged him to show it was a joke but he hardly smiled back. Poor Ray, he must be feeling really awful.

They stood at the top of the steps, near the front door and well away from the horses. There were dozens of riders on their mounts. Men – mostly older chaps, in red jackets and black boots – and glamorous women, some riding side-saddle, with tall hats and hairnets and crimson lipstick, laughed and called to each other. Hounds raced around, sniffing and barking excitedly. There was a thrill of anticipation in the air.

It was freezing but there were hot toddies and despite her vow never to drink again, Maggie took one from a waiter gratefully.

Lady Ashford was there, in the thick of it all, on her wild black horse. It was as lively as ever and she was having to turn it in circles to bring it back into place.

'Quite a spectacle, isn't it?' Lord Ashford asked, emerging from the front door. He was wearing his thick winter coat and a hat. 'I wasn't sure whether to hold the meet here this year, given the situation, but my wife can be very persuasive.'

'You don't ride yourself, Sir?' Ray asked.

'Good gracious, no. I leave all the dangerous stuff to my wife. She's in her element, as you can see.'

Maggie wondered whether Lord Ashford minded all the attentive men gathered around his wife, like bees around a honeypot.

'I always tell her,' he continued, 'as long as she comes back in one piece, she can do as she likes. You should see the size of the hedges they jump.' He lifted his hand to his forehead. 'Nearly as tall as me.'

Lady Ashford would have made a good Spitfire pilot, Maggie thought. Or a spy! She was so brave, it seemed rather a waste that she spent all her time charging about on a horse or living it up at The Dorchester.

'Right, I'd better go and say a few hellos.'

Lord Ashford trotted down the steps, pulling his coat around him and started greeting riders, most of whom were now sipping from the stirrup cup.

'Hard to believe there's a war on, isn't it?' Ray mused.

Maggie nodded. 'That's what I was thinking. But I suppose life has to go on. We can't all sit around being miserable and feeling sorry for ourselves. We have to get on with it. I think, as long as you're not hurting anyone else, you have to enjoy yourself, wherever you can.'

Ray looked at her rather strangely and his mouth twisted. 'Quite the little philosopher aren't we, these days?' He held up the empty glass in his gloved hand. 'I'm going to have another. Do you want one?'

She shook her head, smiling to herself as she watched Ray approach one of the waiters. He was getting used to this way of life. They all were. How would they cope when the war finally ended and they had to go back to their humdrum lives?

She turned and looked up at Snowden Hall, with its honey-coloured stone, the huge front door and the rows and rows of white-framed windows. A palace, that's how she'd thought of it when she first arrived.

One day, this would all be Jack's. It could be hers, too. She could look after Vi and Mutti, bring them here to live with her, in the country. Vi could have a horse – she could do this, if she liked, ride to hounds. Although, knowing Vi she would feel too sorry for the fox. And Mutti need never cook or take in sewing again.

Maggie would be rich. She could have all the compacts and lipsticks she wanted, not to mention dresses and shoes with heels and furs and hats and she'd never be mistaken for a waitress ever again.

But, would she be happy? Look at Lord and Lady Ashford. They had plenty of money – enough for sleek motor cars and horses and visits to The Dorchester – but they didn't seem awfully happy to her.

* * *

Ray knocked back his second hot toddy. Goodness knew what was in it but whatever it was, it was having the right effect.

He'd hardly slept last night. When he had managed to drop off, he'd had nightmares involving that bloody airman's face, in a Spitfire, flying at him.

He gazed out at the horses and the riders in their bright red jackets and the hounds, one of which was busy digging up Tonks' vegetable patch.

He was a bloody fool. He'd left it too late.

Maggie, standing beside him, was quiet. 'Penny for them,' he asked.

She blushed and he guessed she was thinking about Call-me-Jack, her *fiancé*. He'd thought 'heartache' was only an expression but he was feeling an actual pain in his chest.

Of course, Maggie hadn't mentioned Rosman's proposal. She'd probably guessed he couldn't stand the fella; he didn't exactly hide his feelings. What would he say when she finally told him the news? It would be hard to keep his voice even, to sound pleased. He wondered whether, under those mittens, Maggie was wearing Rosman's ring.

He was torturing himself but he couldn't stop. The irony of it all. That trinket box he'd made Maggie for Christmas would come in handy now. She wouldn't be short of jewellery when she married Jack Rosman.

'Excellent Father Christmas, Maguire, by the way!' Lord Ashford said, coming back up the steps and slapping him on the shoulder. 'My own papa made a good one but I think you even surpassed him.'

'Thank you, Sir.'

Lady Ashford had said the same to him yesterday.

'Perfect, Ray!' she'd said. 'Goodness me, you got into the part. A natural!'

He hadn't thought of it before but he supposed he was good with nippers. Probably because he was still one himself. He wasn't a grown-up; grown-ups enlisted, grown-ups had proper jobs, grown-ups got the girl.

No, he wasn't a grown-up. Perhaps he never would be.

Chapter 48

It was a few days after Christmas and the weather was grey and cold.

The bank staff were back into the routine of work, the excitement of the festive season was over and, as Elsie constantly complained, there was 'nothing to look forward to'.

That morning, when she grumbled again, Ray looked up from his desk and coughed. 'Excuse me, Miss Davenport. I think you're forgetting the forthcoming delectation and delight of the recital!'

She frowned. 'You what?'

'He means the concert in the village hall,' Pam said drily.

'Oh, that.' Elsie shook her head.

Maggie and Ray exchanged rueful smiles. He'd been acting queer since Christmas, moping around and not his usual chirpy self. One of the older chaps, Mr Whitehouse, had actually asked if he'd had some bad news.

After morning break, when Maggie was helping to stack the used crockery onto a tray, Mrs Mason spoke quietly to her. 'I've got an errand for you,' she said. 'How d'you fancy a little trip to The Smoke?'

Maggie frowned. 'To London?'

'That's right. Her Ladyship's gone to The Dorchester for New

Year but she needs a few items taking. She's staying longer than expected.'

'But …' Maggie wanted to ask "why me?" but it would sound as though she was inviting a compliment. What about her work with Lord Ashford? Surely, she'd have to ask him if he minded?

'It was his Lordship's suggestion,' Mrs Mason said, reading her mind. 'He knows her Ladyship's got a soft spot for you. You'll be quite safe with Brummie. He's what her Ladyship calls SIT – safe in a taxi.'

Maggie smiled. She wasn't worried about being alone with the driver but what would the other girls say when they discovered she'd been singled out yet again and this time for a spree to The Dorchester? They'd reached a kind of truce in the last few weeks. She didn't want to do anything to upset the apple cart.

'Can't Brummie take it?' she said. 'He's in and out of London all the time.'

Mrs Mason looked aghast. 'The driver? Certainly not! These are lady's items and should be taken by a female. Her Ladyship doesn't have a lady's maid anymore.' She crossed her arms and sniffed. 'That's the sacrifice she made for the war.'

It seemed rather silly, but Maggie bit her tongue. She'd learned not to question how the gentry went about things.

Now she thought about it, an outing to London was rather tempting. Besides, she might get away with not telling the others. She'd be returning in style too, in a chauffeur-driven Bentley. Not that anyone would see her – they were hardly going to drive down the cobbled back streets of Poplar, but it would be an experience, something to look back on. If they wanted to give her time off and a trip to London, she oughtn't really to complain.

She still hadn't given Jack her answer. He wasn't rushing her; he'd gone back to his squadron and assured her he would wait. But she couldn't keep him hanging on much longer. Perhaps, on the journey to and from London, she'd finally be able to make her decision.

Mrs Mason nudged her. 'You could call in and see your folks while you're there.'

That was an idea. She could go and see Dad and make the peace, if he'd let her, and end 1940 on a good note.

'Very well,' she said. 'I'll do it. When do we leave?'

* * *

'Here you are, Miss. The Dorchester,' Brummie announced from the driver's seat, as he pulled in and braked sharply outside the entrance.

Maggie looked out. On either side of the hotel's front door, sandbags were stacked ten feet high and a doorman in smart livery and top hat was stepping towards them.

They'd had an early start and Brummie had told her on the journey that, after the lull over Christmas, the bombing had started up again overnight, with a vengeance. He'd heard it on the wireless. The fires were still raging. Maggie had a moment of doubt but then dismissed the thought. Nothing bad would happen. It was a flying visit. They'd be heading back to Snowden before she knew it.

In London, there were shells of buildings, shrapnel and rubble on the streets and firemen and fire engines everywhere. Those old familiar barrage balloons were still bobbing overhead.

The red double-deckers and black taxi cabs were still trundling along, doing their best to get through. It was business as usual; life was carrying on. Maggie felt a sudden burst of pride in the city and the people who lived here. They were made of stern stuff.

The doorman opened the passenger door and Maggie got out, remembering how Charity had instructed her to keep her legs firmly together at the knees and to 'swivel'.

'There's a case in the boot, if you don't mind, chum,' Brummie called out. He tilted his head towards Maggie. 'And, Miss, remember, don't be late!'

Maggie was checking the angle of her hat in the reflection of the car window. She nodded. Brummie had warned her he'd be leaving London at three o'clock on the dot, before it got dark.

'Them's my orders. You're to meet me outside the bank, understood? And if you're not there, Miss, I can't wait. I shall have to leave without you.'

There was plenty of time; she'd easily be there by three. She'd leave the case at the reception desk for Lady Ashford and then catch a bus over to Poplar, to face the music. She was finally going to see Dad.

Brummie revved the engine and drove off with a cheery toot of his horn.

Maggie hesitated, suddenly feeling like an imposter. Thank goodness she was wearing Charity's outfit. Without it, she'd probably have been sent round to the servants' entrance.

Charity had insisted on lending her a grey woollen overcoat and it was quite the smartest thing Maggie had ever worn. It had a sheepskin collar and cuffs and three large buttons. As Maggie walked, it swung out effortlessly from the waist. There was a matching hat, too: grey wool, with a feather at the side, so different from her usual pudding basin felt hat.

Charity had placed the hat on Maggie's head and stood back to admire her handiwork. 'There, you look quite the part!'

'You're quite sure you don't mind?'

'When do I ever get the chance to wear them here, spreading manure or digging up sprouts? No, the coat and hat will enjoy themselves tremendously, swanning about on Park Lane!'

Maggie had laughed. She was hardly going to be 'swanning about' but at least she didn't look too out of place. She watched now as another woman walked confidently up the steps and into the hotel on the arm of a uniformed officer. *Yes*, Maggie thought, *I look as good as her*.

She felt a twinge of guilt about keeping Jack's proposal from Charity but she didn't want to be dissuaded. Charity didn't approve of him; in fact, she didn't really approve of marriage at all. This was something she had to decide for herself.

'Could I leave this suitcase for one of your guests, please?' Maggie asked at reception. She'd had to wait a few minutes to be attended to but when she added, 'It's for Lady Ashford,' the man behind the desk perked up.

'Yes of course, Madam! And who shall I say—'

'MARY!'

Maggie turned. She knew that plummy voice. Lady Ashford was almost skipping across the reception towards her. She looked exquisite, in a blue day dress, nipped in at the waist, with padded shoulders and high heels, her dark hair tumbling to her shoulders.

She sashayed towards Maggie like a mannequin in one of Miss Sharp's *Vogue* magazines and everyone turned to look: the man on the desk, the bell boy pulling a luggage trolley towards the lift and other guests milling around in the reception. A woman placed her hand under her husband's chin and shut his mouth. Not gently, either.

'This is awfully good of you, Mary,' Lady Ashford said in her clipped voice. 'Now, no dashing off. I insist you stay for morning tea, at the very least.' She must have noticed Maggie's hesitation because she added, 'Or coffee, if you prefer?'

Maggie bit her lip. It was bound to be real coffee here, not that horrid treacly Camp coffee they served at Snowden which was only good for tanning your legs and which, Jack had assured her, was nothing like the real thing.

Why shouldn't she have a treat? She'd got up at the crack of dawn and a cup of coffee might perk her up. Besides, it might be the only chance she ever had to take a seat in The Dorchester. It would be a shame to go back to Snowden without a tale to tell. She was trying to remember Charity's advice to say 'yes' more often.

Maggie nodded. 'Thank you. Lovely. And by the way, your Ladyship, my name isn't Mary. It's Maggie.'

Lady Ashford looked confused. 'Oh. But didn't it used to be Mary?'

'No,' Maggie said firmly. 'It's always been Maggie. My name is Maggie Corbett.'

They sat on padded armchairs in the hotel foyer, a small table on the marbled floor between them, which was laid with cups, a plate of biscuits and linen napkins.

Maggie suddenly had an awful thought. Did Lady Ashford know that Jack had proposed? Perhaps her errand to The Dorchester was nothing to do with bringing a suitcase of clothes. Maybe it was a ruse to get her here, to discuss Jack's proposal? But to encourage Maggie to accept it or to turn it down?

As a waiter poured their coffee from a silver pot, a voice called, 'Esther!' and a rather dashing man, in a smart black suit, rushed across the lobby towards them.

'There you are, darling,' he said, in an American accent. 'Gee, I thought I'd missed you!'

Maggie gave a jolt of surprise. *Darling*?

The waiter was leaning over, asking if she wanted cream – *actual cream* – and Maggie nodded quickly.

The man probably didn't mean anything by it. Perhaps it was simply what toffs – or Americans – called one another.

'This is Maggie,' Lady Ashford said, pronouncing Maggie's name carefully. 'Silly me. I've been calling her by the wrong name all this time. She works with my husband, at the bank. Maggie, this is Lewis Carlton III, a very good friend of mine.'

Maggie smiled and said, 'How do you do?' and he did the same, shaking her hand warmly and looking straight into her eyes. Maggie's gaze moved to the floor. Something didn't feel right.

The awkward moment passed, as one of the hotel staff approached the American and whispered something in his ear.

'I'm so sorry, ladies.' He held up his hand. 'Do excuse me. I have to take a call. Very nice to meet you, Miss.'

He gave a little bow and, in a trice, he'd gone.

There was a moment's silence. Lady Ashford watched as her friend disappeared from view and then stirred her coffee thoughtfully. 'He works at the Embassy. I dote on those letters after his name. Lewis Carlton "the third". Like a French king!' She laughed.

Maggie tried to sip her coffee but it was too hot. She put the cup down. She couldn't quite shake off the feeling that she'd been complicit in something – and disloyal to his Lordship – by meeting the American.

It was a relief when Lady Ashford changed the subject.

'It's an awfully big world out there, you know, Maggie,' she said. 'Bigger than Snowden, or London or England itself.'

Maggie frowned, wondering where the conversation was going. But in the next moment, her Ladyship brightened and changed topic again.

'Now,' she said, 'do let me set your mind at rest. This is one of the safest buildings in London. Reinforced concrete, everywhere. There was terrible bombing last night of course but we were absolutely fine here. And if the sirens do go off …' She sighed. 'Oh, what a terrible bore that is – but we can pop down to the Turkish bath in the basement.' She laughed. 'I know, it's amazing, isn't it? It's perfectly warm down there and the jazz band plays in one of the neighbouring rooms, so it's not too shabby. They bring us champagne and smoked salmon if it drags on for too long. But …' She held her elegant finger aloft. 'Half the time we simply don't bother going down. There's too much fun to be had up here!'

Maggie felt lightheaded. She'd thought Snowden Hall was an oasis from the war but this place was another world entirely. She could hardly wait to report back to Charity.

Lady Ashford put down her coffee cup and as if reading Maggie's mind, said, 'You know, you'd probably better not mention any of this, when you get back. People get the wrong idea.'

When it was time for Maggie to leave – and to her relief Jack Rosman hadn't been mentioned once – Lady Ashford insisted on accompanying her to the hotel entrance. She twisted her hands and looked uncharacteristically unsure of herself.

'I'm not … that's to say, I may not be back at Snowden for some time, Maggie. So, do look after the place for me, won't you?'

She laughed and then, suddenly more serious, she took Maggie's hand and squeezed it gently. 'Do be careful, Maggie. It's awfully blitzy out there,' she said. 'So long! Farewell.'

* * *

On the bus ride to Poplar, Maggie felt as though ants were running round inside her. There was something fishy about Lady Ashford and that American chap. What on earth would she say if his Lordship asked about her visit? If he knew what Maggie suspected about his wife, it would break his heart.

As she stepped off the bus to walk the last hundred yards to her street, a fire engine tore past, its bell clanking. The noise made her wince and she waited for it to pass. Then she hesitated before walking on. Her stomach was turning somersaults. It wasn't too late to turn around and go back. Dad would never even know she'd been here.

No, on second thoughts, she would go. Because you had to stand up to bullies, or else they carried on. And besides, it was her home too and why shouldn't she go there? She had every right.

She'd willed the bus to slow down the whole way to Poplar, to give her more time to think. What would Dad say to her? They'd had no contact since she'd left home in September. She'd sent him a handmade Christmas card, with a note and, finally, giving him her address at Snowden but she'd heard nothing back.

Of course, he might be at the docks today, working. Or he might refuse to come to the door. She wouldn't put it past him to give her the cold shoulder.

Maggie took a deep breath and rounded the corner into her street.

She stopped. It took a moment for the view to register. She had to close her eyes, shake her head and look again.

It was a scene of utter devastation.

The street wasn't there. Or at least, only half of it was. Houses had simply gone, replaced by piles of rubble: bricks, doors, window frames and dust. Oh, so much dust. Hoses snaked across the craters in the street and there was a terrible, burning smell.

People swarmed everywhere: policemen, ARP men and firemen with grimy faces were shouting orders and climbing over the piles of bricks. A baker's van was parked in the road and bundles of rags were being brought out of the rubble on stretchers and doors and being loaded into it. It was a makeshift ambulance. She realised with a jolt that the bundles of rags were bodies.

There were ordinary folk in the street too. Men and women shuffling around aimlessly, looking as bewildered as Maggie felt.

She took a few steps forward, coughing and stumbling on debris, shaking her head. It felt like an awful nightmare. It couldn't be happening.

A warden in a black helmet approached and put his hand out. 'No further, Miss. It's too dangerous. They're still clearing up.' His eyes creased in concern. 'Is anything the matter, Miss?'

Maggie's mouth felt as though it were full of sawdust, so dry she could hardly speak. 'That's my house down there. Number eleven. Or leastways, it was …'

She blinked and gazed at the view again, making quite sure it was real.

Not every house had been hit. Those to one side of where her house had been, had their windows blown out but were still standing; others were simply a shell. They'd been opened up, the walls peeled back like a can of sardines. You could see the stairs going up to the bedrooms and the furniture inside them, like a dolls' house.

Her house though, looked like it had taken a direct hit. What was the word? Yes, that was it: obliterated.

Maggie started to shiver and shake. 'That's my 'ouse,' she said again.

The warden touched her coat sleeve gently. He asked her a question that he'd clearly asked a hundred times before. 'Do you think a member of your family was in the house when it was hit?'

She nodded. 'Yes, I do. My dad.'

He took Maggie's arm and steered her back up the street, past dust-covered men frantically digging through the rubble with shovels and pickaxes. 'Is there any chance he'd have made it to a shelter, Miss?' he asked.

She shook her head. 'He'd never go. Would rather die in his own house. He used to sit under the stairs. Said it was the safest place.'

'Come on, love. Let's get you a cup of tea.' He guided her across the street and around the corner, to where a canteen van was parked. WVS women in bottle-green uniforms were pouring tea from a large urn, while dusty-faced men and women stood around, clutching cups. Dazed.

'Plenty of sugar, please, Joan,' the warden said at the hatch, nodding at Maggie. 'Someone's had a shock.'

He took off his helmet to scratch his head and put it back on with a sigh. Then he took a list of out of his pocket. 'Number eleven,' he said. 'Reg Corbett?'

Maggie nodded. Her teeth were chattering.

'They're still searching,' he said gently. 'I can't tell you anything yet, love.' He sighed again wearily and headed off, back in the direction of Maggie's street.

She found herself being pressed down gently into a chair and a motherly woman in an apron brought her a steaming cup of tea and a bun.

'There, nice and sweet. Get that down you, love.' The woman lowered her voice. 'Sugar might be on the ration but we have our own special supply here.' She tapped her nose.

It was worse when people were kind to her. Maggie started to sob; she thought she'd never stop.

'Aw, love. Don't take on so. Your dad, was it, did someone say? You've lost your poor old dad? There, there.' The woman leaned down and put a comforting arm around Maggie's shoulder. 'You must've been ever so fond of him …'

Maggie shook her head. That was just it – she hadn't. She hadn't been fond of him at all. She'd lost track of the number of times she'd wished he were dead and that the rows and the shouting might stop. And yet, for all his faults, he'd been her father. And now, he was almost certainly gone and she'd never get the chance to make it up with him. The thought of it was breaking her heart.

Maggie pulled a handkerchief from her bag, wiped her nose and sniffed. What good was crying, after all? She had to pull herself together.

Mutti. What would she say to Mutti? She'd have to let her know. And on top of the shock of losing Dad, they no longer had a home. Nowhere for Vi or Mutti – or her – to come home to.

She started to ask the WVS woman what she needed to do because there must be a procedure but the woman shushed her. 'There now, love, don't take on so. All in good time. Try to drink your tea and eat your bun. Don't try to speak. You've had an awful upset.'

And then, as if things couldn't possibly get any worse, the sirens went off.

A collective cry of 'Oh no!' rang out. Men – and women – muttered and swore. Heads were shaken and eyes, white in dirty faces, opened wide in alarm.

The WVS women nodded at each other and calmly started to pack up and shoo people away.

'Come along! To the shelters. That's the siren. Off you go!'

Maggie was helped to her feet, the cup was snatched away and a woman linked her arm. She tried to object. She couldn't go into a shelter now; Brummie would be waiting. She tried to explain but no one listened. She was hurried and bundled down into an Underground station.

It was only once they got down the flights of steps and were among the crowds on the eastbound platform, that Maggie managed to disentangle herself from the WVS woman and slip away.

The dank platform was heaving with people, some loaded up with suitcases, others already getting ready to bed down for the night with blankets and mattresses.

Not this again. The thought of spending the night down here was almost more than Maggie could bear. And in Charity's best coat too. She didn't dare take it off – she'd freeze – but she'd have to choose her bit of ground carefully.

Maggie picked her way through the masses of people, looking for a space. The floor was filthy – was that blood there? – oh, and the stench of sweat – and worse – was enough to turn your stomach.

She finally found a spot at the back of the platform where she could lean her back up against a wall. She sat down wearily.

A blonde woman in a headscarf, sitting nearby, nodded at Maggie. 'We was here all night, last night. 'Spect we'll have to do it again. Might as well live here, eh?'

The woman looked up as a group of kiddies raced along the platform, making plane noises. 'George!' she yelled. 'Pipe down! And come back 'ere NOW!'

The boy ran on, ignoring her. She sighed and made a 'what can you do' gesture at Maggie.

If Rudi was here, he'd be doing the same – running wild.

An image of Snowden Hall, and all her friends there, flashed through Maggie's mind. She hadn't told anyone about her trip to London. Not even Ray. No one would know what had happened to her. What would they be thinking? Would they be worrying?

She tried not to think about Brummie and the lift back to Snowden that she'd almost certainly missed by now.

Oh, how she wished Ray was here with her. There was no one else she'd rather see. He'd make her feel better; he always knew the right thing to say.

She bent forward and put her head in her hands; she'd never felt so utterly wretched.

The sheepskin cuffs on Charity's coat were already dirty. She might be dressed up to the nines but she was sitting on a filthy floor in a stinking Tube station, with a load of strangers. She'd thought those days were behind her when she moved with the bank, but she was right back where she'd started.

Once an Eastender, always an Eastender. You couldn't escape where you'd come from.

Except, of course, she could. She had a way out. And not only for herself, but for Mutti and Violet too, if she married Jack.

Was it wrong to think of him as her 'way out', her escape? No, it wasn't because she was his escape, too.

She hadn't understood on the night that Jack had proposed. But she understood now. It all made sense when he'd mentioned prison and she thought of Mike and she remembered asking Jack if Mike had someone who cared about him. Yes, had been the answer. And that someone was Jack.

Time passed. She had no sense of how long she'd been sitting there, although she was feeling the hard floor now, so it must have been a while. A man in a gaberdine mac sat down heavily on the ground next to her. He bumped her arm and didn't apologise.

Maggie tried to inch away but when she shifted along the platform, so did he. He was pressing against her. Maggie's chest tightened. Who the heck did he think he was? She glanced down and watched as his dirty fat fingers edged along the ground, towards the hem of her coat.

She thumped her fist down on them, making him yelp and pull his hand away. 'Oi! Leave it out!' she yelled. 'I've had just about enough!'

Everyone around turned and gawped at them. A few people jeered and laughed, as the man got to his feet and hastened away, red-faced.

'Good for you, love,' the woman in the headscarf said. 'Dirty old man. There's enough of them down 'ere. Say, there's room with us. Come and sit over here.'

They sat together for hours in silence. Maggie was grateful that the woman seemed to understand she didn't want to talk.

The stone floor was as hard and cold as ice beneath her but she didn't dare move, not even to find a lav. If she left her place, she'd never get it back again. She slept in fits and starts, dozing for a few minutes and then waking again with a jolt, because of the cold or someone coughing or a baby crying.

The next time she woke, the woman in the headscarf had gone and two men had taken her place.

People were starting to stretch and yawn and stand up around her, folding up their blankets, pulling up mattresses.

It must be morning. Perhaps the all-clear had sounded.

Maggie's limbs were so stiff with cold they hurt as she tried to move them.

Couples and families – white-faced and exhausted – were slowly making their way along the platform towards the exit.

She'd wait here for a while. There was no point getting up yet, if she was only going to join a queue at the bottom of the stairs.

The men asleep beside her were lying close to each other. One had his head on the other's shoulder. Their blanket had slipped down and she could see they were holding hands. Maggie reached forward and gently pulled the blanket back over them.

People could be funny about that kind of thing.

Her face was tight and her eyes were sore from all that crying and lack of sleep. But at least she'd got through the night and one thing was now clear, she was going to say yes to Jack, she'd marry him on condition that she could still do her bit. She still wanted to take up that post that Lord Ashford had found for her, using her German. So, they'd have to marry quickly and go off to their postings, or else wait a while.

It would be a marriage of the head, not of the heart, but that was all right.

Marrying for love didn't get you anywhere. Look at Mutti and Dad; presumably they loved each other, once. And Lord and Lady Ashford, too. That must have been a love match. Maggie remembered the first time she'd seen them, on the lawn at Snowden House. She'd thought they were the perfect couple. But Lady Ashford practically lived at The Dorchester and now she had this American man. This 'very good friend'.

No, love didn't last; there were no guarantees but if you were friends – and she and Jack *were* friends – and went into marriage with your eyes open, then you had as much chance – more, in fact – of being happy.

Chapter 49

Maggie pulled Charity's coat around her and shivered as she emerged from the Underground. She squinted in the bright morning light. You never knew, after a night of bombing, how the city landscape might have changed, so she stood for a moment to get her bearings.

She was buffeted by people rushing past, desperate to get home. If they still had a home to go to.

Maggie remembered, with a shivery sick feeling, that she didn't.

She'd make her way back to her street, where they'd still be clearing up and ask someone there, what she needed to do next.

Perhaps the WVS canteen van would be back and she could get a cuppa. She couldn't stomach anything to eat but her mouth was so dry she doubted whether she could even manage to speak.

Maybe things would turn out all right. Dad might have been down in a shelter, after all. Or perhaps he'd been with Kath Deacon in her house? Kath's house was still standing, from what Maggie had seen. If he'd been in there, he might have survived.

Her eyes roved over the passers-by. Please, please. She'd give anything to get a glimpse of him now. She could even cope with the sarcastic greeting he'd be bound to give her. 'Oh, found your way home, at last, did you?' or 'Who are you? Who? Maggie who?'

'Course, he mightn't be talking to her because she'd disobeyed him for the first time in her life and run off to the country. She wouldn't care. She could stand up for herself these days. He could say what he liked; she'd simply be glad that he was alive.

There, that was him! Her heart lifted. And fell, a second later. No, it wasn't. It was another chap in a grey overcoat and cap, hands in his pockets, shuffling along the street towards her.

Maggie braced herself and turned into the street, as she'd done yesterday. This time, she was prepared for it.

It was the same mess as before: smoke, dust, craters and ten-feet-high piles of rubble that used to be people's homes.

'Stay back, Miss! No further! They're defusing an unexploded bomb down there,' the warden – a different man from yesterday – called out angrily.

She nodded.

There were crowds of people at the end of the street, gazing at the mess in undisguised delight. Sightseers, if you could believe it. No wonder the warden was cross with her; he thought she was one of them.

'MAGGIE!'

The yell came from behind. Maggie turned. It was as though she'd wished him there.

Ray. It was Ray. He was standing in the ruins of the street. In the ruins of everything.

She was hallucinating again. First Dad, now Ray.

She rubbed her eyes. She must be dead. That was it; a bomb had fallen on the shelter last night and Ray was here now to guide her through the pearly gates. But that didn't make sense. Why Ray? Ray wasn't an angel.

'Maggie!' he said again, running towards her. His face was etched with concern. No, it really was him. He wrapped her in his arms and it was the best feeling in the world. His embrace was warm and she was safe. She could smell that comforting scent of coal tar soap. She'd been so cold, so lonely. She closed her eyes, as he kissed the top of her head. 'Thank God,' he whispered. 'We've been worried sick.'

He loosened his grip and pulled back to look at her. His eyes – he did have the loveliest brown eyes – were full of anguish. He licked his thumb and wiped her face. 'There,' he said, brightening and giving Maggie an encouraging smile, 'that's better.'

'What—? What are you doing here?' she asked.

'You weren't at dinner and no one knew where you'd gone. And then Mrs Mason – and Brummie – told us. I was beside myself when you didn't return. This morning, I persuaded Brummie to drive us back. Miss Sharp looked in the staff files and gave me your address. I guessed you'd have come home.' Ray surveyed the wreckage of the street. 'What there is of it.' He shrugged. 'I came to find you.'

She was glad, so grateful, she couldn't put it into words.

'Oh blimey.' Maggie reached up and patted her head. 'I've lost my hat, Ray. It was Charity's best one.'

He frowned. 'Is that all? You're not hurt, though?'

Her eyes filled up. 'The house has gone. My—'

'Oi! This ain't Lover's Lane, it's a bomb site, in case you hadn't noticed. Move along now, you pair!' The warden was back, angrily ushering them away. They moved off to the corner of the street, where people were hurrying by.

Ray looked like he was steeling himself, his face, normally so pale, was flushed and he couldn't look her in the eye. She felt a pang of something for him.

'Ray—'

'You need to go,' he said, suddenly all businesslike. 'The sirens could go off again any minute and Brummie's waiting for you at the bank. He could get the sack for this.'

'But … but what about you?'

He shook his head, distracted. 'No, there's something I've got to do. You get out of here, Maggie, do you hear? Get out!'

It hurt as much as if he'd struck her. Just when he'd found her, he was leaving her alone again.

She wanted to argue with him but he looked determined. 'I'll see you back there, then?' she said. 'At Snowden?'

But he was shaking his head, starting to walk away.

'Ray!'

He twisted around to face her but he was still walking. He was walking backwards. He'd taken his trilby off and he was pointing it at her. 'Do you think he's good enough for you, Maggie?' he yelled.

What? He knew! And it hit her then, why he'd come to find her. Ray knew about her and Jack and he wanted to put her off marrying him. She shook her head. No, she wouldn't listen. She'd spent half the night working it out. Her decision was like a little sparrow, perching on a tiny branch. Ray Maguire wasn't going to knock it off; her mind was made up.

'Because he's NOT!' It was Ray's parting shot. He'd turned again, rammed his hat on, shoved his hands in his pockets. He was striding away.

Maggie started to lose sight of him as he disappeared into the crowd. She ran after him, dodging people, knocking elbows.

'Oi, watch out!' a woman shouted.

'Steady there, Miss!' a man said.

Finally, she reached him, grabbed his arm and swung with all her weight, pulling him to a halt.

She was out of breath. 'It's all right for you, Ray Maguire, fella-me-lad, laugh-a-minute!' He was staring at her, stony-faced. 'Some of us have people to worry about and look out for,' she said. 'We can't all be carefree! What are you gonna do? Laugh and joke your way through the whole blimmin' war?'

He looked at her in astonishment and apparent disbelief. 'Ha!' He did a kind of mock laugh. 'Is that what you think?' He bit his lip. 'You really think this is a laugh? That I don't worry? Don't you think that maybe the only reason I find something to laugh about is because, if I don't, I might start blubbing and never stop?'

She shook her head. No, she couldn't bear it. Not him, not Ray. If Ray felt fed up and scared, like the rest of them, then there was no hope. No hope at all.

'Because, you know the funniest part?' he shouted. 'The biggest joke of all?' He was holding his trilby, swapping it from hand to hand, searching for the right words. 'It's never telling you!' he burst out, finally. 'It's never telling you how I felt before it was too late!' He suddenly reached forward, put his hand around the back of her neck and, pulling her towards him, landed a kiss on her lips.

'There!' he said, pulling back. He was breathless, his eyes bright – oh and angry. That was the strangest thing, he was so angry.

'I bloody love you, Maggie Corbett. There! Oh, blast! Here, have it all. My heart is yours. Do you hear? Now, do what the heck you like with it. Take it and—' He flung his arm out and a passing soldier had to duck. 'Throw it on the rubble with the rest of the wreckage from this whole, bloody *war*!'

He turned on his heels and stomped away. In seconds, he was gone, swallowed up by the crowds and it was as though he'd never been there.

Maggie touched her lips. She stared at the space where he'd been. She didn't have the strength or the courage to follow him. She turned and walked slowly back towards what remained of her street, trying to make sense of what had happened.

Ray was cross and confused and he'd confused her because, somehow, he knew that Jack Rosman had asked her to marry him and he didn't want her to.

Ray loved her.

'Oh!'

There was another face in front of her – someone else she knew – and all thought of Ray and what he'd said and where he'd gone disappeared.

It was Kath. Kath Deacon. Her face pale and pinched, her eyes red. She looked exhausted.

'Oh, Maggie, it's you,' she said. Her eyes filled with tears. 'It's no good, love. I saw the stretcher bearers bringing him out. I've been up to the mortuary.' She shook her head and her voice cracked. 'I'm sorry, Maggie. It's your dad, love. I'm afraid, he's gone.'

Chapter 50

For once in her life, Charity Richmond was lost for words.

She put her shandy down on the bar and stared at Maggie, aghast. 'Jack Rosman asked you to marry him?'

'Sshh!' Maggie said, glancing around. She gestured at Charity to lower her voice. The pub was almost empty but Derek the barman was only a few feet away and a couple of the old chaps were sitting up at the bar.

'Gosh!' Charity said, shaking her head. 'Was he drunk? Sorry, but – what on earth did you say?'

Maggie shrugged. 'I said I'd think about it and when I was stuck down in the shelter that night, that's what I did.'

Charity ran her fingers through her hair. 'Oh yes. The night you went AWOL and gave us all a nervous breakdown.'

Maggie managed a smile. She felt hopeless. Like someone had pulled the plug in her and drained out every bit of strength and light.

'My dad had gone, my house had gone, I didn't know how I was going to take care of everyone, so …' She shrugged. 'I decided to accept him.'

Charity gasped and put her hands up to her face. 'That's one reason for chaining yourself to someone, I suppose. But do you love him? Does he love you?'

Maggie shook her head.

Jack Rosman didn't love her, she knew that now. He loved someone else and although he was probably very fond of her, he didn't love her in the way that a man should love his wife.

Charity frowned. 'And what about your posting? Your essential work?'

'I'd still do that. The wedding would have to wait.'

Charity winced. 'So, do I need to buy a new hat?' Her voice was tentative, as though she was braced for the worst. She certainly didn't seem happy about the news.

Maggie shook her head. 'No hats required,' she said softly. 'In the end, I turned him down.'

She'd spent a long time thinking of the right words to say to Jack. She'd written to him as soon as she got back from London, her head still reeling from the shock of everything that had happened.

She'd thanked Jack for his kind offer and told him she couldn't marry him, not now, not ever. But she hoped they could still be friends and wished him all the very best.

And then, she'd waited and waited, in vain for Ray to come back to Snowden.

Charity was signalling for more drinks to the barman. 'Well, I can't say I'm not relieved. Apart from anything else, you're too damn young to be getting married.' She waggled her finger at Maggie. 'You've got a lot of living to do, first! When are you off?'

'I'll get these,' a man's voice said, from a few feet away. It was an older chap with a patch over his eye. Maggie had seen him in here before. He was handing some coins to the barman, for their drinks.

'That's awfully kind, Ted, but what's the occasion?' Charity asked.

The man nodded at Maggie. 'Little bird tells me this young

lady's off on war work. Important posting.' He tapped his nose. 'Hush-hush and all that. I'd just like to wish her Godspeed.'

There were no secrets around here, Maggie thought, as she and Charity exchanged wry smiles. Ted could ask all he liked about where she was going and what she'd be doing and there was no danger of Maggie spilling the beans because she didn't know herself.

She'd passed the language test and the security clearance and in a few days' time she'd receive an envelope containing a railway warrant for her new destination.

It was exciting and terrifying all at the same time.

And before that, she still had her dad's funeral to get through.

* * *

Joseph slammed down the telephone receiver and stood up.

'Yeees!' He clenched both fists in the air and tilted his head towards the ceiling. He wasn't a religious man but if there was ever a time to send a small thank you heavenwards, this was it.

He glanced at his watch. He had a couple of hours to kill. Now, what?

He should have a smoke, to celebrate. He opened the cigar box on his desk, thought better of it, slammed it shut again, put on his jacket, marched to the window, turned and marched back to his desk.

He snatched up Sebastian from the desk. 'We've done it!' he told the bear. The glass eyes stared at him impassively. 'If only Miss Corbett were here, old chum, eh?'

Joseph put the bear down and drummed his fingers on the desk. For the first time in his life, he wished he could dance. Like Fred Astaire. The thought of twirling a cane and tap-tapping his way down the Long Gallery, between the rows of desks, was suddenly immensely appealing. The look on everyone's face! Miss Sharp – oh, he'd pay good money to see Cynthia Sharp's face!

And then, they'd all clap. And Mr Maguire would rope him in to do a turn at the concert in two days' time.

Ha! The thought of it made him laugh out loud.

But Maguire wasn't there. That was a bad business. Joseph didn't blame him for requisitioning his car and driver and making a mercy dash to London to find Miss Corbett. He'd probably have done the same. Of course, Joseph had had to give Brummie a ticking off – essential journeys, rationed petrol and all that – but they'd both known he hadn't really meant it.

There'd been no sign of Maguire since that day, almost two weeks ago. New Year had come and gone. It was 1941 now and the lad had disappeared off the face of the earth. It was a worry.

Miss Corbett had come to his office. Black didn't suit her, she looked thin and wan, poor thing, she'd been through such a lot. She'd told him the rumour was that Maguire had joined up.

'He and Brummie had a talk about it, you see, Sir, on the journey down to London, to find me. Brummie had suggested he join the Sappers.'

'The Royal Engineers?'

'Yes. Because it's not fighting, as such. He wouldn't be sent overseas. It would be …' Her voice had faltered. 'Bomb disposal.'

Joseph rubbed his chin and tried not to show his shock.

'And I said, "Isn't that very dangerous"? And Brummie said it was and then he said …' She started to get upset. Joseph reached into his top pocket and passed her his handkerchief. 'Then Brummie said, "If it was me, I'd rather take me chances with the Hun. But I think he might have just done it, the barmy devil. I think he might have just gone and signed his life away".'

And then she started to cry. 'And I think it's partly my fault too, Sir – if he has gone and signed his life away because …' She shook her head. 'Because of lots of things.'

'My dear young lady,' Joseph said, 'I don't believe for one minute that Mr Maguire has enlisted.'

She looked up then, with hopeful, watery eyes. 'You don't?'

He put his hand up. 'And not because I think he's a coward but because he wouldn't simply leave Snowden like that.' He believed it; these were not merely words of consolation for Miss Corbett.

'To go, without a word to you or any of his other colleagues? Or to me? No.' He shook his head. 'He has more integrity than that. If he'd wanted to enlist, goodness knows I wouldn't have stood in his way. He only had to say.'

Miss Corbett dried her eyes then and seemed a little less despondent.

'I'm going back to London, Sir, as you know, for the funeral and, well, I'm hoping – and half expecting – to bump into him there.' She gave a helpless shrug.

'Stranger things have happened,' Joseph agreed.

'And I've written to him, too. Miss Sharp got me his address. I couldn't think what else to do. But … I've not heard back.'

'Not yet! Hope springs eternal, Miss Corbett!' He sounded much more optimistic than he felt.

Joseph brought himself back to the present. It was no good, he couldn't stay in here, like a caged animal. He yanked the study door open and flew out. Dakin appeared as though from nowhere.

'Will you be wanting the motor car, Sir?'

Joseph patted his arm. 'No. Yes. Tell Brummie I'll need the car brought round to the front at three o'clock. Overnight trip, Dakin, if you could pack me a few things, please. But now, I'm going to walk down to the village.' He called for the dogs.

Dakin produced his overcoat. 'You might be needing this, Sir.' He held it out while Joseph put it on. 'It is January, after all, Sir. Chilly. And your hat.'

Dakin's face was as serene as ever, but he must have been wondering what was happening. Joseph never went to the village.

As he reached the front door, he stopped and turned back.

'Dakin,' he said, 'do you happen to know where Mrs Nicholls lives?'

Joseph set off down the drive, Snowden Hall behind him. The

dogs were excited, bounding on the grass either side, delighted by the unexpected outing. His arms swung, he was almost marching now, the rhythm was satisfying. He breathed in the cold air.

He should do this more often. He was the landlord, after all, of all those cottages in the village. Yes, it really was his moral duty to make sure everything was in good order.

At the end of the drive, he walked through the iron gates and turned right.

'Heel!' he called to the dogs and they came.

It was indeed bitterly cold but it was bright, too. The kind of day that held the promise of spring, of better days after a long cold winter.

There were swathes of perfect white snowdrops on the verges. He'd never noticed them before. Even in the midst of this terrible war, flowers still bloomed, trees sprouted leaves, hedges grew. And the birds – all around him there were birds – singing their little hearts out.

As he walked, Joseph started to hum. Then he whistled a tune.

He couldn't remember the last time he'd whistled. He was surprised to find that he still could.

Chapter 51

On the day of the concert, Maggie was called in to Lord Ashford's office. She'd been back to London for the funeral and all her hopes had been dashed: there'd been no sign of Ray. It had been stupid to even think she might see him.

'Ah, Miss Corbett. Welcome back, if only briefly,' Lord Ashford said. 'When are you leaving for your posting?'

'First thing tomorrow morning, Sir. I could have gone straight from London, of course, but I wanted to … well, say goodbye properly to everyone and, of course, it's the concert tonight. I wouldn't miss that for the world.'

He nodded. 'Good, good. Never easy to lose a parent. My condolences, once again. I trust it all went as well as these things can?'

Maggie nodded and thanked him.

'I've got something that might cheer you up a little. I've been away myself for the past couple of days and I've brought a special delivery back with me.'

Maggie's heart lifted. Ray! Oh, please let it be Ray.

He beckoned her with his finger. 'Come with me.'

But it wasn't him. There were two strangers – a man and woman, in their thirties, wrapped in coats and hats and scarves – standing in the drawing room.

The woman spun around as they entered the room and looked disappointed that it was only Maggie and his Lordship. She was serious and pale, with dark rings beneath her eyes. There was something familiar about that face.

'Miss Corbett, these are Rudi's parents,' Lord Ashford said.

'You did it,' Maggie murmured.

'*We* did it,' he said. And then, to the couple, he said, '*Hier ist Fräulein Corbett!*'

Hearing Maggie's name, the young woman gasped and ran across the room to embrace her. Maggie was almost knocked off her feet. She hugged the woman back. She was a frail little thing. Maggie could feel the bones of her back through her thin coat.

'I've sent the car for Rudi and Mrs Nicholls,' Lord Ashford was saying. 'They'll be here any moment. It was my intention for you to be the first to hear the good news but you were away when I took the call. Mrs Nicholls knows but Rudi has no idea.'

'*Danke schön*,' Rudi's mother whispered in Maggie's ear and then she pulled back and took both of Maggie's hands in hers and gazed at her with huge brown eyes. '*Danke schön*.'

It was all she had to give: her thanks. But it was enough.

* * *

That evening, in the village hall, Charity and Maggie took sixpences on the door as the audience filed in and started to take their seats.

'Still no word from Ray?' Charity asked gently.

Maggie shook her head. 'Still no word.'

'Well, it's a great turn out!' Charity said brightly. Villagers, Hall and bank staff, old and young, were streaming in, wrapped up against the cold night in coats, hats and scarves. The hall was soon full of laughter and chatter.

'You'll help with tea and biscuits in the interval, will you,

Maggie?' Charity asked. 'Oh, and something else. You will stay in touch, won't you?'

The girls looked at one another. Goodness, Charity looked suddenly incredibly sad.

'Of course!' Maggie said. 'When I get some leave – maybe in the spring – I'll be back. I've promised Miss Sharp I'll try out her "skin airing".'

'You're going to swim naked in the pool? That's brave. Oh, go on then, I'll do it too but only on condition there are no peeping Toms – or Norms or Bills!'

They laughed.

Maggie raised her eyebrows, as, just then, Miss Sharp and Big Bill appeared at the desk. Talk of the devil, she thought, greeting them warmly and holding out her hand for their money.

'And you will try to go and see Vi for me, once or twice, won't you?' Maggie asked Charity. 'She's happy as Larry on the farm but it would set my mind at rest.'

Charity gave a firm nod. 'Absolutely. I can't promise it'll be on a tandem, though!'

Maggie smiled, remembering, with a pang those happy days with Ray. 'And while you're there,' she said, 'be sure to ask to meet Seth. He's a farmer, sounds like quite a catch. But he's waiting for a goddess. He might just be your cup of tea.'

* * *

The concert was halfway through and it was going well. Maggie stood to one side of the stage, put her head around the curtain and peered out at the audience.

Lord Ashford was sitting on the front row. Lady Ashford was still at The Dorchester, as far as anyone knew. But Maggie was glad to see that his Lordship wasn't on his tod. Gwen was sitting next to him – right up close – and she did look smart. She'd curled her hair and she was wearing what looked like a new blouse. On her other side was Mrs Mason – smiling, for once – and then Rudi's parents.

Rudi was sitting on his mother's knee and his father was teasing him about something and oh, they were having a good laugh.

Even though Maggie's heart was aching for all she'd lost, she couldn't help but smile, seeing the little family together at last.

She knew she wasn't supposed to blow her own trumpet but she was allowed to think it because Lord Ashford had said it to her when it was just the two of them. He'd said he blessed the day she came to Rosman's and if it hadn't been for her, Rudi would have drowned. Without a doubt. Even if she did nothing else worthwhile for the whole of the war, Maggie knew she'd always remember that.

* * *

It was the interval and tea and biscuits were being served from the kitchen hatch at the back of the hall.

'I'll fetch one for you,' Gwen had told Joseph and he was sitting pulling faces at Rudi on his father's lap when his driver, Brummie, interrupted them. There was someone at the back door to see him.

'Come in, man!' Joseph said to the shadowy figure standing outside. It took a second to recognise him – he was bandaged around his head and arm. 'Maguire! You're back! Excellent. But not entirely sound, I'm sorry to see. Goodness, man, what's happened to you?'

Maguire waved his right – unbandaged – hand in a dismissive gesture, making it clear he didn't want to discuss his injuries. Apart from the dressings, he seemed in fine fettle. Which was a relief. Just wait until Miss Corbett saw him! Joseph attempted to hurry Maguire into the hall but he shook his head and stood firm inside the back door.

'There's … erm … a teddy bear, Sir,' he said, frowning at

Joseph's jacket pocket, from which Sebastian was peeping out. He rubbed his eye, thinking he was seeing things.

'Are you coming in, Maguire?' Joseph said again but clearly the fellow had something he wanted to get off his chest.

'Sir, when we moved here from London, you allowed married men to bring their wives.'

Joseph frowned, wondering where this was heading. It sounded like a prepared speech. 'I did,' he agreed.

Maguire nodded. He was standing straight, staring ahead, as though to attention. His back was straight. Gracious, that Home Guard lot had done a good job on him. This wasn't the same man who'd stood in front of him back in September and reluctantly taken on the role of 'Head of Morale'.

'I don't have a wife, Sir—' Maguire said.

'Wise man,' Joseph muttered.

'—and if you don't mind me saying so, Sir, that seems rather unfair, that I'm not permitted to bring—'

'Yes, yes,' Joseph said. His mind was a maelstrom. What on earth was all this about? 'You want to bring someone here, Maguire? To Snowden?'

'Yes, Sir. You need more house staff, after all, Sir.'

Joseph wouldn't say it now but he already had two new members of staff to introduce to Snowden. Rudi's parents – both doctors – would make a rather overqualified under gardener and housemaid but they'd assured him they didn't mind. And it wouldn't be forever.

Joseph sighed. 'Go on, then,' he said. 'Let's hear it.'

Suddenly a woman's voice piped up from the other side of the door. 'I'm a grafter! I'll earn me keep!'

Maguire nodded. 'That's her, Sir.'

'What? Out there, in the freezing cold? Well, whoever she is, bring her in, man, for goodness' sake!'

* * *

'Hello, you.'

Maggie turned and almost dropped the huge teapot she was carrying.

She recognised that voice but not the person attached to it. At least, not for a moment. It was Ray, all bandaged up. But it was, undoubtedly, him. She could barely believe her eyes. 'What's happened to you? You haven't enlisted! Have you?'

Someone, probably Charity, took the teapot carefully from Maggie, leaving her free to stand on tiptoe, take Ray's face gently in her hands and kiss him.

The grey-haired woman standing beside him, chuckled. 'Oh, I see it all now, Raymond. No wonder you was so keen to get back!'

'We thought you'd joined up!' Maggie said. She thought her heart would burst with happiness. He was here, he was safe and he wasn't angry with her anymore.

Ray sighed. 'No. Not that. I went to fetch Ma. Ma, this is Maggie, the one I've told you all about.' He turned back to Maggie. 'When I saw the state of those streets back home, I couldn't leave her there. I was going to bring her straight to Snowden. That was my plan. Only Hitler had other ideas.'

His mother chuckled. 'We got bombed out, love,' she said, matter-of-factly. ''Ospickle. That's where he's been all this time.'

'I can look everyone in the eye, now though, eh?' Ray said, pointing to his bandaged head.

'Luckily, 'is head is rock hard,' his mum said.

Charity appeared and gave Maggie a look. 'Mrs Maguire, is it? Would you like to come and have a seat at the front of the hall – best view in the house – and I'll bring you a nice cup of tea? The interval's nearly over and Ray's going on next, aren't you Ray?'

* * *

Ray poked his head around the curtain. 'They're ever so quiet out there. They've all got faces as long as fiddles,' he said. He rubbed his face. 'I'm feeling nervy all of a sudden, Maggie.'

'You'll be wonderful!' she said.

'As soon as I step on that stage, I'll be right as rain.'

'They might be quiet because Pam did a turn, just before we stopped for the interval,' Maggie said.

'Bloody hell. What did she sing?'

Maggie winced. 'A sort of operatic version of "We're Going to Hang Out the Washing on the Siegfried Line".'

'No! And you let her?'

'You try stopping Pam when she's set her mind to something. It's like trying to stop an express train. And the show had to go on. And you weren't here.'

He reached out and touched her face. 'I'm here now.'

Maggie stroked his hand. 'Some people actually found it funny,' she said. 'But most were confused.'

They looked into each other's eyes.

'I wrote you a letter,' Maggie said and then, remembering what she'd written – that she'd take good care of his heart, on condition that he'd do the same with hers – she blushed. 'But anyway, I need to tell you, I'm leaving tomorrow.'

Ray frowned. 'Where are you going?'

'I'm going to do my bit.' Maggie nodded at the stage. 'It's time for you to do yours.'

They'd done everything else: Nancy's tap dancing, Bill's trombone, Norm's magic tricks, one of the footmen was a great juggler and Brummie had sung. Who'd have guessed he'd be such a fine baritone? Miss Sharp had recited a couple of poems off by heart, Charity got everyone singing – that was the best part – and then Pam, of course, had put a dampener on proceedings with her bloomin' operatics.

'Everyone else has done their act. There's nothing left now, Ray, except you. We've saved the best for last, eh? Oh, and mind your language, nothing saucy. There are kiddies out there,' Maggie said.

He stepped forward. 'Wish me luck!'

'Blimey, what's happened here then?' Ray said, as soon as he stepped out onto the stage. 'You lot look a bit glum. Don't tell me Pam's been singing, eh?'

Everyone laughed. Even Pam. She probably thought it was a joke.

'I've got a little story for you,' Ray said. 'A fellow was out motoring late one night. He pulled up at a little tiny village inn. It was long past closing time and he knocked on the door.

'A terrible female apparition put her head out of the window. "Well, what is it?" "Is this The George and Dragon?" he asked. "Yes," she said, "what is it?" "Well," he said, "where's George?"'

That laughter filled the space, loud enough to lift the roof off the little village hall. Maggie could see Ray breathing it in, like oxygen.

'Our gardener, Mr Tonks – there he is, folks, at the back, in the cheap seats, give him a wave – is being ever so creative this year with his herbs. Oh yes, he is. He's put them all in alphabetical order. I said to him, 'That's awfully clever, Sir. How do you ever find the time?' And he answered – come on, what did he answer?'

Everyone yelled, 'It's next to the sage!'

Maggie glanced out a little further. She could see all her colleagues from the bank. And there was Ted from the pub, with the eye patch, sitting on the second row and Cook nearby. People were catching each other's eye and nudging each other and laughing. All their troubles, at least for now, forgotten.

'… The clerk is sympathetic and decides to allow the man to change his unfortunate name. "What do you want to change it to?" asks the clerk. The man replies, "Maurice Stinkfoot!"'

How could she ever have thought Ray wasn't the man for her? That he wasn't someone she could look up to, in a uniform or not?

'I'm in the Home Guard!' Ray was saying. 'And believe me, that's no joke!'

Everyone roared.

He'd been on the stage for half an hour – how did he remember so many jokes? – and Maggie was still standing at the edge of the wings, next to the curtain, watching him, when Ray stopped his banter and glanced back at her.

He held his hand up for silence. 'Just a moment, ladies and gentlemen! There's something I need to do.'

He ran from the front of the stage and faced her. 'I got your letter,' he murmured. 'That was, Maggie Corbett, a very nice letter, indeed. Just what a man needs when he's laid up. Got me back on my feet, that letter did. In fact ...' He reached inside his jacket pocket. 'I might just read it out—'

'NO!' she shrieked, grabbing his arm. The audience started to laugh, even though they mustn't have had a clue what was happening.

Ray laughed and kissed the top of her head. 'Don't be daft. As if I would. It's not in my pocket, in any case. It's not here at all, but ...' He stopped grinning and gazed into her eyes, suddenly serious. 'I know that letter off by heart. Every bloomin' word.' He thumped his chest. 'It's in here.'

And then, in the next breath, he put his mouth to her ear. 'Marry me?'

Maggie nodded, too choked up to speak. She hadn't needed a moment to make up her mind.

Ray grinned and took her hand and pulled her on to the stage and she was laughing, unable to resist.

'Ladies and gentlemen,' Ray said, holding up her arm, 'a big cheer please, for my fiancée, Miss Maggie Corbett!'

There were thunderous cheers, clapping and whooping. Some folk stamped their feet on the wooden floor. Ray put his face up to hers. He looked hopeful and happy, his lovely brown eyes were shining. 'Yes?' he asked her. He had to shout over the noise. 'Yes?'

Maggie laughed. 'Yes!' she said. She'd never been so sure of anything in her life.

Ray kissed her, with his one good arm wrapped around her, and there were more whistles and shouts. It was deafening.

All those people staring at her, making a spectacle of herself!

Honestly! Maggie could feel herself blushing. Oh, she was blushing like a tomato and she didn't care.

'Oi! Is this part of the show?' someone yelled from the front row.

Yes! Maggie felt like shouting back. Oh, yes. The very best part of all.

Acknowledgements

Although a work of fiction, *A Wartime Secret* is inspired by the true story of a bank that moved to a country house for the duration of World War II. Many thanks to the staff and volunteers at Upton House in Warwickshire (now owned by the National Trust), whose magnificent exhibition 'Banking for Victory' sowed the seeds of an idea which, many years later, resulted in this novel.

Many thanks to all the friends (virtual and 'real') and students, past and present, who have inspired and encouraged me along my writing journey.

Special thanks to Chris Morgan, at whose evening classes in Birmingham it all began and to Chris Cherry, my writing-partner-in-crime, for all the fun and laughter we've had, chasing our dreams. Long may it continue.

Without my agent and publisher there would, of course, be no novel and I'm grateful to the Kate Nash Literary Agency and to Robbie Guillory, who saw the book's potential when it was only half-written and, of course, to the brilliant team at HQ, who fell in love with Maggie's story.

Thanks to my writing buddy, Sally Jenkins, for her much-valued support and *Vielen Dank* to my friend Michaela, for kindly checking my (rusty!) German.

I owe a debt of gratitude to the fabulous folk at the Romantic Novelists' Association and to Janet Gover and Alison May, whose enthusiasm for the initial story idea helped to spur me on.

Last but not least, thanks to my husband, Alan: a calming influence, an excellent sounding board and always supportive. He vowed not to read the book until it was finished. Well, finally, now he can.

Dear Reader,

We hope you enjoyed reading this book. If you did, we'd be so appreciative if you left a review. It really helps us and the author to bring more books like this to you.

Here at HQ Digital we are dedicated to publishing fiction that will keep you turning the pages into the early hours. Don't want to miss a thing? To find out more about our books, promotions, discover exclusive content and enter competitions you can keep in touch in the following ways:

JOIN OUR COMMUNITY:

Sign up to our new email newsletter:
http://smarturl.it/SignUpHQ

Read our new blog www.hqstories.co.uk

https://twitter.com/HQStories

www.facebook.com/HQStories

BUDDING WRITER?

We're also looking for authors to join the HQ Digital family!
Find out more here:

https://www.hqstories.co.uk/want-to-write-for-us/

Thanks for reading, from the HQ Digital team

If you enjoyed *A Wartime Secret*, then why not try another sweeping historical novel from HQ Digital?